distress signal

dusk valley — book 2

amanda chaperon

content warnings

Dear reader,

Please note that *Distress Signal* contains the following material that may be triggering for some readers: mentions of PTSD and loss related to time in the military, death of loved ones (off page but discussed), discussions of grief, receiving a phone call that a loved one is dead, instance of having to visually identify the dead body of a loved one, finding a family member after they were physically assaulted, car accidents that cause bodily injury (one off page but discussed, one on page), drugging and abduction, gun violence, graphic sexual content, and explicit language.

If you're sensitive to any of these subjects, please use this warning to make an informed decision about whether or not to proceed reading this story.

As always, your mental health comes first. Please take care of yourself.

Xoxo,

Amanda

For my sissy.

*And for my fellow firstborns, who would go to hell
and back for their younger siblings.*

one

. . .

REAGAN

I POINTED AT MY ASS. "That belong to you?"

On the final night of our hiking trip, my twin sister, Lainey, and I wandered into the local dive bar, which happened to be the only bar in this entire county. She wanted to dance, and I wanted to drink something that wasn't water.

Unfortunately, as I'd been on my way to the bar for another round, several guys had gotten handsy, and the latest offender now faced my ire.

What the fuck was it with men, anyway? Putting their hands —and other things—places they didn't belong?

This whole trip had come to fruition because I'd caught my ex-boyfriend balls deep in another girl, and Lainey suggested we get the hell out of dodge. The timing couldn't have worked out better, lining up perfectly with spring break, the final one of our college careers. While the bulk of our classmates headed south for warmer, more tropical locales, Lainey and I traveled north and west, ending up in southwestern Idaho in a place I'd never heard of.

Dusk Valley.

An idyllic name for, I had to admit, a damn charming little town.

Chuckling and shooting me a wink, the offending asshole said, "Not yet."

Stepping forward until I was in his face—eye level, because we were the same goddamn height—batting my lashes like some doe-eyed school girl, I said sweetly, "You ever touch me again, and *I* will own your dick after I break it off your body. Understood?"

"*Oooooh,*" his friends chorused, laughter bubbling out of both of them, but the man in question sneered. Red crept up from the collar of his worn flannel shirt, spreading to his cheeks. Beneath the brim of his hat, I was certain a vein pulsed in the center of his forehead.

"You bitch," he hissed, some spittle landing on my cheek. "I ought to teach you a lesson about respect."

I moved backward. Not because I was afraid of him, but out of sheer desperation to get away from the reek of beer on his breath. "Seems like you missed that lesson yourself."

If such a thing were possible, steam would've come pouring out of his ears then, and he sputtered for something to say.

Satisfied with a job well done, I turned away, intent on continuing my journey to the bar, but I was once again pulled up short by something colliding with my back.

I knew how to take care of myself when it came to drunk men. In addition to the regular self-defense classes Lainey and I had started taking on a whim last fall, I'd put myself through college by waiting tables and bartending. But now fear gripped me, even as the self-preservation instincts that had been drilled into me rose to the surface. Coming after me with my back turned was a fucking coward's move, and the only way to ensure I couldn't mount a proper counterattack.

"I'm so sorry," the person who bumped into me said when I faced them, and I realized it wasn't the man who'd been hitting on me but a woman, the front of her shirt wet from a spilled drink.

"What happened?"

She waved a hand behind her, then accepted a stack of bar napkins from another woman who appeared at her side.

"Pissing contest between a couple guys."

Shoving past me, she and her friend disappeared, and the scene unfolded before me.

A man—a *big* man, thick arms nearly covered with tattoos— had my offender slammed face-first onto a nearby table. Glasses and bottles went flying, shattered pieces skittering across the floor. People nearby fled in gasps of annoyance and shouts of alarm.

Mr. Tall and Tatted twisted the guy's arm behind his back at an unnatural angle, and the man's face contorted in pain. Then the big guy leaned in and said something too low for me to hear.

"I'm sorry!" the asshat shouted in anguish. "It'll never happen again!"

The big man's eyes lifted and scanned the crowd until they landed on me.

Damn, even from ten feet away, his bright blue irises were piercing, reminding me of the watering hole Lainey and I used to spend hot summer days in as kids. We were too poor to afford the community pool, but we had the *best* times on those narrow shores.

"Say it to her," the big guy told his captive, nodding in my direction.

"I'm sorry!" he groaned in my direction. "It won't happen again!"

"You're damn right," I said, then flicked my gaze back to Mr. Tall and Tatted. "You can let him go now."

He did as I asked, saying, "Get the fuck out of here, Tony, before my brothers and I *make* you leave."

Tony held his hands up in surrender, then slowly brought one to his back pocket, withdrew several bills from his wallet, and tossed them on the table before disappearing into the crowd, his flunkies in tow.

All sound in the bar had died at the altercation. Even the band had ceased playing, and my ears rang in the silence.

"Round on me!" Mr. Tall and Tatted shouted, whirling his finger around, then shooting the female bartender a wink as the crowd resumed its evening, the band kicking up an old Alan Jackson tune.

"Very impressive," I said when he approached.

I knew I could take care of myself, but I'd be damned if that display of masculinity didn't give me ideas that would set feminism back a few hundred years. This man…he was *that* hot.

He shrugged. "I've learned a thing or two over the years." Jerking his head toward the bar, he asked, "Can I get you a drink?"

"This round's on you, remember?"

"What'll it be?" the bartender asked when she approached.

"Two vodka sodas, please," I said.

"Two?" the man asked as the woman stepped away to fill my order. "You're here with someone?"

"Yes."

"Damn," he muttered.

"Oh!" I realized my mistake and chuckled. "I'm here with my sister."

The man visibly relaxed, his shoulders dropping, and he made an exaggerated show of wiping sweat off his brow.

"Thank fuck," he breathed. "I was actually on my way over to ask if I could buy you a drink when the whole thing with Tony unfolded."

With a smirk, I gestured to the bar. "Looks like your plan worked."

Wait, was I *flirting* with him?

I wasn't the girl who turned on the charm to get guys to buy me drinks. That was all Lainey's domain. Maybe I *had* been that girl once upon a time. Before life had thrown curveball after curveball at my head, and I spent too long fighting them off to pay much attention to anything else. Now, I was only along for the ride, making sure she didn't get in too much trouble.

You know, typical big sister shit—even if all that separated us in age was a measly five minutes.

My back pocket vibrated, and I withdrew my phone to find a text from Lainey.

> **LAINEY**
>
> Where the fuck are you? I can feel myself sobering up by the second.

I rolled my eyes. *Such dramatics.*

The bartender returned with my drinks, and though I was loath to walk away from this sexy as sin mystery man, I needed to get back to Lainey.

Lifting the glasses in the air, I did an awkward shrug-head nod combination and said, "Well, it was nice meeting you. Thanks for these."

Before he could say anything else, I walked away.

Between sending that text and my reappearance, Lainey seemed to have forgotten all about the alcohol and was instead wholly focused on a different kind of drug: male attention.

Spotting me, she left the guy in question with a caress to his arm and crossed the short distance back to our table.

"Sooooo…" she began when I slid the glasses onto the round high top. Stepping close to me, she leaned in so she could speak directly into my ear to be heard over the crowd. "I'm leaving."

Over her shoulder, I took a moment to study the guy. His back was to us, and he was giving high fives to the two guys seated with him—clearly in celebration that he'd managed to bag my sister. There wasn't much to say about his appearance since I couldn't see his face, but he stood no taller than six feet. His hair was a nondescript shade of brown, and his shoulders weren't broad exactly, but wide enough to suggest he did some sort of hard labor for work.

Arguing with Lainey wouldn't do any good, only drive her out the door faster, so I didn't waste my breath. I simply pulled her into a hug, whispered, "Be safe," and sent her on her way.

"I love you too!" she yelled over her shoulder as she allowed the man to lead her through the crush of people toward the exit.

"Well, fuck," I muttered.

There was no way in hell I was staying here alone. Leaving the drinks untouched on the table, I started working my way through the crowd in the same direction Lainey and her flavor of the evening had disappeared.

With my head down, I unashamedly elbowed my way toward the door—until a large hand caught me around the upper arm and pulled me to a stop.

Not again.

"Look, pal," I started, whirling around, guns blazing, ready to lay into this asshole.

Only to find myself staring up into those gorgeous blue eyes belonging to Mr. Tall and Tatted.

He let me go, raising his hands. "Sorry. I saw you on a mission and couldn't let you leave."

I quirked a brow. "Oh?"

"I wanted to buy you a drink, remember?"

"And you did…"

"Then where is it?"

"Oh, I…" *Damn.* Why was I so flustered? Something about his eyes had knocked me off balance, clearly. "Look, my sister ditched me for a hookup, and I don't really want to be here alone."

One side of his mouth ticked up in a half grin. "You're not alone."

"You mean you?"

He shrugged. "Why not?"

Why not, indeed?

Other than the fact that I had no idea what this man's name was, I didn't have a good reason *not* to stick around.

You know, for science.

Deciding it was time to fix our lack of proper introduction, I stuck my hand out. "Reagan," I offered.

He accepted my handshake, his large palm entirely engulfing mine. An electrical current zinged up my arm and spread through the rest of my body, illuminating my nerve endings in a way I'd never experienced before.

Chemistry.

Was it possible? Could I be experiencing that elusive lust-at-first-sight with the hottest man I'd ever laid eyes on?

"Finn," he supplied, his voice a low rasp that sparked across my skin and settled deep in my belly, pooling heat in my core.

"Suits you."

The answer to the question I'd asked myself earlier was a resounding *yes*. I was *absolutely* flirting.

"How so?"

I shrugged. "Sexy name for a hot guy."

He ducked until we were eye level. "Pot, meet kettle."

I'd never blushed a day in my life, but under his bright blue gaze, my cheeks flamed.

Awkwardly clearing my throat because I had no appropriate response to *that*, I deflected by saying, "So how about that drink?"

Another smirk tilted his full lips, surely remembering the one he'd already gotten me that I'd abandoned untouched. "Lead the way."

The crowd parted like the Red Sea around us, easily paving the way to the bar, likely in deference to the large man behind me. He didn't touch me, but I could feel his hand hovering near my back, ready to reach for me if the need arose.

The bartender smirked. "You can't stay away, can you?"

Finn grinned. "Not from you."

My brow creased, annoyed to find him flirting with her right in front of me—and further annoyed for being annoyed in the first place.

What the fuck was going on with me?

"Round for my brothers, except—"

"Yeah, Finn," she said, cutting him off with an eye roll. "Except Crew, I know." Then she looked at me. "And for you?"

"Whatever they're having is fine with me."

"Six IDs, coming right up." When we didn't move, she shooed us away. "Go. I'll bring 'em over. You're takin' up space we ain't got."

Finn chuckled, then grabbed my hand. He stared at me in surprise, like he hadn't meant to. But when he tried to pull his hand away, I held fast, giving him a reassuring smile. He returned it before heading toward the back corner, skirting the dance floor and towing me along behind him. I told myself I wanted to hold his hand because it made following him easier than trying to fight through the crowd myself.

Really, though, that was a lie.

Secretly, I loved the way my nerve endings lit up with his touch. My whole body was electrified, making me feel more alive than I had in months.

"What's an ID?" I asked, loud enough to be heard over the din.

"Local brew," he replied over his shoulder. "Hope you like IPAs!"

I didn't, but I wasn't about to tell him that. I'd find a way to choke it down. Growing up in the south, my manners had been drilled into me from a young age. If this sexy ass man was buying me a drink, I'd say, "thank you" and finish the whole damn thing with a smile on my face. *Especially* since I'd already wasted the first one.

Maybe I wasn't *quite* the southern belle Mama and Daddy had raised anymore, but there were some things I'd never shake.

"The prodigal son returns!" someone, who I couldn't yet see around Finn's massive body, yelled before we'd even reached the table. Though we were out of the thick of the crowd, we still had a perfect view of the stage and the people line dancing to "Fake ID" by Big & Rich.

"You and your fucking hero complex," a different man said.

"Don't you know, little bro?" Finn responded. "The hero always gets the girl."

"Don't call me that. And if you *got* her, where is she?"

Finn stepped to the side, giving me a full view of the table full of ridiculously good-looking men. These must've been his brothers and, *damn*, the *genes* in this family didn't fuck around.

"Everyone, meet Reagan. Reagan, these are my brothers," Finn confirmed. "Owen, the oldest." He pointed at one sitting at the end of the long, rectangular table, a backward ball cap settled on his head, his sandy blond hair long enough to brush his shoulders. Something about him was vaguely familiar, but I couldn't put my finger on what. "Trey, second oldest." Trey's hair was short on the sides and long on the top. He was more leanly muscled than the others, but equally as tall and with the same shade of hair and eyes. "Lane."

"That's Sheriff to you," the guy said, his muscles rivaling Finn's. Every inch of skin I could see from where the sleeves of his tee strained against his biceps down to the words "love free" across his knuckles was covered in ink.

"You've had the title for like three days," Finn retorted. Then he murmured to me, "You don't have to call him that."

"We all call him a pain in the ass," one of the two remaining brothers said happily, earning him a slap on the back of the head from the sheriff.

When I turned my attention to him, I gasped, doing a comical double take between him and Finn.

Finn grinned, and his his *twin* said, "Surprise! I'm West, his better half."

Sighing heavily through his nose, Finn pinched his eyes shut and tilted his head back, as though praying for strength. "How many times do I have to tell you, dipshit? That doesn't mean what you think it means."

"As many times as you want," West said. "I'm never going to stop saying it."

"I should've eaten you in the womb."

As though sensing a fight was brewing, the final guy rose from the table and extended a hand to me. Same hair, same eyes, tall, muscular build, only the upper half of his left arm engulfed in tattoos.

"I'm Crew," he said as we shook. "The youngest of these idiots."

"Nice to meet you all," I said, feeling a tad shell-shocked.

What had I gotten myself into?

A LOT OF FUN, as it turned out.

When the bartender arrived with a tray of drinks for me and the boys, they slipped easily into the sort of not-so-gentle ribbing and shorthand only possible between siblings. Sitting next to Finn, I watched it all, wishing Lainey had stayed to experience it with me. I found myself marveling at the sheer gorgeousness of these men. How was it possible that their parents had created not one or two, but *six* stunning creatures? With the muscles, tattoos, mesmerizing blue eyes, and straight, white smiles, it was clear to me they'd each left a trail of women with broken hearts in their wake.

Was I about to be another one?

Honestly? I fucking hoped so.

Lainey and I were leaving town in the morning. This didn't have to be anything more than a good night of sexy fun.

The band, which had been playing a mixture of throwback and recent country hits, launched into their rendition of "The Bones" by Maren Morris.

"I love this song," I murmured, closing my eyes and swaying to the beat, softly singing the words.

In addition to the beers, we'd taken several shots of tequila, and that delicious buzz had settled over me, loosening my limbs.

A touch fell on my shoulder, and my eyes popped open, immediately connecting with Finn's.

He held his hand out. "Let's dance."

Like hell was I about to say no.

I slipped my palm against his, and he led me out onto the floor.

We found ourselves right in the middle of the couples already dancing. A few of Finn's brothers had also made their way out. Lane was nearby with his arms wrapped around a brunette of average height, her curled hair a long curtain that fell to her butt. Beyond him, Trey was laughing with a tall blonde in his arms. Owen and Crew had remained at the table, and West had disappeared a while ago.

Finn drew me into his embrace, his hands sliding low on my hips, fingers spreading wide against the upper curve of my ass. For once, I was grateful for my own height, because I easily looped my arms around his neck. He settled his cheek against my temple, and we gently stepped side to side, swaying in a small circle.

Goddesses, it felt good to be wrapped in someone's arms again—but, inexplicably, *especially* his. Strong, sturdy, and incredibly warm. I barely knew him, yet I knew without a doubt I was *safe* with him.

As that sense of safety spread through my system, it morphed into something totally different.

Desire.

I *wanted* this man. In a bone-deep way.

As if able to read my thoughts, Finn's fingers flexed, digging into my flesh, scorching my skin through the thin material of my dress. Though no space remained between us as it was, he pulled me closer. His heart beat out a staccato rhythm against his chest, echoing the pace of my own.

"Finn," I breathed, shifting to look up at him.

Our lips were inches apart.

"Let's get out of here."

"*Fuck yes.*"

two

. . .

FINN

REAGAN HAD STOOD out like a beacon in the dark, dirty bar. And not only because she wore this tight, short, sexy red dress either, sticking out like a sore thumb amongst the Carhartt pocket tees, dusty Wrangler denim, and array of well-worn work boots.

She was easily the most beautiful woman I'd ever encountered, like an angel in a room full of devils. I'd never seen her before, but I *wanted* to see a *lot* more.

"Dibs," I'd called to my brothers like the complete asshole I was.

But I'd be damned if I didn't immediately *know* she was mine, at least for the night.

The moment that "fuck yes" left her lips, I captured her hand in mine and rushed toward the exit, Reagan's excited laughter following.

When the cool evening air greeted us, I crowded her back against the side of the building, planted my hands on the sides of her head, and stared down at her.

"Damn, you're pretty."

Ducking my head, my lips found her throat, that soft spot

over her pulse where her shoulder curved up. Reagan tilted her head, giving me better access. The first kiss was soft, chased by a flick of my tongue and a nip of my teeth.

Reagan's responding sigh was music to my ears.

I worked my way up to her jaw, across her cheek, until my lips hovered right above hers.

Waiting. Silently daring her to take this where we both wanted it to go.

"Do it."

My mouth crashed to hers, tongue instantly seeking entrance. She tasted exactly as I thought she would: sweet and perfect, like the small, wild strawberries that grew on my family's ranch. The bitter bite of beer and sharp, lingering sting of tequila combined with her signature flavor was addictive as hell.

She was soft and pliant under my touch, plump lips fitting perfectly against mine. We found an easy rhythm, tongues flicking against each other, teeth against lips, biting and pulling. I shifted my pelvis into her, my cock painfully hard against her lower stomach, and I hissed at the pressure.

Reagan reached between us and palmed me, eliciting a groan.

"Let's go to my room," she said. "Take care of this."

Slipping my hand under her dress, I skated my fingers over her panties, encountering her heat and soaked gusset. Her breath hitched.

"And this. Fuck, I want to taste you so badly."

Reagan shoved lightly at my chest, and through my lust-filled gaze, I studied her. The way the red neon glow from the bar sign cast a sexy spotlight on her.

Lacing our fingers together, Reagan inclined her head. "So my room then?"

"Fuck yes," I said.

The walk to the lone motel in town was short—barely two blocks—but I couldn't keep my hands to myself. Tangling my fingers in her hair, pulling her to a stop every few feet so I could indulge in another kiss.

I felt like a teenager again. The urge to touch her, to taste her, was uncontrollable.

The beauty was, she seemed to be as caught up as me.

When we reached the motel, she led me to her door, fumbling in her little clutch in search of the key. I wrapped myself around her, pressing her back to my front and wrapping my palm around her throat, angling her head back.

"Hurry up," I growled.

Reagan moaned, the sound morphing into a cute little squeak of triumph when she latched onto the key and withdrew it.

Taking it from her hands, I spun her around and slammed her against the door, mouth coming down on hers once again, scooping her into my arms at the same time. Reagan's clutch fell to the ground as her legs and arms wound around me. By feel, I shoved the key in the lock, pushed the door open, then kicked her clutch in.

The heavy wooden door slammed against the wall loud enough to wake the dead—but not with enough force to tear my mouth away from Reagan's.

All night, I'd been damn near crawling out of my skin, ready to drag her into my lap and take her right there in the middle of the bar. The casual touches we'd shared had set my skin on fire. So had the way she'd constantly studied me, as though she didn't want to look away for too long, worried I might vanish if she did.

I'd been afraid of the same thing.

This connection was undeniable, had struck me straight and true.

"Fuck, Reagan," I groaned against her skin, shifting my attention from her lips to her cheek, her jaw, the delicate column of her throat. "If I wasn't already drunk, your kiss would do it."

"More," she gasped, echoing my thoughts.

I needed more of *everything*: more of her skin, her little sounds, her nails in my back.

More of *her*.

I crossed to the bed in two long strides and tossed her onto it.

Grabbing one boot then the other, I yanked them off and threw them across the room.

"Strip," I demanded.

Reagan surprised me by rising onto her knees. I didn't take her for a woman great at following directions—not based on the way she'd handed Tony his ass earlier. But her eyes never left mine as she gripped the hem of her dress and slowly dragged it north. Every fresh inch of exposed skin heated my veins until my blood flamed, sent it all rushing south to my cock, further hardening the already engorged flesh.

It cleared the apex of her thighs and the lacy black underwear covering her cunt, her trim waist and belly button with a pink and gold ring through it. When the bottom curves of her tits appeared—bare—I knew I was a fucking goner.

At last, the dress came free, and she tossed it away.

"My god, you're beautiful."

With a grin and flushed cheeks, her thumbs dipped into the waistband of her panties, but I stopped her.

"Keep them on."

"I thought you wanted a taste," she teased.

"We'll get there, baby. We've got all night."

"All night, huh?"

"And I plan to use every single second to unravel you."

I stepped forward and knelt on the bed, placing my palm gently on her chest and forcing her onto her back. Crawling up, I straddled her hips and bent, kissing her again, inhaling deeply. As though I could brand every sensation of this moment on my memory, keeping it with me to carry through endless dark days when West and I went back overseas in a few days.

Mentally, I shook myself. I wouldn't go there. Not now. The future didn't exist. Only this moment with her.

My mouth traveled lower. Sealing my lips over the flesh of her neck, I suckled, pulling away with a *pop*. Satisfied by the red mark left behind, knowing it would still be there tomorrow.

Next, I fixated on her tits, the perfect, perky handful with rosy nipples tightened to points. Darting my eyes up to hers, I lowered my head and wrapped my mouth around a peak, flicking my tongue against it, swirling it around. I repeated the process on the other side before sliding lower. At her sides, Reagan's hands fisted the sheets.

"You okay?" I asked with a chuckle.

"Don't stop."

When I dipped the tip of my tongue into the hollow of her belly button, she arched against me, my name leaving her in a breathy gasp.

I fucking loved how responsive she was. How every inch of her body seemed to be an erogenous zone.

Shifting backward, I dropped to my stomach so I was face to face with her cunt, the tip of my nose nudging her panties right over her clit.

"If you taste as good as you smell, I'm about to be ruined."

"Never had someone talk so much in bed."

"You want me to stop?"

"Fuck no."

Grinning, I brushed my thumb over her mound, and she twitched, her hips arching up, seeking more when I pulled my hand away. I was about to shift the soaked fabric covering her pussy to the side and dive in when she stopped me.

"Hey Finn?"

"Yes?"

Lifting onto her elbows, she looked down at me, her bottom lip stuck between her teeth. She batted her lashes, though her lids were at half-mast, a lust-filled expression that made the feral beast in my chest who loved nothing more than pleasuring a woman roar in satisfaction.

And she hadn't even come yet.

"Would you mind taking your clothes off, please?"

Her drawl had gotten thicker than it'd been when I first clocked it earlier. The vowels stretched the more we drank, and now they were pure honey.

"Such manners," I said, rising to stand, my hands going to my belt.

"Well, I am a southern lady, after all."

Kicking my pants off and whipping my shirt over my head, I returned to her, leaving us similarly clad in only our underwear.

I knelt on the bed and smirked down at her. "My sexy little belle."

"Nah," she said, shaking her head, her blonde hair a corona on the ugly paisley comforter beneath her. "You're the sexy one."

"I think we can both be sexy."

"Stand up," she demanded, and I did as she asked. "Now spin."

Though confused, I followed that command as well, turning in a slow circle.

When I faced her again, she groaned, throwing her head back.

"Goddesses, your body is unreal."

"Goddesses?" I asked, brow raised.

"You don't think I'm going to pray to a *man*, do you?"

I chuckled. "Fair enough. Now let's go back to the part about my body being unreal."

Reagan huffed out a sigh, but her lips twitched in amusement. "What do you do for a living?"

"What do *you* do?" I retorted.

"Currently, I'm in college," she answered quickly. "But my sister and I are starting our own photography business once we graduate next month." Then she stood on the bed, tall enough that she had to duck to avoid bumping her head on the drop ceiling, and peeled her panties off. Leaving her completely naked—and me drooling. Her underwear flew at my face. "Your turn."

I snapped to attention. "Guess," I said as I shucked my boxer briefs and crawled back onto the mattress, capturing her by the waist and tackling her backward. The bed groaned and squeaked, leaving no doubt any neighbors we had would know *exactly* what we were doing in here.

Let 'em listen. I planned to give them a hell of a show.

She ran her hands up my stomach, my abdominals bunching under her touch, over my chest, and down my arms. Her palms were cool against my overheated skin. Her fingertips followed the outlines of my tattoos, the mountains and trees on my left arm, the compass, flowers, and map of the world on the other.

"Well, you don't get muscles like this at a desk job."

"I work out regularly."

"I'm sure you do," she agreed. "But not out of some misplaced sense of vanity."

"Misplaced?"

"Please." She rolled her eyes. "You know you're hot."

I grinned. "As long as you think so."

"Your job?" she prompted, not letting me go that easily.

"I'm in the Army."

I didn't want to talk about it, so it didn't make sense to give her more than that, to delve further into the details of what exactly I did on behalf of the United States government. For starters, ninety-nine percent of my missions were classified, and the parts that weren't didn't exactly qualify as pillow talk.

"When do you head back?"

"Three days. West and I only managed to get leave because Lane was elected sheriff."

"I'm kind of the ideal one-night fling then, aren't I?"

"What do you mean?"

"There aren't any strings attached to this. You're leaving. I live across the country. You won't have to go back to war worrying about making some woman back home a widow. After tonight, we'll never see each other again."

I blinked in surprise. How had she known that was one of my greatest fears? If something happened to me or West—or, god forbid, both of us—leaving our family behind to mourn us would be one thing. But I couldn't, in good conscience, put a woman through that—asking her to wait for me, knowing I might never return.

So why did the thought of never seeing Reagan again fill me with so much dread?

Playing it cool, I said, "Better make the most of it before I go back overseas then."

"My sexy soldier," she mused, hands sliding to my shoulders and pulling me close.

"Reporting for duty," I replied, a breath away from her mouth.

She lifted her head and captured my lips.

The rest of the world faded away as we lost ourselves in each other.

three

. . .

FINN

SEVEN YEARS LATER

I CLICKED MY TONGUE, and the miniature horse I was working with in the paddock next to the barn trotted over to me.

"He's healing up nice," Abel, my foreman, said from where he watched outside the fence, his arms resting across the top board.

Nodding, I reached for the horse's reins and led him to the nearby water trough.

As a rescue ranch, we took in all kinds of lamed and otherwise wounded animals, as well as ones that were unwanted and abandoned by previous owners. The mini horse, who came to us as a foal, was the king of mischief around here. His most recent escapade involved him breaking free from the barn in the middle of the night and going on a jaunt across nearby fields. Unfortunately, he'd fallen into a ditch and broke one of his front legs. We got him patched up, which meant surgery to properly reset the bones and two months of physical therapy. Finally, though, he appeared almost back to normal—but we were keeping a close eye on him lest he tried to do something similar again.

After he drank his fill, I walked him into the barn and secured him in his stall.

I was about to enter my office when my phone rang, and I peeled off my glove, tilting my hat back to wipe the sweat off my brow before answering.

Sheriff, the readout said.

Couldn't be anything good if big brother was calling.

"Hey, Lane."

"You and West busy?"

I glanced at the mountain of paperwork on my desk, then to the manure fork resting against the wall on my left, then down the alley and twelve stalls I knew needed mucking.

Yeah, I had time.

I had a slew of stable boys to do the shittier parts of this job, but sometimes, I liked to come out here and do it myself. As the boss, I didn't *need* to get my hands dirty, but I liked to remind my employees I wasn't above doing the same hard work I asked of them.

"I don't know about him, but I'm free. What's up?"

"I need you to fly the SAR chopper out to a scene. A couple hikers reported a suspicious campsite, but it's dicey getting in there with anything bigger than an ATV, and it's several miles off the closest access road. Figured having you to evac if need be was a good idea."

My dark little brain brightened some at that.

"You think there's someone there?"

"A woman recently filed a missing person's report for her sister who was supposedly in the area. Could be nothing."

Helping someone was exactly the kind of distraction I needed.

"I'll wrangle West and we'll be on our way. Send me the coordinates."

We disconnected, and I dialed my twin.

"Yo."

"Get your ass up to the house. Lane needs our help on a call."

"Fuck yeah," West said. "Anything to get out of changing sheets in these fucking guest cabins."

I could hear movement in the background, a muffled curse, and West saying, "Peace out, losers!"

"You still haven't found a new housekeeper?"

"No!" he whined. "Good help is so hard to find."

"So are brothers who aren't dramatic as fuck."

West chuckled. "You love me."

I did. Loved all my brothers, and Aria, but as twins, it was different with West. Especially given the shit we'd done and seen together in the service. Those kinds of situations bonded you for life, and having endured it all with him by my side was both a blessing and a curse.

"Hurry up," I grumbled

A door slammed, a loud diesel engine turned over, and West shouted, "Aye, aye, captain!" before hanging up.

After tidying a bit and letting my foreman know I'd be taking off for the rest of the day, I walked toward the big house—the house we'd all grown up in—where Mama and Aria still lived. I poked my head in long enough to tell them where we were headed and chug a glass of water before West arrived.

Crossing the Lawless family ranch land from his dude ranch to my rescue ranch took five minutes on a good day, but West must've been desperate to get out of cleaning cabins, because he made it in less than half.

He'd barely pulled to a stop when I hopped into the passenger seat.

"Where to?"

"Airport."

West nodded and stepped on the gas, peeling away from the ranch.

Owyhee County airport wasn't a commercial affair. In fact,

its small hangar only housed two aircraft—a Cessna 172 Skyhawk, which happened to be mine, and a Bell 429 search and rescue helicopter, which we'd be taking out today. There was no real runway, only a strip of hard-packed dirt cut into the field from years of little planes taking off and landing.

West pulled to a stop in the gravel lot next to the hangar, and we rounded to the bed where he kept extra gear stored for situations like this. We quickly suited up, easily shedding our ranch owner personas for the Rangers we'd been barely six years ago.

Though Lane made it sound as though this was nothing more than a routine recovery, I'd walked into too many "routine" situations only to have them go sideways to head into the mountains without my tactical gear.

"Hello, wee birdie," I murmured to the chopper when we got inside, approaching it to do my checks while West opened the hangar door and loaded equipment, like ropes and harnesses, as well as EMS supplies like a rescue basket, neck brace, and various bandages, tapes, and gauze.

My brother wasn't fazed by me speaking to the helicopter; he'd long since gotten used to my antics where aircrafts were concerned.

The sky was my happy place.

We'd been given numerous opportunities thanks to the Army, especially as far as what we did while we were enlisted went. I'd always known I wanted to be a pilot, and West hadn't given a fuck what he did as long as he had a gun in his hands.

We were simple creatures like that.

Being able to get my pilot's license and provide aerial support for a number of highly classified government ops over the years truly wasn't where I'd seen my life going, growing up in this small town. But I was grateful for the experience—even more so because, when we were ready to retire at the ripe old age of 28, the Army let us go with little fanfare and a lot of money in our bank accounts.

Money we put right back into Lawless Rescue & Dude Ranch.

Personally, I was happy to be free of the military, where, while we'd been paid handsomely after joining the Rangers, we were treated as little more than a set of numbers. Cogs in some great machine with no idea who pulled the strings.

I didn't like the power those unnamed, faceless forces had over us, oftentimes turning us and our unit into contract killers to carry out vendettas that had no rhyme or reason.

Sometimes, though, I thought West was a little…listless without it. Many men and women made lifelong careers out of it, but that was never on my and West's radars. Still, it had been the only thing we'd known from the time we'd signed on the dotted line at eighteen to the day we walked away a decade later.

The dude ranch was good for him. It gave him a place to channel his energy, to fuck around and act like his crazy, reckless self without causing too much damage.

And nights like this helped, when we soared off into the sky on a mission like the good old days.

Pre-flight checks finished, I gave West a thumbs up, and he climbed into the passenger seat beside me. We both donned our headsets, strapped in, and sealed the doors shut.

Then I ran through my next set of checks, including the pedals, throttles for both engines, emergency equipment and lights, communications systems, and a slew of other shit that was all muscle memory to me now.

When I'd first moved home and been asked to take over for the previous rescue pilot who was getting ready to retire, I'd had to certify in order to fly this specific helicopter, but I hadn't minded. Any chance I had to get up in the air, I was taking it.

Once we lifted off and reached cruising altitude, I had West punch in the coordinates Lane had texted me. Our comms system was connected to the same channel as Lane's sheriff's satellite phone, and we'd been airborne for maybe five minutes when it crackled to life, our older brother's voice coming down the line.

"Sheriff Lawless to N652AA. Come in. Over."

West and I shared a look, more of a glare at our brother's formality, before I opened the line and said, "Captain Lawless of N652AA here. What do you want, *Sheriff?*"

West's chuckle resonated through my headset, cut off by Lane's world-weary sigh as he opened up his end of the line again.

"What's your ETA?"

I glanced down at the nav system, the topography of the Idahoan landscape speeding past, and calculated our distance from the scene.

"Ten minutes."

Another sigh from big bro. "There's a clearing about a quarter mile out to the west that you can touch down in. I texted those coordinates." West pulled his phone out, then punched the new numbers into the system, and our course altered slightly. "One of Crew's guys will be waiting on the ground to lead you in."

"You've got the fire department out there too?" West asked.

"They assisted with the search."

I noticed how he pointedly didn't mention the second half of what SAR stood for—*and rescue*. That combined with the lack of urgency told me we would not find someone who could be saved, and my heart twisted in pain for the friends and family of this lost soul.

"So it's a recovery."

"Yes."

"Where was our call?" West said. "You know we've got more experience than our baby brother and his guys."

"You were busy."

I snorted. *Bullshit*. Ranch business didn't come before the welfare of Dusk Valley citizens or lost campers, and he damn well knew it. Shit like this was the whole reason I even had access to the SAR chopper. Hell, I was the only person within a hundred miles of this place who could even fly the damn thing.

But after the whole ordeal our youngest brother, Crew, and his now-fiancée, Aspen, had gone through last summer, Lane was wary of letting his family anywhere near cases.

Especially if foul play was suspected.

Suffice it to say, my curiosity was officially piqued.

West and I shared a look that told me he felt the same.

"What do you think we're walking into?" he asked after Lane severed our connection.

"Honestly? I have no fucking clue. Before that strange conversation, I would've guessed a camper who died from exposure. But he's being cagey, and when he gets like this, you know there's more to it than that."

"Been a minute since we had a murder around here," he said, almost conversationally, though that twin-speak thing we had going for us allowed me to read between the lines.

Allowed me to understand the subtext, how below the off-handed remark, he was remembering last summer when Crew had been taken hostage by the woman who had committed Dusk Valley's last murder.

Crew's abduction wasn't anyone's fault but Kelly Saunders', and he'd gotten the love of his life out of the whole mess, but that didn't stop the rest of us from remembering the fear that came with realizing he'd been taken, and the seemingly interminable hours we spent trying to figure out where the fuck he'd been.

I wondered: would this case hit as close to home?

Ten minutes later, I touched down in the field and found Crew himself at the tree line, waiting to lead us in.

"What've we got?" I asked as I opened the back door of the copter and extracted the basket, leaving the bag of medical supplies.

"Female vic," Crew said as West and I fell in line behind him, ducking under low-hanging tree branches and stepping on newly sprouted saplings, trampling a path back to the site. "Mid- to late twenties if I had to guess. No idea how long she's been out here, because the ME hasn't arrived yet, but body is fairly well preserved."

"Well, it's been cold as fuck," West said. "So I'm sure that helped. She's not a popsicle, is she?"

"I don't think so, but rigor mortis has set in, so it's hard to tell."

"Time of death is within the last day or so, then?" I asked.

"Most likely," Crew said. "Lane's MP was reported this morning, and by then, the call from hikers had already come in."

Conversation stalled as he led us up a steep incline that plateaued slightly at the top. When we reached it, West and I stopped to survey the scene.

Off to the side stood Crew's subordinate firefighters: Tuck, Childers, and Burns. They murmured amongst themselves, waiting for instructions from their captain, but each gave us a nod of acknowledgement. Several of Lane's deputies also milled around, fanned out at regular intervals, presumably searching for evidence.

Johns was here, but he wisely stayed far away from Crew— likely on Lane's orders.

Someone had obviously been camping here. Off to one side, tucked up against the sheer cliff face that jutted up behind it, was a single-person tent. Larger vegetation in the area had been recently cleared. A firepit had been dug in the dirt in the center and circled with rocks. A fallen log served as seating and a large boulder was being used as a rudimentary table. Atop it were two slabs of meat, raw steaks of some sort already being picked over by flies.

The victim was lying in the brush off to the side, right at the edge of the clearing, her limbs tangled around her like the branches of the trees above. Long, honey blonde hair trailed out around her, limp and lackluster in death.

Crew, West, and I drew closer until we stood right over her. Eyes, once full of light and life, were now milky in death, turning the irises some undetermined shade. Her mouth was open, as though parted on a scream for help no one would ever hear. The back of her head rested against the base of a birch tree, her chin resting on her chest.

My first glance didn't give me any indication of cause of death, but as I shifted around to her side, I saw it: dark purple streaks of bruising around her neck—each in the shape of fingers.

"Sooo…strangulation then?" West said conversationally.

"What gave it away?" Lane said wryly, walking up with Sutton Rausch, one of the paramedics who worked out of the firehouse with Crew. Her partner, Thomas, wasn't far behind.

"Lucky guess."

"Have some fucking respect," Sutton said fiercely, glaring at each of us in turn. "She died horrifically."

None of us were religious by any stretch, but we all took a moment of silence in the wake of Sutton's admonishment. Lane went so far as to make the sign of the cross before speaking again, as though sealing some prayer that the woman's soul found peace in the beyond.

"I know you're not a doctor," Lane said to Sutton, "but break it down for me."

"Well, in my inexpert opinion, she's been out here since sometime yesterday. Clothes are still intact, so I'd guess the crime wasn't sexually motivated. Based on how deep the bruising goes, whoever did this to her held on for a lot longer and with far more force than was necessary. I wouldn't be shocked if the autopsy reveals her neck was also broken. I'd guess this was personal for the killer. Either they knew each other, or she represents a trigger."

"You and your fucking psychology," Lane muttered.

Sutton rolled her eyes, and I shared a look with my two other brothers.

The comment was too…familiar, like Lane was privy to some information about Sutton the rest of us weren't. There was something that simmered beneath the surface of every one of their interactions, and I genuinely had no idea if they wanted to fight to the death or fuck it out.

It was a fine line.

"Isn't that one of the first things you look for, *Sheriff?*" she sneered. "Does the motive not play a major part in who did this to her?"

"Uh oh," West stage whispered. "Mom and Dad are fighting again."

"Fuck off," Lane gritted out.

"You know she's right," Crew said. Lane cut him a glare that could've killed, and Crew merely shrugged.

To Lane, I said, "What do you need from us?" steering the conversation back to the matter at hand: getting this victim out of the elements and to the morgue.

If we let them, Sutton and Lane would run away with their argument, and the results could be catastrophic enough to level the forest around us.

"Get some gloves on and help us load her on the backboard," Sutton answered.

"Then Tuck, Burns, Childers, and I will bring her to the copter," Crew supplied.

"Will personnel meet us in Boise?" I asked Lane.

Owyhee County didn't have its own medical examiner since its population consisted of more farm animals and wildlife than people. Any suspicious deaths found their way onto the state-appointed medical examiner's slab.

"No. Bring her to town."

I blinked slowly, not positive I heard him correctly.

"We're taking her to *our* morgue?" West asked the question I'd been about to, mirroring my surprise. "The morgue that *never* gets used?"

"Yep," Lane said as he passed out nitrile gloves to each of us, which would then go into an evidence bag and logged into the file in case anything transferred to us when we moved the body. "Stockman said he'd come to us."

"Look at you, moving up in the world," I said, clapping Lane on the shoulder. "Solve one case and now you're a big dog who's got the ME on speed dial."

Lane rolled his eyes, but the corners of his mouth tipped up slightly.

Until Crew stole his thunder.

"Actually, my girl solved that case," Crew piped in.

Lane flipped Crew off.

"C'mon, fuckers. Let's get this show on the road."

four

· · ·

REAGAN

"I FEEL AWFUL."

"You look it too," Lainey said, grinning at me.

Rolling my eyes, then wincing as the movement aggravated the headache I'd been unable to shake for the last three days, I pinned her with a look. "You're an asshole."

"You love me."

When I grumbled noncommittally, Lainey threw one of the pillows from our couch at my head.

"I meant about the trip," I explained. "You know it's my turn."

She gestured to me, where I was curled into the fetal position on one side of our sectional, dressed in sweats and layered with blankets to ward off the chills that had plagued me as long as the headache. "You're on your deathbed, Rea. You're hardly in a position to fly across the country."

"It's just the flu," I protested, albeit weakly.

The truth was, I hadn't been this sick in a long time. The up and down fever, the body aches, headache, and occasional bouts of nausea and vomiting had sapped all of my energy. For the last several days, I'd barely been able to shuffle between my bed and the couch.

As much as I hated to admit it, she was right.

After graduating college nearly seven years ago, Lainey and I had started our own photography business. Though it had taken a few years, we'd built a large social media following. Thanks to our online popularity, we frequently fielded inquiries about jobs across the country. Long ago, my twin and I had come to the agreement that we would alternate who took the trips. Our styles were similar enough that we'd never encountered an instance where a client preferred one of us over the other.

We were simply Twin Flames Photography, the faces behind *the cameras.*

"Are you sure it's even a good idea for you *to go, though? You know, since you-know-who…"*

I trailed off. Lainey knew who I was talking about. In fact, I didn't even know the guy's name. When we'd come back from our spring break trip to Idaho seven years ago, Lainey had brought a stalker with her.

Maybe stalker was the wrong word. As far as we knew, the guy had never come to our small town in eastern Tennessee. But for six and a half years, he'd refused to leave Lainey alone digitally. He would call and text at all hours of the night. Lainey would block him, but he'd reappear with a new number in days. He'd also harassed us both on our business and personal social media profiles.

Begging Lainey to come back. Asking her to give them a chance. Reminding her what a good time they'd had together that night in Dusk Valley.

Over the years, I'd pleaded with her to go to the police, especially after he threatened to leak some naked pictures he'd taken of her while she slept that night.

But she hadn't, claiming he'd eventually get bored and find someone else to bother.

"Besides, I'm hot as fuck. Having my nudes leaked would hardly ruin me," *she'd said once.*

That was Lainey—irreverent as hell, almost to a fault sometimes.

About six months ago, though, her prediction had come true, and she hadn't heard from the creep since.

Still, sending her back to that place alone was difficult, knowing he was likely still around.

Lainey dropped onto the couch and reached for my hand. "I'm going to be fine."

"I wish you'd at least stay at the motel where there's some security."

Now my sister rolled her eyes. "That place has about as much security as a paper bag," she quipped.

"Hey, they could've upgraded since we were there last."

"I'm camping, and that's the end of it."

Lainey had that look in her eye that told me no amount of pressing the issue would change her mind. She'd dug her feet in and planted roots. There'd be no moving her.

That deep-seated stubbornness was a quality—like many others—we had in common.

"You have your SAT phone?" I asked.

She dug into her bag and withdrew the black, boxy device. Thanks to that trip seven years ago, and numerous ones closer to home since, we knew the signal out in the wilderness was dicey. While I enjoyed the occasional camping and hiking trip, my sister had a habit—more like a penchant—for going off the grid when the voices in her head got a little too loud. I'd purchased the phone for her a few years ago when she disappeared for three days without a word, leaving me with a mountain's worth of worry.

I didn't judge her for it. Goddesses knew there had been days when I'd take off on the road with nothing but my camera and the desire to find a sliver of peace and quiet away from my own demons.

But she was the only family I had left, and I wouldn't survive if something happened to her.

Lainey zipped her bag after returning the phone to the disorganized mix of clothes and toiletries. In contrast to the haphazard jumble of her duffel, next to it, her camera bag with all of its equipment was neatly packed.

Then she faced me, one hand on her hip, the other raised, fingers folding over her palm. "Out with it."

"Out with what?"

"The big sister lecture you always give me before I take off like this. Even if you are only five minutes older," she added with an eye roll.

I snorted. "If you know it's coming, you should remember it from all the times I've given it before."

"Humor me."

Shifting slightly on the couch, though every bone and muscle in my body protested, I reached out and clasped her cheeks in my hands. Most people never got to see their face with their own eyes, but I found mine in Lainey every day. The same green eyes, same naturally honey-blonde hair, the same mouth—though hers had a small white scar cutting through her top lip thanks to a bar fight with a sorority girl in college.

The same girl my ex had cheated on me with.

Lainey had always had my back, and now I would have hers.

"Be careful. I know you're a pro at this, but if something feels off, you bail. Get a hotel room. Ask for help." I stressed that last one with a playful tug on her hair. "There's nothing wrong with asking for help."

"I know."

Lainey was the most free-spirited, independent woman I'd ever known. I was the more careful of the two of us, the level head. The planner. The worrier.

But Lainey was a grown woman, and I had to trust she could take care of herself.

I hauled her to me even though I ached, hugging her tightly, not wanting to let go.

I couldn't explain why, but I was more anxious than I'd ever been for her to leave.

"I'm going to be fine," she said with a laugh, eventually pulling back from my embrace after I allowed it to drag on longer than normal.

As she did, a car beeped outside—her ride to the airport.

"I know," I sighed. "You have everything?"

"Yep."

Unable to help myself, I brought her in for one more squeeze.

"I love you."

"I love you more."

five

. . .

REAGAN

IN MY LAP, my phone rang, pulling me from the memory of my final face-to-face conversation with Lainey.

That final hug.

The last time I heard her say she loved me.

Watching as she skipped down the porch, loaded her bags into the waiting car, and waved as they pulled away.

If I had known what would happen, I never would've let her leave.

Because though the readout on my iPhone screen showed an unknown number, the area code was one I recognized to be from Idaho, and *I knew*.

I knew I wasn't going to like whatever the person on the other end of the line had to say.

The thought almost had me letting the call go to voicemail, but there was no prolonging the inevitable.

Sooner or later, I would have to face this.

With shaky fingers, I slid the bar across to answer, and my voice was barely above a whisper when I said, "Hello?"

A deep, stern male voice asked, "Is this Reagan Lindsey?"

"Yes, this is she," I replied, tone shaky.

"My name is Lane Lawless, and I'm the sheriff here in Dusk Valley, Idaho. I…this is going to be difficult to hear, but we've located the body of a woman. Her driver's license identifies her as Lainey Lindsey. We were able to locate your number as her emergency contact."

We've located the body.

The last fucking words I ever wanted to hear.

Not, *we've located your sister and she's okay.*

Not, *we've located your sister and she's in the hospital undergoing treatment.*

We've located the body.

Four words like gunshots to my heart.

"Oh, goddesses, my sister," I managed to gasp through the panic choking me.

"I am so sorry," he offered lamely.

I didn't thank him for his condolences, only said, "What do you need from me now?"

"If possible, we'd like you to come out here and give us a visual ID, then we can proceed with the autopsy."

That pulled me up short.

"What do you mean, autopsy?"

I assumed she'd taken things a little too far while on a hike and died doing what she loved.

Even if her final message to me had been strange, I never anticipated *this*.

An *autopsy*? That shit was serious.

"We have reason to believe your sister's death was…not accidental."

"She was m-mur—" I couldn't make myself spit out the word.

"We suspect foul play." A diplomatic response, but it said enough.

The world warped around me, my perspective shifting, like I was detached from my body and viewing this whole thing as some unaffected bystander. Like my brain was doing what it could to protect me from the agony it knew was coming.

Still, I appreciated this sheriff's no-nonsense approach to delivering the news of my sister's death.

I didn't need to be coddled right now.

After our parents died, I'd been doted on enough, been spoken to *so* gently and tip-toed around like I would break at any second.

In the end, *that* had been what nearly broke me.

That and the survivor's guilt.

And now I'd have to go through it all again.

I was the only one left.

Fuck.

"I'll be there as soon as I can."

"Your best bet is to fly into Salt Lake, catch a connection to Boise, and—"

"And drive down. Yeah, I know. I've been there before."

Back on *that* night, which now seemed like the beginning of the end.

When Lainey had met the creep who refused to leave her alone.

And I'd met the man I'd never been able to forget.

"Great," he said. "Then we'll see you soon."

"Is this a good number to reach you at?"

"Yeah, this is my personal cell."

"Thank you," I said. "I'll be in touch."

I hung up before he could utter another word.

I breathed out slowly, impending tears prickling my nose.

My vision blurred, and a sob wrenched free from my throat as I dropped my phone onto the couch next to me.

My sister was gone.

My *twin* was *dead*.

Someone had taken her from me, left me completely alone in this world.

Pain like nothing I had ever experienced before arced through my chest, doubling me over. Curling myself into the smallest ball I could manage, I shattered.

The waves of grief crashed and crashed and crashed, pulling me under over and over, leaving me gasping for air. Every time I thought I was coming out on the other side, like the surface was within reach, the realization that the worst was yet to come dragged me down again.

Goddesses, how the fuck was I supposed to get on a plane across the country knowing at the end of it, I'd have to look into my sister's dead face? How could I make myself go there knowing I would see her but never be able to speak to her again?

How was I supposed to handle this alone? Lainey had always been my rock. Through every moment since birth, I had walked this world knowing even if I had nothing else, I had her.

And now, that one constant had been ripped away from me.

A few hiccups escaped as I calmed at last, wiping the tears off my face and rising to blow my nose, my body creaky from disuse. I'd finally come out on the other side of the flu only to be punched in the gut again.

Desperate to not be alone, there was only one person I could call right now. I picked up my phone and dialed before I could fully think it through.

He answered on the second ring.

"Hey, stranger."

"Tr-oy," I croaked, my voice cracking his name in half. Damnit, I thought I'd gotten myself composed enough for this.

"Baby, what's wrong?"

We weren't together anymore, but I didn't admonish him for using the pet name.

My ex having delusions about our reconciliation was the least of my worries.

Though I tried to get the words out, nothing escaped but another sob.

"I'm on my way."

Forgetting he couldn't see me, I nodded then hung up.

That was the thing about Troy: he was so good at *anticipating* my needs or understanding my moods, yet so horrible at *dealing* with them.

He'd come because I called, but he wouldn't know what to say.

And in truth, there wasn't anything he *could* say, no magic combination of words in any language that would make this pain go away.

Besides, I didn't need reassurances or empty platitudes tonight. I didn't need someone to serve as a sounding board while I talked my feelings out.

I only needed to be held. *That* he could handle without diffi-culty—even if inviting him back in had the potential to be a slip-pery slope.

I knew he'd be confused that I called, that I was sending mixed signals, but I wasn't exactly in my right mind.

Troy lived in Knoxville, about an hour north of our small town near Tennessee's borders with Georgia and North Carolina. He didn't bother to knock when he arrived, only came inside, found me in the fetal position on the couch, wrapped me in his arms, and held me as I once again fell apart.

Sometime later, I'd managed to collect myself enough to put some distance between us, though he kept a tight grip on my hand. Anchoring me.

"What happened?" he asked softly.

"Lainey is dead."

The words were flat, but they still struck Troy like a punch. He reared back, blinking rapidly, mouth gaping.

"What?" he asked dumbly.

I shot him a pleading look. "Please don't make me repeat it," I whispered.

Swallowing hard, he nodded. "Start from the beginning."

I told him everything. The client in Idaho. How I'd been supposed to go but had been too sick, so Lainey had gone in my place. How I hadn't heard from her since Tuesday—two days ago—which was entirely unlike her. How I'd made the call to report her missing this morning, hoping like hell my gut instinct had been wrong.

"And now," I said through my tears. "I have to go out there and fucking identify her body."

Troy gathered me to his chest and rocked me as I once again lost myself to gasping sobs.

"Do you want me to go with you?"

I was already shaking my head before he'd fully asked the question. "No. I need to do this on my own."

There was, of course, more to it than that. Troy and I weren't together, and this relapse into my old habits didn't change that.

Still, when the day neared its end, and I was so emotionally and physically exhausted I could barely keep my eyes open…I didn't ask him to leave.

I let him carry me to bed, let him crawl in behind me, the big spoon to my little. Fell into a fitful, nightmare-laden sleep wrapped in his arms.

six

. . .

FINN

I GATHERED my horse's reins and swung us back in the direction of the barn. West and Aria were at my sides on their own horses.

A few months ago, the ranch was asked to take in a badly abused Appaloosa mare. She was skittish as hell around everyone and everything: me; Aria and Mama, who were the gentlest souls on the planet; the highland cows and goats we sometimes penned her with to get her to socialize; the ranch hands and all of my brothers; the other horses.

But with a lot of patience and one-on-one work, she'd come around.

Today, we'd taken her running with the three of us, seeing how she'd react to the wilderness and being surrounded by other horses—especially West's, who, like his rider, was full of piss and vinegar and preferred to lead the pack. Rogue was bossy as hell, and other horses either fell in line or pushed back.

Thankfully, the Appaloosa, whose name was Zigzag, handled the new environment beautifully. My brother, sister, and I took turns trotting along holding her reins, keeping her close lest she decided she had enough human interaction for one lifetime and took off into the wilds.

Sometimes, when a horse like her came into my care, I *wanted* to let them go, allow them to heal themselves and find peace in their freedom.

But she wasn't mine to decide for, and her owner—the woman who'd saved her from her previous life of neglect—was paying Lawless Rescue good money to help her heal.

"A few more rides like this, and she'll be ready to go," Aria said, grinning ear to ear beneath the brim of her caramel-colored Lucchese hat, stealing the words right from my mind.

West and Rogue sidled up to Zigzag, and my twin placed a palm on her broad, brown-and-cream-spotted back, brushing it gently over her coat. Like she would have when she first arrived here, she didn't startle. Merely turned her head, eyes fluttering closed, like she was relishing that soft, loving contact.

How anyone could ever hurt a horse—or any animal—I'd never understand. When Zigzag showed up here and we led her out of the trailer, I damn near collapsed. She'd been all skin and bones, her long ribs pressing harshly against her sides. Her mane, forelock, and tail had been so badly matted we'd had to cut it all off and let it regrow. She'd been filthy, too, like her abusers had left her to fend for herself in the elements for weeks and weeks.

I wanted to kill people who did that to animals.

And believe me—I could do it.

The important thing was, we'd rehabilitated her. The next step was getting her new owner out here for some socialization and, in a few weeks, a ride.

Then she'd be ready to send on her way, another happy customer.

"Thanks for coming out with me today," I told my siblings as we loped back toward the ranch.

Though the days were lengthening the closer to summer we got, the sun hung lower in the sky, dusting the tops of the trees.

Almost time for dinner then, which was a good thing, because my stomach chose that moment to emit a loud, demanding grumble.

Days on the ranch were long, especially when I had a full barn like I did currently. As the only rescue in the entire state of Idaho, we took in all kinds of animals, most often lamed horses, and dogs and cats that were about to be euthanized. There weren't currently any dogs roaming around, but we had eight cats that had been dropped off a few months ago and made their home in the storage shed. Plus the eight horses that belonged to me, my siblings, and Mama, the ten in the remuda, the two highland cows Aria insisted we get because they were "cute", the mini horse, and four small fainting goats.

That wasn't including the dairy cows, either.

Like I said—I had a full barn, and a lot of shit to get done still.

"You're welcome," Aria said, pulling me from my thoughts. She flicked her wrist to check her watch and added, "But if we don't hurry the fuck up, we're going to be late for dinner, and Mama will kill us."

"Shit," West hissed, not bothering to wait for us as he dug his heels into Rogue's sides and took off at a gallop. Aria and I shared a look and took off after him. I gave Zigzag her head, and she kept up easily.

When we pulled the horses to a stop in front of the barn, the three of us quickly dismounted and handed them off to some of my ranch hands, who would be responsible for untacking, grooming, and cooling them down before bedding them down for the night.

My sister, brother, and I headed for my office and the small bathroom attached, where we washed up and brushed as much dust off our clothing as possible before heading for the house.

Mama stood on the porch, arms crossed over her chest, foot tapping.

"Barely made it."

"Sorry," I muttered. "We took Zigzag out and lost track of time."

"How's she doing?" Mama asked, softening. She had that same bleeding heart for animals as the rest of us did.

"Amazing," Aria breathed. "She kept right up with the boys, kept her head when Rogue needled her. I reckon she's ready for a rider."

Aria looked to me, waiting for confirmation, and I gave her a nod. "I want to get her owner out here to socialize with her first. You know, grooming, trotting around the pen, feeding. Easy stuff before we try to get her on for a ride."

Mama nodded. "I think that's a wonderful idea. Now, if y'all don't mind, I slaved all day over this meal, so get your butts inside and start bringing stuff to the table."

We murmured a chorus of "yes ma'am" before clearing the rest of the steps.

Before we could even open the door, a vehicle slid to a stop on the gravel drive. We all turned to watch Lane get out from behind the wheel, but I noticed he didn't turn the engine off.

And he was driving his department SUV, which was odd considering he wasn't on shift tonight.

"Where the fuck have y'all been?" he asked, eyes darting between me and West. "I've been calling for over an hour."

"We were out on a ride," Aria responded before West or I could.

"What's going on?" West asked.

"The sister of that vic is here to do an ID, so I have to miss dinner." He glanced apologetically at Mama, who merely nodded. Police business, of course, waited for no one.

"What vic?" Mama asked.

Lane tried to wave her off, but West said, "We found a dead girl out in the woods yesterday. Looks like murder."

"Murder?" Aria gasped. "What the fuck?"

"Aria," Mama scolded, though absently. Then she sighed, glancing between us three boys. "I suppose if it's important…"

I frowned. "What does that have to do with us?"

"Need you both to come give your statements."

"*Now?*" My stomach grumbled, reminding me I hadn't eaten in hours.

Lane nodded, shifting on his feet like he was anxious to get back to town.

"West and I will come by when we get home," I said to Mama, bending to press a kiss to her cheek, a farewell gesture West repeated on her other side. Lane climbed the stairs and pulled her into a hug, apologizing again for ruining dinner.

"It's fine," Mama said to him, shooing us. "Trey and Crew will be here."

"Actually…" Lane started with a wince. "I need Crew too."

Mama huffed, threw her hands up, and disappeared inside without another word.

Aria hugged us, then wagged her finger in Lane's face. "Be gentle with the sister."

"What's that supposed to mean?"

"You can be a bit…" Aria trailed off, searching for the right word, which West supplied for her.

"Of an asshole."

Lane growled at him. "I don't need you three telling me how to do my job."

Aria shrugged. "Don't say I didn't warn you," she quipped, then disappeared inside.

"You guys wanna ride with me?" Lane asked. West shook his head, answering for us both, and Lane nodded. "See you at the department."

West and I both lived within walking distance of the ranch. In the more temperate months, I boarded Raider at my house so I could ride him to and from work, even though he had a stall here with his name on it. West had driven over since he usually kept Rogue here, so we headed for his truck and took off toward town.

When we reached the department, Lane was already in an interview room with the victim's sister, but Crew had arrived, the three other members of his fire department team in tow, so the six of us stood around, shooting the shit with a few of big brother's deputies while we waited for him to come out.

Nothing could've prepared me for the moment he did.

I heard him before I saw him, murmuring gently to the woman as he led her down the hall toward the bullpen.

"We'll find who did this to her," Lane promised, then paused when he caught sight of us. "Hey, guys. This is—"

Introductions weren't necessary, as I realized the second I laid eyes on the blonde woman beside my brother.

It had been seven years, but I'd never forget that face.

I knew this woman *biblically*, had that long, honey hair wrapped around my fist as I pounded into her from behind.

I knew what her pussy tasted like.

The sounds she made when she came.

How fucking good she looked riding me.

Our eyes met, and the whole fucking world faded away.

Something tugged insistently in my chest, like there was a hook behind my sternum, and she was at the other end of the chain.

This woman was a sexy blonde tornado that had blown through town seven years ago and turned my world upside down. There wasn't anything I could've done to prepare. The only course of action had been to let myself be swept away.

And now…she was back.

For seven years, that face had haunted my dreams. Demanded I remember her and our singular night together.

As if I could ever forget.

"Reagan?" I choked out.

"Hey, Finn," she said—and goddamnit, that single word, the

breathy utterance of my name, went straight to my cock. *What the fuck?* I was thirty-four, not fourteen. "I wondered if I'd see you."

Get it the fuck together, Lawless.

"Holy shit, it is you."

"Wait…*Reagan?*" West asked at full volume, breaking the trance I'd found myself in. "Like one-night-stand, spun-you-out-for-a-minute Reagan?"

I smiled sheepishly when she blinked in surprise, but I wasn't embarrassed.

Reagan had marked me in a way that lasted a hell of a lot longer than the scratches she'd left down my back.

"Yes, cocksucker," I said to my twin, punching him in the arm. "*That* Reagan."

"What're you—" Crew started to ask, then stopped himself when realization struck. He glanced wide-eyed between me and Reagan, and it suddenly dawned on me as well.

Oh, fuck.

Lainey Lindsey was Reagan's sister.

"Fuck, Reagan," I said softly. "I'm so sorry."

Reagan nodded, mouth flattening and eyes blinking rapidly as though fighting off tears.

"Thank you. You guys were at the scene?"

"Yeah, we—"

"We can do all this later," Lane said, cutting me off. "Right now, Miss Lindsey needs to identify her sister."

West cursed.

All the blood drained from Reagan's face, skin instantly losing its healthy glow, replaced by an almost sickly paleness, and her entire body tensed with obvious dread.

"Okay, right," I said, awkwardly cupping the back of my neck and averting my gaze. God, this was fucking uncomfortable. "We can catch up later then? If you want to, of course."

Reagan didn't answer, and I braved looking at her.

When our eyes locked again, that same spark I'd experienced

all those years ago flared to life once more, back like it never left. And maybe it hadn't. Maybe the time and distance had only banked it until it dimmed to a glowing coal.

Now, being together again seemed to breathe new life into it, reigniting the flames.

"I…" she started. "I don't know how long I'll be around."

"Sure, of course."

I tried—and likely failed—to hide my disappointment.

Oblivious to the tension between me and Reagan—or willfully ignorant—Lane called for one of his deputies, and Johns appeared from around the corner.

"Yeah, boss?" he asked, eyeing us all warily.

"Take statements from Burns, Childers, and Tuck, will you?"

Johns nodded, then jerked his chin at Crew, asking, "What about…that one?"

Crew took a menacing step toward the deputy, but West threw out an arm, barring his path.

There was no love lost between Crew and Johns. Their animosity dated all the way back to high school, when Crew hadn't exactly been the best guy, and Johns took every opportunity to remind him of that fact. Things had only gotten worse after Crew punched the deputy in the face at an incident scene last summer.

Ignoring Johns' comment, he said to us, "Head to my office. I'll be back in a bit."

Crew and West ambled off, muttering about something too low for me to hear, but I lingered, eyes on Reagan.

With a final smile at her that was surely more of a grimace, I turned to follow my brothers.

"Finn?"

Reagan's voice stopped me, and I faced her once again.

"Yeah?"

"Will you come with me?" she asked quietly.

"Anywhere," I answered without thinking. A moment later,

what she was truly asking sank in: she wanted me to go with to identify her sister.

That didn't change my response, and I extended my arm, reaching for her hand.

With zero hesitation, she accepted and laced our fingers together, leading me away.

seven

. . .

I RECOGNIZED Sheriff Lawless the minute he arrived at the station and led me into that stark, too-bright interview room, but he obviously had no memory of me, and for that I was grateful.

The last thing I needed was reminders of that night, of his brother. Not when my mind and my entire life was already a fucking mess. Not when, once this horrific day was over, I'd have to go home and figure out how to move on with my life without Lainey at my side.

Adding Finn to the mix would only make things more complicated.

Finn *Lawless*.

I hadn't known his last name until the moment I laid eyes on the sheriff, and I couldn't stop myself from wondering if he was around town, if he was still in the service, or if he was off somewhere else with a wife and a few kids by now.

Why did the idea of Finn having a family depress me so much?

"I'm sorry we had to meet like this," the sheriff said as he took his seat across from me at the interview table.

"Actually, we've met before."

He stilled, eyes slowly coming up to meet mine before darting all over my face, scanning what he could see of my body.

"I'm embarrassed to say I don't remember."

I gave him a wry smile. "That's okay," I assured him. "It's been a while. I spent most of that night with Finn anyway."

"Holy fuck," he cursed as recognition dawned. "You're *that* Reagan?"

"Sure am."

"Small fucking world."

I choked on a laugh. "Sure is."

"Well, for what it's worth, it's good to see you again. I wish it was under different circumstances."

"Thanks," I murmured, throat clogged with emotion. He gave me a few minutes to collect myself before I asked, "What can you tell me about…it?"

I couldn't bring myself to say *her death*. The reality hadn't fully sunk in yet, and some deeply rooted, delusionally optimistic part of me hoped it wasn't true.

"We found her in a fairly remote part of the ridge west of town. Almost at the Oregon border."

I blinked in confusion. "Wait…you found her in the woods?"

"Yes. It looked like she had cleared the area herself to set up camp."

"That's so…odd."

"What is?"

"She called me on Sunday, complaining about the cold." I chuckled at the memory. The same thing had happened seven years ago, where the nights had gotten too frigid to sleep outside, so we'd gotten the motel room for the last two. "So she checked into the motel."

The sheriff scribbled in his little notebook. "I'll be in touch with the owner," he mused, more to himself than to me. Then he looked up. "You reported her missing on Thursday morning, correct?" I nodded. "Have you ever had to report her missing before?" A shake of my head. "Then why this time?"

"I knew something was wrong," I said quietly. "I had a bad feeling before she even left, and when she sent me this text on Tuesday evening, that nagging in my gut got worse. But I waited, hoping she'd turn up."

"What text?"

I fished my phone out of my purse and navigated to my messages with Lainey, then passed it over to him.

Lane studied it, then handed it back. "Who is this *he* she referred to?"

I debated whether or not to tell him about the stalker, given Lainey's stubborn refusal to involve law enforcement of any kind.

But Lainey was gone now, and if her stalker had something to do with this, the sheriff needed to know.

As best as I could, I boiled down six and a half year's-worth of creepy texts, calls, emails, and social media DMs into a succinct explanation.

"So you don't even know this guy's name," he mused, leaning back in his chair and crossing thick, tattooed arms over his chest. "Were you and your sister not close?"

"She's my best friend," I ground out, growing irritated with his irreverence. "But we both had secrets, and this was hers. Her phone is going to be your best bet to get info on him."

"Unfortunately, her phone is missing."

I didn't have a response for that, and Lane leaned forward again, picking up his pen and plowing ahead.

"Can you tell me why she was in the area? From Tennessee to Dusk Valley is a long way to travel for some hiking."

"We own a photography business, and we had a client from the area reach out, wanting us to do an engagement shoot."

More scribbling.

"I'm going to need the name of the client."

Scrolling through my phone, I found the inquiry email and

relayed the information. The *scritch*ing of his pen on the paper filled the silence between us.

"If you haven't been able to locate her phone, how did you find me?" I asked.

"Ran her name through some databases and found you paired as next of kin. Your parents died some time ago, yes? Car accident?"

My eyes slammed shut with the reminder, the horrible images of that night flashing across the backs of my lids.

"Yeah."

"Shit, sorry," he said, catching my reaction. "You were with them, right?"

I nodded. "We were on our way to Knoxville. Got caught in a bad thunderstorm. Hydroplaned, went off the road. I survived; they didn't."

I spoke the words as flatly as I could, having gotten good over the years at never letting talking about it penetrate too deeply, lest I lose control completely.

Losing our parents had nearly broken both of us, but in the end, it had also brought Lainey and I closer together.

That first trip to Dusk Valley had been our re-entrance into society, the moment we decided to stop letting our grief control us and start living again.

And now, she was gone too.

"Do you have any idea where her phone might be since we didn't find it on her body?"

"No. She never went anywhere without it." Then another thought occurred to me. "Did you find her SAT phone?"

"SAT phone?" Lane asked like I was speaking a different language. "Like a satellite phone?"

"Yeah, I bought her one a few years back when it became obvious I couldn't stop her from going on these little excursions alone."

Lane hummed thoughtfully. "There was a tent at the scene,

but we didn't find any other personal effects besides what she was wearing. If she'd moved into the motel for the remainder of her trip, that would explain why."

"Odd that she wouldn't take the tent, though," I mused, more to myself than him. "That thing wasn't cheap."

The fucking tent doesn't matter, Reagan. Your sister is gone.

I dropped my head into my hands, and Lane gave me a beat before speaking again.

"I'm sorry," Lane said, correctly interpreting my distress. "I know this is a lot."

I looked up at him, and his expression softened at whatever he saw in my gaze. "Where do I go from here?"

Lane winced. "Not to pile on, but…we do still need to get that visual ID."

"Fuck."

Fuck, fuck, fuck.

I didn't want to do it, but there was no getting out of it.

Squaring my shoulders and lifting my chin, I rose from my seat.

"Now?" Lane asked, standing up as well.

"Now," I confirmed.

With a nod, Lane moved to the door and held it open for me.

"We'll find who did this to her," he promised me as we walked down the hallway, but my attention wasn't on him.

Instead, my gaze locked on the group of men gathered at the edge of the bullpen.

I recognized three of them.

Crew, the youngest Lawless brother and a firefighter, if I remembered correctly.

West, everything about his physical appearance except his longer, shaggier hair an exact match to the man between them.

When Finn's eyes caught mine, the entire world seemed to stop spinning. Everything narrowed to that moment, that reconnection.

Memories flashed quickly through my mind.

Skin.

Tattooed hands.

Sighs of pleasure and screams of his name.

A deluge of sensation, and I almost let it drag me under.

This man had *haunted* me. Had me questioning over the years if I'd ever find a connection with anyone like what we'd found together on that single night.

A one-night stand wasn't exactly grounds for a solid relationship, but there'd been something in the air that night. A force greater than us drawing us together—the same force that had likely never let me forget him since.

Did he feel the same?

He looked at me as though he'd seen a ghost, like he'd been as haunted all these years as I had been.

Lane spoke, though his words seemed to come from miles away, snapping the world back into focus.

"Hey guys," the sheriff said to his brothers. "This is—"

Finn cut him off.

"Reagan?" he asked hoarsely.

"Hey, Finn," I said, not recognizing the breathy tenor of my own voice. "I wondered if I'd see you."

"Holy shit, it is you."

"Wait...*Reagan*?" West asked at full volume, reminding me we weren't standing here alone. That our reunion had an audience. "Like one-night-stand, spun-you-out-for-a-minute Reagan?"

I blinked in surprise.

Spun him out?

Maybe I *hadn't* been the only one plagued by memories of that night, cursed to remember.

"Yes, cocksucker," he gritted out to his twin, going so far as to sock West on the arm. "*That* Reagan."

"What're you—" Crew started to ask but quickly stopped

himself. His eyes went almost comically wide as realization dawned, darting between me and Finn.

I wanted to hide, to do whatever I could to avoid the expression of pity that passed over Finn's face when he came to the same conclusion as Crew—the reason for why I was back in Dusk Valley.

"Fuck, Reagan," Finn said softly. "I'm so sorry."

I could only nod and look away, rolling my lips between my teeth and blinking furiously, trying to fight off the tears that threatened.

I knew I couldn't hold them at bay forever. The dam would break today, likely the moment I set my sights on my sister's lifeless body.

But I wasn't going to break *here*. Not in the middle of the fucking sheriff's department bullpen with too many eyes on me.

"Thank you," I managed to croak out. "You guys were at the scene?"

"Yeah, we—"

"We can do this later," Lane said. "Right now, Miss Lindsey needs to identify her sister."

"Shit," West hissed.

I swore I could *feel* the blood drain from my face and my hands, my fingertips going cold and shaky.

I didn't want to do this.

"Okay, right," Finn said awkwardly, scratching the back of his neck uncomfortably and looking away from me. These were not ideal circumstances for a reunion, and I hated more than anything that it had to be like this. "We can catch up later then?" he asked hopefully. "If you want to, of course."

I didn't answer right away—truthfully wasn't sure *how* to answer.

This was simply another thing added to my plate, pulling me in another direction.

Find who killed my sister.

Somehow keep my and Lainey's business afloat in the face of all this uncertainty.

…Rekindle things with Finn?

His reappearance in my life seemed too good to be true, a bright spot in an otherwise black hellscape of loss.

I wasn't sure I deserved it, and I'd learned the hard way once before that jumping into a relationship when grieving was a recipe for disaster.

Still, when he finally looked at me again, I couldn't deny that the same current, the same magnetism that had drawn me to him before, was still there. I hadn't misremembered the way my body awoke in his presence, like an instrument only he knew how to play.

"I…" I started. "I don't know how long I'll be around."

"Sure, of course."

Disappointment flashed across his eyes before he averted them, and I hated that I'd been the one to put it there.

"Johns?" Lane called, breaking the moment. A beat later, a deputy appeared at his side.

"Yeah, boss?"

I tuned them out as they discussed taking statements from the unfamiliar men, my attention focused wholly on Finn. Wanting to do something—*anything*—to erase the hurt I'd caused. Compelled to draw him back in when he was about to turn his back on me to follow his brothers.

Which was *insane*.

After all, was I not hurting? And over something far bigger than being unable to catch up with a one-night stand?

Ignoring all of that, I did something crazy, something that was maybe a little too reckless given my fragile emotional state.

"Finn?" I called.

"Yeah?"

"Will you come with me?"

"Anywhere," he answered quickly.

I waited for him to change his mind, to realize exactly *where* I was asking him to come and back out.

But he didn't.

Instead, he surprised me by extending his arm, reaching for me.

I didn't pause to think about it before accepting his hand and lacing our fingers together, leading him to my doom.

eight

. . .

REAGAN

ONCE HIS BROTHERS WERE GONE, Finn squeezed my hand.

"Ready?"

"Fuck no," I chuckled humorlessly. "But let's get this over with."

I didn't know what to expect when we descended into the bowels of the building. We crossed through a short underground tunnel that connected what appeared to be file rooms and evidence holding to the subterranean morgue of this small county. I hadn't expected there to be so much light, though. Wall sconces with high-wattage bulbs were placed frequently enough to give the space a warm glow and keep it from being creepy.

The theme continued in the morgue itself, with the walls painted a creamy beige and the linoleum floor a few shades lighter, worn though clean.

Along one wall was a collection of six doors, presumably lockers for bodies, though I doubted they'd ever been full at once.

A man stood in the center of the room, wearing a white lab coat and gloves on his hands, which were clasped in front of him, waiting for us.

The medical examiner, I guessed.

Lane approached and said, "Hey, Stockman. This is Reagan. She's here to do a visual ID on the woman."

"Relative of yours?" Stockman asked. Then he extended a hand. "I'm Clay, by the way."

I accepted his handshake, though the entire situation was so surreal, as though happening to someone else.

What a strange question to ask, I thought. Surely, he'd done a cursory examination of the body? Surely, he recognized I wore the same face as the deceased?

The same sense of *wrongness* I'd experienced yesterday when Lane first called with the news settled over me again, but I couldn't put my finger on *why*.

"She is—*was*," I corrected awkwardly, practically choking on the word, "my sister."

"I am sorry for your loss. This will only take a few moments."

Stockman moved to the table on one side of the room—the portion of the space I'd carefully avoided looking at until now. But as my eyes traveled over it, over the shape under the white sheet, I began shaking uncontrollably. My feet were anchored to the floor, suddenly made of immovable concrete instead of flesh and bone.

"I can't do this," I murmured to Finn, wanting to turn into him and bury my face in his chest.

His hands found my upper arms, and he shifted around so he faced me, ducking until we were eye level.

"This is going to be the worst thing you'll ever endure in your life," he said.

I snorted, saying sarcastically, "Thanks for making me feel better."

Finn shook his head. "You won't feel better until you get it over with. Until you confirm it's her and can start moving on, start healing."

I knew he was right. That didn't make what I was about to

do any easier, but like ripping the bandage off, it would only be a few seconds of intense, stinging pain before eventually dulling to an ache. I knew the pain of the loss of my sister would never fully recede, but this was the first step in making it slightly easier to bear.

Plus, I had to identify her before we could figure out who the fuck had done this to her. Lane had told me Stockman wouldn't begin the autopsy until I confirmed Lainey's identity.

With a final, deep sigh that I held in for four counts, willing myself to relax a bit, I opened my eyes and nodded at Finn, who shifted to my side.

"Okay," I said softly, my voice so small it barely echoed in the cacophonous space. "I'm ready."

"Atta girl," Finn said, rubbing a hand up and down my spine.

Honestly, I didn't think I could've done this without him. His steady presence meant more to me than I'd ever be able to tell him.

With light pressure, Finn ushered me forward until I stood at the side of the metal table, across from Stockman.

The ME gripped the edge of the sheet.

From there, it all seemed to happen in slow motion—his hand pulling the fabric back, revealing inch by excruciating inch of the dead woman's face. Stockman folded the sheet neatly across the top of her chest, revealing her entire face, neck, and shoulders, stopping above the curves of her breasts.

I stared in horror at the woman's neck, the long, ovular bruises decorating the flesh—the shapes of fingers, I realized— marring the deathly pallor of her skin, a purple so dark they were nearly black.

Her cause of death was obvious.

My gaze traveled slowly north, over her jaw and chin, full mouth, long nose, high cheekbones and the dark slashes of her brows over her closed eyes.

To her hair, honey blonde but dark at the roots, fanned out

around her on the shiny steel surface of the medical examiner's slab.

So shocked by the sight before me, I stumbled backward, tripped over Finn's foot, and landed hard on my ass on the cold floor.

"Are you okay?" Finn asked, rushing to help me up.

I was shaking uncontrollably now, but not from grief and despair.

No, this was all *rage*.

What the actual fuck?

"That's not my sister."

"But her ID—"

"I don't give a fuck about the ID!" I screamed at Lane, panic rising in my chest. I turned to Finn. "Does she look like me?"

"W-what?" he asked, clearly stunned by my outburst.

"Does. She. Look. Like. Me?"

Reluctantly, Finn shuffled closer to the dead woman, taking a moment to study her, eyes darting between the two of us. Goddesses, I wanted to laugh—if hysterically. This was un-*fucking*-real.

"Ahh…no?" he said, though his inflection made it sound like a question.

"What's your point, Miss Lindsey?" the sheriff asked impatiently.

"We're *twins*," I gasped out. "That woman is *not* my sister."

"Well, there's a certain degree of change a body undergoes after death—" Stockman started, but I cut him off.

"I *knew* it," I hissed.

The inkling I'd had a moment ago fully formed.

Lainey wasn't dead.

"Knew what?" Stockman asked.

"Lainey's not dead," I said aloud. "I'd be able to tell if she was." Once again, I locked my attention on Finn, the only person in this room who could possibly understand. "Right? If some-thing happened to West, you would *know*."

Like a deer caught in headlights, he stared wide-eyed at me for a beat—then nodded before turning to Lane. "She's right, bro. If he was gone, I'd know."

Lane rolled his eyes. "You know I don't believe in that woo-woo shit."

"*You* don't have to," Finn said evenly. "You just have to trust that *we* do. Like when West got shot in that raid?" I had no idea what he was talking about except it likely had to do with his time in the Army. The sheriff clearly understood the reference because he nodded, if a bit warily. "I *knew*, Lane. Felt the pain as surely as if the bullet had gone through my own chest."

The sheriff looked at me—studied me, his shrewd cop's gaze seeming to see right through me, down to my core.

"Are you absolutely certain this isn't your sister?"

Did he…did he think I was lying? That I'd deluded myself into thinking this woman wasn't my sister simply so I wouldn't have to deal with the grief?

What a fucking joke.

"Without a doubt. Do a DNA test if you need to. I'll happily give a sample. But we're *naturally* blonde," I said, tugging on my own hair, which I'd never once dyed. Lainey hadn't either. "No dark roots to be found. Or, you know, you could just check her left foot." Placing a steadying hand on the edge of the table, I slipped off my tennis shoe and sock, lifting my foot and showing them all the tattoo, the tiny camera, inked on the inside of my left heel. "She'll have a matching one if it's Lainey."

Stockman moved to the foot of the table and lifted the sheet, his gloved fingers twisting the woman's leg gently to the side, searching for the ink.

There was nothing to be found save smooth, unmarred skin.

"Believe me now?" I said triumphantly.

Lane scrubbed a hand over his face, letting out a world-weary sigh, his eyes never straying from the woman on the table.

"I'll want to do a DNA test to be absolutely certain," he said, almost absently. "But if this isn't your sister…who the fuck is she?"

"I don't know," I said. "And I'm sorry for what happened to her. But my sister is still out there somewhere, and we need to find her."

Lane nodded. "Let's head upstairs. I've got some more questions for you."

"I have no doubt," I muttered, and Finn snorted.

"Before you go," Stockman said, stalling us. He held a long cotton swab in his hand. "Can I get that DNA sample?"

"Oh, right." I approached him, opening my mouth. He swept it along my cheeks before sealing it in its plastic tube and turning away to scribble on the label.

That completed, Finn steered me from the cold room, his hand a comforting presence at the small of my back. Lane hung back momentarily to speak with Stockman before following us upstairs.

This time when Lane and I took our seats at the table in the interview room, Finn was at my side. He seemed reluctant to leave me, and I was more than a little grateful for his presence.

Cutting right to the chase, Lane said, "If your sister isn't dead, what do *you* think happened to her?"

My mind whirled with possibilities. She'd never willingly leave me like this, never disappear without a trace—without a word.

Not unless she didn't have a choice.

"She was here for a shoot. I told you that earlier."

"A shoot?" Finn asked.

"We're photographers. Own a business. We have a reputation across the country thanks to our social media following, and we're always willing to take on out-of-state projects. About three months ago, we booked an engagement shoot with a couple here in Idaho, local to Boise."

"When was the shoot supposed to take place? Getting an idea of Lainey's movements when she arrived in town is going to be helpful in discovering what happened to her."

"Tuesday evening and midday on Wednesday," I said quickly. "The couple wanted to do some shots at sunset as well as daytime ones. Then Lainey was supposed to fly home yesterday."

My head fell into my hands, a headache appearing and taking up residence behind my right eye. Goddesses, this had been the day from hell.

"Let's reconvene in the morning," Lane said, saving me from having to ask for a break. "Does ten o'clock work for you?"

"Yeah, that's fine." I stood, as did Finn and Lane.

"For what it's worth," Lane began as we moved toward the door. "I'm sorry for the...drama. I never would've brought you down there if I thought for any reason—"

I waved him off. "I understand."

Now I'd have nightmares about my sister *and* that poor dead woman, but he didn't need to know that.

So many questions still swam in my brain, but I needed headache meds, a meal, a shower, and at least eight hours of sleep before I could make any sense of them.

"I promise, my department will do everything in its power to find your sister."

"Thank you."

With another nod, Lane turned and headed through the bullpen toward a closed door at the back, the white placard on it reading SHERIFF LAWLESS in black letters.

Finn remained nearby. "How long are you in town for?"

"Until Sunday," I said.

"Maybe we can—"

"No," I said, gently but firmly. "I can't...There's too much going on up here." I tapped my temple. "And until I find my sister, I can't take on anything else."

Though his expression fell from earnestness to disappointment for the second time today, he said, "Okay, I understand."

"I'm sorry. All of this is a lot right now."

"No, I get it. Don't worry about it." Hands stuffed awkwardly in his pockets, he inclined his head toward Lane's office and said, "I better go."

"Right. Well…see you around."

"Yeah, see you."

I didn't move from the spot as he walked away, watching as his long legs ate up the distance to his brother's office, his broad shoulders hunched forward, head down.

Wondering if this was the last time I'd lay eyes on Finn Lawless.

nine

. . .

FINN

"WHAT THE FUCK, LANE?" I fumed as I stalked into his office and slammed the door shut behind me. Placing my palms flat on his desk, I leaned in, getting right in his face.

"I swear to god, Finn, I had *no* fucking idea."

"You just put that woman through hell for *nothing*," I gritted out.

"I know, I know," Lane said, raising his hands in surrender. "And I'm sorry. But honestly, I could not have predicted *that*. No one could have."

As furious as I was for Reagan's sake, he was right, and it took some of the wind out of my sails.

"Somebody please tell us what the fuck is going on," Crew demanded.

I straightened and began pacing, mind spinning, while Lane filled West and Crew in on what had happened.

"So…the sister isn't dead?" Crew asked.

"Not as far as we know. She and Finn"—he glared pointedly at me—"seem to agree that she would *know* if her sister was gone thanks to some woo-woo twin shit."

West nodded in understanding. "Makes sense."

Lane rolled his eyes. "Not you too."

West shrugged. "I can't explain it, Sheriff. I just know it's real." He tapped a spot on his chest, right over his heart, then jerked his chin at me. "I'd know if something happened."

I smirked at Lane.

"Like when you got shot," I said. "I knew right away."

"Yeah, can we not bring that up?" he asked, palm moving slightly to the left, to the point where a specially designed armor-piercing bullet had shredded through his Kevlar vest and pierced his body. "I swear it fucking...*pulses* every time someone mentions it."

"Sorry," I muttered.

"The point is," Lane said, redirecting our attention to the matter at hand, "now I've got a fucking missing person's case *and* an unidentified dead girl in the morgue."

He leaned back in his chair and squeezed his eyes shut, pinching the bridge of his nose.

"Might have to bring Trey in," Crew said.

"We'll see," Lane replied.

"'We'll see'? Are you serious?" Crew asked, incredulous. "I get you're pissed you got this one so wrong, but there's a missing woman out there and we have a tech genius for a brother. You don't think that could help?"

Lane's hand scraped down his face, and he blew out a long breath. The set of his shoulders—hiked up damn near to his ears—told me his patience was wearing thin.

"Can we get these statements done with?" West asked, sensing what I had. "I'd like to get home sometime before midnight."

"Shit, yeah," Lane said, rocking forward and pulling his work phone out of his pocket. He clicked on the voice recorder, stated the case number and purpose for the interview, then nodded at Crew to go first.

Before Crew could start speaking, Lane's personal phone rang, and he paused the recording to answer.

"Sheriff Lawless." A beat. "Hey, Reagan. What can I do for you?"

Reagan?

Whatever she said had Lane's brows rising in surprise. He flipped to a new page in his notebook and started scribbling. "You got a plate?" Lane asked.

A plate for what?

"This is great, Reagan. Thank you. We'll run this down, and I'll see you in the morning."

When he disconnected, I looked at him expectantly.

"Just another lead to run down," he said, being evasive. "Let's get these statements done."

Though I wanted to press, I didn't. I had no authority here, and he wasn't obligated to tell me shit.

An hour later, we'd finished rehashing our memories of the recovery of the dead girl.

Though after ten p.m., and it had been a long day for all of us—except maybe Crew, who wasn't on shift that day—Lane stalled us before we could get up and leave.

"What do you guys remember about that night seven years ago?"

"We were out celebrating," Crew said slowly. "You'd just been named sheriff, so West and Finn were home on leave, and Owen and I had come too."

Back then, only Trey and Lane had resided in Dusk Valley. It had been the first time in far too long that all my brothers and I were in the same place.

"I remember Tony Walter acting like a fucking asshat and making a pass at Reagan," I said.

"Do you think he could be the one?" Lane asked. "Revenge for her rejection and all that?"

My eyes fluttered shut as I conjured memories from that

night, but I ultimately shook my head. "Reagan went back to her table after I told Tony to leave, and her sister left sometime after that. I think it's safe to say Tony was long gone by then. Even so, this isn't his style. He'd smack her around in the parking lot, not abduct her."

Though it had been a long time since that night, Tony Walter hadn't changed much. In fact, he may have gotten worse. I was genuinely surprised his liver hadn't given up on him yet—or that his wife hadn't packed up herself and her kids and left.

"True," Lane said, jotting down notes in the ever-present spiral-bound pad he kept in his pocket. "Who else was there that night?"

"Christ," West said. "It's been so long, and we'd holed up in the corner, remember? As far away from the door as we could get."

That was typical of us, especially during those infrequent trips home when all I'd wanted to do was spend time with my family and decompress before West and I shipped back overseas. As local boys and war heroes to boot, Dusk Valley's residents had no qualms about interrupting our evenings to shoot the shit or sing our praises.

Of course, that night, I'd made an exception for Reagan. I couldn't have freed myself from the gravitational force dragging me toward her, even if I'd wanted to.

Lane continued scribbling, seeming to lose himself as ideas and memories poured from him onto the pages.

"Anything else?" he asked, at last looking at us.

I shook my head. Crew and West followed suit.

"Honestly, I don't remember a lot about that night except Reagan."

West shot me a shit-eating grin. "You gonna hit that again?"

"Fuck you. Her sister is missing, and she's not staying."

"I didn't hear the word 'no' anywhere in there," Crew supplied with a smirk.

I smacked him upside the head, and he, West, and Lane devolved into a fit of laughter.

Their comments forced me to confront the idea, though. Would I fuck Reagan again?

The answer was a resounding yes.

Although, I didn't love the term in reference to her. That night had been a hell of a lot more than two strangers fooling around, getting off, and going their separate ways. The entire time, it seemed as though some greater force had been at work, guiding us to one another.

And I had to admit, the idea that the same force had brought us back together now had me…hopeful.

Hopeful for a future I'd never dared to allow myself to envision before.

ten

. . .

REAGAN

THE LONE MOTEL in Dusk Valley hadn't gotten any better in the years since we'd last stayed here. In fact, as I pulled up after leaving the sheriff's department, I thought it looked a lot worse.

I didn't think calling ahead and booking a room was necessary, not when I had other ideas about securing lodging.

Somewhere in the two wings that jutted out from the main reception area, there was a room with my sister's things in it.

I needed to get in there before the sheriff's department did. Since Lane hadn't mentioned anything about it during either of our interviews, I assumed it wasn't currently high on his list of priorities. But I knew that would soon change, when he had time to process everything that had happened today and made a plan for moving forward with the investigation.

The portly man behind the check-in counter's eyes lit in recognition as I approached, and I was grateful that I wore the exact same face as my sister.

Seems this will be easier than I thought.

"Miss Lindsey," the man said, standing and smoothing a

hand over the wisps of hair covering the top of his shiny, bald head. "Pleasure to see you again. What can I do for you?"

Smiling sweetly and laying on the charm, I said, "I seem to have misplaced my key. Is there any way I could get a new one?"

His tone was as saccharine as mine when he said, "That'll be a fifty-dollar replacement fee."

I nearly choked. Fifty dollars to replace a key at this shithole? When I could go to the nearest hardware store and have a new one made for less than ten? When anyone could come by and break down the door with a well-placed kick, myself included?

"Fine," I gritted out through my smile. "Can you put it on the card on file?"

Lainey and I shared a credit card for business expenses, and I added that to my mental list of leads to run down, to see if she'd used it for anything that might explain her whereabouts.

He handed me the new key, the tag hanging from it displaying the room number.

Thanking him, I returned to my rental car and moved it to the space directly in front of door number nine, collected my things from the back, and went inside.

The room was about what you'd expect from a roach motel: thin, threadbare comforter on a bed topped with flat pillows. Round table in the corner, the laminate on top peeling, the fabric of the two chairs faded and pilled. At the far end of the room was a large mirror over a counter with a sink in the center. The bathroom sat in the back right corner.

I didn't give myself the chance to get lost in examining my sister's belongings yet, which were strewn all around the room like she'd been here moments ago and had every intention of returning.

Certainly, that had been the case. She couldn't have known what would happen to her—whatever that was.

I was surprised to find her tent propped up in the corner of the room, though. When packed up, it was about two feet long and narrow enough to tuck into the side of her suitcase. That meant the one they'd found in that clearing with the dead girl hadn't belonged to Lainey.

For the first time, I wondered how the girl had ended up with Lainey's ID. Had Lainey lost it? Had it been stolen?

I dropped my own things on the bed, rifled through for some headache medicine, and washed the pills down with the bottle of water I'd picked up at the airport earlier.

Getting behind the wheel of my rental, a thought occurred to me.

Lainey had a rental car.

Racing back into the room, I rifled through her backpack, half of its contents spewed atop the little stand under the TV. Lainey rarely carried a purse, content to wear bottoms or dresses with pockets that fit her wallet and lip gloss. With a cry of triumph, I came up with a receipt from the airport rental car place.

Stepping back onto the curb outside the room, I scanned the lot, not seeing any sign of the vehicle described in the paperwork.

Then I called the sheriff.

"Sheriff Lawless," he answered, sounding exhausted.

That made two of us.

"Lane, it's Reagan."

"Hey, Reagan. What can I do for you?"

"She had a rental car."

"I'm sorry?"

"Lainey had a rental car that she picked up at the airport. A black 2025 Toyota Highlander."

"You got a plate?"

I read off the numbers.

"This is great, Reagan. Thank you. We'll run this down, and I'll see you in the morning."

Satisfied I'd accomplished *something* to help bring Lainey home, my stomach emitted an insistent growl, gnawing at itself.

A quick Google search alerted me to a few places in the area that provided takeout—Mozzy's Pizza Parlor and the diner.

A few greasy slices of pizza would go a long way to restoring some of my energy, so I returned to my car and headed out. I could've walked but, given the fact that my sister had gone missing in this town, I wasn't taking any chances with my own safety.

The main street was brightly lit, both by lampposts and signs and interior lights of the businesses still open at this time of night.

When I pushed through the door of Mozzy's, the kid behind the counter looked up and grinned. "Lainey! Back for more? I told you that blueberry pizza would change your life."

"Oh…" *Fuck.* Tears pricked my eyes. I missed my sister like I'd miss a limb, and this kid mistaking me for her pricked a nerve. "I'm not Lainey. I'm her sister, Reagan."

The guy raised a brow. "Are you fucking with me?"

I chuckled, some of the tightness in my chest easing. "No. We're twins."

"Damn, that's freaky," he said, though it sounded like a compliment coupled with his boyish grin. "Well, it's a pleasure to meet you, Reagan. What can I get for ya?"

"Not gonna lie, that blueberry pizza sounds intriguing," I chuckled. "I'd love some cheese sticks as well."

"Perfect," he said as he punched it into the system. "I'll get that started for you."

"So you met my sister?" I asked as nonchalantly as I could while he ran my card.

"Yeah, she's great. Came in here three nights in a row. Told me she was a photographer and owned a business with her sister. Wait." He paused, eyes brightening as realization struck. "You're the sister."

"Sure am. And look…" I leaned closer, dropping my voice so only we could hear. "I don't want to raise any alarms, but Lainey is why I'm here. She's kind of MIA, and I need to track her down." His eyes widened. "Do you remember the last time you saw her?"

"Monday night," he said quickly, a flush creeping into his cheeks. He had to be in his early twenties, several years younger than my and Lainey's thirty years. "Sorry. We don't get a lot of fresh faces around here, and definitely not ones that look like you guys."

I gave him what I hoped was a reassuring smile. The compliment *was* flattering, if poorly timed. "Did you guys chat or anything?"

"Yeah, we talked a bit while she waited for her food. She told me why she was in town, where she was from. That's pretty much it. She said she'd be back on Tuesday to tell me how she liked the blueberry pizza, but I didn't see her again. She's missing?"

I nodded. "I last heard from her on Tuesday."

"Damn, I'm sorry," he said. Someone called his name—*Trevor*—from the back, and he gave me a sheepish smile. "Sorry, duty calls."

"No problem, and thanks," I said, mind already going a thousand miles a minute away from the current conversation.

I took a seat on the wooden bench affixed to the wall off to the side, pulled out my phone, and opened a new Note.

Lainey likely last seen at the Swallow Tuesday night, I tapped out.

I knew that much for a fact, seeing as how she told me she wanted to check the place out "for old time's sake."

Well, and that was the last place she'd been active on Find My Friends. Shortly after she sent her final text, she went dark, disappearing completely from view. I'd hoped her phone had merely died, but obviously, that wasn't the case.

My fingers flew across the keyboard as I wrote down everything I knew so far, including when she'd arrived in Dusk Valley nearly two weeks ago—coming out way earlier than necessary to do some hiking so she could come home right after the sessions—the names of our clients, and the date and time the two separate shoots were set to begin. I wasn't an investigator by any means, but I owed Lane everything I knew that could help.

"Reagan?" a voice said softly, jarring me from my task. I looked up to find Trevor standing over me, two pizza boxes stacked in his hands. "You're all set."

"Thanks," I said, jumping to my feet and accepting my order.

He nodded. "And I hope you find Lainey."

"Me too. And hey," I added, digging into my purse for a business card, "if you remember anything else, give me a call."

"Will do."

He disappeared into the back again, and I pushed outside, heading back to the motel.

An hour, a shower, and way too many slices of pizza later—Trevor had been right; the blueberry, feta, and ham concoction *was* life changing—I sat on the bed, both my and Lainey's laptops open in front of me.

Ice slid down my spine when I pulled up the iMessage app on her laptop and read that final missive and my responding texts, which had been unread until now, confirming my suspicions.

TUESDAY, 10:41 PM

ME

I think he's here.

REAGAN

Who?

Your stalker?

Lainey???

LAINEY!!!

When my messages had gone unanswered, I'd called.

And called and called and called.

The first five times, it rang through to her messaging system.

On the sixth try, it had gone straight to voicemail, like someone had turned it off, which coincided with the loss of her location in Find My Friends.

I hated snooping. Lainey and I didn't have secrets, but going through her computer felt…icky, made my skin crawl. Like she'd burst into the room any moment, catch me red-handed, and start screaming.

The police would do all of this, but I didn't want there to be any surprises for myself. I wanted to be sure I knew everything there was to know.

Starting with her most recent journal, which I stuffed into my purse, untouched. I wasn't ready to go there yet, but I knew I didn't want the police to have whatever was written on its pages before me. The rest were back home in Tennessee, and I'd hand over the ones from the last seven years as soon as I got back there.

Deep in my bones, I knew without a doubt her creepy ass stalker was behind this.

Her messages didn't yield anything I hadn't already known, and I breathed a sigh of relief. There was our text thread, going back so far I gave up after a few minutes of scrolling. Some correspondence with clients, messages with friends and distant relatives.

Interspersed among all of those were several threads from varying numbers, none of which were saved under any sort of contact information.

That would've been too difficult when they changed so often.

Messages from her stalker.

UNKNOWN

I miss you.

I had fun with you.

Come back and let's do it again.

Those were the first three, sent not long after we'd returned to Tennessee, and they'd all been fairly innocent at first. Unlike me, who had chosen not to share any personal information beyond my first name with Finn that night seven years ago, Lainey was more…trusting and had clearly given the creep she hooked up with her number.

I remembered when the first few came in.

"It's fiiiiine," she said in a sing-song voice. "He's harmless."

Famous last words, I thought.

Things quickly took a turn when Lainey never responded.

UNKNOWN

You will be mine.

I will find you.

We'll be together forever.

UNKNOWN

See you soon.

The last message had come over six months ago, but I found myself shocked by its tone. Lainey had claimed he'd left her alone after that, which, I could tell from my perusal of her messages, wasn't a lie.

But she'd never shared the contents of the final message, or how ominous it came across.

We thought he was gone, that, after over six years of no response from Lainey, of her constantly blocking his numbers and social profiles—though that did little good—he'd finally given up and moved on.

Clearly, that hadn't been the case.

I think he's here.

Irritation, anger, and a sense of dismay rose within me, overwhelming and choking. I slammed the laptop shut and buried my face in my hands.

It should have been *me*.

Had it been me, we wouldn't be in this mess.

We'd both be home in Tennessee, safe and sound and far away from this creep.

Even when we found her—yes, *when*; I refused to accept anything less—I didn't think I'd ever be able to forgive myself.

"Goddesses, Lainey," I whispered to the universe. "Where are you?"

Only silence answered.

eleven

. . .

FINN

OVER THE NEXT FEW DAYS, I threw myself into work, doing everything I could to move past recent events.

To forget Reagan's reappearance in my life.

Even if she came back to Dusk Valley, it wouldn't be for me. It would be to find out what happened to her sister, and I wouldn't stand in her way. I wouldn't be a distraction she didn't need.

Instead, I'd do everything in my power to ensure we found her sister alive—and brought the fucker who had taken her to justice.

Trying, of course, was different than doing, and no amount of working with the horses currently boarded in the barn or feeding the various ranch animals managed to turn my mind away from the Lindsey sisters.

West and I joined the Army because while neither of us had any desire to go to college, we both had delusions of grandeur where our places in the world were concerned. We'd been reckless—and nearly broke Mama's heart the day we signed our contracts.

Those first four years passed in a blink, and somehow, inexplicably, we *liked* it. Liked the structure, the training, the men and women we served with. The service had shaved off the edges of our recklessness, uncovering our natural protective instincts and honing us into weapons instead of agents of chaos.

So we extended another two years.

At the tail end of that extension, we were approached to consider joining the Rangers.

Twenty-four years old and they wanted *us* to join one of the most elite military forces in the world?

The choice had been easy.

Maintaining physical fitness for the normal Army branch had been difficult but nothing compared to the shit we'd faced for the Rangers. We'd pushed our bodies to the brink, endured sleep deprivation, and were subjected to the advanced interrogation techniques we'd later use on enemy prisoners. Ranger training had been grueling mentally as well.

All that to say, there was some deep-seated part of me that, as a Lawless, had always *demanded* I protect those around me. Those weaker, less fortunate, anyone who found themselves down on their luck and in need of saving.

Being a soldier only rooted that desire deeper.

And Reagan was a textbook damsel in distress, signaling for my help. The beast in my chest perked up like she'd given off a distress signal I couldn't ignore.

The following Tuesday, four days after I'd last seen Reagan and a week after the last time anyone had seen or heard from Lainey, I was damn near coming out of my skin from feeling so fucking *useless*.

I took off my hat and wiped a sweaty and dirt-streaked forearm across my equally sweaty and dirty face, doing nothing but spreading both further around. It had been a long ass day in the fields, making sure crops had been planted properly and were surviving. All hands had been on deck, pulling any that hadn't survived. As we sold quite a bit of the corn, wheat, and soybeans, both to other outfits and in other products such as Mama's line of homemade soaps, lotions, and candles, West, our foreman Abel, and I were unyielding in the quality of what we grew.

I clicked my tongue, and Raider trotted over, abandoning the patch of grass he'd been munching on. He was wholly in his element out here, content to roam around, though never too far from me. He was my soul horse, a bond we'd developed over the years that was the strongest connection I'd ever had with a living thing besides my twin.

As usual, I was the last one in the field, the rest of the workers having disappeared back to their homes and families hours ago. But the sun was going down, and a quick check of my watch told me it was nearly eight p.m.

Damn, later than I'd intended.

I'd thrown my leg over Raider and settled into the saddle when my phone vibrated against my ass. Shifting, I withdrew it from my pocket and found Lane's name on the readout.

"Yo."

"You home?" he asked.

"Headed that way," I said, collecting Raider's reins in one hand and digging my heels into his sides, turning us around to head back to my house.

We had a barn with plenty of stalls for boarding him, but when I'd built my own home years ago, I also constructed a smaller barn with stalls for four more horses. I liked having Raider nearby, making it easier to get up and go should the need arise.

Sure, I had a truck, but in my opinion, there was no better way to navigate my family's land than on horseback.

At the edge of my property was my guest house, about a hundred yards from mine. It rarely got much use, mostly from Owen when he and his wife, Delia, came to visit—though they hadn't been to town since their son, Jace, was born last November.

Lately, Aria had been staying there more and more often, though. Some nights, I'd come home after a long day and find the lights on inside. I'd invite her over for dinner as a way of keeping an eye on her. While I knew she loved our mother and all six of us boys, I couldn't imagine how difficult it was for her to be not only the baby of the family, but also the only girl. Instead of growing up with a dad, she'd gotten six alpha-male, overprotective father figures in the form of her big brothers. But she wasn't a little girl anymore, and I got the sense that Aria had been looking for a way out for a long time.

If staying in my guest house gave her a little taste of the freedom she so desperately craved, I was happy to be the one to provide that to her.

I gave Raider his head as we trotted toward home.

"I need a favor," Lane said, reminding me I was on the phone with him.

Warily, I asked, "What kind of favor?"

"You, West, Trey, the Swallow."

"Shit, Sheriff. You askin' me to get drunk?" I teased. I'd been in this position a few times before, and I knew it seriously irked my brother to have to ask for help. There was nothing I loved more than knocking him further off balance.

Lane huffed in annoyance, knowing he'd have to give me more information than that. "I need you to ask around about Lainey Lindsey."

"You got a lead?" I asked, breathless with…hope? I couldn't entirely name it. All I knew was when Raider crested the hill, the downside leading to a little hollow where my house, barn, and small paddock were located, I felt weightless.

Maybe Lainey's story wouldn't end here in Dusk Valley after all.

"Kind of?" he said, though it sounded more like a question. "Before she left, Reagan let me know Lainey had a rental car, and she handed over all of Lainey's personal effects she found in her hotel room, and—"

"Did you do a sweep?"

I could practically see Lane's eyes roll through the phone. "Did I do my job? Yes, Finn, we did a fucking sweep. Sent all the results up to the crime lab in Boise, and we're still waiting on results. Not likely anything will pop since it's not like those housekeepers exactly sterilize those rooms, but we have to exhaust every option."

"So what's this 'kind of' lead, then?"

"We haven't managed to locate Lainey's phone, and it's looking like her ID and credit cards being on that dead girl were a fluke. Likely a theft kind of situation. But her laptop was in her motel room, and I also sent that up to Boise—"

"Let me guess, Addie?"

Addison "Addie" Caldwell was an FBI agent who worked out of the Boise field office. Over the years, she and Lane had developed a close working relationship—though our entire family often wondered if it went beyond that.

But then there was that inexplicable thing between him and Sutton Rausch that always made us question if there was more to *that* relationship than met the eyes.

Whatever.

Not my monkey, not my circus.

"Yes," he said grudgingly.

"And?" I prompted.

"Her phone is turned off, but the last place it pinged was right outside the Swallow. We also found her rental car in the lot. Whoever took her, took her from there."

"That bar really needs to increase its exterior security," I gritted out. "Hire a fucking guard or something."

"You'll get no argument from me."

Last year, right around this same time, Aspen was abducted right outside the Swallow too and held captive for a full day at a remote cabin in the woods before her assailant left her to die in a fire.

Crew saved her life, and now they were getting married in a few months.

Theirs was the kind of love story people wrote books about, and I hoped like hell Lainey's had a similarly happy ending.

"So what do you want us to do?"

"Well, Trey is going in to get security footage from the night she went missing, as well as anything he can get from seven years ago."

I blinked in surprise. Now that Lane had gotten over himself and brought Trey on, but that he thought we'd be able to get our hands on anything like that after so much time had passed.

Raider slowed to a gentle trot as we neared my barn, and I slid off, leading him inside and into a stall. We'd taken it easy on the way back, so there was no need to cool him down. I'd untack him when I hung up with Lane.

"You think they've kept those kinds of records?" I asked as I absently ran a hand down Raider's chestnut flank.

"Honestly? I doubt it, but if anyone can make something out of nothing where this shit is concerned, it's Trey."

True. Our second oldest brother was one of the best in the country, making a pretty penny in private and cyber security after he'd left the Secret Service and returned to Dusk Valley nearly a decade ago.

"I want you and West to ask around," Lane continued. "The good ole boys will talk to you."

Another truth. Small towns treated military vets like super-heroes, and though a lot of what we'd done in the Rangers was classified, they all knew we'd been part of several important missions. To them, West and I were practically gods. If we bought them a few drinks and let them relive their own glory days in the service, they'd sing like canaries.

"You call West yet?"

"I was going to after I got off with you. And I'm going to send you a picture of Lainey that you can flash around, okay?"

"Sure," I said. "Give me an hour to untack and groom Raider, shower, and we'll head in."

"Thanks brother," Lane said, his relief evident. "I owe you one."

"I'll be taking you up on that," I assured him before hanging up, my phone beeping a moment after with the promised photo.

Little did he know, I'd do it for free, no quid pro quo necessary.

If it meant giving Reagan her sister back, safe and whole and unharmed, I'd do whatever it took.

twelve

. . .

FINN

AS PROMISED, sixty minutes later, Raider was clean, fed, and bedded down in his stall. I was freshly showered and dressed in my standard uniform of Carhartt pocket tee, my nicest pair of jeans, and favorite boots. I'd finished brushing my teeth and was applying deodorant when my front door opened.

Though no one in my family ever knocked when they came in, I knew it was West before I saw him. I could sense him through that "woo-woo twin shit" Lane liked to thumb his nose at.

"Ari in the guest house again?" he asked as I came out of the bathroom, meeting him in the center of my great room, the kitchen and dining room to my left.

Moving to the front windows, I flicked the curtain to the side. Sure enough, the lights in the house across the field glowed.

"Must be."

"Wanna check on her before we leave?"

"Nah," I said, shaking my head, swiping my wallet and keys off the sideboard by the door and stuffing them into my pockets. "She'll be fine."

Still, I shot her a text.

ME

House is open if you need anything that's not over there.

ARIA

Love you.

ME

Love you too, Ari.

I grinned. I'd take "love you" over "thank you" any day.

"What'd she say?" West asked as we moved through the house in the direction of the door to the attached garage.

"That she loves me and I'm her favorite brother."

West snorted. "Bullshit."

"Okay, only half true. I'll let you guess which half."

"You're annoying."

"Get moving, baby bro."

"Don't call me that," I mimicked as he said it.

With a laugh, he shoved me hard as we made our way to the truck.

On a Tuesday, the dirt-packed parking lot in front of the local bar was nearly empty. Tourist season wouldn't kick up for another three weeks or so. The rest of Dusk Valley's residents were home, enjoying some R&R, likely preparing for bed.

Trey was already there, climbing out of his SUV when West and I parked. We walked in together, pausing right inside the door to allow our eyes to adjust to the dimness. Four sets of eyes turned in our direction when the heavy wooden door slammed shut behind us.

Unsurprisingly, three men who were permanent fixtures in this place were seated side-by-side-by-side at the far end of the bar. Benny, the owner, stood on the bar's other side, elbows leaned on the counter as he chatted with them.

"Well, well, well," he said, moving to our end and placing

napkins on the bar top in front of us as we took seats. "The brothers Lawless. You want IDs?"

We all murmured affirmation, and he quickly poured our beers.

"Normally don't see you guys here on weeknights," Benny mused. "I assume there's a reason?"

Cutting right to the chase, Trey said, "I need your security footage."

"I heard about that girl that went missing. Shame shit like that keeps happening in this town."

"Shame shit like that keeps happening right outside *your* bar," I growled. "First Aspen, now this woman?"

"Tell me, Benny," Trey said almost conversationally, "am I going to find anything worthwhile on those exterior cameras I installed, or are they going to be as useless as they were when Aspen was taken?"

Benny, who was younger than us and had taken over the bar when his father passed last fall, didn't particularly like me or my brothers. But he put up with us for two reasons.

First, my sister was an amazing fucking singer and brought in huge crowds every time she performed here. Fucking with us meant Aria taking her talents elsewhere, which wasn't something his business could afford.

And second, he knew each of us could kick his ass with one hand tied behind our backs.

Hell, we could do it without any arms at all.

Even so, he sneered at Trey. "Pops never wanted those installed in the first place."

That much was true. Exterior cameras on all local businesses was an ordinance the town council passed several years ago, when a string of break-ins and vandals had cost owners—and insurance companies—a lot of money in repairs and payouts.

The petty crimes dried up pretty quickly after that, and Trey signed a nice little contract to provide all the technology.

Still, quite a few of the business owners had rebelled in what little ways they could. Benny's dad had been the worst offender of all, never bothering to turn the cameras on let alone allow them to record. Claimed it violated the privacy of his patrons.

We all knew the real reason was that he wanted to keep prying eyes away from the drug dealing business he ran out of the back room. It had worked too. Lane and his department had failed to find enough evidence to arrest him before he died, and no one was sure if Benny had taken up the mantle or not.

"Answer the fucking question," West said evenly, though his tone brooked no room for argument.

"They're working," Benny gritted out.

"Get me the footage," Trey said.

In the interest of protecting the privacy people weren't even entitled to in public spaces, Trey didn't record any footage onto the servers at his house. That responsibility fell on the shoulders of the business owners.

Benny gave a curt nod and turned to head to the back, but Trey stopped him.

"Gonna need everything you've got from March seven years ago as well."

Returning his attention to Trey, Benny's eyes were wide. "There's no fuckin' way."

"I'm sure there are old tapes or something around here somewhere," Trey said with a wide, fake grin. "Your dad hadn't always been such a pain in my ass about it."

Benny sighed, dragging a hand down his face in obvious annoyance.

"Probably in the attic," he mumbled.

"Great!" Trey said happily, jumping to his feet. "I'll help."

West and I muffled our snorts in our arms, occupying our mouths with twin swallows of our beers. We knew what Trey was doing, offering to go with, and Benny likely did too. Trey wasn't giving him the option to dick around and pretend he didn't find anything.

We had no time to waste, not when a woman's life hung in the balance.

Two, if you considered what the loss of her twin would do to Reagan.

As a twin myself, it was fucking unimaginable.

Once Trey and Benny disappeared, West and I picked up our drinks and walked to the other end of the bar, pulling up stools at the corner perpendicular to the three grizzled men.

Rusty, Jim, and Dodger were indeterminate ages, though I guessed they were all north of sixty. They were a sure thing in this life. Like death and taxes, finding Rusty, Jim, and Dodger seated in this same spot in this bar on any given night was one thing you could count on.

"Boys," Rusty grumbled, and the other two dipped their chins in acknowledgement.

"Look," West started. "I'm not going to beat around the bush here. There's a woman missing, and this is the last place she was seen. She'd been here last Tuesday night. You guys know anything about that?"

Dodger's rheumy, bloodshot eyes narrowed in our direction.

"Buying us another round might jog our memories."

I rolled my eyes but got up, went behind the bar, grabbed three bottles of Budweiser out of the cooler, uncapped them, and placed them in front of the men.

Each took a healthy drink, smacking their lips as they set them down.

"Now," Jim started. "What's this woman look like?"

Getting out my phone, I pulled up the photo Lane had sent, careful not to linger on it. Mistaking her for Reagan would be too goddamn easy.

"I remember her!" Rusty exclaimed. "Don't get pretty little things like that in here much."

"Was she with anyone?"

They all shook their heads, and Dodger said, "Sat in the corner by herself with a drink, playing on her little phone."

"How did she seem?" I pressed. The fact that these guys even remembered seeing her was a miracle, but I supposed when you spent over half the day drunk, it became a natural state you learned to navigate the same way normal people navigated sobriety.

"Fine?" Jim supplied, like that was a silly question. "I wasn't familiar enough with her to say any different."

"How long was she here?"

"Couple hours. Had a few beers, nursing 'em. Seemed to be killing time."

Like she'd been waiting for someone, possibly?

I shifted my eyes to the side, sharing a look with West that told me he had a similar thought.

"Anything else you can remember?"

The three shook their heads in unison, and I nodded. The fact that they even recognized the photo was an impressive feat. At the very least, Lane now had visual confirmation she'd been here the night she went missing.

Still, the sheriff and his department had their work cut out for them—as did Trey.

Heavy footfalls echoed down the stairs at the back of the building, and Benny and Trey emerged from the hall a moment later. In his arms, Trey carried a stack of dusty banker's boxes.

"Got the goods," he said. "Benny was so helpful."

"The fuck is this?" the man in question said as he moved back behind the bar, seeing the nearly full bottles in front of the old men alongside the empty ones. "Which one of you came behind my bar?"

All six of us—even Trey—raised our hands in similar gestures of, *wasn't me*. Benny huffed, muttering and cursing under his breath about people acting like they owned the place.

"That's our cue," West murmured.

Trey and I nodded, and I said, "Well, thanks for your help," clapping the old guys on the shoulders as I walked by.

"You too, Benny!" Trey threw over his shoulder as we headed outside.

When we were free from eavesdropping, Trey said, "I'd like to ring that fucking guy's neck. If this wasn't the only bar in town, I probably would."

"We could help get rid of the body," West supplied jokingly, holding his fist out, which I bumped with mine. "We've done it before."

Without a doubt, Trey had as well, quietly and efficiently neutralizing threats to the President as part of his Secret Service detail.

"Let's not take it that far," Trey said diplomatically. "There's no reason, even if he is a pain in my ass." We reached his SUV, and he beeped open the hatch, shoving the box in beside the mobile command center he'd outfitted his vehicle with. "The upside is there are tapes from seven years ago, but they're *only* labeled with the year, so it's going to take me some time to comb them."

"Surprised we haven't heard from L—"

West hadn't even been able to get our brother's full name out before Trey's phone rang, his name popping up.

Answering, Trey put it on speaker. "Sheriff."

"You guys still at the bar?"

"Just leaving," Trey said. "I've got the security footage from last week *and* the tapes from seven years ago."

"Great," Lane said. "How long do you think it'll take to go through it all?"

"Well, like I just told Finn and West, they're not organized in any way that makes sense beyond having the year on them. So first, I'm going to have to digitize them, then spend some time compiling everything chronologically. Could be a few weeks, could be a few months."

"*Months?*" Lane asked, incredulous, and I had to admit, I was in agreement. "In months, Lainey Lindsey could be *dead*, Trey."

"I'm going to work as fast as I can, you prick. That's the best I can do."

"Hand it all over, and I'll send it up to Boise."

"We could do that," Trey conceded, "but that's not going to make the process go any faster, *and* you wouldn't be the first in line for information if anything pops. You know bringing the FBI in, even if it's only Addie, makes it look like you can't handle shit on your own."

Lane growled in frustration, but only because he knew our big brother was right.

Letting Trey handle this was truly the best and fastest course of action.

"I don't like this."

"None of us do," I piped in. "A woman is missing, and someone in *our* town is responsible."

I fucking hated that revelation, knowing that, once again, a woman had come here and been targeted. Aspen had survived, thanks in no small part to Crew, but Lainey was still out there somewhere—likely alive and being held against her will if Reagan's gut feeling was anything to go on. Though we weren't law enforcement, we *were* the best chance she had at breaking free without the loss of her life.

The upside was that Trey, West, and I could operate outside the constraints of the law. Crew too, if he wanted to help. Knowing him, he'd be all in. That same strong desire to serve and protect the rest of us had also lived in him.

And I doubted we'd get Crew on board without Aspen offering to help as well, which wasn't a bad thing, either.

"What did you and West dig up?" Lane asked me.

"Rusty, Jim, and Dodger recognized the photo. Couldn't say much beyond confirming they saw her that night. Said she sat in the corner for a few hours, nursed a couple beers, played on her phone, but that was it. Sounds to me like she was waiting for someone or something."

"Hopefully this footage," Trey said, tapping the top of the box, sending dust flying, "will shed some light on that."

"Hopefully," Lane sighed, not sounding the least bit hopeful.

I didn't envy him, being the one burdened when bad things happened to good people in his jurisdiction.

"We'll find her," I said. No, *promised*.

"Yeah," Lane replied, seemingly unconvinced. "Well, keep me posted."

He didn't wait for a response before he hung up.

West and I said our goodbyes to Trey and made for my truck, heading back to the ranch. I dropped him off at his before heading home, unsurprised to find Aria in my living room, watching some reality TV show on my massive flat screen.

I changed into comfier clothes before joining her.

"Rough night?" she asked when I'd thrown myself onto the couch at her side, head tipping against the back.

"Not really," I admitted. "Just been a long week. I can't stop thinking about this missing woman."

"Is it her…or her sister?"

I snorted. Truthfully, I was pretty fucking transparent when it came to Reagan Lindsey. Leave it to Aria to hone right in on the real issue.

"Both," I said honestly. "I can't imagine being in Reagan's position, and…I care about her. Doesn't make a lot of sense since I've never spent a full day with the woman, but I do. I'd do anything to make this right for her."

Aria scooted closer and tucked herself into my side.

"You will, Finny."

She sounded so sure, and I wasn't about to refute her.

If Aria believed in me, the least I could do was make sure that belief wasn't misplaced.

thirteen

. . .

THREE WEEKS LATER

MY SISTER WAS STILL MISSING.

A month had passed without her.

And we were no closer to finding out what happened to her.

Sheriff Lawless had been in touch a few times, mostly to check in and pass on what little new information they'd gathered. In addition to sweeping her motel room for prints and particulates, the department had also canvassed the area, asking anyone who lived or worked nearby if they remembered seeing her that evening, if she'd been with anyone, or if they'd noticed anything out of the ordinary happening.

Naturally, no one had anything to report.

Lainey had seemingly vanished into thin air, which didn't bode well for her safe return. Deep in my bones, I knew she was alive, so I forced myself to cling to that small comfort, protecting the little ember of hope that still smoldered in my chest.

Still, I couldn't sit around all the way across the country, doing nothing while she was out there somewhere. Before I'd even gotten on the plane home from Idaho, I'd made the decision to move to Dusk Valley, at least for the summer. I could operate my business from anywhere, and I had nothing keeping me in Tennessee.

Lainey and I owned our home outright—the same house our parents had purchased shortly after we were born that reverted to our names when they passed. Troy was an attorney, and though he admirably pleaded his case for me to stay, I knew I needed to be in Dusk Valley.

I had no idea how long I'd be gone, but I cancelled all photography jobs we'd scheduled this summer and secured a three-month lease in Dusk Valley. I also offered the same here. My renters were a travel nurse and her husband, who worked from home. I'd had Troy run background checks on them. Both had clean records, excellent credit, and provided glowing personal references. By all accounts, they were upstanding citizens who kept to themselves.

Did I *need* to move to Dusk Valley? Of course not. But I wanted to be there, in Lane's face, reminding him Lainey was still missing. And *maybe* I was delusional enough to think I could help in some way.

Though he was no closer to locating Lainey than when I'd left three weeks before, Lane had been helpful in finding me a long-term rental. Most rentals in the area were short-term, and with the summer tourist season rapidly approaching, I'd had difficulty finding anything myself.

I hadn't seen pictures of the place, but the sheriff assured me it was safe and well-maintained. The price was right, so that was good enough for me.

My doorbell rang as I was packing the last of my clothes.

I was unsurprised to find my ex on the other side.

To be honest, my and Troy's relationship had been ill-fated from the start. We'd met shortly after Lainey and I graduated college. He'd come into the restaurant where we'd been waiting tables, working crazy hours to save enough to get our photography business off the ground. In his bespoke suit, with that expensive haircut and warm brown eyes, I'd been immediately drawn to him. To his stability. How he seemed to see me for *me*. Not Reagan, the twin. Not Reagan, the reformed party girl. Not Reagan, the woman who remained trapped in the backseat of a car with her parents dead in the front.

Simply…*Reagan*, the woman.

Our romance had been a whirlwind, and I'd been so caught up in the glamor of it all—me, fresh out of college pinching pennies, catching the eye of this well-established, successful attorney—that I ignored the red flags for far too long.

Troy had been instrumental in bringing me back to myself, and for that, I would always be grateful for him. But this version of me had simply outgrown him.

Unfortunately, he wasn't taking our separation as gracefully as I'd hoped—as evidenced by him showing up at my house unannounced, once again attempting to get me to stay.

"Damn, it looks empty in here," he said when I let him in.

"That's what happens when you move," I replied, not bothering to hide my annoyance.

"You don't *have* to, though."

Rolling my eyes, I didn't respond. We'd had this same argument numerous times over the last few weeks.

"Please, Reag. Don't do this."

"Don't call me that," I gritted out.

I fucking *hated* when he called me that, like I was some filthy dish rag to be discarded the second it outlived its usefulness.

Troy raised his hands. "Sorry. But can't you see how insane this is? What are you going to be able to accomplish that those Podunk cops can't?"

"You wouldn't understand," I said, angrily shoving sweaters into the suitcase flopped open on my bed, no longer caring about organization.

"You're right," he admitted. "I don't get it. This isn't the first time Lainey has taken off without telling you where she is. Why is this any different?"

Whirling on him, I allowed my fury to rise to the surface, exploding on him.

"She's been gone for a *month*, Troy!" I screamed. "I know you're not exactly my sister's biggest fan, but even you can understand that's not normal. If she could, she would've come back by now. She would've at least *called*."

Unshed tears choked out the final word, but I wouldn't allow myself to cry. Not now, and especially not in front of him.

"Whatever," he said on a sigh.

"Get out."

"Reagan…" My name was a plea.

I shook my head vehemently. "No. Leave. Now."

I was through talking, done giving him the time of day. The time to cut all ties, to remove him from my life once and for all had long since passed.

"Reagan, please."

Not bothering with words, I merely pointed toward the door.

For too long, he didn't move, only stared at me, as though wordlessly willing me to change my mind.

I wouldn't.

Eventually, he got the point and disappeared, but not without a final parting shot.

"You'll be back."

I wasn't sure if he meant to Tennessee or to *him*.

Likely both.

Only when his ridiculous sports car fired up and peeled away did I allow myself to break.

Not for Troy, but because I missed Lainey so deeply. Half of my heart, my *soul* had gone with her. Without her, I'd never be whole again.

Plus, Troy was wrong.

I might never come back.

All the reasons I had to stay here had disappeared right along with my sister.

The circumstances were unimaginable, but maybe this was my chance at the fresh start I'd secretly been craving for years. My opportunity to leave behind the ghosts of my parents, which still lingered in the halls of this home Lainey and I had once shared with them.

Besides, Lainey was in Dusk Valley. I might not have known *where*, but my gut told me whoever had her hadn't taken her far.

And wherever Lainey was? That was where I needed to be.

I'd be lying if I said I wasn't also a bit excited to be living in the same town as Finn, even if my conscience whispered I was a horrible person for thinking such a thing given my sister's disappearance.

I'd been with a fair number of men in my life, but Finn Lawless was the first one to ever elicit such a strong physical reaction from me. My body remembered the way he'd held me, how he'd played and toyed and teased, driving my pleasure higher and higher until it had all come crashing down around me. Like a flesh memory, flashes of that night had assaulted the forefront of my brain the moment he'd taken my hand in the sheriff's department—and they had yet to leave me alone.

Maybe that was all the draw to him meant. My traitorous body remembering how fucking *euphoric* he'd made me feel.

I tried to get myself to believe that, but it didn't ring true. While he'd whispered filthy words against my flesh and fucked me in ways I never imagined I'd experience in real life, he genuinely seemed to care about me.

That made him dangerous.

A physical connection was one thing, but an emotional one?

Given the hellscape my mind had become, one false move would send me headlong into a breakdown—not something I could afford right now.

As badly as I could use the distraction, and as much as I

wouldn't mind tangling with him in the sheets again, I vowed then and there to let go of any delusions I had about Finn Lawless.

He was better off without me and my mess.

THE FOLLOWING MORNING, I rose well before the sun to get on the road.

According to my GPS, it would take me about thirty hours to drive to Dusk Valley from eastern Tennessee, and I pushed myself hard the entire time. Back-to-back sixteen-hour days in the car with nothing to keep me company but my own intrusive thoughts gave me severe cabin fever, and I was bursting at the seams by the time I reached the Dusk Valley town limits.

So much had changed in the month since I'd last been here. Not the town itself, which was as idyllic as ever, but *me*. The ache in my chest of missing my sister was a constant companion I was afraid would never leave me.

A month ago, winter still had the town in its grip, though loosely. Everything had been drab and grey. Now, though, everything was bright and crisply verdant. Each old-fashioned lamppost that lined downtown's main street was decorated with a hanging basket of flowers that spilled over its edges in bright pinks, purples, and an array of other summery shades.

The buildings and storefronts were well-kept, businesses differentiated by colorful striped awnings, hanging signs that swung in the gentle breeze, and plate glass windows emblazoned with large, creamy white logos. Though there were numerous shops, everything from the cafe, Mozzy's Pizza, and the diner to a salon, hardware store, and pharmacy.

The air outside was warm—though not as warm as what I'd left behind in Tennessee. More refreshing than the oppressive humidity of the south, the kind of warmth you could enjoy without suffocating.

I was reminded how beautiful this place was, trying to look at it through the lens I'd first viewed it through instead of seeing its dark underbelly—instead of viewing it as the place my sister had disappeared.

The town was so small it didn't have a single stop light, only a blinking yellow light that cautioned drivers at a particular inter-section, where Cassia connected with a perpendicular road that stretched into the distance in either direction. There was no one behind me, so I grabbed my phone and plugged the address for my new rental into my GPS, on the outskirts of Dusk Valley.

I didn't mind the distance from town, though. That far out, I hoped to have some mountain views. I might be miserable, but having a stunning view wouldn't make things worse. Maybe I'd be able to hike around and take some pictures.

My mind wandered as I navigated the unfamiliar area, not settling on anything important, but my attention focused when I came to a break in the long fence running parallel to the dirt road.

The break was a large wooden archway, two tall, thick pine posts with a third stretched across them. Dangling from the cross beam was a sign, marking the entrance to a farm or something.

No, *a ranch.*

LAWLESS RESCUE & DUDE RANCH

"Oh, Lane," I muttered. "What have you done?"

Maybe there was a reasonable explanation. *Maybe* there was another Lawless family in the area.

Not fucking likely.

The GPS directed me to turn past the gates, and a few hundred yards beyond, another dirt track branched off, shaded by trees on both sides, cocooning me beneath a canopy of broad maple leaves and dappled sunlight.

Despite my rising trepidation, I had to admit the effect was magical.

Idaho was the most beautiful place I'd ever visited.

Less than a mile later, I emerged from the tree cover into a clearing—a yard, I supposed. The dirt road turned to gravel paths that branched off in two directions—one toward a gorgeous, sprawling, dark grey-sided ranch-style home with an attached garage, the plentiful windows framed in a richly-stained wood that matched the entrance and garage doors. Nearby sat a low-slung building with massive sliding barn-style doors, designed to match the house. I quickly realized it *was* a barn, the fenced in paddock giving it away.

I doubted this was the "quaint two-bedroom" the listing the sheriff sent me described, so I decided to continue down the other path. Beyond what I now assumed to be the main house, about a hundred yards away, sat a smaller guest house, a cute miniature of the big house.

My worst fears about *who* owned this place, about *why* Lane had been so helpful, about *how* he'd known so much about this place, were confirmed when my eyes landed on the man waiting on the top step of the little front porch. He was doing that sexy man lean against one of the posts, his thick, sexy, tattooed arms crossed over his chest as he watched my approach.

There was a small gravel lot out front, and I pulled to a stop, shut the car off, and leaned my head back, eyes closing as I begged the universe for an ounce of patience and peace.

When I opened them again, finally mustering up the courage to face the firing squad, I got out to meet Finn.

Goddesses, he was the kind of man wet dreams were made of —and he'd certainly starred in countless of mine over the years. I hadn't given myself the chance to really *look* at him when I'd been here a month ago, too wrapped up in everything going wrong to allow myself that luxury.

The years had been kind to him, morphing him from an attractive but polished twenty-something with his buzz cut and muscles who still maintained some of his boyish charm, into this rugged, sinful *man*. And, goddesses, it made me want to be *bad*.

I wondered, had the metamorphosis been the Army's doing? Experience? Was there a woman in his life? I'd never considered the possibility, and I realized now what a horrible oversight that had been on my part.

One that could epically backfire.

Not that I was interested in Finn Lawless.

Not like that.

At least, that was the lie I'd tell myself.

Still, I couldn't stop myself from picturing how that hard body looked beneath the Carhartt pocket tee and thigh-clinging denim. He'd been strong back then, but now he seemed *bigger*— and had more tattoos.

Was his ass still tight enough to bounce a quarter off? Could I pour tequila into the ridges of his abdomen and slurp it up like the thirsty bitch I was?

Get it together, Reagan.

Giving myself a little internal shake, I closed the distance between us.

"You didn't."

"I did," he grinned. "It was the only way."

"Only way to what?"

"Keep you close."

I hated the way my insides clenched at the promise and sheer alpha male *possession* in those words, my body waking up and remembering.

We like this one, it seemed to say. *He fucked us real good. We should absolutely let him do it again.*

Yeah, yeah, my inner voice was a slut—but only for Finn Lawless.

I remembered the sign out front as I drove in.

"The ranch is yours?" I asked.

"My family's," he said. "West and I run it now."

"So you decided to come home once you left the Army after all."

"You remembered," he said, that grin growing wider.

I merely nodded.

I'd need a fucking lobotomy to forget.

Every nanosecond of that night seven years ago was etched into my memory, a brand I'd never be able to remove. Not only the sex, but the conversation too.

"I can't stay here," I said, turning the conversation back into safer territory.

"Sure you can."

"You live here."

He pointed at the big house across the field. "Technically, I live there."

"Finn…"

"*Reagan.*"

Goddesses, I loved the way my name rolled off his tongue.

"I'll go to the motel until I can find something else," I said, turning away from him.

I'd barely made it a step before his broad palm circled my upper arm.

"Please, Reagan. Stay. I promise, you won't even have to see me if you don't want."

Though my brain screamed at me to tuck tail and run, every cell in my body begged me to stay.

Guess which one won out?

"Okay."

"Okay?" he repeated, surprised.

"Okay," I agreed, hooking my thumb over my shoulder. "Help me with my stuff?"

He released my arm. "Lead the way."

fourteen

. . .

REAGAN

MOVING into Finn's guest house didn't take long. All I had with me was my camera equipment, clothes and toiletries, and Lainey's journals, which I planned to hand over to the police.

Of course, I'd stopped at a UPS store on the way here to make copies of all of them. I wasn't ready to read them yet, but I knew I wanted to have them. Depending on how this whole thing shook out, I might never see them again, and I couldn't risk not keeping *some* piece of my sister close to me.

My first order of business now that I was settled was to sit down with the sheriff and get an update on the case. I wasn't above making myself a nuisance if it meant keeping the pressure on the department, reminding them that a woman had gone missing on their watch, and someone who loved her wanted her home.

After making breakfast on my third morning in town, I took my third cup of coffee—I'd been up for hours, and I needed it—out to the little back porch that looked over the fields and hills that rolled up into the distant mountain range behind the house and dialed Lane.

He answered on the second ring. "This is Sheriff Lawless."

"Hey La—" I stopped, correcting myself. It didn't feel right referring to him by his first name when this wasn't a social call. "*Sheriff.* This is Reagan Lindsey."

"Reagan," he said warmly. "You get all settled?"

"I did. Sitting on the back porch as we speak. This place is beautiful."

He hummed in agreement. "The ranch is my favorite place in the world, for sure."

"I can see why. Thanks for helping set all this up, but you could've warned me this was Finn's place."

Lane chuckled. "I'm failing to see the problem."

"Meddling siblings," I muttered.

"A brother's duty," he agreed.

Conversation died, Lane waiting me out. I took a fortifying sip of my coffee and said, "So look, the reason for my call—"

"You want an update on your sister."

"Yes."

"You're in luck. I've got some time free in a couple hours, and I was planning on calling you anyway. Could you come down to the station?"

"Absolutely."

"Eleven work?"

"Yep. I'll be there."

"Great, see you then."

He hung up, and I relaxed a little, feeling slightly more confident about how seriously his department was taking my sister's case. And maybe, hopefully, they had some break in the case that would get us one step closer to finding Lainey.

Eleven was still a way off, so I went back inside, cleaned up my mess from breakfast, then spent some time getting everything I wanted to hand off to the police in order. My hands shook as I sifted through her journals, the faux leather covers soft beneath my fingers.

I'd bought the first one after she'd mentioned offhandedly

one day that she wanted to start journaling, and I'd given it to her on our birthday that year—our first one after our parents died.

Lainey glared at me as I handed the wrapped present over. "This better not be a book."

I simply shrugged, my smile growing wider as she ripped through the paper to reveal the small journal. I'd found a place to personalize it, and her initials, LML, were stamped in the bottom right corner of the cover.

"You didn't," she said, though her tone held no admonishment, only awe.

Again, I shrugged. "You said you wanted to journal, so I bought you one."

Lainey wrapped me in her arms, holding tightly, and I didn't mention the cold, wetness that dripped onto the shoulder of my tee.

"Thank you, sissy. I love it."

"Just don't use it to talk shit about me," I said with a laugh as I pulled back.

Lainey wiped her eyes. If I'd known it would mean so much to her, I would've bought one months ago when she first mentioned it.

"Never," she promised.

A gentle knock on the front door pulled me from the memory, and I swiped at my own face. I'd been doing that a lot lately—crying without realizing it, the tears silently spilling free from my eyes.

One day, I'd find out if she kept that promise, but not today.

I'd left the inside door open last night, letting the midnight breeze filter in, and as I approached, I saw a tall, broad figure silhouetted in the frame.

Finn.

I had every intention of standing firm in my claim that I couldn't do this—whatever *this*—was with him, that my entire focus had to be on Lainey. But my mind and my body, the traitorous bitch, were on different levels, because every fiber of my being fucking *yearned* for him. Not only in remembrance of the sex, either. I couldn't explain it except to say something deep within me knew I was safe with this man. Every negative emotion and invasive thought settled when he was near.

Staying away was that much harder because of it, even though my brain knew it was for the best.

"Morning, belle," he said when I opened the door for him. His hand instantly went to the back of his neck, cupping and scratching in a gesture I knew to be a nervous tic. "Shit, sorry."

"It's okay," I said softly, stepping back to admit him. "What can I do for you?"

"I wanted to check in. Make sure you've got everything you need."

I couldn't help but smile. This was exactly what I meant. I'd rejected him—and not gently, I might add—and he still came to me, making sure I was doing okay.

Finn Lawless was a giver, always making sure everyone around him was taken care of before he ever spared a thought for himself.

I knew this deep in my bones. Maybe I didn't know much about him on the surface, but I knew the man beneath the muscles and ink.

How he'd come to my rescue in the bar that night seven years ago.

How he'd held my hand through one of the worst experiences of my life a month ago.

Of course, even a grazing thought over the night we met had my mind running away with me, conjuring images of him and me, tangled in those motel room sheets.

The way he'd made me come several times before ever giving into the demands of his own body. The way he'd talked me through it all, the deep tenor of his voice riling me up as much as his hands and cock had.

Oh yes, Finn Lawless was *absolutely* a giver—a generous man in and out of the bedroom.

"I'm okay," I answered, an easy, blanket answer that didn't

even come close to encompassing how I truly felt. "I have a meeting with your brother this morning, actually."

"About the case? Have there been any developments?"

"I have no idea," I told him honestly. "I'm hoping so, but he wasn't exactly forthcoming on the phone.

Finn chuckled, a low, deep sound that rolled over my body and settled on my bones.

"Sounds like Lane," he said.

As if drawn together by some invisible force, our gazes collided and held. I couldn't have looked away if I tried, entirely entranced by the ocean depths of his eyes.

A woman could easily drown there, and I couldn't deny there was a part of me—a big one—that wanted to throw myself into the deep. Surrender to the siren sounds of his presence.

Shaking my head slightly, I discarded that thought and dragged my attention away.

Nothing good could come from giving into my desires.

"Is that all?" I asked, a bit curtly. Goddesses, this man sent my emotions haywire. My mama would be appalled at how badly my manners failed me when he was around.

I refused to look at him again, though I didn't miss the way his brows pinched together as he stared at me, his gaze a brand on my cheek.

"I—" he started but cut himself off. "Yeah, that's all. You'll call or text if you need anything?"

"Sure thing."

"Okay then. Well, good luck with your meeting."

"Thanks."

He lingered for a moment, clearly waiting to see if I'd backtrack and apologize, or offer anything else. Ask him to stay, ask for his help, *something*.

I said nothing, and eventually, he left.

And I took my first full breath since he'd arrived.

AT ELEVEN ON THE DOT, I walked through the front door of the sheriff's department. The woman at the desk behind the bullet proof glass smiled warmly at me.

"Good morning, ma'am," she said after she slid open her little window. "What can I do for you?"

"I'm here to see Sheriff Lawless."

"Name?" she asked, looking down at a clipboard of notes and papers in front of her.

"Reagan Lindsey."

Her finger traveled up and down a list before tapping it with a long, manicured fingernail. "Yes, I've got you right here. One moment while I buzz him." She indicated to a row of chairs by the wall. "Please have a seat."

I nodded, but I was too restless to sit, so I wandered around the small lobby, looking at the photographs on the walls.

One of my favorite pastimes was looking at old photos, studying the composition, framing, and perspective. Wondering what kind of equipment might have been used given the time period, and oftentimes, imagining how I could recreate such a shot with my modern technology.

A gasp left me, hand flying to my mouth, when I eventually stopped in front of a photo proudly displayed in the center of the longest uninterrupted wall, the most recent of all the ones I'd seen so far.

The entire Lawless family, taken the day Lane was officially sworn in as sheriff, if I had to guess.

They looked exactly as they had the day I met them all, and I remembered with a jolt that was because *this* had been the reason they'd all been home. Finn and West had taken leave specifically to celebrate Lane's accomplishment, and the rest of the brothers that had been spread around the country had come back as well.

The only two people I hadn't met that night were the Lawless matriarch and the baby sister, both of whom made an appearance in the photo.

I couldn't remember either of their names, though I was certain Finn or one of the other brothers had told me. Still, the family resemblance between them all was unmistakable. The little sister had hair the same shade as her mother's, more honeyed than the brothers' sandy blond. Their eyes varied in hues of blue, but the shape of each was the same. Baby sister couldn't have been more than sixteen or seventeen, but even then, she was gorgeous. Likely giving the boys at her high school the run around.

Or maybe they'd steered clear of her, given the formidable front her big brothers presented.

There was no father in the photo, though, and I was even more curious about the man who had sired these strong, striking men and that beautiful girl.

I dimly registered the buzz of a door behind me, but I'd finally allowed my attention to linger on Finn in the photo, and I couldn't look away. Seeing him like that—buzzed hair, only a single sleeve of tattoos instead of both arms now engulfed in ink, narrower and less hardened than he appeared today—only reminded me of how much time had passed.

Being back here, back in his orbit, was, for lack of a better word, insane.

I wasn't a believer in a conventional religious deity, but I did believe in a higher power, more like fate, and I was convinced that power wanted me back here.

But why now? And why at the cost of my sister's safety?

"Miss Lindsey?" a deep voice asked softly from behind me, as though not wanting to startle me.

Still, my hand flew to my chest as a little squeak escaped me, heart pumping a little harder, as I spun to face the sheriff.

So we were back to "Miss Lindsey?" Interesting.

"Sorry."

"It's okay," he smiled. "I didn't mean to scare you." Inclining his head toward the photo, he said, "That was the day I was sworn in as sheriff."

"I figured as much," I said. "This wasn't long before we met, right?"

"Right," he nodded. "Only a few days, actually." With a pointed glance at the box under my arm, he asked, "What's that?"

"Oh! Lainey's journals and some of her other stuff. I thought they might be helpful."

Well, minus the most recent one I'd found in the motel room three weeks ago, but he didn't need to know that. Her stalker had backed off in recent months, so I doubted there'd be anything helpful in there anyway.

I wanted to hang onto one piece of my sister in case I never saw her again.

Lane took it from me, then tipped his head backward, toward the door to the inner sanctum, and I dutifully followed.

"It's impressive," I mused. "To have been appointed Sheriff so young."

"I've been working for this department since high school," he admitted as we moved through the bullpen, not toward an interview room like the last time I'd been here, but his office at the back of the space. "Running documents, answering the phone out front. Bertie, the desk sergeant, has been here for years, and I was her little sidekick for a while." I snorted at his use of *little*. Hard to imagine him as anything other than this big, physically imposing man. "I went to college at Boise State, so I was close enough that I could come home on nights and weekends. I went on ride-alongs, sat in on interviews, did pretty much every job possible without being a sworn deputy. I completed the training program my final semester of university, moved home, and immediately jumped in."

"How old are you now?" I asked.

"Thirty-six."

I whistled low. "Sheriff at twenty-nine? Damn."

He winked as he opened his office door and gestured me inside. "What can I say? I'm an overachiever."

Without waiting for an invitation, I made myself comfortable in one of the guest chairs. Once he'd closed the door behind him, he slid the box onto his desk and took a seat behind it.

"So…what's new?" I asked conversationally, like we were old pals catching up. Like I wasn't the sister of a missing woman his department was in charge of locating.

The sheriff chuckled. "Well, in regard to your sister's case, we're at a bit of a standstill at the moment."

"It's been over a month," I blurted. "Surely you have *some* sort of lead."

He regarded me curiously. "You're aware the first forty-eight hours in a missing persons case are the most crucial, correct?" I nodded. "We weren't afforded the luxury of having those hours to work with. We weren't made aware that Miss Lindsey was missing until over seventy-two hours later."

I didn't like his tone—the insinuation in it. "And you're saying that's *my* fault?"

"I'm just saying, had she been reported missing sooner—"

Before he could utter another word to drive my irritation higher, I rose from my seat and cut him off with two words. "Fuck you."

There was absolutely no way I was going to sit there and listen to that bullshit.

How *dare* he accuse me of being the reason my sister was still missing?

I hadn't called right away because I'd been hoping my intuition had been wrong. That she'd simply taken off on her own for a few days and would be in touch when she returned to civilization.

What the fuck kind of place was this, blaming the family of a victim for her disappearance?

As I stormed away, I was even more glad I'd made copies of the journals. With the accusation he'd thrown at me, I didn't have high hopes his department was taking this case seriously—or that they'd ever locate my sister.

The thought was a punch to the gut, and by the time I stumbled out of the station and into the broad June daylight, I was gasping for air—bent over, hands on my knees, chest heaving as I attempted to suck in a full breath. My vision darkened at the edges, a wave of dizziness crashing over me and sending me staggering sideways.

"Hey, hey," someone said softly, the voice belonging to a woman, accompanied by warm, gentle hands grasping my shoulders, steadying me and directing me to sit down. "It's okay. Head between your knees and breathe with me. In, two, three, four. Hold." The woman rubbed soothing circles on my back, and I struggled to follow her directions. "Out, two, three, four. Good, good. And again."

We ran through the exercise three more times before my heart rate finally began to come down. Once I'd collected myself, my limbs now shaky as the adrenaline drained from my bloodstream, I looked up at my savior.

And I blinked in surprise, jaw dropping, when I recognized her.

"Holy shit," I breathed. "You're Aspen McKay."

The woman's peculiar cinnamon-colored eyes flashed with warmth, not a hint of annoyance to be found in her expression. "That's me."

Up to that point, I'd only ever seen photos of the private investigator-turned-best-selling true crime novelist. The first thing I noticed was how gorgeous she was, even more beautiful than photos suggested. Her hair was a bit longer than in the headshot at the back of her book, and she was shorter than I expected. I had seven or eight inches on her.

Lainey and I were into true crime, and we'd devoured her book, *The Shadows of Dusk Valley*. For both of us, it had been crazy to think Kelly Saunders, the Prom Night Arsonist serial killer, had been active when we'd visited and we'd never known it.

Made a chill run down my spine.

Murder, arson, missing women.

This town may have been charming on the surface, but clearly, the welcoming facade masked evil.

Remembering my manners, I quickly apologized and added, "Thank you for that. I—"

She smiled knowingly. "Trust me, I've been through a panic attack or two myself. And the sheriff's department is a stressful place."

"And the sheriff is an asshole," I muttered.

Aspen laughed. "You can say that again." She leaned closer, voice dropping conspiratorially. "Want to hear a secret?"

"Sure."

"He's also my future brother-in-law."

I blinked in surprise. "You're marrying one of the Lawless brothers?"

I didn't make it a habit of looking into public figures' personal lives, so I wasn't surprised I didn't already know this about her. Still…small fucking world.

"Crew, the—"

"Youngest," I finished for her. "Yeah, I'm familiar." Aspen's brow curved, and I realized too late how that sounded. "Sorry, not like that. At least not *him*." Goddesses, I was babbling. My cheeks heated. "I've been here before. A long time ago. Met them all at the bar."

Aspen nodded in understanding, then stood, extending a hand to me. "Let's go get lunch. You can tell me all about yourself and the night you met my future in-laws."

"Are you…busy or something?"

"Nah. I was running a few errands, but they're done, and I've got a few hours before I've got anything else to worry about. C'mon. It'll be fun. We can commiserate about those Lawless boys."

Eager for a friend, I followed along.

fifteen

. . .

REAGAN

WHEN WE ENTERED the diner around the corner from the department, an older woman immediately approached with a smile.

"Aspen, honey," she said, leaning in to press a kiss to Aspen's cheek. "Good to see you, dear."

"You too, Bonnie."

"Table for two?"

"Yes please."

Once she led us to a booth along the windows and we were settled with menus, she looked between Aspen and me, asking, "Who's your friend?"

"Oh, this is Reagan. Reagan, this is Bonnie, the owner of the diner."

"Pleasure to meet you, Reagan," Bonnie said. "I'll be back in a bit."

Wait a minute…

"You know who I am?" I asked Aspen when Bonnie disappeared.

Aspen gave me a sheepish smile. "Guilty."

"How?"

"There's been talk of you floating around the family since you first came to town a month ago," she admitted with a shrug.

My gaze narrowed. "What kind of talk?"

Her grin widened. "Mostly the boys giving Finn shit. You know how men are."

Boy, did I ever.

"It's not like that with us. I'm only here to find my sister."

"I admire your dedication," Aspen said. "But there's something about this town…and those Lawless men. I came here on a case once myself. I had no plans other than finding a killer and moving on to my next adventure." She lifted her left hand, showing off the diamond winking on her ring finger. "I wound up with a hell of a lot more."

"That's not…I'm not looking for a relationship. I just want Lainey back."

I couldn't live my life—could barely breathe properly—until she was home safe.

Aspen nodded in understanding. "I had a sister, so I get it."

"*Had?*"

"She died in a fire when I was sixteen."

"Shit, I'm so sorry."

Waving me off, she said, "I've spent a lot of time in therapy coming to terms with it. I miss her every day. It's an ache that never fully goes away, you know?"

I nodded, rubbing my chest, the spot right over my heart reserved entirely for my sister. "I know."

"Tell me about her."

Before I could, Bonnie returned, and I quickly glanced at the menu, selecting a club sandwich with sweet potato fries on the side and a water to drink. Aspen ordered the same, and Bonnie disappeared again.

Then, I launched into tales of Lainey.

I told her everything good about my sister: her fearlessness, her free spirit, her talent for capturing the heart and soul of any subject she photographed, whether person, place, or thing. Her sharp wit, the way she devoured mystery novels like they were candy.

How she was my best friend, and how badly I missed her.

"I know that feeling well," she admitted. "It's been, hell... almost twenty years since Lola died, and she was six years older than me, but we were inseparable. It's like losing a limb, you know?"

I nodded. "She's my twin, so I feel like half of my soul is gone."

Aspen reached out and patted my hand. "I hope she comes home safely."

"Me too."

"Where are they at with the investigation? You just met with Lane, right?"

Snorting, I said, "Yeah, that went *great*." I shot her a little sarcastic thumbs up.

"Oh no."

"Oh, yes. He essentially accused me of being the reason she's missing because I never reported it. They lost the benefit of the *first forty-eight*."

"I never understood that. I mean, I get it from the standpoint that you're more likely to locate an MP"—I took the abbreviation to mean *missing person*—"when the leads are still hot and fresh, but protocol also dictates waiting twenty-four hours before they'll even file the missing person's report?" She looked at me then, as if searching my face for something. "Why didn't you file a report?"

"My sister can be a bit of a wild card," I admitted. "I'm the more level-headed, even keeled twin."

"Like Finn and West."

I frowned. "Which is which?"

"Finn is like you," she said with a smile, though she didn't elaborate.

That explained why we got along so well, I thought. The old adage was that opposites attract, but I never put much stock in that. Troy was as different from me as you could get, and our relationship had crashed and burned spectacularly.

"He's the older of them, isn't he?" She nodded. "Me too. Anyway," I continued, steering us back on track, "she has a habit of going off the grid without warning. We're both photographers, and while I love photographing *people*, Lainey especially loves photographing *places*. Especially remote, hidden gems. She loves hiking and being in nature. I even bought her a satellite phone for our birthday about five years ago so she had some way to call for help if she needed it." Pausing, I inhaled deeply, pressing down on the emotion welling, threatening to pull me under. My vision blurred as moisture welled.

"Why was she here?"

"On a job. We trade off on travel," I said, diving into a succinct explanation of how our business worked. "It was supposed to be my turn, but I came down with the flu, so she came in my place.

"Between the last time I talked to her and getting the call from Lane about coming out here to identify a body, less than two days had passed." Unbidden, a few tears splashed free, and I angrily swiped at my face. "I should've known though. I *did* know." I tapped my heart. "I could tell things weren't right, but I was giving her the benefit of the doubt. Praying I was wrong."

I'd never forgive myself for that, for not following my intuition.

Especially after that last text.

Goddesses, what the fuck had I been thinking?

Dropping my head, I buried my face in my hands, willing myself to pull my shit together. A gentle touch encircled my wrist, but I didn't move, not yet, content for the moment to let Aspen's silent presence soothe me.

Once I'd collected myself, Aspen asked, "So where does that leave the investigation?"

"I have no idea," I admitted. "After the sheriff threw that accusation at me, I stormed out."

Aspen nodded sympathetically. "As much as I had to admit it, and as big of an asshole Lane can be, he's a hell of a cop."

"I just feel like there have to be more leads they could be running down. Why does it seem like the investigation is stalled out? I handed over Lainey's laptop a month ago. And what about security footage from the bar? I know this is a small town, but there have to be cameras, right?"

"Oh yeah, I'm sure Trey is all over that."

"Why would Trey be working on it?"

"He's kind of a tech savant, and he owns his own security company." Aspen sighed. "Look, these things take time. I know it's not what you want to hear, but you have to trust that your sister is still out there somewhere, alive. And we'll find her."

"How can you be so sure?"

Aspen grinned, looking a little feral—in a good way.

"Because now you've got me."

I blinked in surprise, not entirely sure I'd heard her correctly.

"Are…what?" I asked dumbly.

"You know who I am," she said. "And you know what I do. This is *literally* my area of expertise, Reagan. Please, let me help."

The absolute *last* thing I expected when I came to town for my meeting with Lane today was to run into Aspen McKay.

Having her offer to help me investigate my sister's case was… incredibly generous of her, considering I knew she was busy with her business, burgeoning writing career, and planning a wedding.

But she wouldn't take no for an answer, despite my refusal and attempt to dissuade her. Honestly, it had been for show anyway. Truthfully, I was excited to have someone looking into things who wasn't restricted by the same protocols Lane and his department was.

We spent more than two hours in the diner, chatting over our meals, then dessert, then the iced coffee Bonnie brought us without asking when it became obvious we had no plans of moving anytime soon.

First, we went over what I did know in regard to my sister's disappearance. I passed along what little information I had, told her about Lainey's stalker, and I shared with her all of the lingering questions I still had.

While I spoke, Aspen didn't take any notes or record our conversation. She simply let me ramble, listening intently, her attention wholly focused on me.

Her belief in me, her obvious desire to *help* me, had me deciding to place my trust in her.

Which is why I also told her about the copies I'd kept of Lainey's journals, and the small fact that I hadn't told that to the police when I handed the originals over.

"Have you read them? Has anything jumped out?"

I shook my head, and the smooth skin between her eyebrows creased, so I rushed to clarify. "I haven't read them. I-I'm not ready."

"Understandable," she said. "For years after Lola died, pretty much up until I graduated and left for college, my parents' kept her room exactly as it had been. Though she was getting ready to graduate college by then, little about it had changed since she finished high school. Sometimes, I'd walk by the closed door and hear my mother in there crying, but I never could bring myself to enter."

"Did you ever?"

She nodded. "The day before I left for college."

"How was it?"

"Fucking brutal," she admitted with a humorless laugh. "I couldn't understand how she'd been gone for nearly two years and it still *smelled* like her. How there was still a sweater discarded on her chair in the corner, like any second, she'd come back and retrieve it. How her bed was still rumpled and unmade from the last time she'd slept in it. And I couldn't understand how I got to keep breathing while she was just…gone."

I recognized the pain in her voice, certain the same expression that lingered in her eyes could also be found in mine.

Rolling my lips between my teeth, I fought back tears.

Focusing on the investigation, on bringing her home, was the best thing I could do for Lainey right now.

I reached over and grabbed one of Aspen's hands, offering her the same comfort she'd provided me earlier.

Sniffing loudly, Aspen tilted her chin up, defiant even in the face of her own emotions, and squared her shoulders.

"We'll find her."

Three words I'd heard before—from the sheriff.

But coming from Aspen's mouth?

This time, I believed them—believed *her*.

After all, you could never trust a man to do a job a woman could do better, *and* she'd solved a case four decades of law enforcement in this town hadn't been able to.

"With you working the case, I have no doubt," I told her, grinning.

She returned my smile, and another thought occurred to me.

"Hey, is there anywhere around here I could get some posters printed?" I grabbed my phone to show her the missing person flyer I'd designed last night.

"Go to the library," she said immediately. "Ginny is the best, and she'll be more than happy to help you. Tell her I sent you."

I raised a brow. "You're friendly with the librarian?"

"Oh yeah," Aspen chuckled. "She was a huge help to me when I first got here on the Prom Night Arsonist case last year. I spent a lot of time there, going through old newspaper articles and yearbooks. She's lived here forever and knows her shit."

It seemed to me like Ginny could be a great resource for information on the comings and goings in this town, as well.

Before I could press Aspen further, her phone started buzzing, jumping and vibrating its way across the table. Picking it up, she checked the screen and muttered a curse.

"I'm so sorry," she said, quickly gathering her things, withdrawing her wallet and dropping a few bills onto the table. "It's my agent, and I completely forgot we had this call." Another rifle through her bag had her coming up with a business card, which she passed to me. "Call me and we'll make a plan to sit down and get to work."

Following her lead, I also left some money on the table and moved toward the exit. On the sidewalk outside, she surprised me by turning and giving me a hug, which was almost comical given how tiny she was compared to me, then rushing off without another word.

I added her contact information to my phone before heading back up the block to my SUV.

Once I settled behind the wheel, I noticed the piece of paper under my wiper. I glanced around at other cars, but unease slid down my spine when I didn't spot anything similar on nearby vehicles.

Getting out, I grabbed the note with a shaking hand and pulled it free. The paper was crisp and white, free from any blemishes aside from a small smudge where it had rested under the wiper and a crease from the fold. I opened it, and my heart dropped into my stomach as I read the words printed there in a big, bold font.

WELCOME TO DUSK VALLEY, REAGAN LINDSEY. YOU'LL BE SEEING YOUR SISTER VERY SOON.

What the fuck?

Alongside the fear that enveloped me in its adrenaline-soaked blanket, so many questions ran through my head.

Who had left this?

When had they left it?

Had anyone seen them?

And what the fuck did it mean?

Would I be seeing Lainey soon because she was still alive?

Or because she wasn't?

I didn't stop to consider what I was doing as I grabbed my phone and dialed Finn.

sixteen

. . .

FINN

"THAT'S IT, GIRL," I praised Zigzag as she and her owner looped around the paddock. If all went well, Zigzag would be leaving us today to head to her new home. I wanted to give her one final test to ensure she wouldn't buck her owner.

So far, she was performing beautifully, a totally different horse than the one that had arrived here a few months ago.

Atop her back, the woman grinned and let out a joyous *whoop*.

Damn, I loved my job.

My phone vibrated against my ass, and I pulled it out to see Reagan's name on the screen.

"Reagan?" I asked in surprise when I answered. "Everything okay?"

Her voice shook as she said, "I found a note."

That was it.

I found a note.

No further explanation was required to raise my hackles, adrenaline spiking my blood in preparation of taking on a yet unknown foe.

"What kind of note? Where?"

"On my car."

She was likely in shock and unable to offer more than the most bare bones of sentences.

"Tell me where you are. I'm coming."

"I-in front of the barber shop."

"I'll be right there. Don't move."

She mumbled incoherently before the line went dead.

Shouting at one of my ranch hands to take over with Zigzag, I raced for my truck, grateful I'd driven to the barn today, and peeled out.

I drove well over the speed limit, racing like hell to get to her.

She'd sounded so...scared. I'd do anything to take that fear away, to make it so she never had anything to be afraid of again.

Reaching town in record time, I miraculously found a parking spot only two spaces away from her monstrous SUV. Reagan was in the front seat, unmoving, eyes staring off into the distance, door hanging open.

I approached cautiously and murmured her name so I didn't spook her.

Her attention whipped to me, and then she was climbing out and throwing herself into my arms.

"*Baby*," I murmured as I held her tightly, the endearment slipping free without my permission.

Reagan either hadn't heard it or didn't care to acknowledge it, because she simply clung to me, her hands fisting in the front of my shirt, pressing as close as she could possibly get. I bracketed one arm around her waist, the other cupping the back of her skull, resting my chin atop her head.

Fuck, it felt good to hold her again.

Like two crazy people, we stood there for a long while, until she finally pulled back.

"Thank you for coming," she whispered.

"I'll always come for you."

She gave me a soft smile, then shifted—though, I noted with

no small amount of satisfaction, she didn't let go of me—and pointed to a piece of printer paper resting on the center console of her vehicle.

"What happened?"

"Found that under my wiper. Freaked me the fuck out."

"What's it say?"

"'Welcome to Dusk Valley, Reagan Lindsey. You'll be seeing your sister very soon.'"

As she recited the words, my distress immediately morphed into a rage that had me wanting to raze this entire fucking town to the ground.

"I'll kill him."

Reagan choked on a laugh. "I have no doubt you could, soldier. With your bare hands too. But we don't even know if it *is* a him, and that's not your job."

"What is my job, then?"

"To protect."

Our gazes collided as a third word hung unspoken in the air between us.

To protect me.

Something shifted in that moment. For all her talk of not being able to do this with me, not while her sister was still missing, I'd still been the first person she called when she felt threatened. The sheriff's department was right around the corner, and she'd still called *me*.

"'Protect' is my middle name," I grinned, trying to diffuse some of the tension in her body.

She giggled. "Is it really?"

"Nah, it's Conrad." I brushed a lock of honey hair behind her ear, leaning closer so my lips brushed against the shell. "But I will stop at nothing to protect you and keep you safe, belle. Don't forget that."

Reagan sucked in air, a quick, breathy gasp, and I chuckled as I pulled back.

"Noted," she clipped. "Now what the fuck do we do about that?"

"We call my brother."

She groaned, and I remembered they were supposed to have a meeting this morning. I wondered what had happened during it to make her apprehensive to call him now.

"I'm working," my brother said when he picked up. "What do you want?"

"Reagan found a creepy note on her car. Seems like something you might want to check out."

Lane swore creatively, then mumbled something about being grateful he'd at least been informed of the note before several months had passed this time.

"Where are you?" he asked me.

"In front of the barbershop."

"We'll be right over."

Less than five minutes later, my brother rounded the corner a block away, a small squad of deputies following in his footsteps like eager little ducks trailing after their mother. I would've laughed at the sight if the situation didn't seem so dire.

Lane approached us, his hands already encased in nitrile gloves.

"Where is it?" Reagan pointed into the car, and Lane asked, "Anyone but you touch it?"

"You mean other than the sick fucker who left it there?" I said with a snort.

"No," Reagan told Lane.

Pinching the corner between two fingers, Lane pulled it out of the vehicle and held it in front of his face. His deputies gathered at his back, reading over his shoulders.

"Looks like standard printer paper," he mused. "Nothing remarkable about it at all."

"Other than the fact that it's a fucking taunt," I ground out.

Reagan elbowed me, and I snapped my mouth shut.

"We'll get it up to Boise," he told Reagan, turning to one of the deputies who held out an evidence bag. Lane tucked the note inside, open, smoothing the crease down the center once he sealed it in. He handed it back to the deputy who, with a dismissive nod from Lane, turned and went back to the department.

"I've got an FBI friend at the field office who I know will want to help," Lane continued. "I'm also sending her your sister's journals. She's got some background in profiling, so I'll let her take a look and see if anything pops."

"Thank you."

"We're going to need to take the wiper too," Lane said, nodding at one of the other deputies, who stepped forward with a larger bag, popped the wiper off, and sealed it away. "There's a hardware store up there on the corner—"

I cut him off. "I can handle it."

"You don't have to—" Reagan started, but Lane interjected.

"Fine." To his remaining guys, he said, "You guys can go. I'll be back in a bit."

They dutifully trotted away, and I wondered why the fuck so many of them had come out in the first place.

Likely to get a peek at the freak show, which annoyed the shit out of me.

"We have to find this fucker," I gritted out to my brother.

"You think I don't know that?" he retorted, swiping a hand down his face—which he only did when he was stressed to the max and needed to throw his fist into something. "This is my fucking jurisdiction, Finn. *My* town. And now I've got another fucking crazy on my hands."

My brother only let his carefully constructed, do-gooder sheriff's demeanor slip when he was around people he trusted.

I wasn't surprised it fell around me, but I was that he let it go so easily in front of Reagan.

His attention locked on her, and he said, "I'm sorry for earlier. I was out of line."

"It's fine. It wasn't anything I haven't asked myself a million times in the last month."

"What are you talking about?" I asked Reagan, then turned to Lane. "What did you say to her?"

"If she wants to tell you, she can," my brother said, stepping away, taking his phone out of his pocket. "Fuck!" His abrupt and rather loud shout drew the attention of several people nearby, including glares from a number of families with small children. "I can't believe this is happening again."

"Aspen," Reagan said, surprising both me and Lane.

"You know about that?" Lane asked.

Reagan shrugged, feigning nonchalance, but her cheeks pinkened a bit in embarrassment. "I've read her book," she admitted. "And I had lunch with her today."

"What?" I blurted. "How did that happen?"

"After your brother so kindly accused me of being the reason my sister is missing," she said, shooting a glare toward Lane that could've killed if such a thing were possible, "I sort of had a panic attack when I came out of the station. She talked me down and invited me to lunch."

My gaze narrowed on her as the wheels in my head spun.

Aspen was a private investigator.

Reagan had a missing sister.

"What'd you talk about?"

"Girl stuff," she said quickly, an obvious lie I didn't buy for one second. "Did you know her sister died when she was a teenager?"

"I did," I said slowly. "She told you about that?"

Aspen was tough as nails, a bad ass with the backbone of steel her chosen profession demanded, hardened further by all the shit she'd endured in her life. She wasn't exactly an open book, preferring to handle all of her problems on her own—or with Crew's help, though that had taken a long time. We'd all come to accept that about her, knowing she'd share with us when she was ready. Telling a virtual stranger about Lola was out of character.

"We bonded over our losses."

"Your sister isn't dead," I reminded her, tone vehement. Placing a palm over my chest, I said, "You'd feel it, right?"

She mirrored my stance. "I would," she agreed. "I know she's still out there somewhere."

And I guaranteed she'd conscripted the help of Aspen McKay, top-tier private investigator, to find her.

Lane butted into the conversation by clearing his throat, though his attention remained on his notebook.

"I need to get back to the station and set up a canvass of the area," he said as he continued to scribble. "And I need to call Trey to check the cameras. I'll catch you guys later."

Yet again, we relied on fucking technology, and for Reagan *and* Lainey's sake, I was getting goddamn tired of the waiting game. A month without anything resembling a lead would drive even the strongest person insane. This guy was dust in the wind, it seemed, and Reagan's shoulders were stiff with tension. The lines around her eyes appeared a little deeper, coupled with purple bruising beneath them.

Clearly, she hadn't been getting enough sleep, and all the unknowns surrounding her sister's disappearance were starting to take their toll physically.

"What happened earlier with Lane?" I prompted.

"He…questioned why I didn't call in a missing person's report on Lainey sooner."

God, my brother could be such a prick sometimes.

I gently cupped her face, and she leaned into my touch, her eyes fluttering closed.

"This isn't your fault, Reagan. Do not think for one second that it is. The blame for all of this rests solely on the shoulders of the creep who took your sister." I swiped a thumb along her cheek, her skin so smooth beneath my calloused fingertip. "Look at me, belle. Tell me you understand."

Her eyes popped open, and I immediately lost myself in the hypnotizing green depths, the shade the same as the soft, pale underside of a maple leaf.

"I understand."

"Good," I murmured, then quickly pressed a kiss to her forehead before she could stop me. Gauging her reaction, I was deeply pleased to find her lips twitch at the corners, an almost smile appearing on them. "Now let's go get you a new wiper and head home. Sound good?"

She nodded, following me toward the hardware store. Less than ten minutes later, we were on the road, headed back to the ranch.

I followed her all the way to the turn off toward my house. She rolled her window down and waved at me as she headed into the trees. I wasn't entirely comfortable letting her go back there alone, without me nearby to keep an eye on her, but I wasn't going to press the issue. I didn't want to suffocate her, and I had to get back to work.

Besides, I was utterly gone for that girl, and the proximity only made things worse.

seventeen

. . .

REAGAN

I PULL *up to the old house, the dirt driveway shaded by towering maples interspersed with oak and birch trees. The sky above is a crisp, perfect blue, the sun hanging high. There is no breeze to be found, and when I get out of my car, I'm instantly coated in a thin sheen of sweat.*

Wiping my clammy palms on my linen shorts, I turn toward the house, heading for the porch and the front door beyond. The exterior of the home is painted green, a shade that had likely once been bright now faded with time and exposure to the elements.

There seems to be no one around for miles.

There isn't even another vehicle parked in the drive, and a quick survey of the surrounding area doesn't reveal a garage or carport of any sort. Only a badly dilapidated barn with a giant hole in the roof.

So why am I here? *Where* am I?

Sensing those questions will be answered in time, I approach the door, gently rapping my knuckles against it. The boards of the porch beneath my feet are weathered grey—not artfully or intentionally, but the kind of patina that can only be accomplished with time. They rock and pop as I shift my weight, and I'm not entirely certain they won't collapse beneath me.

As though pushed by a phantom wind, the door creaks open, revealing a sliver of the dim interior.

I don't know why, only that I need to get inside the house, so I settle my hand on its surface and push the door open wider. The hinges screech horribly, making me wince and cower, preparing for the owner of the home to appear and demand to know what the fuck I'm doing.

Several tense moments pass where nothing happens, so I release my held breath and cross the threshold.

In keeping with the exterior, the inside is equally as outdated. The entry way floor is lined with cracked and filthy linoleum, looking like it hasn't been cleaned once in the years since this place was built. To my right is the living room, with a sagging sofa I somehow know has a pull-out bed hiding within. Ahead is the kitchen, the doors of the cabinets hanging slightly crooked, the backsplash tile caked with grime.

"Hello?" I call.

There is no response.

Tentatively, I tiptoe deeper into the home. Past the kitchen is a small dining room with a sliding door that leads to a narrow patio and the fields beyond. In the center of the room is an oblong table set for six, though the china is thick with dust, like at any moment, the family who once lived here will come rushing into the room to enjoy a meal together.

Something tells me it has been a long time since any sort of joy could be found within these walls.

The floors creak beneath my feet like the porch did. I make my way around slowly, shoulders hunched up to my ears, as if bracing for some sort of confrontation.

Nothing happens.

I continue to explore the main floor, peeking into closets and checking under beds, wandering through every room and searching each thoroughly.

I get the feeling I'm looking for something specific, but I have absolutely no idea what it could be.

There is one final door I haven't yet opened, and with a fortifying deep breath, I square my shoulders, settle my hand on the knob, and twist.

It pops open to reveal…darkness.

I allow myself a few moments for my eyes to adjust, and when they do, I see a set of carpeted stairs leading to a basement.

Go to the creepy basement, *I think*. The start of every great horror film where the pretty blonde girl dies.

Though I still don't know what it is I'm so desperate to find, I know without a doubt it's at the bottom of these stairs. So I muster all the bravery I possess and descend.

When I reach the bottom landing, I feel along the wall to my right, finding a light switch and flipping it on.

The floor is covered in the same shag carpet as the stairs and the living spaces above. It's a horrifying mix of dark brown, amber, and cream that kind of reminds me of chocolate, vanilla, and caramel ice cream. I've spent so long staring at it that the patterns are starting to swirl together, making me feel as though I've entered a time warp or that I'm on some psychedelic trip.

The same deep wood paneling from upstairs also continues down here.

The whole space feels…cozy, despite the seventies vibe.

It seems warm and inviting.

At least, that's what I think—until my eyes land on the bed in the corner.

And the chain leading from the wall, a manacle wrapped around the ankle of a woman sitting atop a dirty mattress—wearing my face.

I woke up screaming.

eighteen

. . .

FINN

SHOOTING UPRIGHT IN BED, I strained my ears. My heart was already racing, and it took me a moment to adjust to the world around me as I attempted to figure out what had awoken me.

I heard it again, recognizing instantly what had dragged me from sleep.

Screaming.

I was out of bed before I made the conscious decision to do so, throwing on joggers and a tee. I made a quick detour to the gun cabinet in my closet, punching in the code and grabbing my favorite pistol before rushing toward the door and stuffing my feet into my boots.

Because if I could hear screaming, there was only one explanation.

Reagan.

Bursting outside, my feet crunched against the gravel as I took off at a run down the pathway that connected my home to the guest house, crossing the hundred or so yards in record time. After years of being in the Army, I kept physically fit, if only because it helped me around the ranch and because I didn't know any other way to live. By the time I reached the guest house, I was barely out of breath, but my adrenaline was high. I didn't bang on the door, not wanting to announce myself in case there was an intruder. Instead, I punched in the code for the security system, rushed in, and disarmed it before the obnoxious beeping could turn into a full-blown alarm cutting through the night.

Slipping my boots off, I tiptoed on bare feet in the direction of the bedroom. The house seemed to be still, but…

There.

The creak of a floorboard echoed down the hall, and footsteps fast approached me. I flattened my back against the wall, gun at the ready, and waited.

Before I could react to the intruder, light flared, catching me off guard, and another scream echoed in the silence.

"What the *fuck*, Finn!" Reagan screamed. "What are you doing? Is that—is that a *gun*? How did you even get in here?"

She tossed questions at me so fast I couldn't answer a single one, but they penetrated enough to have me lowering my weapon and taking stock of her.

Starting with her face, I gave her a once-over. Her skin was sallow, and there were dark smudges beneath her eyes. With her arms crossed over her chest, the hem of her tee rode indecently high on her thighs—and my attention shot back to her face.

She was fine.

Then what the fuck was I doing here?

"I was wondering the same thing," she said, hand to her chest as she moved around the wide peninsula that separated the kitchen from the living area.

I must've spoken those words out loud.

Okay.

"I heard screaming."

With a wince, her cheeks turned pink, then she downcast her gaze.

"I-I had a nightmare," Reagan stammered.

She turned her back on me, and my more basic nature finally got the better of me. I allowed my eyes to dip down—and down and down.

Goddamnit, the tee was so fucking short, it barely covered her ass, the bottom curves of the cheeks peeking out of the hem.

And her legs were as long and shapely as I remembered.

They'd looked so fucking good wrapped around my face and my hips.

I gave myself a shake. *Not the time, Finn.*

She took a glass from the cupboard and filled it to the brim with water, chugging eagerly until there was only an inch or so remaining in the bottom.

Even the woman's throat was sexy, the way it worked as she swallowed.

I remembered it swallowing a few other things that involved both of us wearing a lot less clothing.

And there I went, thinking about sex again.

Clearing my throat and swinging my eyes upward again, I asked, "Are you okay?"

Her lips were pursed, an eyebrow slightly curved upward, as if to say, *really?*

Shit, she'd caught me checking her out.

Whatever. I was a red-blooded male who hadn't fucked in a long damn time, and I knew exactly what fucking this particular woman was like.

No one I'd ever met had managed to get me going quite like she did.

Sue me.

In answer to my question, she finally said, "I'd be a lot better if you put that gun away."

"Shit," I hissed, realizing my pistol was still in my hand. I flipped the safety on and let it hang loosely at my side, not exactly having anywhere to store it in this house. "Sorry."

"It's okay," she said, draining her glass of water. "I'm sorry I woke you up and made you go all…Rambo."

I chuckled. "Kind of second nature. I am a soldier, after all," I reminded her.

"Oh, I'm well aware."

Silence descended between us. Not exactly awkward, but fraught with something I couldn't quite name. The air was charged with tension, and I recognized this moment as a tipping point. We could part ways and pretend like nothing happened, or…

Ultimately, I decided to leave the ball in her court.

"Well, I'm gonna head back," I said, hooking my thumb toward the door and my house. "Gotta be up early. But call if you need anything."

Honestly, I had no idea what time it was, only that dawn was coming faster than I'd like. And I'd surely struggle to fall back to sleep after this, too worried about her and wired about the threat of danger to let myself relax.

My hand was on the doorknob when she stopped me with a single word.

"Stay."

I whipped back around. "Are you sure?"

"Yes," she whispered, but the word was firm. "I need someone here. So stay. Please?"

The question came out as a plea, softly begging.

As if I'd ever deny her anything.

"Okay."

She blinked in surprise but tamped it down quickly, though I noted how she bit her bottom lip as if holding off a smile.

After setting her glass in the dishwasher, she moved out of

the kitchen and headed toward the bedroom. Once I ensured the security system was properly armed, I followed along, shutting the lights off as we went.

The master was situated in the back corner of the house and had its own set of French doors that led out onto the back deck. I'd positioned the bed to face the fields and hills beyond, which were bathed in moonlight, glowing silver and faintly illuminating the room.

My own master was set up similarly, because honestly, nothing beat the sight of this land, the tall country grasses and the distant snow-capped peaks of the mountains first thing in the morning.

Reagan crawled into bed, which I noted was a tangled mess of sheets. She curled up on the side closest to the door and patted the other one.

I shook my head. "Move over, belle."

"Why?"

Leaning close so she could see the seriousness of my expression, I said, "If someone breaks in, they'll have to go through me to get to you. And I won't make it easy. Now move, please."

Her eyes widened at the command in my tone, but she wisely did as I asked, mumbling a breathy little, "Yes, soldier," before doing so.

Setting the gun on the bedside table, I shucked my sweatpants, leaving myself in only my tee and boxer briefs, before getting in next to her. I settled in, tugging the sheets as far as my waist and tucking one arm behind my head.

After years in the Army, I could fall asleep on command, anywhere, at any time.

Tonight was different. I was wired, tightly wound, as if waiting for some other shoe to drop.

I didn't know how long we lay there, me waiting for Reagan's breathing to even out as she dropped into sleep, before she shifted to face me and said, "Can I tell you about my nightmare?"

I turned my head toward her in surprise. "I—if you want to?"

She nodded. "It's going to sound crazy, but I think you're maybe the only person in the world besides Lainey who would understand it."

Her voice cracked on her sister's name, and without thinking, I reached for her, gathering her up and tugging her to my side. Reagan came willingly, tucking her face against my chest, one hand coming to rest on my stomach, her thigh hooking over mine. My arm came around her instinctively, rubbing soothing circles on her back.

This, I thought. *This is how I should be falling asleep every night and waking up every morning.*

"There was this old farmhouse," she started. "Somewhere in the woods."

"Just any old woods?" I asked.

There was a reason she was telling me this, and something told me we both needed her to be as specific as possible, some gut instinct leading me through this conversation.

Shaking her head against my chest, she said, "No. There were mountains in the distance. But not Tennessee mountains," she continued before I could ask. "Like…"

"Idaho mountains?" I guessed.

"Yeah. Idaho mountains." Absently, her fingers drew nonsensical patterns on my stomach. My abdomen tightened beneath her touch, and goosebumps raised along my skin. "I had no idea why I was there," she continued. "Only that I felt like I was… searching for something."

"What was it?"

Reagan gave my stomach a little slap. "I'm getting there."

She explained how she went inside, how this old, rambling

farmhouse which seemed to have not been updated since the seventies, was completely empty.

"And then I found the basement."

Unease trickled down my spine. I knew it had only been a dream, but it had terrified her enough to wake up screaming bloody murder, and had this been a real-life scenario—well, it seemed like the kind of place I would've done whatever possible to prevent her from entering.

Still, I admired her bravery, even if she was perfectly safe.

"And what did you find down there?" I whispered.

She tilted her face up to look at me, her eyes damn near glowing in the darkness. Them and a flash of teeth were all I could see as she said, the words barely more than a breath, "Lainey. I found Lainey."

That was *not* the answer I'd been expecting.

"Do you think..." I trailed off, unsure how to phrase the question in a way that didn't make me sound insane. But I was starting to understand *why* she'd wanted to share this story with me—why she thought I, of all people, a twin myself, would latch onto the potential meaning behind the dream.

"I think my sister is trying to tell me where she is."

There wasn't anything I could say in response to that, and Reagan didn't seem to expect me to speak anyway. She merely snuggled closer and let the silence envelope us.

Eventually, she drifted off, but sleep never found me.

As I lay there with the girl of my dreams in my arms, making her feel safe enough to fall into unconsciousness, my mind whirled.

With the exception of the decade West and I had spent in the service, I'd lived my entire life in Dusk Valley. There wasn't a square inch of this town I didn't know. Hell, the same could be said for most of the county, which was dominated by Lawless land.

We'd been operating under the assumption that Lainey's

abductor was local, and Reagan's dream only drove that point further home for me.

Which meant this farmhouse was nearby, likely no more than a few hours by car.

As we lay there, as the sky outside turned from inky black pricked with stars to grey to the yellow-orange of the rising sun —a plan began to form.

A plan that required my twin and my plane.

nineteen

. . .

FINN

I MUST'VE FALLEN asleep at some point—though with the way my body protested and the grittiness of my eyes when I blinked them open, it couldn't have been long—as Reagan attempted to slip out of bed.

"Planning on running off with my shirt again?" I asked, my voice a low rumble.

She whipped toward me, a sheepish grin appearing on her lips.

"Considering I'm wearing my own?" She toyed with the hem, reminding me how fucking high the hem sat. Making me wonder if she wore panties or if her perfect pussy was bare beneath. "And considering I'm not running off?"

"Then where are you going?"

"To make coffee, *sir*," she said in a way that had my dick twitching. The sass turned me on something fierce. "That okay with you?"

I gave her a mock salute, and her giggled followed her out of the room.

The shirt she was wearing wasn't hers, though. In fact, it had once been mine—the same shirt she'd thrown on the morning

150

after our tryst. It had looked so good on her, I couldn't make her take it off. I loved that she still had it, that she still *wore* it. Had she forgotten she'd stolen it from me? Or did she wear it and remember that night I'd been unable to forget?

You could imagine how well that conversation had gone with West when I called for a ride back to the ranch the next morning and asked him to bring me a new shirt too.

To this day, he still made fun of me for it.

Waking up next to her *this* morning, though short-lived, was too damn good, something I had to remind myself not to get used to. She wasn't mine to keep—she'd made that clear.

But I'd be damned if I couldn't imagine doing every day for the rest of my life.

Still, something had changed last night. Sure, I'd barged in uninvited, but she hadn't turned me away. She'd trusted me. Let me in. Shared her nightmare, knowing I'd understand the significance.

Finally, I dragged myself out of bed, stuffed my legs back into my sweats, and padded barefoot out into the kitchen, greeted by the scent of freshly brewed coffee.

Reagan poured me a mug.

"How do you take it?"

"Black is perfect," I replied, accepting the cup and taking a sip.

Damn, was I glad I stocked this place with *my* favorite coffee. I'd be perked right up in no time.

Unable to keep my eyes off her, I watched as she moved around, navigating the kitchen like she'd lived here for years instead of a week. Reagan, as it turned out, did *not* take her coffee black, and I made a mental note of the caramel oat milk creamer she splashed into her mug before leaning on the counter across from me to sip it.

"Thank you for coming for me last night," she said, almost conversationally, as though she didn't want to make a big deal out of it. I didn't like the way she avoided my gaze when she said it, either.

I fixed that in a hurry, setting my coffee down and clasping her chin between my thumb and pointer, turning her face to me until her eyes met mine.

"I will *always* come for you," I assured her.

That was the second time I'd said as much to her, and I wondered how long it'd take for her to believe it.

Those gorgeous green orbs darted around my face, testing the seriousness of my statement, before she nodded once and pulled free.

My attention snagged on the clock on the stove over her shoulder.

"Fuck," I hissed, lifting my coffee to my mouth and chugging it down, not giving a single fuck about the burn in left in my throat.

"What's wrong?" Reagan frowned.

"I didn't bring my phone over last night, and I should've been at the barn hours ago. I have to get going."

I passed her the empty mug and said, "Thanks for this."

She gave me a small smile. "Thanks for last night."

Nodding, I left before I could do something crazy like say fuck work and drag her to bed, give her something to *really* to thank me for.

A wall of notifications greeted me when I lifted my phone off my nightstand back at my house, the top one a phone call from my foreman.

I dialed him back.

"Hey, I'm so sorry," I said when he answered, not letting him get a word in.

"Everything okay?" Abel asked.

"Yeah, it's fine. Just a personal thing I had to deal with. And speaking of, can you handle things on your own today? I've got something else I need to take care of."

"Of course," Abel said. "That's what you hired me for."

"Thanks, Abel. I owe you one."

"Get your mama to make her baked mac and cheese for lunch one of these days, and I'll consider us even."

I chuckled. "Deal."

That call completed, I immediately dialed my twin as I headed into the bathroom, stripping out of my clothes so I could shower.

"Sup."

"You busy today?"

West snorted. "I'm a business owner. I'm *always* busy. And so are you."

"I know, but there's something I need to do that's more important than work, and I want you to come with me."

"More important than work," he mused. "Let me guess: this involves Reagan."

"Of course it does," I snapped. "You gonna help me or not?"

"Obviously. I'll head over now."

"Great. I'm hopping in the shower, so let yourself in."

"Always do," West said, then hung up.

I raced through the shower, using my shampoo as body wash, which I spread around with my hands, not bothering with the loofah Aria had bought me ages ago.

Had to admit, though…women knew what the fuck they were doing with those things. It got into all the nooks and crannies and made my skin smooth as fuck.

By the time I toweled dry, dressed, swiped on some deodorant, and brushed my teeth, West was waiting in the living room, scrolling through his phone.

"Took you long enough."

"Fuck you. It took fifteen minutes."

"And I've been here for ten."

I walked over and kicked his feet. "Get up and let's go."

"Where exactly are we going?" West asked once we were in his truck.

"Airport."

He caught my eye, a brow raised in question, so I quickly explained about Reagan's dream.

"That hero complex is gonna get you in trouble one day," he chuckled. "Bursting into women's houses without permission."

"Technically, it's *my* house, and I thought she was in danger."

"So what's our plan?" he asked.

"Grid search."

"Off the record?"

I glared at him. "You know Lane would never condone this. He'd insist on calling in the fucking National Guard or something, and the last thing we need is a bunch of those assholes hogging my airspace."

"Fair enough."

When we arrived at the hangar where my Cessna Skyhawk was stored, West pulled his truck right inside and killed the engine. We climbed out and headed for the long table along one wall, above which hung several maps of the area and state.

Focusing my attention on the one of our county, I tapped the surface. Thankfully, the map was already divided into a grid, each square representing ten square miles. Dusk Valley was located in the southernmost county of Idaho along its shared border with Oregon. I dragged my finger to the quadrant in the bottom left corner of the state. "We'll start here, work our way east until we hit the edge of the county, then head north and back to the west."

"And you're sure this fucker is keeping Lainey somewhere in the county?"

I shook my head. "Not entirely. I mean, I don't have any reason to suspect that except a gut feeling. But if they met here seven years ago and she was taken from here, I think logic dictates he's local, right?"

"Agreed," West said, then picked up one of the maps on the table—replicas of the ones on the walls, this one the same as the one I'd been pointing at. "So let's go."

While I went through my pre-flight checklist, West sat in one of the chairs we kept in here and started jotting down notes and coordinates, which is precisely why I'd brought him along. While I focused on flying, he'd be responsible for keeping us within the grid by updating the nav system. He was also responsible for ruling out any areas we could safely do so, mainly our ranch land and any bordering farms we were familiar with, where we knew no such house like the one from Reagan's dream existed.

We didn't speak. Didn't need to. We simply relied on the "woo-woo shit" to guide us, communicating in looks and gestures.

Plus, this wasn't the first time we'd set off on a mission like this. In the Rangers, there had been a time when three of our team members had gone MIA. Our team only contained six total, so the remaining three—me, West, and a guy we'd nicknamed Spike—were responsible for locating them, extracting them, and bringing them back to our basecamp safely.

And that was precisely what we planned to do with Lainey. We only had to find her first.

Once I ran through my checklist, we loaded up and locked in, taking off once the air traffic controller confirmed all was clear. Our little airport was too small to have its own, so when I made an impromptu flight, we relied on the guys at the Boise airport to help us out.

We'd taken off toward the east, so I swung us around and headed west, toward the first quadrant.

"Alright," West said through the headset. "Remind me what exactly we're looking for."

"Maple, oak, and birch trees. Fields with mountains nearby. Reagan seemed to think this was some sort of old farmhouse, and she said the mountains weren't particularly tall, but it was difficult to judge because of the distance."

"So likely somewhere near the end of the range," West mused.

"That's what I'm thinking."

The first square we'd fly over fit the bill perfectly.

The tallest mountains in the state sat more northerly and centrally. Boise, for example, was located right on the edge of the Northern Rocky Mountains, which dipped down into the Columbia Plateau. But smaller ranges cropped up all over the state, and there was one located right at the edge of our county —the ideal place to begin our search.

I cut across the area until I reached the southwestern corner of Idaho, then tipped it back toward the east, flying along our border with Nevada. The plan was to note anything that looked promising from the air before passing our findings along to Lane.

There was no denying my brother was a great sheriff and a hell of a cop to boot, but West and I agreed we weren't going to bring him in on this until we had a more complete picture of the area and something concrete to share. Better to ask forgiveness than permission.

Besides, we weren't doing anything illegal or interfering in the investigation in any way.

If anyone asked, we were simply taking a joy ride—missing it from our days in the service.

There was nothing better to me than being in the air, anyway. Up here, I could think clearly and breathe more freely than I could on the ground.

Sometimes, though, these trips to the sky hit a little too closely to memories that ought to stay buried. Flyovers of decimated towns, bodies blown apart and strewn in the streets. Racing against the clock to save a comrade, only to arrive too late—a recovery, not a rescue.

I'd gotten good over the years at accepting the things from

my past I couldn't change, but that didn't mean the memories didn't still assault me with all the finesse of an AK-47 now and then.

"Do you ever have war flashbacks?" West asked softly, as though reading my mind.

"Yeah." Sidelong, I glanced at him. "You?"

"All the time. Nightmares too."

"More like night terrors," I muttered. "At least nightmares are figments of our imagination. But the shit we've seen?"

"Yeah. *Real.*"

"I'm always here for you, brother," I said, lifting my fist, which he bumped. "And I won't judge you if you need to talk to someone else. Seems to be working well for Crew."

West nodded, his knuckles resting against mine for a fraction longer than necessary.

Right back at you, he said wordlessly.

The longer we flew, naturally, my thoughts turned to Reagan.

I wondered if I could talk her into taking a ride with me. I wanted so badly to show her this side of me, to experience my favorite thing with her.

As if he could sense where my mind had gone, West asked, "You gonna tell her about this?"

I shook my head. "Not yet. I don't want to get her hopes up, and there's no guarantee we'll find anything. Hell, there's no guarantee that dream meant anything."

"You and I both know it meant something," he said.

On the surface, West was the good-time twin. The one always down to party, always down to fuck, always quick with a joke to diffuse a tense situation. The flipside of his coin was me, the one who was more serious, more in my head, more…reserved.

But there wasn't a fucking thing West wouldn't do to protect the people he cared about, something me and all of my brothers had in common. And while he played the part of a himbo well, I also knew—likely only because I was his twin—that he felt things deeply, possibly even deeper than me, who had been open about the way the shit I'd gone through in the service had affected me.

All that was to say, whether he ever spoke the words aloud, West was as concerned as I was with bringing Lainey home safely, though for entirely different reasons.

"Storm's rolling in," West said. "We better get back."

We'd spent two hours in the sky, but we didn't find anything that fit Reagan's description, which left me irritated by the time we landed. I wanted to keep going, but if we were late for family dinner, Mama would have our asses. Plus, we barely touched down before the storm broke.

As we pulled out of the hangar to head home, West clapped me on the shoulder.

"We'll find her, bro."

"You're goddamn right," I answered.

For Reagan's sake, I'd accept nothing less.

twenty

. . .

REAGAN

LAST WEEK, when I'd gone in to meet Lane for an update on the case, I'd had every intention of hanging some missing person posters. I planned to offer a reward for any viable information provided, as long as it helped bring Lainey back.

But after I'd found that note on my car, all thoughts of anything else had flown from my mind.

Today, I was going to fix that.

After locking up the house, I headed straight for the library as Aspen had suggested.

When I pushed inside, I was instantly greeted by an older woman, her hair a gorgeous mix of white and grey, secured in a neat little bun at the base of her skull. She wore a long, flowing white skirt, decorated in pale purple flowers, a matching sweater covering her upper half, feet stuffed into lavender orthopedic shoes.

"Hello, dear," she said, her voice warm and inviting. "What can I do for you?"

"I'm Reagan Lindsey," I said as I approached where she stood near the chest-height counter. "Aspen McKay sent me here for some help. Are you Ginny?"

"I am," she said, smiling brightly. "Aspen is such a doll, isn't she? This town owes her so much."

"She's great," I agreed. "She's helping me out with a case of my own, and told me I could come here to get some missing person fliers printed?"

She regarded me thoughtfully, mumbling my last name a few times, snapping her fingers when realization dawned. "*Lindsey*. Your sister is Lainey."

"Yes ma'am."

"I was sorry to hear she went missing," Ginny said, clasping my hands in hers. I was shocked by how warm her skin was, instantly soothing me.

"Thank you," I replied awkwardly. What the fuck else was I supposed to say?

"Come, dear," she said, leading me toward a room at the back of the library. The space was lined with tables, likely workspaces, and she beelined for one, pulling out two chairs and sitting down as I took the other. "What sort of leads do the police have?"

I didn't get the sense she asked because she wanted to feed the rumor mill around town—which, as was the case in small towns, had likely been at work for the last several weeks, speculating about what happened to Lainey.

"At the moment, not much," I admitted. "That's why I want to hang up these posters." I navigated into my phone and my Canva app, where I'd spent a few hours designing something eye-catching but informative.

My reward offering was a measly thousand dollars, the most I could spare at the moment, when work was fairly low on my list of priorities.

"Let's get them printed then," she said.

I spent a few minutes connecting to the wireless network and locating the printer, then Ginny and I went back and forth over how many I should print.

Ultimately, we decided on a hundred with the understanding that I could always come back and get more if need be.

While we waited for them to finish printing, she helped me create a list of local businesses with community boards that would let me hang them up, as well as suggesting I walk around the area and pass them out to residents.

"You know," she said as we headed back out front, where she left me to go behind the desk and grab the sheaf of papers, "you should also run this as an ad in the paper. And think about joining a few of the local Facebook groups and sharing it there."

"That's a great idea," I said, annoyed for not having thought of it myself. "I really appreciate all of your help, Ginny."

"Of course, dear. Any friend of Aspen's is a friend of mine. And besides, we take care of our own around here. That includes taking out the…*trash*," she said diplomatically, though I caught her meaning. Before handing the stack over to me, she asked, "Do you mind if I take a few? I'd love to hand them out to the girls at my knitting circle, and I'll hang one up here."

"Be my guest," I assured her, handing a handful over. "And I have another small favor to ask, if you don't mind."

"Not at all, dear."

"One second," I told her, then ran out to my SUV. The sky overhead had darkened considerably while I'd been inside, the leaves on nearby trees flipped upside down, signaling an oncoming storm.

Grabbing the box, I went back in.

"What have we here?" she asked, gingerly lifting the lid.

"Photocopies of my sister's journals. I was hoping to get another set to pass onto Aspen."

"Of course," Ginny said, taking the entire thing behind the circulation desk, setting it down on a chair, and lifting out the first rubber banded stack.

While she worked, I wandered. The library was homey, warm and welcoming, the scent of books wrapping around me comfortingly. The shelves seemed to stretch on endlessly, divided into easy to recognize sections.

I'd selected a book of poetry off the shelf in the non-fiction section and was thumbing through it when Ginny called for me.

My stack of papers had doubled in size, but thankfully, the bankers box I'd stored Lainey's journal pages in was big enough to fit the second set.

"How much do I owe you?"

Ginny waved me off. "On the house."

"Oh, no. Please, let me pay something."

"Absolutely not," she insisted. "You can repay me by bringing your sister home."

I gave her a small, sad smile. "That's all I want." I held up the posters. "Thank you for this."

"Of course, dear. Good luck out there."

When she turned her back on me, I quickly stuffed the twenty I had in my pocket into the donation jar and took off before she could try to give it back.

The sky outside had gotten even darker, and the temperature had dropped considerably. If I wanted to get these posters up today, I needed to move quickly.

Inexplicably, that thought made me guilty as hell. How was it fair that I could continue to walk *free*, to enjoy the simple plea-sures life offered, while she was locked in that creepy basement somewhere, waiting for me to find her?

With renewed vigor and purpose, I left my car parked and decided to walk, taking Ginny's advice to knock on the doors of homes as I passed on my way toward the main strip of businesses.

A lot of my solicitations went unanswered, so I left fliers stuffed in door jambs. The few who did open their doors were kind, accepting the paper and promising to call me with any information.

The same could be said of the businesses in town, who all happily allowed me to hang posters on their community boards or right there on the front door. Once that task was completed, I took the long way around back to my car, passing by more homes and passing out more papers, and stopping at lampposts to tape them up.

I was nearly back to my car when the sky opened up, dumping rain all over me. Doing my best to shield the posters from damage, I raced for my SUV and threw myself behind the wheel.

Safely inside, I tossed the remainder of the posters on the passenger seat then put the car in drive and headed toward the grocery store to restock on some essentials.

An hour later, I rolled to a stop in front of the house. The rain hadn't lessened, so I parked as close as I could, backing up so the hatch opened onto the porch. Across the way, a big black truck with the Lawless Ranch logo on it pulled up in front of Finn's. He got out of the passenger seat, saying his goodbyes to whoever drove—the tint on the windows was too dark for me to see inside—before slamming the door. The truck pulled away immediately after.

As if sensing my presence, I could practically feel Finn's eyes find me from a hundred yards away and through the deluge, so I raised my arm in greeting before heading to the back hatch to get my groceries.

Naturally, he made his way over.

"I thought you had to work today," I asked when he reached me, noting his navy cargo pants and matching tee. He looked like he'd been out on some sort of military mission, not working at the ranch.

The shirt clung to him indecently, outlining each ridge and hollow of his abdomen, suctioning to his biceps in a way that had me wanting to sink my teeth into them. Damn, the man looked good wet. There was something so delicious about the way drops of water clung to his veiny forearms and plastered his hair to his forehead.

"Had something more important to take care of."

I nodded, the comment not warranting a verbal response.

"Well," I said awkwardly after several long moments passed. "I better get this stuff inside."

"Here, let me help."

"Oh, you don't have—"

My words died as he ignored me, lifting a heavy, reusable grocery bag in each arm and moving toward the house.

Men.

I grabbed the remaining one and followed after him.

When I stepped inside, sliding the bag onto the peninsula, he said, "You know, if you don't want to cook…tonight is family dinner, and my mom and sister have been begging me to invite you."

His hand cupped the back of his neck, those damp biceps flexing and bulging, and I was momentarily lost in the show.

Remembering what they looked like when he was over me, holding himself up as he pumped his hips into me, his cock hitting that spot so deep…

"Reagan?"

"Sorry," I said, dragging my eyes away from his muscles to his face, which was split wide open in a knowing grin. "What did you say?"

"Will you come to family dinner tonight?"

"Family dinner, as in…"

"The *whole* family," he confirmed. "Well, minus Owen because he doesn't live here. Like I said, Mama and Aria have been dying to meet you."

"You told them about me?"

"You've come up in conversation."

Something about that deeply pleased me, that he talked to his family about me. Likely only in the course of discussing my sister's case, but still.

"I didn't tell them anything specific about…*us*, if that's what you're worried about." I hadn't been, but appreciated the discretion nonetheless. "I mean, of course my brothers know we, uh, hooked up all those years ago, but that's it. They've still given me endless shit about you since you came to town, but they don't know what we've done or anything…"

I grinned. "You're cute when you ramble."

"I'm not cute," he argued. Once again, that hand found the back of his neck. "I don't know why I'm nervous. I've seen you naked, for fuck's sake."

A laugh burst free from me, which seemed to ease the tension in Finn, because his arm fell and he smiled wide enough for the corners of his eyes to crease.

"So I can expect more of the endless ribbing like the night we met, then?"

He nodded. "You don't have to come."

"Hell no," I said. "I look back on that night fondly. I don't have any regrets. Do you?"

"Absolutely fucking not."

"Good, then I'll see you tonight."

twenty-one

REAGAN

OKAY, I could admit it: I was nervous as fuck to go to dinner with Finn's *entire* family.

What if they didn't like me?

And why did that possibility bother me so much?

Before dinner that evening, which Finn told me started promptly at six p.m., I ran back into town to get flowers and a bottle of wine. He hadn't told me I needed to bring anything, but the southern hospitality deeply rooted in my DNA refused to let me show up empty-handed.

Hands that shook against the steering wheel as I navigated to a stop in front of a gorgeous farmhouse. A few hundred yards away down a gentle slope stood a big red barn, a paddock, and some other ranch-related buildings I couldn't begin to guess names for.

From a distance, it looked like an impressive outfit. Maybe Finn would show me around one day.

I'd barely gotten out of the vehicle before two women appeared on the front porch, the screen door slamming shut behind them triggering memories of childhood summers, running barefoot through our neighborhood with my sister at my side—my constant companion, my other half.

Shaking those images off before they pulled me under, I swung around to the passenger side. Once I grabbed the bouquet of flowers and Sauvignon Blanc—the perfect summer wine, in my opinion—I faced the women.

There was no mistaking them as anything other than mother and daughter. Though the older woman's blonde hair was threaded with white, the strands that remained untouched by age were identical to her daughter's. The same blue eyes peered out from identically shaped faces, matching mouths pulling up at the corners and spreading into twin grins.

Damn, the genes in this family were fucking *impressive*. The beauty shared by Finn's mom and sister made me even more curious about his dad.

"You must be Reagan!" the older woman crowed as she rushed down the steps to greet me, not waiting for a response as she pulled me into a hug.

I sank into that embrace, deeply comforted by her warmth and the scents of yeast and honey that clung to her.

"I am," I said when she pulled back. "You must be Birdie."

"And this is my daughter, Aria," she replied as Aria stepped forward.

"It's *sooooo* nice to finally meet you," Aria gushed, dragging me into an embrace when her mother released me. "You're even more gorgeous in person."

I blushed, wondering where in the hell they'd seen pictures of me.

"Thank you." Then I thrust out the wine and flowers. "These are for you."

"Oh, these are lovely," Birdie said, lowering her face into the bouquet and deeply inhaling. Aria accepted the wine. "But you know, you didn't have to bring anything."

Shrugging, I said, "I'm southern. It's the way I was raised."

"Explains the accent," Aria giggled. "Where are you from?"

"Tennessee," I said proudly. "Small town near Knoxville."

Birdie whistled low. "You're a long way from home. This must be so difficult for you and your family."

"I—" The rest of whatever I'd been about to say died in my throat. "It's just me and Lainey," I murmured. "Our parents passed almost eight years ago now."

"Oh dear," Birdie said, her hand flying to her chest. "I'm so sorry to hear that. We lost our Jace a long time ago, but it never gets easier."

"No, ma'am." My voice cracked, and I struggled to regain my composure. The last thing I wanted to do was break down in front of these people—this woman who, after the loss of her husband, had raised six boys and her daughter all alone. That was a level of strength I'd likely never understand.

"Mama," a deep voice said right before a warm, broad hand curled around my shoulder. Instantly, I knew who. No one else would touch me like this. Hell, no one else's touch made me *feel* like this, like a host of butterflies had taken up residence in my stomach, like live wires were attached to his fingertips, sending electricity through my body. "Aria. I see you've met Reagan."

I hadn't heard him approach, but goddesses, I was grateful for his appearance. He provided a distraction that allowed me to tip my face down and away from him. Swiping at my eyes, I swept away the tears that had collected on my lower lashes but hadn't fallen.

Fuck, I missed my sister.

"She's lovely," Birdie said happily. "She even brought gifts!"

"Well, let's get them inside, then," Finn said.

As Birdie and Aria turned and headed back into the house, Finn moved around to face me, his hands coming up to my cheeks, tilting my head so I met his gaze.

"You okay?"

I nodded, clearing my throat. "Yeah." I surprised myself by how convincing I sounded. "It's just…hard. I miss Lainey."

He arced his thumb across my cheek, the callous there scraping against my skin. My blood heated at the intoxication combination of his proximity, natural masculinity, and the sexy eucalyptus and sandalwood scent of his body wash. It wrapped around me, cocooning me in a bubble I never wanted to leave.

And, goddesses, I loved his hands. They were broad, tan, thick-fingered, the backs decorated with veins that snaked up his forearms beneath his tattoos. I loved how rough they were, so at odds with how gently he handled me.

I leaned into his palm, my eyes fluttering closed, allowing myself to linger for a moment.

"If it gets to be too much, don't hesitate to leave," he said. "They'll understand."

"Okay," I whispered, opening my eyes again.

He gave me a small, reassuring smile, then slipped one hand from my face, down my arm until he captured my hand, lacing our fingers together.

"You look beautiful, by the way," he said as he led me up the steps to the front door.

"Thank you."

Because I knew I'd be seeing him, I had taken some pains with my appearance, swiping on an extra coat of mascara, using my favorite rose-colored eyeshadow to make my green eyes pop. My long hair fell in soft waves down my back, and I'd dressed in my favorite white eyelet blouse and nicest pair of black shorts, my feet in my most comfortable gold sandals.

Call me crazy, but I wanted to make a good impression on Finn's family—well, his mom and sister. I couldn't care less what his brothers thought of me.

Except, maybe, West. I understood the connection between twins better than anyone, and if he and West were anything like me and Lainey, I knew he would never bring someone into his life that West couldn't stand.

Lainey and I had each done it a time or two, most recently and notably for me, of course, being Troy, and it never ended well.

But at the end of the day, the only opinion that *truly* mattered was Finn's.

The interior of the Lawless home was as welcoming and beautiful as the exterior, with soaring ceilings in the foyer, a grand staircase that led to upper levels, and multiple wings branching off the entrance. Finn led me toward the left, past a formal dining room, through a kitchen, and into another more casual dining space. A long table dominated the center of the cedar-paneled room. Finn's brothers were already seated at benches on either side, conversing while they waited for the rest of the party—me and Finn—to join.

There didn't seem to be any sort of seating arrangement, so we ended up on one side, with West and Aria across from us.

Finn's twin grinned at me. "Good to see you again, Reagan."

"You too," I said, meaning it.

The rest of the brothers chimed in with similar sentiments, and then Birdie said, "Now that we're all here, let's eat."

The boys dug in with an impressive gusto, like they hadn't had a meal in days. The feast was impressive, and I couldn't help but wonder if Birdie had gone the extra mile because I joined them.

"Everything looks amazing," I said to her, leaning forward to catch her eye across the table, where she sat at the opposite end with Lane at her side and Trey across from her. "Thank you for having me."

"Anytime, dear. You're always welcome here."

Finn's hand found my thigh under the table, squeezing in a way that told me he liked the sound of that—me at his side for a thousand more nights like this.

I liked it too.

At first, I was quiet. There were so many personalities in the room, making it almost impossible to catch onto a thread of conversation and follow it meaningfully. This family seemed to have a shorthand for the way they spoke to each other, born from years at each other's sides. None of them seemed bothered by the fact that several different topics were being discussed at once, all between bites of Birdie's delicious meal.

I was content to sit back and observe. Growing up, it had only been me, Lainey, and our parents. Mom and Dad had both been raised in New England and moved to the south after they graduated college, so any extended family we had was spread across Massachusetts, Vermont, Rhode Island, and Maine. Every few years, we'd head north or some of them would head south, but we didn't have a close relationship with them. Two of our grandparents had passed before we were born, the other two when we were in high school.

Those funerals were the last time we'd seen any of our parents' relatives—until their own funeral, of course.

Lainey and I always discussed our family dynamic, curious if there was more to the story of why we weren't close with them outside of literal distance driving a wedge into those relationships.

But we never figured it out before Mom and Dad died, and now we never would.

Once everyone returned home after the funeral, we never heard from them again.

For our entire lives, it had been me and Lainey against the world.

Being surrounded by these people, this warm, big family, was surprisingly comforting. I expected the opposite, to be an odd man out, to be reminded how fucking alone I was.

And I did feel that way, mostly in the way that I wished Lainey were here to experience it with me.

Otherwise, being here was…easy.

Finn was a solid presence at my side, carrying on a conversation with Crew, but frequently checking in with me. Giving me space to navigate this setting on my own but letting me know he was there to lean on if need be. Silently reminding me I could leave if it all got to be too much.

Eventually, though, when the boys had polished off their second helpings and dessert made its way onto plates, conversation turned to me.

"You said you grew up in Tennessee, right?" Aria asked me, the first time since West's welcome that I'd been addressed directly.

"Yep, about an hour south of Knoxville."

"How close is that to Nashville?"

All movement, conversation, hell, *breathing*, at the table stopped in an instant, like all the air had been vacuumed from the room with Aria's question.

Unperturbed by the silence that followed it, she merely stared at me expectantly, cutting off a small bite of her peach cobbler and putting it in her mouth, chewing slowly.

Clearing my throat awkwardly, unsure of what the hell happened, I said, "About three and a half hours. We're tucked in the southeast corner of the state, right along the borders with North Carolina and Georgia."

"I've always wanted to move to Nashville," Aria mused, her lips twisting into a wry smile—almost like she knew her brothers would erupt.

They didn't disappoint.

Lane: "Absolutely not."

Trey: "You're fucking crazy."

"You're not moving halfway across the country without any family nearby, Ari," West grumbled from next to her.

"I personally think she could benefit from getting out of this town," Aspen said from the other side of Crew, who hummed noncommittally in response.

"Yes, well, no one asked your opinion, *little phoenix*," Trey snarled from next to her.

"You don't get to call her that," Crew replied lowly.

A nickname from her fiancé, then, I surmised.

"I can't get my singing career off the ground if I stay here," Aria said.

"You're not moving, and that's final," Lane said.

"It's not up to you," Aria retorted.

"How come you guys didn't put up this kind of fuss when Owen decided to stay in Michigan when he retired?" Aspen asked.

"Because Owen can take care of himself," West said.

Aria reared back from him like she'd been slapped.

Angrily, she tossed down her fork and rose to her feet, lifting her hands in the air, middle fingers raised at her outspoken brothers.

"Fuck you." She spared an apologetic glance for her mom, then Finn, Aspen, and me in turn. "Except you four."

For the first time, I noticed Finn hadn't uttered a word in all that chaos.

Then Aria swept from the room, and Birdie made to get up, but Finn waved her off.

"Stay, Mama. I've got it."

With him gone, I wasn't entirely sure what to do, so I sat there silently.

"I hope you're happy with yourselves," Birdie chastised her boys. "For that, you can clear the table."

"Yes, Mama," they mumbled, all of them rising and taking their plates to the kitchen before coming back to get the various serving dishes.

"C'mon, my dears," Birdie said to me and Aspen, getting up and moving over to the small fridge in the corner of the room I hadn't noticed until now. She grabbed three wine glasses from a nearby sideboard, extracted the Sauvignon Blanc I'd brought, and inclined her head toward the exit.

Aspen and I dutifully followed behind her until we entered a large den-like room, filled with cozy, oversized furniture—likely in deference to the massive men she had for sons. The mantle above the unlit fireplace was lined with family photos, and I took a moment to study them, lingering on one of the twins as teens, arms slung around each other, dressed in dirty baseball uniforms and grinning ear to ear.

Hanging against the shiplap facade was a candid family portrait, all of them gathered around a football player in the center—Owen, I realized. The boys were tall, though all gangly limbs, and wide smiles. Aria was so cute and tiny, barely coming up to Lane's waist, missing one of her front teeth, hair in little blonde pigtails. At Owen's sides, bracketing him, were Birdie and Jace.

"That was the last one we took before Jace died," Birdie said, catching my attention. "Owen played for the University of Oregon, and that was homecoming his junior season. Jace passed about a month later."

"The boys look just like him," I said. Then, glancing at her over my shoulder, added, "I'm sorry."

"Thank you," she said. "It happened a long time ago. Been twenty years now."

"How did he…"

"Aneurysm. He was out putting up a new fence along one of the pastures with some of the ranch hands. There one second, gone the next."

"Sudden."

"Extremely."

"My parents died suddenly too."

"How?" Aspen asked.

"Car accident. I—" I hated admitting the next part.

Survivor's guilt was fucking brutal. "I was with them. I lived. They didn't."

Aspen gasped, and Birdie crossed the space to pull me into a hug.

"Seems we've all lost people we loved very much."

When I broke from Birdie's embrace, I nodded, blinking rapidly, willing myself not to cry.

"I don't know what I'll do if Lainey doesn't come home," I admitted.

"We'll find her," Aspen vowed. "I promise you."

Birdie glanced between us, not saying anything as she reached for the wine and poured out three glasses—draining the entire bottle.

She held hers aloft in front of her, and Aspen and I grabbed our own glasses and met her, clinking them lightly together.

"To strong women," Birdie said before sipping.

Aspen and I echoed the sentiment and followed her lead.

We made ourselves comfortable, Aspen and I were on one side of the massive sectional with Birdie in a chair across from us.

Seemingly desperate to steer the conversation away from the losses we'd all suffered, Birdie said, "So Aspen, how's wedding planning going?"

Crew, who had appeared in the archway leading into the den, turned on his heel, attempting to sneak away.

"Not so fast, young man," Birdie said, snapping her fingers and pointing at the spot beside Aspen. Head hanging, though not seeming too put out to cuddle up with his girl, Crew took a seat.

Finn entered next, beelining for me and taking up a similar position on my other side. I didn't balk at him slinging his arm along the back of the couch and curling it around my shoulders, or the way he tugged me closer so we were pressed together, his warmth seeping into me.

The rest of the brothers filtered in and took spots on the opposite side of the couch. Nobody else in the room seemed to think anything of my and Finn's position, as though curl up together like this—like a couple—was the most natural thing in the world.

"How's Aria?" Birdie asked Finn.

"She's okay. I talked her off the ledge…for now at least."

"I'm disappointed in you," Birdie said with a glare at Trey, Lane, West, and Crew in turn.

"That's fine," Lane said. "As long as we're all in agreement Aria isn't moving anywhere."

"We're definitely *not* in agreement."

All eyes in the room swung to the man with his arm around my shoulders.

twenty-two

. . .

FINN

"*WE'RE DEFINITELY NOT IN AGREEMENT.*"

My brothers' eyes found me, widening or narrowing in varying degrees of surprise and irritation.

I wasn't going to stand down on this, though. Aria deserved to have one of us—actually *all* of us—go to bat for her.

For as long as I could remember, my little sister wanted to be a singer. Almost like her name had been a self-fulfilling prophecy. She was insanely talented, and that talent deserved to be displayed somewhere outside of the Swallow every weekend.

"What do you mean?" Trey asked.

"I mean she's twenty-four. An adult. If she wants to move, there's not a single fucking thing any of us can do to stop her. Not to mention," I continued, "as her *family*, we should be encouraging her to chase her dreams, not holding her back under the guise of protection."

"We just want to keep her safe," West muttered.

"And right now, you're suffocating her. Why do you think she spent so much time at my guest house? Because it's away from your overbearing asses, who show up here and act like your word is gospel when it comes to how she lives her life."

Next to me, Reagan gasped, realizing she'd taken over Aria's safe space. I settled a hand on her thigh, squeezing gently, letting her know it was okay.

I'd been indulging in similar touches all evening, unable to resist the feel of her smooth, golden skin beneath my palms. Her fucking legs went on for miles in her little black shorts, and it had taken everything in me not to grab a handful of her ass when I'd walked up to greet her, Mama, and Aria out front earlier.

I was glad she indulged as well, not pushing me away or subtly distancing herself when I got close.

Almost like, maybe, her "I can't do this with you" walls were crumbling.

But I wasn't going to push her. I was happy to have her here, at my side, and I wouldn't risk this little bit of common ground for anything.

Before any of my brothers could open their mouths to argue with me, Mama cut them off.

"I'm not going to listen to you all argue about this. You know where I stand on the matter."

Her disappointment in the four of them said as much: she was in favor of Aria doing whatever made Aria happy.

"And I think you're crazy," Lane muttered.

Mama glared, and he wisely shut his trap, at least having the sense to look guilty.

"Moving onto more important things," Mama said pointedly. "I'd just asked Aspen how wedding planning was going before you all so rudely interrupted."

Groans rose from my brothers, and all but me and Crew made to get up, but Mama pinned them in place with a look.

"This is your punishment for being mean to your sister," she said.

"Better than having our pie privileges revoked," Trey muttered.

"The night is still young," Mama quipped, then fixed her attention on Aspen.

Aspen wore a shit-eating grin on her face. She secretly loved it when the boys got scolded by Mama, presumably fondly remembering *her* first family dinner in this house. Mama had learned Lane tried to run her out of town and had given his slice of pie to Crew as punishment. Crew had savored that fucking pie while Lane watched, fuming.

"Wedding planning is basically done. Linens have been ordered, chairs and tables have been rented, flowers are booked, and I had my first dress fitting. Oh! And we finally have a caterer," she added with a pointed look at Crew.

"What?" he asked. "That first guy was a fucking creep, and the second one fucked up the ribs."

"Okay, fair," Aspen conceded. "Those ribs were dry as shit. But the first guy was not a creep."

"He kept looking at your ass," he told her flatly. "He's lucky we left with his face intact."

Ignoring that comment, Mama asked, "What about a photographer? The big day is in like two months."

For the first time all evening, Reagan willfully waded into the conversation.

With a little gasp, she asked, "You don't have a photographer this close to the big day?"

Aspen shook her head. "Where *he*"—she jabbed a finger into Crew's chest—"was picky about the food, I've been picky about pictures. I haven't found anyone whose work I'm in love with, you know?"

Reagan nodded, turning her attention from Aspen to me as Crew muttered something about picking one already.

I met Reagan's gaze, her eyes narrowing a little, a silent question posed in them.

Somehow, I *knew* what she was asking without a word exchanged between us, and I gave her a small nod.

"I could do it," she said quickly, whipping her head back to Aspen and Crew, interrupting their whispered argument.

Aspen's eyes widened comically as Crew's mouth split in a grin.

"You would?"

"Of course," Reagan insisted. "I'd be happy to help."

"You're hired!" Crew yelled, and the room erupted into laughter.

"You're insane," Aspen said, turning to give him a kiss, then getting up and walking over to Reagan, hauling her up into a hug. An impressive feat, given Reagan was several inches taller.

"Thank you, thank you, *thank you*," she murmured. When they pulled apart, Aspen was grinning. "I secretly hoped for this, you know." Then she glanced pointedly between the two of us. "And I'm still hoping for *this*."

I smiled back at her. "Me too."

Reagan blinked slowly at me, as though she couldn't believe I admitted that out loud, and in front of my entire family, no less.

What she failed to realize was I'd fucking get on my knees and *beg* for a shot with her if I thought it would help.

For now, I'd content myself with letting her curl up against my side as the wedding conversation continued.

"How about the guests?" Mama prompted. "Do you have a head count yet?"

"RSVPs don't officially need to be in until next week, but right now we're looking at around two hundred."

"One big ass party," West said, grinning.

"Speaking of," Crew started, angling his body toward my twin. "We're still waiting on an RSVP from Tyler."

"Who is Tyler?" Reagan whispered to me.

"West's…something."

Her brows drew together in confusion.

I leaned closer, my lips brushing her ear. She shivered against me, reacting to the sensual touch—which is precisely why I'd done it.

"Can we talk about this later? They have a long and complicated history."

And, truthfully, not my story to tell.

West groaned. "She, uh…" he trailed off, his hand coming up to scratch at the back of his neck in an imitation of my own nervous tic. "She didn't text me back the last time I reached out."

My brothers erupted, tossing out jeers and teasing words.

"Hell must have frozen over," Trey mused.

Usually, West was the one leaving women on read, not the other way around.

But things with Tyler had always been different.

"If she doesn't show up, who can you possibly have slutty wedding sex with?" Lane asked, giving West a suggestive nudge in his side.

"I have more women on my roster than just Tyler," West mumbled, clearly pouting.

I seemed to be the only one who heard it for the lie it was.

Mama placed her fingers in her ears. "I don't need to hear this."

Ignoring that comment, Trey said, "Don't you think it's about time you two stop fucking around and admit there's more happening there than just sex?"

West shot to his feet, towering over Trey as he said, "That's a little hypocritical, don't you think?"

I couldn't see West's face, but the rigid set of his shoulders told me his was pissed right the fuck off, that Trey had taken it too far.

However, I *could* see Trey's face, and it had completely drained of color.

We all may know how to rile West up, but that knowledge ran in both directions, and West had pressed on Trey's sore spot.

Wyatt Saunders.

A bit of a sore subject for the entire family these days, after her mother tried to kill both Aspen *and* Crew last year, but she'd been Trey's best friend forever, and none of us were blind to the fact that he'd been in love with her for nearly as long.

After her mother died, Wyatt and her dad had picked up and left town in the middle of the night without a word to anyone—including Trey.

He didn't talk about it, but we all knew he'd been trying to reach her for nearly a year with no luck.

I didn't miss the look Crew and Aspen shared.

"What, baby bro?" I said to him. "You got something to say?"

Crew swallowed hard, clearly in a tough spot, but Aspen was the one who spoke.

"We invited her to the wedding. And she RSVPed…yes."

It went so quiet in that room, you could've heard a pin drop.

"It'll be good to see her," Mama hedged. "Let her know we don't blame her for any of it."

West, who still stood in front of Trey, pulled his phone out of his pocket.

"I'll call Tyler," he mumbled before leaving the room.

I had half a mind to go after him, but I wasn't going to intrude on that conversation, if there even *was* one. The one thing we knew unequivocally about Tyler Atwood was that she was as wild and free as a damn bird. That woman wouldn't be caught unless she wanted to be.

I didn't know if he meant to call her or simply needed an excuse to slip free of the scrutiny. Likely a combination of both. The front door closed, and he appeared on the porch, his back to the windows.

"And what about you?" Mama stared directly at Lane. "Will you be going stag?"

"It's my brother's wedding," he said. "I don't need a date."

"But you have one," Crew supplied happily. "The sheriff is bringing a plus one."

"Sutton?" Mama asked with a brow raised, voicing the thought we all had.

Surprisingly, Lane shook his head.

"Addie," he rasped out.

Oh shit.

Trey snorted. "That's gonna get messy."

"Sutton is coming," Aspen supplied. "She was one of the first RSVPs I received."

Reagan sat silent at my side, head turning back and forth, tracking the conversation, likely not having a single fucking clue what was happening.

"I'll break it all down for you later," I whispered, once again eliciting that tremble in her body, grinning as her flesh pebbled with goosebumps.

"I'm gonna need diagrams and a manual to keep all of these people straight."

I liked that she wanted to know, no matter how complicated explaining it all would be.

That meant she wanted to stay.

twenty-three

. . .

REAGAN

WHEN FINN and I walked outside a little while later, my head spun like a helicopter propeller.

All those names of people I didn't yet know but found myself *wanting* to meet.

I didn't grow up with a big family, certainly wasn't used to the chaos of one, but I couldn't deny how enticing being a part of this one was.

"Did you drive here?" I asked Finn.

He shook his head. "I had to wrap up a few things at work, so I rode my horse over."

"Do you want a ride home?"

He nodded eagerly, turning to accept the stack of leftovers his mother carried out to us. Then he bent and gave her a hug before carrying the food to the backseat of the car.

Only he didn't get in the passenger seat, instead walking around to the driver's side of *my* car and getting behind the wheel.

Birdie chuckled at my expression. "I raised my boys well."

"You sure did," I mused.

Then Birdie surprised me when she approached me next, drawing me into that warm, baked goods-scented embrace.

"I meant what I said earlier," she murmured to me. "You're welcome anytime. With or without Finn."

I squeezed her a little tighter before letting go, but when I did and looked down into her face, I whispered, "Hopefully with."

A smile broke across her face, and she patted my cheek. "You're a good one, Reagan Lindsey."

"You too, Birdie Lawless."

With a wave goodbye, I climbed into the passenger seat, and Finn and I set off for home.

"You're driving my car."

"My woman doesn't drive as long as I'm around."

I quirked a brow. "Your *woman*?" I asked, though I secretly loved the claim and the surety behind it. Heat pooled low in my belly.

I was completely and utterly fucked where this man was concerned. How had I ever thought I could stay away from him?

"Yep," he quipped, popping the *p*. "So you just sit there and be my pretty little passenger princess."

Silence descended between us, thick with tension and desire.

"We should probably talk about us," I hedged.

"Agreed."

"Now?"

"Let's get home first," he said, glancing quickly at me as he turned onto the access road to his house. "I have a feeling I'm gonna need bourbon for this."

Having the confidence boost of some alcohol certainly sounded like a good idea.

"Mine or yours?" I asked.

"It's *all* mine."

The look he gave me told me wasn't talking about the houses.

I was a feminist, damnit. I didn't believe in God. I put my faith in goddesses, the ancient Greek variety, simply because I refused to give my prayers to some fucking masculine power in the sky. For my entire adult life, I'd supported myself by working my ass off.

I indulged in sex on occasion simply because I liked it. I wasn't promiscuous, but I was open and honest about my sexuality. I wanted a husband and children, but I wouldn't accept either at the cost of my own freedoms.

I wanted a *partner*, an equal, a man who wouldn't look at me and think my place was in the kitchen, barefoot and pregnant with a toddler on my hip.

I didn't do the whole possessive alpha male bullshit.

At least, I *hadn't*.

But Finn claiming me?

My panties were fucking *soaked*.

What if we didn't talk when we got inside? What if, instead, I jumped his bones? Honestly, that sounded like a much better use of my time. After all, it had been seven *long* years since I'd last had this man inside me, and I fucking *ached* for him.

When we pulled to a stop in front of the guest house, I climbed out before he'd fully put the SUV in park, needing some fresh, Finn-free air to get my head back on straight. He made me crazy.

Gulping down a few large lungfuls, I didn't wait for him as I climbed to the porch and unlocked the house.

As I stepped inside and flicked the lights on, an inexplicable sense of unease overcame me. I didn't know *why*, only that something seemed…wrong.

I halted in the doorway, and Finn's heat appeared at my back a moment before his hand settled between my shoulder blades.

"You okay?"

"Fine," I said, though I sounded unsure. "Something seems weird, but I'm not sure why."

Without another word, Finn pushed past me and stalked deeper into the house, disappearing down the hall. I heard the doors to the guest room and closets open and close as he checked for intruders. He returned a moment later, shaking his head.

"Everything looks normal," he admitted, as though he hated to disappoint me.

"Good," I said, breathing a little sigh of relief but not relaxing entirely.

I moved to the sideboard in the small breakfast nook, grabbing two rocks glasses and filling them with three fingers of bourbon, handing one off to him. We clinked them together before I took a heavy pull.

It burned all the way down, the good kind of sting that was immediately followed by warmth suffusing my limbs.

Finn inclined his head toward the couch, and I followed him over, kicking off my sandals by the door on the way. Tucking my feet up under me, I dragged a pillow onto my lap—my last line of defense against this man.

"So you wanted to talk," he said.

"Thank you for tonight," I started.

He shook his head. "No need to thank me. But I should've given you a better warning before dragging you into the lion's den like that."

"I had fun."

"My family is insane."

"I *love* your family," I admitted. "Y'all are so real. And even through the bickering, it's obvious how much you love each other. I envy that."

"You don't have that kind of relationship with Lainey and your parents?"

"Lainey, yes. You know how the twin thing is." He nodded. "But my parents are dead."

"Fuck," he hissed, then reached for me, looping his thumb and pointer around my wrist. That gentle, innocent point of contact set my heart racing faster. "I'm so sorry, Reagan. How did it happen? If you don't mind me asking."

For once, I found myself *wanting* to talk about it—about them and the night that changed everything.

"We were on our way up to Knoxville," I started. "Lainey and I were in college at UT, and we lived close enough that we commuted from home. That weekend, she had a showing at an art gallery. She'd been in the city all day, getting things ready, while I'd been home. I had a waitressing shift at our local diner, which was why I wasn't with her."

The fall of our senior year was when we started getting serious about making careers out of photography. Had our paths diverged, that would've been cool too, but it was so incredible to me that photography wound up being another thing we each loved and could do together. One of our professors had seen a few of Lainey's photos from a hiking trip we'd taken through the Smokey Mountains over the summer and wanted to display them in her gallery.

We both had jobs too. Even though we'd been living at home and didn't have to pay rent, our parents had instilled in us the value of hard work. Earning our own money was impor-tant to us. Hence my job at the diner, where Lainey also worked.

"This freak thunderstorm came out of nowhere. We were less than five miles away from Knoxville when it came on. Dad was driving, and the rain was coming down so hard he could barely see. He was going too fast."

I didn't realize I was crying until Finn reached out and swiped at my cheek.

It all came flooding back at that moment.

The steady cadence of the rain hammering the roof of the car.

Mom begging Dad to go slower.

Dad swearing everything was fine.

Hydroplaning. Dad slamming on the brakes, the worst thing he could've done.

The oncoming headlights blinding me as our car cut across the opposite lane of traffic.

The way my body jerked forward when we hit the tree. The seatbelt digging into my chest and stealing my breath. The fiery pain in my leg.

Screaming for help, begging Mom and Dad to answer me.

"They died on impact," I finished, tipping my bourbon back and draining the glass. "So I suppose I have that to be thankful for. On the other hand, I sat in that car with my dead parents for two hours while first responders arrived at the scene and worked to extract me. I'd been their main concern, of course, because I was still breathing. By the time they finally pulled me free, I had screamed myself hoarse."

"How badly were you injured?"

"A broken fucking leg," I said, laughing humorlessly, extending said leg out in front of me and pointing to the thick, white scar that cut across my shin.

"I remember this," he murmured, fingers gently brushing over my skin. "From that night."

This time, my laugh was real, though a little choked with unshed tears. "I was so scared when you pulled my boots off," I admitted. "I remember thinking you'd find me repulsive and take off before we got to the good part."

Back then, even six months after the accident, the scar had been pinky and puffy. Nothing like the now smooth, pale flesh.

"Fuck no," he said, his hand fully encircling my ankle now, right below the spot where the scar stopped. "I honestly didn't even notice it. You were the hottest woman I'd ever laid eyes on. I couldn't believe I was there with you, that you'd even given me the time of day. Hell, I still think you're the most beautiful woman in the world."

"I never could figure out how I managed to bag a real-life Rambo."

"Simply by being you, belle."

If he knew all of these things about me, had seen my scars both real and figurative, and he wasn't running…why weren't we at least *trying?*

"I don't know if I can do this," I said, gesturing between us. My voice dropped to barely above a whisper as I continued. "But I do know I can't stay away."

Finn reached for my empty glass, sliding it onto the table alongside his before hauling me onto his lap.

"I think we're inevitable, Reagan. And I'll wait forever if that's what you need."

Curling against him, I fit my head beneath his chin. His arms wrapped me up tightly, so close I could feel his heart beating out a steady rhythm in his chest.

That's what Finn was. *Steady.* A solid presence, willing to walk at my side while I figured shit out—for however long that took.

"My sister is my number one priority," I reminded him. "I *need* to find her."

"And we will."

So many people kept promising me that.

The sheriff.

Aspen.

And now Finn.

The sheriff's department I didn't put much trust in, truthfully.

Aspen was damn good at her job, and I knew she meant it when she'd told me we'd bring Lainey home.

But when Finn said it—hope sprouted in my chest for the first time since Lane had called to tell me about the body they found.

Besides me, he had the most on the line if Lainey didn't come home.

Because without my sister, I would cease to exist.

And without me, there would never be an *us.*

I wanted that future with him so badly I could taste it, could almost see it like a mirage shimmering in front of me, slightly out of reach.

A future with Finn meant nothing if my sister wasn't there too.

FINN LEFT SHORTLY AFTER THAT, leaving me alone with nothing more than the noise in my brain—and the lingering unease I'd experienced when I got home after dinner. Something *seemed* wrong but I couldn't put my finger on *what*.

With Finn gone, I walked through the house, turning on every light, peeking into every dark nook and cranny, ensuring myself there wasn't someone lying in wait for me. Nothing appeared to have been moved or taken, but I still couldn't shake the sense of *wrongness*.

And when I finally allowed myself to crawl into bed, a heavy liquor bottle on the nightstand as a makeshift weapon, I wasn't entirely able to relax. All night, I couldn't help feeling like there were eyes on me. Every time I drifted off, I woke with a start and shot up in bed, certain someone had been standing in the corner of the room, watching me.

Finally, at the ass crack of dawn—no joke, the sun had barely crested the horizon—I dragged myself from between the sheets.

After dinner last night, Aspen had texted asking if I'd want to meet her today. Crew was on shift, so I was planning to go to their house, where we could talk about the case and execute the photography contract for the wedding.

Last night would've been the ideal time to drop the bomb on the Lawless boys that Aspen was helping me on the case, but when Aspen didn't offer up that information, I kept my mouth shut as well.

As evidenced by the gross overreaction they had to the mere *suggestion* of Aria moving, those boys were overprotective as hell, and I didn't have the energy to get into an argument with them about putting myself in danger.

I didn't *feel* like I was in danger.

After spending a few hours straightening the house, running some laundry, and responding to the work emails I'd let pile up in the time since I arrived in Dusk Valley, I had to get ready to meet Aspen.

Turning the shower as hot as I could physically stand, I stepped under the spray, a moan leaving me as the delicious heat pounded against my flesh and seeped into my weary bones.

I took my time, washing my hair then applying a deep-conditioning mask, exfoliating and shaving my legs. The self-care was much needed and, by the time I climbed out, my mood had perked up considerably.

The worst of the unease from the night before had dissipated, and I did my best to shake the remainder off, assuring myself I was safe here.

As long as Finn was around, no harm would come to me.

Except…all of my worst fears slammed back into me when I stepped in front of the vanity to go through my extensive skin-care routine before getting dressed.

There, on the mirror, revealed by the steam from my shower, were three words. The edges of them blurred, dripping with condensation that, given the contents of the message, reminded me far too much of blood.

My blood ran cold as fear, a terror like I'd never known before, sluiced down my spine.

SEE YOU SOON

Stumbling backward, my towel came loose from around my

chest, and I tripped on it. Falling to my ass, I scooted backward until I'd managed to wedge myself in the corner between the toilet and the wall.

And then...I screamed.

twenty-four

· · ·

FINN

I WAS GETTING out of the shower when I heard the scream.

Reagan.

Hastily, I threw on clothes, my worry over her damn near suffocating as I once again raced down the gravel path between our houses. She could've still been sleeping, awoken by another nightmare. But I was mobilized by the idea that she was in danger.

"Reagan?" I shouted when I burst into the house. I hadn't thought to grab my gun this time, so I reverted into combat mode, mentally drawing up all my years of hand-to-hand training should I need it.

My body *was* a weapon, and I'd use it against anyone who attempted to harm my girl.

No sound greeted me except faint sobbing coming from the back of the house.

I moved swiftly down the hallway, my head on a swivel, waiting for an ambush, but the coast to the master remained clear. The sheets on the bed were a twisted, tangled mess; Reagan likely hadn't slept well.

And she was nowhere to be found.

"Reagan?" I called again.

"I-in here." Her voice was so, so small, coming from the bathroom.

I stepped inside, not seeing her at first. Then I caught a flash of blonde in the corner, and I rushed across the room, dropping to my knees before her.

I barely registered that she was naked, her body curled into a tight ball.

My hands shook as I reached for her, but I held back from making contact. "Are you okay? Are you hurt? What happened?"

Reagan shook her head, still crying too hard to speak. Instead, she lifted a shaky finger and pointed toward the vanity.

Standing, I moved back across the room, first looking at the counter, the sink, the floor around, searching for whatever had freaked her out so badly.

"The m-m-mirror," she managed to gasp around her sobs.

My eyes flicked up.

Horror and rage fought for purchase in my chest, my anger ultimately winning.

I was going to fucking *destroy* whoever was doing this to her.

Grateful I'd at least remembered to shove my phone in my pocket on the way out my door, I pulled it out and called my brother.

"Awfully early for a social call," Lane said in lieu of greeting.

"Get out here now."

"Where?"

"My house. The guest house."

I could barely grit the words out from between my clenched teeth. I was trying my fucking best to keep my temper in check, not wanting to distress Reagan any further, but keep it together was difficult.

"What happened?"

"Just get here."

I hung up before he could say anything else.

This fucker had been in this house, and that realization made me want to burn the whole goddamn thing to the ground.

"Baby," I whispered when I once again crouched in front of Reagan. "Can I…can I hold you?"

Reagan's head barely shifted into a nod before I was pulling her into my arms, carrying us into the bedroom and reclining on the bed. She was shivering, whether from fear or the chill caressing her damp skin, I didn't know.

Likely both.

Knowing my brother would arrive shortly, I finally shifted us to sitting and slid her off my lap, reluctant to let her go. Reagan folded herself in half over her lap, head in her hands.

I rifled through the dresser drawers, coming out with underwear, a sports bra, a pair of leggings, and a baggy tee, laying it all out on the bed.

"Do you need help?" I asked gently.

She shook her head, unfurling herself and standing before me—still entirely unembarrassed to not have a stitch of clothing on.

No, not unembarrassed. *Numb*. Which was so much worse.

I faced away, ignoring the way my body responded to the soft rustling of clothes behind me.

A knock came at the door when she said, "I'm decent."

"That'll be Lane," I said, glancing at her over my shoulder. "You okay for a second?"

Though she nodded, she trotted behind me when I left the room.

"What the fuck is going on?" Lane demanded loudly when I let him in, bursting the safety bubble I'd attempted to create around Reagan.

"First of all, keep your voice down," I warned, cutting my eyes to Reagan, who had dropped onto the couch. Her legs were tucked up against her chest, her arms wrapped around them, eyes vacant with a thousand-yard stare. "Follow me."

Lane spared Reagan a glance, forehead creasing in concern.

I led him back to the master and into the bathroom.

His eyes immediately went to the mirror, the words fading as the steam dissipated.

"What the fuck?"

"She must've found it when she got out of the shower," I explained, noting the glass door to the enclosure was still open, a damp towel strewn carelessly across the floor. "I heard her scream and came right over."

When he faced me, his eyes were wide, expression grim. "Someone has been in this house, Finn."

"I *know*."

"Who has access but you two? Anyone know the code?"

"Aria," I said pointedly.

"Yeah, there's no fucking way our little sister is responsible for this," he said, agreeing with the warning in my tone.

"It could've been unlocked," I admitted. "I don't know."

"Ask her when she calms down," he said. "It's obvious we're not getting anything out of her right now."

"I didn't lock the door when I went to dinner last night," Reagan said from the doorway. Some color had returned to her face, and her green eyes flashed with anger. "I've only been locking it at night. I figured it was safe. I'm so sorry."

"It's *supposed* to be safe," I said, going to her and drawing her into my arms. "And you have nothing to apologize for, belle. This isn't your fault."

"Is anything missing?" Lane asked her. "Or disturbed?"

Reagan shook her head, stepping out of my arms to face my brother. "I had this weird feeling when we got back from dinner last night that something wasn't right, but Finn cleared the house, and I did another check myself before I went to bed."

"What kind of feeling?" he asked, withdrawing his notebook from his pocket and clicking a pen open.

"Like my space had been disturbed," she said, eyes cutting to the mirror. The message had completely faded, but the imprint lingered in illegible streaks, reminding us of what hid in plain sight.

"I'm going to call some deputies out to do a sweep and get photos of this," Lane said. "From now on, make sure your doors are locked at all times."

"Fuck that."

Both of them turned to me with identical confused expressions. It would've been funny if I wasn't still battling the fury in my blood.

"What do you mean?" Lane asked.

Ignoring him, I looked at Reagan.

"Pack your shit."

"What? Why?"

"You're moving in with me."

"But—"

I cut her off, not in the mood to entertain her strong, I'm-an-independent-woman shit right now. I was going full caveman, and I didn't give a single fuck.

"No arguments. I'll fucking throw you over my shoulder and *carry* you home if I have to. Now pack. Your. Shit."

Lane snorted, and I cut him with a glare that had him raising his hands and leaving the room, letting Reagan and I have our little battle of wills without an audience.

Unfortunately for her, she wouldn't win this battle.

Reagan's eyes widened at the complete, unrelenting demand in my tone. I half expected her to fight me, to put her foot down and tell me to fuck off.

But this woman continued to surprise me, because she listened for once.

There was a lot of foot-stomping and cursing my name under her breathing happening, but she rooted around in the closet, coming out with two giant rolling suitcases, opened them up on the bed, and started haphazardly throwing clothes into them.

"You're an asshole," she muttered, and I knew she purposely said it loud enough for me to hear.

"An asshole who wants to keep you safe."

She paused, fists resting on the gentle swell of her hips, and faced me. "I can go stay at the motel."

I chuckled darkly. "Absolutely not. That place has absolutely no security to speak of."

"It's just a creepy message," she retorted. "It's not like it caused me physical harm."

"Reagan," I said softly, closing the distance between us and cupping her face in my hands. "I found you curled up in the corner, sobbing. It may not have caused *physical* harm, but it still hurt you."

"Scared the fucking shit out of me," she admitted.

"And your scream did the same to me."

"You got here so fast."

"I will *always* come for you," I reminded her. "I need to keep you safe, belle. Please, just…*please.*"

Our eyes held then, the moment stretching, time around us warping to a standstill. Fuck, I wanted to kiss her so badly but now was absolutely not the time.

Still, the thought must've been on her mind too, because her tongue darted out to trace her bottom lip, almost as if trying to direct me where she wanted me.

There would come a day—in the near fucking future—when I'd take her up on that offer, when I'd give into the pull once again.

But today was not it.

I shook my head at the same time Reagan blinked, pulling us out of the moment.

"Can I help?" I asked.

She nodded. "There are some boxes of things in the guest

room. Would you bring them out to the car? I can drive every-thing over."

Before she could walk away from me, I captured her wrist and hauled her in for a hug, needing to feel her warmth and vitality against me, to reassure myself she was okay. I pressed a kiss to her temple and walked away.

Reagan Lindsey was badass. Strong, independent, didn't take shit from anyone. The fact that she let me in, was letting me care for her the best way I knew how, was a goddamn miracle.

I was making my third trip outside when two sheriff's depart-ment vehicles pulled up, four of Lane's deputies getting out.

"Where's the boss?" Johns asked.

"Here," Lane said, stepping out of the house before I could speak. "Did you bring what I asked?"

One of the other deputies ducked into the back of the SUV and came out with a large crime scene camera and a briefcase-looking toolbox that likely had CSI equipment inside.

"Good," my brother nodded. "Master bath. You'll have to turn the shower on. I want the entire house swept and dusted for prints, but start there."

The deputies shared looks of confusion at the mention of the shower but wisely didn't press the issue as they disappeared inside. They'd figure it out soon enough.

My own task completed and not liking the idea of Reagan alone with those guys, I followed them.

"You done?" I asked when I entered the master.

She pulled the zipper closed on the suitcase she was wrestling with, the other one already shut, and said, "Yep."

"Do you need us for anything else?" I asked Lane when he appeared.

He shook his head. "I know where to find you if I do."

With a nod, I collected both of Reagan's suitcases, carrying them instead of wheeling them simply to see the way her eyes glazed over with lust at the flexion of my biceps.

"Like what you see, belle?"

Her eyes snapped to mine. "I'd *like* to see a lot more of it."

Blood rushed right to my cock, and I was grateful for the stiff denim keeping it in check behind my zipper.

"All you have to do is ask, baby."

Reagan smirked but didn't say anything, merely lifted the canvas bag off the floor by her feet and followed me out the door.

A half hour later, her belongings were safely unloaded in one of my guest rooms.

I didn't tell her how badly I wanted her in *my* bed.

We'd get there eventually. For now, I was giving her space and time, exactly like I'd promised last night.

Once she was settled in, I said, "So as much as I hate to leave you, I need to get to work."

My phone had been blowing up all morning, ranch hands and my foreman demanding to know where I was. I'd already spent too much time away from my duties, and there was a pregnant mare who needed my attention today. West and I *had* agreed to take the plane out again today, but it could wait until later. I shot him a quick text saying so.

"That's okay," she said. "I've got a meeting with Aspen this morning anyway."

"Great. I'm glad you won't be alone."

"See you later?" she asked.

I nodded. "It might be late. West and I have to take care of something this evening."

"Okay."

"Okay," I repeated. Before I thought better of it, I stepped forward, pressed a kiss to her cheek, and left.

twenty-five

. . .

FINN

UP TO THAT POINT, the only women I'd ever lived with were my mother and Aria, and I was worried how adapting to having Reagan in my space would go.

I shouldn't have been worried.

Living with Reagan was as easy as breathing, like we'd been cohabitating for years instead of a few weeks.

Easy if you completely ignored the unspent sexual energy that pulsed in every one of our interactions.

Both of us were busy, though, so we usually only came together for dinner and rotting on the couch for a few hours before bed. While I was at work, I'd usually see her car up at the big house, Aspen's parked right alongside it, likely working on wedding details together. The two of them had grown close during Reagan's time here, and I was grateful she had a friend to keep her company when I had to be at work. Mama and Aria also absolutely adored her; she folded into my family so easily, it was difficult to remember a time when she hadn't been around.

Everyone looked at and talked about us like a couple, and I supposed from the outside looking in, we sure seemed like one.

But she hadn't made a move in the physical sense, though

we'd grown so much closer emotionally over meals and glasses of bourbon before bed. There was no doubt in my mind this woman was *it* for me, and I wanted to show her that, hoping she felt the same way.

The opportunity presented itself perfectly almost two weeks after she'd moved in with me. There hadn't been any movement on Lainey's case, though I knew Reagan called Lane regularly for updates. Trey was taking his sweet ass time going through the old security footage from the Swallow, and honestly, I was getting as impatient as Reagan. Waiting for some tangible lead we could follow to her sister's whereabouts was painful.

West and I had gone up in the plane four more times, clearing half of the area we were currently focused on, and managed to locate five properties that had potential to be the one from Reagan's dream.

Every day, every time her hopes were dashed by my big brothers, it grew harder and harder to keep those clandestine trips to myself. I wanted so badly to tell her, but I didn't want to get her hopes up more only to disappoint her.

The sounds of cooking greeted me when I walked into the house after work that night. Once I'd shed my boots and hat, I found Reagan in the kitchen, barefoot, long golden legs on display in a pair of tiny white shorts. Her tank's thin spaghetti straps exposed the gentle, tan slopes of her shoulders, the lines of her collarbones, the long column of her neck.

She had yet to notice my presence, likely because of the music blasting from the surround sound, so I leaned against the wall and watched her.

I loved the easy way she moved around my home. She seemed to know exactly where everything was, not having to dig or open multiple cupboards before locating what she needed. I *wanted* her to think of this place as hers too. I wanted it to be *ours*.

When she bent over to pull a tray of what I quickly realized was lasagna from the oven, the sight of her ass had me unintentionally clearing my throat, fighting off a groan at the perfect peach shape, ripe and *right there* for the taking.

The tray of lasagna clattered to the stovetop as she whirled on me, hand to her chest.

"Sorry," I said with a grimace, loud enough to be heard over the dulcet tones of Hozier crooning about how someone was too sweet for him. "Didn't mean to scare you."

Grabbing her phone off the counter, she turned the volume down.

"It's okay," she said. "I was a little distracted."

"This looks amazing." Moving into her space, my body pressed against hers, I took a giant whiff of the lasagna and cheesy garlic bread.

Reagan inhaled sharply, then shoved me out of the way, grabbed both with oven-mitted hands, and carried them to the table.

"There's salad and wine in the fridge too," she said, and I grabbed them before joining her.

After she shed the mitts and set them on the island, I pulled out her chair. Once she sat, I opened the wine and poured us each a glass. Truthfully, I wasn't a big wine guy, but since Owen had married into a family who owned a winery, I'd been known to drink it more than I used to. Chateau Delatou was the only label I kept in my house.

Reagan caught me studying the bottle of Pinot Grigio and said, "I hope you don't mind. I found it on the rack in the pantry." She took it from me, squinting at the label. "I've never heard of this winery before."

"It's my sister-in-law's," I said. "Owen's wife's family owns a winery in northern Michigan."

Setting the bottle down in favor of her wine, she sipped. "It's delicious."

"I'll take you there one day," I promised. "You'd love Delia and her sisters."

Reagan smiled but didn't say anything, and I quickly realized my misstep.

Mention of my sister-in-law and her sisters was likely a sore spot for my girl.

While I searched for a safer topic of conversation, Reagan blurted, "I want to scout the ranch for photo locations for the wedding."

I blinked in surprise. "Okay…"

"Is there an ATV or something I could borrow? And maybe a map?"

"Not necessary," I said quickly.

"What do you mean?"

"Have you ever ridden a horse?"

She pursed her lips and narrowed her gaze. "I'm southern. Of course I have."

I grinned. "Perfect. Horseback is the best way to see the ranch."

"I can borrow one?"

"Of course. We'll go out tomorrow if you want?"

"*We?*"

"You didn't think I'd let you see my family's ranch for the first time without me there as a guide, did you?"

Reagan smiled, almost reluctantly, but it dropped quickly. "Tomorrow is Friday. Don't you have to work?"

"I can take the day off."

"You don't have to do that for me."

"I want to."

"But you shouldn't."

"Stop arguing with me, woman."

"But it's so much fun," she grinned.

I merely growled in response, though my lips twitched with a barely leashed smile of my own as I returned my attention to my meal.

When we finished, I cleared the table and did the dishes—

exactly like at Mama's, whoever didn't cook, cleaned. Reagan should've been used to the dance by now, but she still tried to help me. I had to shoo her out of the kitchen with a pat on her ass—and, okay, maybe I snuck a squeeze, which had her squealing before heading down the hall and disappearing into her room for the night.

Once I finished cleaning and got the dishwasher running, I shut myself in my own room and called my mom.

"You're calling late," she said when she answered. "Everything okay?"

"Everything is fine," I assured her. "But…I'm taking Reagan on a tour of the ranch tomorrow, and I was hoping you'd help me put together a picnic."

Mama was silent for a moment. "You're not proposing, are you? The last time I had to make a picnic for one of you boys, he came back with a fiancée."

"No!" I said, a little too loudly. Dropping my voice, I repeated, "No, I'm not proposing. We're not…" I sighed. "It's not like that."

"But you want it to be."

"Have you seen her?" I responded with a chuckle.

Mama laughed as well. "I have, and I've seen you together. There's something there, isn't there?"

"Yes," I admitted. "Hence this phone call."

"I'll have it all ready in the morning," she said. "Swing by before you head down to the barn."

"You're the best, and I love you so much."

"I love you too, my boy."

THE FOLLOWING MORNING, Reagan and I rode over to the barn together. I parked at the big house and told her to go along to the stables so I could run inside and grab the picnic.

The basket was ready to go, and I didn't bother to question what was inside, knowing Mama would take good care of us. I gave her a peck on the cheek, ruffled Aria's hair, and set off across the yard.

When I walked into the barn, I found Reagan standing at one of the stalls, cooing at and scratching the nose of one of the horses.

As luck would have it, *my* horse.

"That's Raider," I said when I reached her side. "He's a sweet old thing."

"He really is," she agreed as Raider leaned in to nuzzle her cheek. Reagan giggled, and it might've been the most beautiful sound I'd ever heard.

"He's mine."

"Makes sense."

"How so?"

"Soft guy, soft horse."

With a smirk, I patted my stomach and adopted a thick, country-boy drawl as I said, "Baby, there ain't nothin' soft about me."

"Don't I know it," she agreed with a grin.

"Let me get him out and tacked up, then we'll pick one for you."

As I led Raider out of his stall, plying him with a few peppermints, Reagan asked, "Are all of these yours?"

"My family's and the remuda for the ranch hands, yeah. West has stables on the dude ranch that hold a dozen more, but since this is closest to the big house, it's where we keep ours."

"What are all of their names?"

"Outlaw, Rebel, Bandit, Raider," I said, pointing at each stall in turn and pausing to brush a hand along Raider's coat. "Rogue, Rascal, and Scamp."

Reagan chuckled. "Really leaned into the whole 'lawless' thing, didn't y'all?"

"It made the most sense. Plus, we let Aria name them."

She'd been a little tike when all these horses had come to the ranch before Dad died. When she asked if she could name them, Dad agreed. He'd never been able to say no to his little girl.

Conversation died out as Reagan watched me tack up Raider, even going so far as to prove she knew her way around a horse by getting his bit and bridle in place while I focused on the saddle.

Keeping my attention on Raider was goddamn difficult with Reagan looking as good as she did. Tight jeans, feet stuffed into black cowboy boots I remembered from our first night together, and a white ribbed tank that clung to her torso. Her blonde hair a braided rope down her back, topped by a fucking cowboy hat I wished was mine. That old wear-the-hat rule would come in handy right about now.

I was damn near drooling, and it took every ounce of self-control I possessed not to drag her into my office and have my way with her.

But I wanted a lot more from Reagan than another single night romp in the sheets, and today was my chance to show her that.

Once Raider was ready to go, I headed back down the alley toward the stall at the end, where Scamp sat ready and waiting. She whinnied happily when I approached, and I held out an apple for her before leading her out.

"This is Scamp," I told Reagan. "Aria's horse. Since you guys are about the same size and she's a sweetheart, I figured she'd be perfect for you."

"She's gorgeous," Reagan breathed, running her palm down the length of Scamp's neck.

Scamp was a stunning grey Arabian with a fully black mane and tail. Compared to the warmer coats of my and my brothers' horses, she stood out—which was ideal for Aria, who was born to be in the spotlight.

We worked in tandem to get her tacked up then set off.

Reagan kept pace with me easily as we headed across the nearest pasture toward a nearly hidden trail that snaked through the woods, leading us to my favorite private spot.

Each of my siblings and I had our own such place on the ranch, the one spot where we could disappear. Sort of like a *Happy Gilmore*-style happy place. Crew had taken Aspen to his to get engaged, and now I was bringing my girl to mine.

But first, I took her to Crew's spot, mainly because that was where their wedding ceremony would take place.

"Holy Aphrodite," Reagan breathed when we trotted up to the ridge overlooking the valley below. She climbed down from Scamp's back, and I took the horses' reins, looping them around a nearby tree branch before following Reagan to the edge. "This is…breathtaking. The perfect spot to get married."

She'd stowed her camera away in one of Scamp's saddlebags, and she had it in her hand now, raising it, the shutter clicking away as she captured the landscape around us.

I didn't want to disturb her as she lost herself in the motions of doing the thing it seemed she was put on this earth to do, so I stood by and watched. Before my eyes, the tension I hadn't realized she'd been holding in her body since the day she came back to Dusk Valley seemed to bleed from her, like she was finally fully relaxed. At one point, she lowered the camera and simply tipped her head back, eyes falling closed as she enjoyed the moment of peace. The sunshine on her skin, the gentle breeze blowing the strands that had come loose of her braid off her face. A simple, easy moment where it didn't seem like the weight of the world rested on her shoulders.

I knew a little off-the-grid excursion didn't erase the fact that Lainey was still missing and we had absolutely no leads to speak of, but I was grateful I got to be the one to give her this moment of peace.

At last, she opened her eyes. They landed on me, a serene smile on her face.

"C'mon," I said, inclining my head toward the horses. "There's more to see."

We spent the next few hours crossing over a small section of the ranch. Reagan peppered me with questions about it, my ancestors, and what it had been like to grow up here.

"Honestly, all of us except Owen had been hellions. Crew, West, and I were the worst offenders, though. I think a lot of that stemmed from the need to act out after Dad died. Our way of coping, you know? We weren't emotionally mature enough to deal with our grief in a healthy, constructive way, so we fucked around. Got drunk and ran rampant through these pastures and hills. Broke bones. Broke hearts. Did all the shit teenagers were *supposed* to do—and a lot of things we shouldn't have."

"That sounds amazing," Reagan said, her head always moving as she tracked all the natural beauty around us. "We grew up close to the mountains, but home isn't anything like this. There weren't tens of thousands of acres to use as our own personal playground." She looked at me then, her smile melancholic. "We were happy, though."

"That's all that matters."

Reagan only nodded.

"Where to next, soldier?"

She called me by the nickname so infrequently, even a completely innocent use of it had my dick getting hard.

Still, I grinned at her, ignoring the situation in my pants. "My favorite spot."

Less than ten minutes later, we pushed through the overgrowth on either side of the path—which I kept that way on purpose, not wanting anyone else to discover this place—I told Reagan about how I discovered it.

"We used to play hide and seek," I started.

One of those perfect, dark-blonde brows curved. "On this much land?"

I chuckled. "We had rules in place to make it a little easier.

Boundaries too. I'd never come this way before, mostly because West and I rarely went anywhere without each other—"

"So nothing has changed," she quipped.

"—but that day," I pressed on, ignoring her, "I decided to go in a different direction instead of following his lead and sticking closer to the big house. I thought this was a thick stand of trees I could lose myself in."

"It's not?"

"It's not," I confirmed, breaking through the brush a moment later, directing Raider to the side and turning so I could see Reagan's reaction as she took it in for the first time.

Straight ahead was a scene straight out of a fairytale. A small but mighty stream gushed over the edge of a fifteen-foot cliff face, filling a pond below with water so clear you could see everything below the surface, all the way to the bottom ten feet below.

Reagan's jaw dropped, and she blinked rapidly.

"This cannot possibly be real." She looked at me in awe. "It looks like some magical fairy pond."

"It's my favorite place to come and think." I slid off Raider, gathering the picnic basket and a blanket from his saddlebags before walking toward the edge of the water. "And now it can be yours too."

twenty-six

REAGAN

I WAS SPEECHLESS, and tears welled in my eyes.

This man…there weren't words for what sharing this meant to me, or what *he* was coming to mean to me.

Lainey was always on my mind, sitting right at the forefront, commingling with any other thought I happened to have at the time.

But for a little while today, for the first time since I'd gotten the call about the body, it felt like I could *breathe* and simply *exist* without the grief crushing me.

Finn didn't press me to fill the silence as he spread out the blanket and our picnic, and I appreciated him even more for it. He was content to leave me to my thoughts, to let me enjoy this peace. To simply bask in this moment where the weight of the world lifted from my shoulders.

Too soon, we had to head back to the ranch.

We arrived back at the barn with only about ten minutes to spare until family dinner started. I wished I had time to go home and rinse the dust off, or at least change, but there was no time. When we walked the horses into the barn, Finn set to untacking Raider, and I did the same with Scamp, hanging up her saddle, blanket, bridle, and bit, then brushing her down quickly before leading her to her stall. A ranch hand appeared to feed her and get her bedded down, and after a final pat to her side, I left them to it.

Suddenly, I was dreading dinner.

Had I been grateful he'd taken me out today? That he'd spent time he could've been working by showing me around the ranch and treating me to a romantic as fuck picnic lunch? Of course. I'd made sure to thank him, and I had enjoyed myself more than I expected.

But my sister was still missing, and here I was, fucking around and playing house with him.

My head was a jumbled fucking mess. Living under the same roof as him was driving me insane. Going to bed knowing he was right down the hall, that all I had to do was walk the twenty or so feet and I'd be right there with him.

I was genuinely shocked, and possibly a little (a lot) dejected he hadn't sought me out. He'd agreed to give me space, but I was starting to think there was such a thing as *too much*, and Finn was too far on the other side of the line.

Maybe, I didn't want *any* space anymore.

Or *maybe*, this whole thing—coming here, thinking I could help find Lainey—had been a mistake.

Finn and I met in the middle of the alley between stalls, staring at each other for so long we were sure to be late for dinner.

I didn't know what he wanted from me, and I was starting to think I had no idea what I wanted for myself. Now was neither the time nor the place to answer those questions.

With a disgusted sigh—mostly at myself—I moved past him, ready to head up the hill for dinner. The last thing I wanted to do was keep Birdie waiting, and I'd never hear the end of it from the boys if I delayed their mealtime.

I only made it two steps before Finn's hand caught my wrist.

"What're you doing?" I asked when I angled toward him, my voice low. They were the first words I'd spoken to him since we left his special place more than an hour ago.

His mouth opened and closed once, twice, as though searching for the right words. Ultimately, he snapped it shut and, with a slight shake of his head, let me go.

Okay then.

I got another step in before he muttered, "Fuck it," from behind me, grabbed my arm again, and spun me so my back was to the wall of the barn.

There was no warning before his mouth descended on mine.

That first brush of his lips, a gentle, teasing glance, had me whimpering, wordlessly begging for more.

And he gave it to me, coming back to me with more pressure, angling his body closer so there wasn't a millimeter's worth of space to be found between us. His thigh came between mine, the hard muscle connecting perfectly with my core which, after only a few moments, already pulsed in time with my heartbeat. Aching for him.

Grinding down against him, I gasped at the pressure, and Finn took that as an invitation to sweep his tongue in my mouth. Caressing, exploring, twisting with mine. Refamiliarizing ourselves with each other, with this heady physical connection we'd gone too damn long without.

I'd forgotten how much I loved the way this man kissed, with his whole entire body, like he couldn't get close enough, like his hands couldn't find every inch of my body fast enough, like he'd never get enough of the way our tongues danced and lips glided and sighs of pleasure mixed together.

Kissing him again was like coming home, like some piece of me I hadn't known was missing—or maybe *had* and chose to ignore—finally locked into place, completing me.

That wild thought had me pushing him away, tipping my head down and brushing a hand over my mouth, gasping for air.

"What?" he asked, and I risked peeking up at him to see if he was as affected as I was. Honestly, I thought he was worse. A thick bulge pressed against the front of his jeans, and his hat had gone missing—I hadn't even noticed I'd knocked it off—his hair a rumpled mess from my fingers. He brought a hand to his kiss-swollen lips. "Did I do something wrong?"

"You didn't do anything wrong, but we're going to be late for dinner," I finished lamely.

"I don't give a fuck about dinner, Reagan."

"I can't do this with you right now!"

Gripping my hair by the roots at my temples, I yanked, as if that would knock some sense into me.

"Can't…or are afraid to?" he asked softly from behind me.

And that was the crux of it, wasn't it?

"I'm going home," I said. "Send my apologies to your family."

"I don't fucking think so," he growled, grabbing my wrist, *again*, as I tried to walk away. Then, gentler, added, "Stay. Please."

Sparing him a glance over my shoulder was a horrible idea, because the second I met his blue gaze, the depths still stormy with desire in the wake of that kiss, my resolve to get as far away from him as possible crumbled.

"For Birdie," I murmured, then tugged out of his grip and stomped toward the house.

When I got closer, I found Birdie out on the porch, hands on her hips, expression stern. But she must've sensed something was wrong, because she pulled me to a stop and said, "Are you okay?"

"Fine." I tried to assure her with a smile that felt brittle, and I knew it didn't meet my eyes. "Finn is right behind me."

I kept moving, not stopping until I was in the family dining room. I reached for the first bottle of alcohol I saw—vodka, but top-shelf at least—poured a healthy serving into a glass and downed the whole thing.

"Rough day?" one of the guys asked, but I didn't look around to see which. I refilled the glass, dropped onto an empty space at the end of the bench, which happened to be next to Aspen, thankfully, and kept my attention on my lap.

"Ahh, that explains it," West said when Finn entered the room a moment later. The air in the room changed. Now that we'd given in, if I thought kissing him was enough to take the edge off how badly I wanted to tear his clothes off every time I saw him, I'd been sorely mistaken.

"You okay?" Aspen whispered to me.

"Fine."

"You wanna talk about it?"

"Later."

She nodded, giving my hand a squeeze, and let the subject drop.

DINNER WAS TENSE. Everyone in the room was aware something had happened between me and Finn. For one, we sat as far away from each other as we could get. Secondly, we made it a point to speak to everyone in the room *but* each other.

The longer I sat there, letting the tension twist my muscles into knots, I realized I wasn't mad or embarrassed about what had happened in the barn.

Actually, I *was* mad. But only because I *wasn't.*

I wanted it to happen again, and that made me feel so fucking guilty when my sister was out there somewhere, being held against her will under goddesses knew what kind of condi-tions. Being able to enjoy this incredible man who was so sweet and caring with me when she was likely stuck with one who only wanted to harm her—and me—wasn't fair. I hated myself for wanting him but couldn't imagine a universe in which I could deny myself having him, either.

Our ride home was tense and silent, and I hated to admit I

couldn't wait to get away from him, if only so I'd have a moment to breathe and get my head on straight.

The night we'd sipped bourbon and talked, I thought I wanted this. But my brain was a jumble of conflicting thoughts, and I was starting to wonder…what would it cost me to truly give into this attraction between us?

I feared the price was too high. The last thing I wanted to do was hurt him, and I was afraid we were on a runaway train in that direction.

The moment we stopped in front of his house, I was out of the car and rushing inside, not stopping until I'd safely shut myself in the guest room I now called mine.

A reckoning was coming, but tonight was not the night I'd face it.

So like the fucking coward I was—I locked the door behind me.

twenty-seven

. . .

FINN

REAGAN STILL WANTED ME.

Despite her little tantrums before and after dinner, and locking herself in her room, the knowledge had me grinning as I got ready for bed that night.

Was I hoping that by kissing her, we'd end the evening tangled up in my sheets together? Of course.

I also hadn't been counting on it. I'd merely wanted to remind her that the spark between us was still there for me, simmering beneath the surface of my skin, all day every day.

And I wanted to remind her she still felt it too.

I'd promised her time, promised to take things slow. I made *myself* a promise to tread lightly with her, knowing she was an emotional mess without her sister.

But *she still wanted me*, and I was going to do everything in my power from here on out to show her how good we could be together.

I JOLTED UPRIGHT IN BED, not entirely sure what had awoken me.

Something was…wrong, the energy in the house slightly off.

Tossing the covers back, I swung my legs over the side of the bed but stilled when my door burst open. A panting, clearly distraught Reagan appeared in the frame.

"Belle?"

"Nightmare," she rasped.

I opened my arms, and she came to me, crawling into my lap and fitting herself against my chest like she was always meant to be there. Falling backward, I relaxed against the pillows with Reagan sprawled atop me.

For a while, I simply held her as she shivered against me, rubbing soothing circles up and down her back while she calmed down.

Eventually, her heart rate slowed and the shaking subsided. She tilted her head to look up at me, pressing a light kiss to the underside of my jaw.

"Thank you."

"Wanna talk about it?"

"It was the same one. That creepy fucking farmhouse and my sister chained in the basement."

"I've been looking for it," I whispered, the darkness allowing me to finally make the admission. "Well, West and I have."

Reagan sat up and shifted so she was straddling me. "You have?"

I nodded, my hands going to her bare thighs. There was no intention behind the touch except the visceral *need* to feel her skin beneath mine. To remind myself she wasn't some fever dream I conjured, a fantasy only brought to life in my dreams. That she was real and here with me.

"Since you first told me about the dream, West and I have been taking the plane out and doing some aerial recon, looking for properties that fit the general description."

"Does Lane know?"

Shaking my head, I said, "We didn't want to tell him until we'd covered all the ground we wanted to and had some solid information to pass along."

"And have you found anything?"

"There are a few areas that are promising."

Without warning, Reagan bent forward and crashed her mouth to mine. Though she'd surprised me, I sank into the kiss easily. The way her soft, plush lips moved against mine ignited a fire in my blood that was impossible to ignore.

It didn't help matters when she started rocking her hips against me, impossibly stiffening my already rock-hard cock further.

We were both gasping for breath when she pulled away. "Thank you."

"Haven't I made it obvious by now that I'd do anything for you?"

"Even though I'm such a mess?"

"*Because* you're a mess," I quipped, reaching up to pull her hair free from the bun atop her head, tossing the tie across the room so I could wrap a handful around my fist. "You're *my* mess."

"I'm not sure I know how to do this," she admitted. "Not when everything up here"—she tapped her temple—"is so fucked up. That's why I acted so crazy earlier."

Sitting up so we were face to face, I cupped her cheeks and rested my forehead against hers. "We're going to find Lainey," I promised with a vehemence that surprised even me. "She's going to come home safe."

"Do you really believe that? Everyone keeps *saying* it, but I'm not sure I should trust it. There's this little flicker of hope, a tiny match flame in my chest that threatens to go out with every day that passes without a single lead. And honestly? I'm not sure how much longer I can do this. When does it stop? When do I accept the fact that she won't come home?"

"*Never*. Not until we've exhausted every avenue, overturned every stone, walked through every farmhouse in the entire fucking state of Idaho if that's what it takes."

"How can you be so sure?"

I tapped her chest, right over her heart. "You'd know," I reminded her. "What's your gut telling you?"

"She's still out there," she said firmly. "Alive."

"Exactly. Trey will get the security footage sorted, and West and I will give our findings to Lane. Things will come together. I know waiting fucking sucks. You're wondering what you could've done differently, what you could be doing *now*. But the truth is, belle…you're doing *everything*. And *when* Lainey comes home safe, it'll be because you didn't give up on her, not because of anything I or Trey or Lane and his department did. Understood?"

She nodded but didn't say anything, instead sinking her teeth into that juicy lower lip.

Goddamnit, I wanted to be the one putting those little dents in her flesh, not only on her lips but on her neck, shoulders, breasts—insides of her thighs.

Experimentally, I shifted so the hard ridge of my cock nestled against the apex of her thighs.

Realizing for the first time that she wasn't wearing panties.

Only the thin fabric of my boxer briefs separated us—the front of which were now wet with her arousal.

"Belle," I rasped. "You're soaked."

"Always am around you."

I groaned, a low, throaty rumble that vibrated from deep in my chest.

"Can I…can I touch you?"

"I think I might die if you don't."

Everything within me settled, then ratcheted up again as her words, her permission, shot adrenaline into my blood.

The fire we'd banked to an ember between us with all the time apart flared into an inferno.

With her still above me, my hands crept slowly higher on her thighs, my mouth latching onto the pulse point at the base of her neck where it sloped out to her shoulder.

Twin sighs left us when my thumb brushed through her slit.

I withdrew my hand, holding it in front of my face. Even in the dimness of the room, which was lit only by the full moon beyond the windows, my thumb glistened.

Eyes locked on hers, I sucked it into my mouth.

Her flavor exploded on my tongue, and I moaned as my tongue swirled around my finger, collecting it all, not wanting to waste a single drop.

"Fucking delicious," I murmured.

Before she could react, I shifted and flipped her off me so she landed on her back. I crawled between her legs, placing my hands on the insides of her thighs and pushing them wide. Reagan's chest heaved, and I wanted her naked and spread out beneath me so badly, but at the moment, I had a single-minded focus for her perfect cunt.

Dropping to my stomach, I scooched forward so I was eye level with her sex.

"Do you have any idea how much I've thought about this pussy?" I mused, leaning in to swipe my tongue up one side, right at the crease of her thigh. She squirmed, trying to put me where she wanted, but I held her firmly in place with a palm spread wide over her stomach. "How many times I found a quiet corner on base to fuck my hand after our night together, remembering how good you tasted?"

"Probably about as often as I fucked myself with my vibrator, wishing it was your cock."

"Fucking hell, woman," I swore, blowing a stream of air

across her drenched cunt, grinning when she shivered and goose-bumps broke out across her skin beneath my hands.

"Finn," she gasped.

"Yes, baby?"

"Stop talking and *eat*, soldier."

"Yes, ma'am," I murmured, rewarding us both with a long, slow lick from back to front.

"Oh, goddesses," she moaned.

I chuckled, having forgotten that about her. That she didn't pray to God, but the ancient Greek goddesses.

As long as another man's name wasn't on her lips—the almighty or not—I didn't give a fuck.

Adding to the teasing strokes of my tongue, I thumbed her clit with the head on her stomach, gentle taps and brushes. Reagan buried her hands in my hair and bore down on my face, hips circling.

Fuck, that was hot. Her *taking* what she wanted from me.

I stiffened my tongue and drove it into her entrance, pumping in and out like I'd do with my cock, and Reagan's ragged breath filled the air around us.

"Finn."

My mouth didn't leave her flesh, but I looked up her body, and our eyes collided.

"I want to taste you."

Immediately, I backed off and stood at the foot of the bed.

"Come here," I directed. She sat up and crawled to me. "Arms up." When she complied, I pulled her shirt off. "Now get on your back with your head off the bed."

Reagan eagerly complied, flipping herself around so her head hung off the mattress. I stripped out of my boxer briefs, and Reagan's mouth popped open, tongue out, when my cock sprung free.

"Good girl," I praised. She reached for me, tugging my shaft, urging me closer. "Good *fucking* girl."

My bed was tall enough that my cock slipped easily into the wet heat of her mouth with little maneuvering, and I bent over her, once again burying my face in her pussy.

I slid my tongue between her lips, collecting her arousal and spreading it around, mixing it with my saliva as I traveled up to her clit. Reagan's hips jerked toward me when I shoved two fingers into her at the same time I flicked my tongue against the swollen nub, and I chuckled.

Soon, though, the finesse I usually possessed when it came to pussy eating turned to disjointed licks. With her tongue swirling around me, her mouth bobbing up and down, I found it difficult to think straight let alone tongue fuck her the way she deserved. Especially not when my hips moved of their own accord, pumping my dick deeper into her mouth and down her throat.

I expected her to gag, to push me away, but she merely swallowed around my tip, squeezing me like a vice, and backed off before repeating the process.

"*Fuuuuuuck*," I moaned, lifting my head from her cunt. "You don't have a gag reflex, do you?"

Reagan's laugh reverberated through my shaft, and my balls drew up tighter to my body.

Oh hell no.

I wasn't about to blow my load before I even got inside her.

In a smooth move, I pulled free of her mouth, hopped on the bed, and dragged her into the center of the mattress.

Reagan pouted. "I was having fun."

"You were going to make me come."

She grinned. "Exactly."

"No, baby. The only way I'm coming is buried balls deep in this pussy." I punctuated the statement with a slap to her cunt, and Reagan gasped.

"Then get to it."

I tried to move away from her, to reach for the condoms in

my nightstand, but her legs locked around my hips, holding me in place.

When I looked at her again, she was shaking her head. "Bare. I want to feel all of you, Finn."

"You're sure? I've never fucked anyone without one, and I haven't been with anyone since my last physical, which came back clear."

"I've never been with anyone without one before, either, and I have an IUD," she admitted. "There is no one I trust to take care of me more than I trust you."

Ducking my head, I captured her mouth with mine, a deep kiss that left us both breathless when I pulled away.

I was helpless to deny this woman anything.

"You are my fucking dream girl, Reagan Lindsey."

My cock slipped through her slit, sliding through her lips easily. When I pulled back, the head notched itself at her entrance, almost like my body knew that's where I was meant to be—buried in and claiming Reagan. Making her mine in a way no one else ever had been.

Finally, I slid home.

twenty-eight

. . .

REAGAN

FINN SLID IN, barely an inch, and I was already dizzy with pleasure and anticipation.

"Fuck," I swore. "I forgot how big you are."

He grinned, his muscles straining as he held himself up, the striations of his deltoids pressing against his skin with the effort. The eagle on his chest rippled, the tattoos on his arms flexed.

"You can take it. Just relax."

I hadn't realized I'd been clenching my pussy around him, but I allowed myself to take his direction, loosening some of the tension coiled in my muscles so he could slide in another inch.

The stretch wasn't painful, exactly. A slight sting, a pinch, but he worked into me slowly, allowing me time to adjust before he kept going.

Both of us were panting hard by the time he was fully seated, his head dropping against my shoulder.

"You're going to kill me," he muttered into my skin.

"What a way to go."

At last, the last of my tension fell away, replaced by pure pleasure at the delicious stretch, how fucking *full* I was. My clit throbbed insistently, and I rotated my hips against him, the rough hair at the base of his cock providing the perfect pressure.

Finn made a choking sound.

"Yeah, definitely going to kill me."

Then he started to move. A slow retreat I felt the entire way, the ridges of his cock dragging against my walls, the friction making my toes curl.

Being with him again was…glorious. There was no other word for it. Every nerve in my body was fine-tuned to respond to his presence, and I couldn't figure out how I had gone so many years without this. The connection was unreal, divined by the goddesses themselves.

Finn set a slow, languid pace. Each advance and retreat was a delicious torture that had me scratching at his back, digging my nails into his ass, wrapping my legs around his waist. Begging with my body to go faster, to put us both out of our misery.

I had no idea how he was holding it together, especially since he'd nearly come down my throat earlier.

But when I blinked my eyes open, my vision hazy from the pleasure, I found his own scrunched closed in concentration, brow furrowed, like it took everything in him to *wait*.

Reaching up, I brushed a curling lock of hair off his forehead, using my fingers and the sweat beading on his forehead to push it back.

"Let go, baby," I urged. "You're not going to break me."

His thrusts stilled, his cock buried so deep, I couldn't hold back a moan. He managed to hit *the* spot, the one no one else but him had ever come close to. Then his eyes flew open in surprise, though I couldn't figure out why. This was *me. Us.* There was nothing he could do that would drive me away. Especially not now that I'd had him again, now that I knew there was nowhere in the world I was safer than at his side, in his arms.

Now that I thought about it, he *could* break me.

But not my body.

Only my heart, which rested wholly in his calloused palms.

"I don't want to hurt you."

I shook my head. "You thinking you need to hold back is what hurts me, soldier." I clasped his face between my palms, making sure he *heard* me when I said, "*Fuck. Me.*"

The words barely left my mouth before he pulled back and slammed in, hard enough that the entire bed rocked, his hip bones slapping against my ass, and my back bowed upward at the intrusion.

"*Again.*"

He obeyed, this time not slowing as he pounded into me relentlessly, recklessly, the headboard snapping against the wall with every thrust.

Thanks to his slow teasing of before, I was already dangerously close to the edge, and the pressure in my core reached an unbearable level.

But I wasn't going without him.

Squeezing my pussy tighter around him, I reached around until I found his balls and rolled them in my palm.

"Come, Finn."

Finally given permission, but before letting go entirely, Finn found my clit with his hand, circling it lightly before pressing his thumb down hard. Like hitting a button, my release barreled through me, my back bowing off the bed like my soul was being sucked from my body.

With a groan, he followed me down. Finn buried himself as deep as he could go, throwing his head back with a roar as he spilled long and hot inside me.

"Good boy," I murmured, brushing my fingers through his hair as his body shook in my arms.

I barely noticed him collapsing on me, both of us spent, bodies slick with sweat, chests heaving from exertion.

For long moments, we laid like that, Finn pressing me into the bed, his softening cock still inside me.

At last, he moved, lifting himself up and pulling out, then reclining back on his heels. His attention went to my pussy, where I could *feel* his cum dripping out of me.

"Fuck, that's hot," he said, a bit dazedly. Reached down, his pointer finger lightly brushed through my sensitive flesh to collect his release—and stuffing it back inside.

I twitched at the intrusion, but fuck. I'd never had a man do something so filthy to me, and I thought I might let Finn come inside me every day if it meant he'd do it again.

Without a word, he got up, and I watched, entirely blissed out, as he disappeared into the attached bathroom. A moment later, he returned with a wet, warm washcloth and set to cleaning me up. His strokes were gentle as he dragged the fabric across my skin, his gaze so full of adoration, it had emotion clogging my throat.

"Thank you," I managed to rasp out.

"Anything for my girl," he grinned, tossing the cloth across the room. "Aftercare is important."

Then he settled on the bed at my side, drew me into his embrace, and promptly fell asleep.

I followed not long after.

I NESTLED DEEPER into the warmth surrounding me, not opening my eyes yet, content for the moment to bask in other sensations.

The warm, smooth skin beneath my cheek and fingers, slightly raised because of the tattoos decorating it.

The soft breaths that fanned across the top of my head, and the rise and fall of his chest.

Turning my head, I pressed a kiss to pec, right over his heart, against the lifelike feathers of the eagle's wing.

"Good morning, beautiful," he murmured sleepily.

"Morning, handsome."

"What time is it?" he asked, eyes still closed.

Sitting up slightly, I glanced at the alarm clock on the opposite nightstand.

"Just after seven."

He groaned. "I told West I'd be ready at eight, but I have no desire to get out of this bed."

"More aerial recon?" I asked with a grin, sliding over and on top of him.

His Adam's apple bobbed as he swallowed and nodded, his eyes finally flying open when I rolled my hips, his cock—which was, unsurprisingly, already hard—sliding against my slick pussy.

My nails dug into his chest, anchoring me there, as I rocked again. Asking a silent question with my body.

Finn grinned. "Be my guest."

I lifted enough to grip his length, giving him a few tugs that had him hissing through his teeth, eyes slamming shut in an attempt to marshal his self-control. Then I notched the tip at my entrance and sank down, taking all of him in one go.

I was still sore from our last go round, which had only been a few hours before. We'd awoken several times in the night, half-asleep but still reaching for each other, coming together without words. Letting our bodies do the talking. I adjusted to his size easily now, my head falling back in ecstasy.

"So fucking full," I murmured, not yet moving.

Finn's hands came to my thighs, sliding up to my hips, where he lifted me until only the blunt head of him remained inside me, then pulled me back down.

I rolled my pelvis, sighing happily when the coarse hair at the base of his cock rubbed perfectly against my clit. Knowing I could get off so easily, I undulated faster. Finn let me work, his hands coming up to cup my breasts, rolling the nipples between his fingers. The friction, the gentle tugs combined with the rough scrape of his skin, was perfect.

"I pictured this," he murmured, eyes heavily-lidded. "When we went horseback riding. Watching you—fuck, I knew you'd look spectacular on top of me." My hands found his, threading our fingers together and leaning forward until I pressed our clasped hands to the bed above his head, still undulating my hips. "Fuck, belle. That's it. Take what you need."

I'd wanted to go slow, his plans with West be damned, but instead, I moved faster, bouncing on top of him, Finn meeting every one of my down strokes with an upward thrust of his own.

As always—because he wouldn't have it any other way—I came first, crying out his name and collapsing on top of him as I shook from head to toe. Finn fucked me through it, prolonging my orgasm until he found his own.

We were still coming down from the high when Finn's phone buzzed on the nightstand. I crawled off him and threw myself down on the bed while he rolled over to answer it.

"Hey, West." A pause. "Yes, I still want to go. Yeah, eight o'clock. I'll be ready. I am up!" he shouted, right before hanging up, muttering about goddamn meddling twins.

Turning back toward me, he quickly placed a kiss on my shoulder then got out of bed, heading in the direction of the bathroom. I couldn't resist checking out his ass, the sexy musculature of his back, the tattoos there he didn't have the last time.

He smirked when he faced me again and caught me staring. I only grinned back, entirely unashamed.

"Why don't you come with me?"

"To shower?"

"That too," he said. "But I meant with me and West. You can even bring your camera."

I wasn't about to say no to spending time with Finn, regardless of what we'd be doing, but he knew he had me when he mentioned my camera. Though I'd taken a lot of great shots of the ranch yesterday on our ride, I'd never been given the opportunity to take aerial photos anywhere.

Plus, if it meant helping look for my sister?

"I'm in."

WEST WORE a shit-eating grin when Finn and I stepped out of the house a half hour later, freshly showered and completely blissed out.

What we'd been up to was obvious, and West, knowing his twin as well as he did, didn't miss a thing.

"You guys fucked."

He didn't phrase it as a question, and Finn didn't treat it as such.

"Mind your own business."

"You are my business, big brother," he quipped, hooking Finn around the neck with his elbow and ruffling his hair. Though Finn tried hard to remain stoic, he was laughing by the time he managed to break free.

Being so happy was honestly a fucking crime, especially without Lainey.

But I knew Lainey would want this for me. Hell, she'd brought Finn up on numerous occasions over the years, begging me to look him up, to reconnect, to see if the spark was still there.

It would've been easy to find him. This town wasn't that big, and he was a war hero. A simple Google search surely would've yielded more than one news article about his and West's service.

But I hadn't been ready. In fact, if Lainey hadn't come out here and gone missing, Finn and I likely never would've seen each other again.

After losing my parents, I couldn't risk losing anyone else. My night with Finn all those years ago had been so fucking special. Something only he and I shared, a moment in time I'd hold dear for the rest of my life, wherever I ended up, and whoever I ended up with. I hadn't been willing to sully it with the possibility that he no longer existed.

War had a habit of taking people away from their loved ones, and I had been too afraid to learn if he'd been one of them.

The dichotomy was painful, knowing that if Lainey hadn't gone missing, I wouldn't have reconnected with this man who felt like the missing piece of my soul. Knowing that, without the pain of her absence, I wouldn't have the joy of knowing Finn again.

I still couldn't believe he'd been spending free time—of which I knew he had little—since I told him about my dream searching for areas where my sister might be. I'd already been half in love with the man, but my heart had expanded further with that knowledge.

We climbed into West's truck, and as he turned to back out of Finn's drive, he shot me a wink that had me shaking my head and grinning.

I was grateful he was taking the news that our relationship had turned physical so well, but I didn't think it would surprise anyone. The way we moved around each other…it had started to feel more like an inevitability than a possibility.

"I'm happy for you both," West said, breaking the comfortable silence as we drove out to the tiny airstrip outside of town.

"Thanks, West," I said, and Finn mumbled a similar sentiment.

In an abstract sort of way learned through conversations with him and the family, I'd known Finn got his pilot's license while he was in the service. Being confronted with the fact that *he* was the one about to take me up in the air was an entirely different concept.

The airport was nothing more than a field of close-cropped glass surrounded by woods on three sides, the runway sitting parallel to the main road. We pulled to a stop in front of a tall, corrugated metal building and climbed out. At the opposite end of the field was a tower, a red light blinking atop it.

"How does this all work?" I asked when we headed inside the building. West hit a button on the wall, and the massive garage door at one end rolled upward.

"We don't have full-time air traffic control out here, so we have to call up to Boise to make sure everything is clear before taking off."

"What about a flight plan?"

"Before we went up the first time, we developed a search area and have been checking it off grid by grid. Since we fly lower than larger commercial and private passenger planes, we're not at risk of disrupting their air space, so we file coordinates the day of," Finn explained as he led me over to one side of the hangar, where a Cessna sat. The other bay held a search and rescue helicopter.

"I texted them in last night," West said, joining us. "If there had been an issue with other trips in the area, they'd have called us off, so we're good to go."

The whole production was impressive, to say the least. The way the brothers moved around the hangar, Finn going through his pre-flight checklist, walking me through each step as he did it, while West ensured the path on the ground was clear, then spent some time consulting the map tacked to one wall.

I wandered over at one point, leaving Finn to finish his checks.

From what I could tell, the map was of Owyhee County, of which Dusk Valley was the seat. A copy was pinned next to it. While one was free of markings other than the ones it came with, the other was highlighted and scribbled on.

"These are all the spots we've searched already," he said, indicating the portions highlighted in yellow. Some of them had circles, exes, and other markings within the squares. Pointing to the circles and exes, West explained, "Those are spots we think may be your farmhouse, or ones we've already managed to exclude."

"I can't believe you guys are doing this for me…for *Lainey*."

West snorted, but his big hand clamped around the ball of my shoulder. "I like you, Reagan, and I think you're good for my brother, but trust me when I say this was *all* him."

"Still…I appreciate you."

"I don't feel good about your sister being held against her will somewhere. And because she's important to you, she's important to Finn, which makes her important to me. We'll find her, Reagan. I promise."

All I could do was nod, not even able to look at him lest he see the tears that had welled in my eyes.

"You guys ready?" Finn asked from behind us.

Taking a brief moment to compose myself, I turned and headed for the plane.

Ten minutes later, we were in the air.

I thought Idaho was stunning on the ground, but it had absolutely nothing on the beauty and majesty of the landscape from the air. Though we were in an area not as mountainous as other parts of the state, peaks still jutted high into the sky, some of them snowcapped despite it being the middle of summer. Everything was lush and green, threaded and dotted with vibrant blue rivers and lakes. I captured it all as best as I could, the constant shutter click of my camera lost to the whirring of the plane's engine and Finn and West's chatter in my headset.

I had no idea what to look for considering I was unfamiliar with the area, and I'd only seen the farmhouse on the ground—and in a dream. It might not even be real, but it meant more to me than these men would ever know that *someone* took me seriously.

Methodically, Finn flew back and across the quadrant they'd sectioned off for that day. They located a singular area that looked promising.

By the time we touched back down several hours later, I was feeling lighter than I had in weeks.

twenty-nine

. . .

FINN

"FINN," Reagan whispered, half-asleep, from my side. "Your phone."

I rose fully to consciousness then, recognizing the particular sequence of beeps and buzzes for what they were: a security system alert.

Sitting up as adrenaline spiked my blood, I scooted to the edge of the bed and reached for my phone.

Before I could fully make sense of *where* the alert had come from, my phone rang with an incoming call from Trey.

"What the fuck, dude? I thought Reagan was at your house."

I glanced over my shoulder, confirming my girl was, in fact, still there. Her brow furrowed.

"She is. I'm looking right at her."

"Then why are the alarms going off at the guest house?"

We seemed to come to the conclusion at the same time, for we said in unison, "Aria."

"I'm heading over," I said, already on my feet and swiping an abandoned pair of sweats off the floor. "Call Lane."

Hanging up before he could respond, I tossed my phone on the bed, pulled on a shirt, and walked into my closet. My lockbox beeped as I tapped in the code, clicking as the locks disengaged, and I opened it, withdrew my gun, and closed it again.

"Finn." Reagan stood directly behind me when I turned to leave the closet, now dressed in one of my tees. "What the fuck is going on?"

"Something tripped the alarm and motion sensors at the guest house," I said. "Stay here. I'm going to check it out."

"Like hell am I staying here."

"Reagan," I growled, gripping her upper arms lightly. "*Please.* I have no idea what I'm walking into, and I can't put you in danger."

She surprised me by nodding at my vehemence, then stepped closer until she was toe to toe, rising up slightly to press a single, hard kiss to my mouth.

"Be careful."

"I'll be right back," I promised.

She followed me as far as the front door, where I left her on the promise that she'd arm the security system once I was out. I'd barely made it all the way off the porch when West slid to a stop in front of the house and threw himself out of his truck before he fully parked.

"What's going on?" he asked. "Trey called."

"Disturbance at the guest house. I'm going to check it out." My eyes darted to the door, to Reagan's silhouetted figure. "Will you stay with Reagan?"

He saluted me before climbing the steps. As soon as Reagan let him in, I took off.

When I reached the guest house, I did a quick perimeter sweep, making sure no one was lying in wait outside. Though the exterior was clear, I cursed under my breath when I found the bottom left windowpane in the door—the one closest to the knob —smashed in, the door itself slightly ajar.

As gently and quietly as I could, I pushed the door wider. I did my best to step wide to avoid it, but the broken glass crunching beneath my feet was as loud as gunshots, alerting anyone still inside to my presence.

The living room appeared to be clear, the high, full moon providing enough illumination to make out all the furniture in the room. Everything was where it should be.

Gun out in front of me, I turned right into the kitchen, crouched low as I rounded the peninsula.

A figure was sprawled out on the floor, the under-the-microwave light casting them in an orange glow. They were face down, head angled so they faced away from me, arms bent awkwardly beneath them.

Blood pooled around their head.

Matted in bright blonde hair.

Broken glass nearby.

"Aria!"

"Finn?"

Not my sister's voice, but one of my brother's.

"Trey. Clear the rest of the house. I've got Aria."

He muttered something to someone else, and I heard a deep voice respond. Crew, I realized.

Not wanting to move her for fear of making things worse, I knelt at Aria's side, dialing nine-one-one as I pressed my shaky fingers to her wrist, checking for a pulse.

I gasped in relief when it thumped, weakened but there, against my touch.

"Nine-one-one, what's your emergency?"

As calmly as I could, I explained the situation, relayed my address, and told them to *fucking hurry* before I hung up.

Crew rounded into the kitchen to find me still on the floor at Aria's side, her chilled hand clasped in mine. He knelt at her opposite side, careful to avoid the blood, and checked for a pulse exactly as I had. I let him without comment, both because I understood the compulsion and because he had paramedic training.

Sliding on some nitrile gloves, he gently probed her skull, his fingertips coming away stained.

"There's a contusion there. Head wounds always bleed a scary amount," he explained. "As long as there isn't internal bleeding, she should be okay."

Trey joined us then.

"House is clear. Looks like point of entry was the front door." His tone was flat, likely trying to distance himself from the scene until we had more information.

The same could not be said for the emotions swirling within me, coalescing into a dangerous tornado one second away from touching down and tearing this entire fucking world apart in search of who had done this to my baby sister.

"Call West," I said. "He's at my house with Reagan."

Trey nodded and stepped away, and I heard the front screen door open and close a moment later.

As gently as I could, I brushed my hand over my sister's head, a comforting gesture surely meant more for myself than her.

"Your house is secure," Trey said a moment later, phone still pressed against his ear. "What do you want West to do?"

"Stay there. I'm not leaving Aria, but I can't—"

Trey nodded in understanding.

I couldn't focus on the task at hand if Reagan was vulnerable, and the only person I trusted with her right now was my twin.

Hours seemed to have passed before sirens distantly cut through the night, gathering steam as they got closer to the house. At last, the cavalry pulled up outside.

Lane led the charge, the ambulance and a few more sheriff's vehicles close behind. Throwing himself out of his SUV, Lane stomped up the porch steps, but Trey cut him off at the top.

"What the fuck?" Lane asked, trying to push past our older brother.

Ignoring him, Crew shouted, "Rausch?"

"Here!" came Sutton's reply a moment before she appeared in the glow of the porch lights. "What've we got?"

"Twenty-four-year-old female," I said, joining the conversation, offering details in a detached sort of way. "She's in the kitchen. Appears to have suffered blunt trauma to the skull. There's…a lot of blood."

"Twenty-four…" Lane whispered, eyes widening, all the blood draining from his face. "Aria?"

I could only nod, shifting out of the way so Sutton and her partner, Thomas, could enter the house. When they were gone, Lane turned to me.

"What the *fuck* happened?"

"I have no idea," I told him honestly, though I hated the admission.

My baby sister was in there, unconscious on the kitchen floor, blood pouring from her head, and I had no fucking idea *why*.

Trey was moving toward his own vehicle before Lane could make the demand, and we all followed along, Crew rushing to catch up after handing Aria's care off to Sutton and Thomas. In the hatch of Trey's SUV was a mobile command center of sorts, with all kinds of complicated looking equipment designed to allow him to check security systems remotely if something—like this—came up while he was on the road.

"There aren't any cameras over here," I reminded him, silently kicking myself for drawing the line there when he asked if he could install them. I thought the motion detectors, flood lights, and security system would be sufficient. I didn't exactly live in a high crime area.

But I should've known better, should have realized there was no such thing as *too much* where the safety of my family was concerned.

And now, because of me, because I swore nothing bad could ever happen out here, my sister had been hurt.

As if sensing my distress, Crew put a hand on my shoulder

and squeezed. I knew he meant well, so I did my best not to shake him off.

I didn't need to be comforted right now, though. What I needed was to beat in the face of the fucker who had done this to my sister.

"I know there aren't cameras over here," Trey said in answer to my comment. He withdrew a laptop and fired it up, tapping around on the screen until a set of feeds appeared. "But there are at your house."

Trey rewound the footage an hour, and my brothers and I watched the screen raptly, waiting for the commotion we knew was coming.

The distant porch lights provided a small bit of light. Trey zoomed the feed in as close as he could, and I had to admit, I was impressed. While the picture became a little grainy, I thought it had more to do with the darkness than the loss of quality.

"I got the motion sensor alert at three seventeen," he muttered to himself, stroking a few more keys that fast-forwarded the footage to the correct time stamp.

Right on cue, the flood lights mounted to the corners of the covered porch clicked on, illuminating a dark, hooded figure.

Seemingly without a care in the world, they ascended the stairs and walked right to the door. Trying the knob and discovering it locked, the fucker wasted no time turning and driving their elbow into one of the glass windowpanes.

"And that's when I got the breach alert," Trey said.

I watched the timestamp in the corner of the footage, waiting as five minutes ticked by where nothing happened. The flood lights extinguished, tossing the whole scene back into darkness.

Inside the house, the kitchen light flicked on, and we all watched in horror as two figures struggled, framed by the window that overlooked the yard. One of the figures disappeared from view while the other moved back through the house, sprinting through the door. The flood lights popped on again, catching the black-clad person running toward the left and out of the frame.

"Aria wasn't the target."

I could feel three sets of eyes snap to me, and Crew asked, "What do you mean?"

"Whoever this was…they're after Reagan. No one but us knows Reagan moved in with me. Aria's assailant broke into the place they thought she'd been staying and attacked the tall, blonde woman they encountered."

"Then why is Aria still here and not being held hostage somewhere like Reagan's sister?"

"They realized they made a mistake. Saw Aria's face, realized she wasn't who they were after, and bolted."

"I suppose that does make a certain amount of sense," Lane gritted out. "Doesn't change the fact that our sister was *attacked*," he added in a hiss. He turned to Trey. "Send this to me so I can forward it onto Addie. The FBI might be able to get more out of it than you can."

"Fine."

I knew Trey only agreed so easily to avoid an argument. Emotions were high enough at the moment; we didn't need to add infighting to the mix. But I also knew he'd spend hours in front of his computer, scouring the footage from some usable information to figure out who'd done this to Aria.

Speaking of Aria, behind us came commotion at my front door, and we all turned to see Sutton and Thomas wheeling our baby sister out toward the ambulance.

"We're taking her to Boise!" Sutton shouted. "Any of you want to come with her?"

"I'll go," Crew said, stepping away from us. But he paused suddenly and swung around. "Has anyone called Mama?"

"Shit," Lane and Trey swore in unison.

"I'll do it," I said wearily. This was, after all, my fault.

Crew once again clapped me on the shoulder, then the three

of them dispersed, Trey and Lane toward Lane's SUV, Crew toward the ambulance.

With a deep breath, I withdrew my phone from my pocket and dialed Mama.

"What's wrong?" she asked when she answered.

She sounded far more alert than I would've expected so early in the morning, and I had to guess her mother's intuition had woken her.

"There was an…incident."

"Are you okay? Is Reagan?"

"Reagan and I are fine," I assured her. "But Aria was staying at the guest house, and she was attacked."

Mama sucked in a gasp, then let her breath out on a soft curse, a rarity for her. "I didn't even know she left. Is she okay? What's going on?"

"I don't know much right now," I admitted. "She got hit on the head, and there was a lot of blood. But she's in the ambulance, and they're taking her up to Boise. Crew is with her."

"Come get me. I'll be ready in five."

"Yes ma'am," I said, then hung up. My attention focused on my house across the field, where two figures stood backlit on the front porch.

My legs felt like lead as I trudged through the country grasses in that direction. A maelstrom of emotions tangled in my chest: rage, fear, and most insistent of them all…guilt.

"What happened?" West asked when I reached the base of the stairs.

"Aria was attacked," I said flatly. "Blunt force trauma to her head. They're taking her up to Boise."

"Let's go then," he said.

Not bothering with the steps, he jumped straight from the porch to the ground and beelined for his truck. He climbed in and turned it over, his headlights illuminating Reagan, staring at me wide-eyed. She had on one of my shirts and a pair of my sweats, her arms crossed over her chest.

"Is she going to be okay?" she asked softly.

I gave her the truth. "I don't know."

Without another word, she reached for me, and I grabbed her hand, holding it tightly as I helped her down the steps, like she was my lifeline, the one thing keeping me grounded in this hellscape.

When I climbed into the back with her, West shot me a confused look, and I said, "We have to pick up Mama."

He jerked his head in the approximation of a nod and sped away from my house, taking a right at the end of the long drive, heading toward the big house.

As promised, Mama waited on the front porch, her normally tan skin almost ghostly pale. Worry lined every inch of her face and body. She got in the passenger seat, and West reached for her, holding her hand the entire drive to Boise.

Walking into the hospital lobby hit me with an intense force of déjà vu. It hadn't even been a year since we'd rushed here in the middle of the night for a different sibling, waiting to see if Crew would be alright after being assaulted, abducted, and thrown fifty feet through the air in the wake of an explosion.

Mama approached the desk while I followed my twin into the waiting room, Reagan's hand clasped tightly in my own. She hadn't spoken a word since we left, and I didn't press her as we took a seat alongside my brothers. Truth be told, I didn't much feel like talking either.

We'd only been sitting there for about ten minutes when I saw a familiar brunette head weaving through the lobby, and I jumped to my feet, racing out to meet Sutton.

"What's going on?" I asked. "The front desk wouldn't give Mama any information."

"She woke up on the drive here," Sutton said. "She got hit pretty good on the head, but it seems to be more of a flesh wound. Split her skin open and turned into a bleeder. I assume they'll run tests to rule out a brain bleed. Worst she'll come out with is some stitches and a concussion."

Sighs of relief echoed from behind me as my body sagged with the same emotion, and I glanced over my shoulder to see my family standing behind me. Reagan reached for me, twining her fingers with mine, and I dragged her into my side. Wrapped my arm around her, needing to feel her warmth and vitality against me.

She was okay.

My sister was going to be okay.

Everything was *okay*.

Except it wasn't.

So fucking far from it, in fact.

Mama pushed past me and gathered Sutton in a hug. "Thank you," she whispered. "Thank you for taking care of our girl."

Sutton smiled at my mom. "Just doing my job, Birdie. Plus, y'all are like family."

Her eyes swept over the Lawless crew, though I didn't miss the blip of…was it pain? that flashed across her eyes when they presumably landed on Lane.

One day, I'd have to sit my big brother down and ask him what the hell happened between them.

Once Sutton and Thomas left, we retreated to the waiting room.

The chairs were horribly uncomfortable, but I slouched down and did my best to shut my mind off for a while.

Naturally, it didn't work, though I must've zoned out for a lengthy period of time, because the next thing I knew, a doctor was pushing in the room, calling for Aria's family.

All of us stood, and the doctor blinked in surprise at the five hulking men standing before him.

"How is she?" Mama asked.

"Stable," the doctor said, and we breathed a collective sigh of relief. "She sustained a concussion and needed twelve stitches to patch up the wound on her skull, but the CT scan didn't reveal any internal bleeding or brain swelling."

"Oh, thank the goddesses," Reagan whispered.

"When can we see her?"

"I can take two of you back right now," the doctor said. "She's awake and asking for her mom."

Mama stepped forward, then turned and faced us. Before my brothers and I could launch into an argument about which of us was going first, Mama reached for me.

"You found her, Finny."

Hardly a good enough reason for me to face her first, but I wasn't about to say no to my mother. Still, as we walked down the long hall behind the doctor, into the emergency area, I couldn't stop my hands from shaking.

Mama merely squeezed tighter.

As we approached the end of the cordoned off emergency bays, the only one with the curtains entirely concealing it, the doctor explained, "She's not in a room because we'll be discharging her shortly."

"Oh, that's excellent news," Mama said.

"Like I said, there's no cause for concern. The concussion of course will have to be monitored, but I can send you home with infor—"

Mama cut him off before he could finish. "No offense, doctor, but I have six sons. I know how to handle a concussion."

Doc grinned. "Fair enough."

He reached for the curtain and pulled it back, revealing Aria laying on the hospital bed. A bandage wrapped around her head, and tubes ran from her arms, one connected to a bag of fluid, the other to one of blood, though both were nearly empty.

"She lost quite a bit from that head wound, which caused the loss of consciousness," he explained. "We needed to replenish it."

Aria's face was as white as the sheets she laid on.

"Please tell me you brought me other clothes," she said, her eyes still closed. She picked at the gown. "This thing is fucking horrible, and what I was wearing is ruined."

"Language," Mama said automatically, though there was no heat behind it. She walked around to Aria's side and bent to press a gentle kiss to her forehead, smoothing back her hair. "You scared me, my girl."

"I'm sorry," Aria whispered, a tear breaking free from her eye and tracking down her cheek.

"No," I said firmly, going to her other side and gathering her hand in mine. "*I* am the one who's sorry."

Aria's eyes flew open. "Finny," she breathed.

"Hey, Ari."

Her brow furrowed, but she winced, eyes falling shut again. "What do you have to be sorry for?"

"I left you unprotected."

Aria snorted weakly. "I've stayed in that house hundreds of times before with no issue. This is *not* your fault," she stated with a vehemence that belied her current invalidity.

"She's right, Finn," Mama said. "The only person at fault here is the fucker who attacked her."

"Mama!" Aria and I gasped in unison.

Mama's grin was a bit feral. To me, she said, "Find whoever did this, Finny."

"I will," I promised.

thirty

. . .

REAGAN

THE LONGER I sat in that waiting room, the more one thing became abundantly clear to me: I didn't belong there.

I wasn't part of this family.

In fact, I was the reason they currently suffered. I was the reason Aria laid in a hospital bed with her head split open.

I'd never forgive myself for that.

Panic crested higher and higher, choking off my air, blurring the edges of my vision. The walls seemed to be closing in around me, and though I tried my hardest to marshal my breathing, to calm, my heart rate still spiked.

I needed to get out of here.

And fast.

Glancing around the waiting room, I searched for the easiest escape route. Even if I got free without alerting the family, the ranch wasn't exactly up the street. I was *miles* from there. Hell, we weren't even in the same county anymore.

But...we were in Boise, which meant I had Uber at my disposal.

Mind made up, I tapped West on the shoulder. "I'm going to

run to the bathroom," I said, surprising myself when my voice came out even.

He nodded, not worried about me in the slightest. We were, after all, in a hospital.

I *did* go to the bathroom, but only to be away from prying eyes while I called for a car and got myself together.

Splashing cold water on my face, I met my own wild gaze on the mirror and spoke softly.

"You're okay," I assured myself. "You're fine. Aria is okay. Just get out. Get out and everything will be okay."

With shaky fingers, I got out my phone, pulled up the Uber app, and booked a car. The fee to get back to Dusk Valley was astronomical, and I knew my disappearance would send the entire Lawless family into a tizzy, but I couldn't sit around, acting like nothing was wrong while also serving as a blatant reminder of Aria's attack.

My ride arrived in under five minutes, the sky a pre-dawn grey. I quickly snuck out of the hospital, taking one final look at the family. Finn and Birdie hadn't yet returned, and the rest of them stood around, chatting, tentative smiles on their faces over the fact that the youngest of them would be okay.

The trip back to Dusk Valley was silent, which was preferable, though as we got closer to the ranch, I did have to speak up to direct the driver to Finn's house. GPS out here wasn't entirely reliable.

Once we pulled to a stop in front of Finn's house, I navigated back into the app, left the driver a hefty tip for taking such a long trip in the middle of the night, thanked him, and headed inside. The security system beeped insistently when I opened the door, so I quickly typed in the code to disarm it. Then I armed it once again and walked around the house to make sure all the doors and windows were secure. Being here alone after what happened to Aria was surely playing with fire, but I wasn't so reckless as to not ensure I was safe.

Or at least had the illusion of safety.

I hadn't been living with Finn long, but two weeks was enough that my things were strewn all over the house. Clothes in the laundry downstairs, toiletries and other personal care products in the guest bathroom. My favorite coffee mug—the one I'd bought as a souvenir when Lainey and I had visited all those years ago—sat dirty in the kitchen sink, and my laptop, glasses, and an old, dog-eared paperback were strewn across the coffee table in the living room.

I went to the guest room and dug my suitcases out of the closet, throwing my clothes directly from the dresser into the biggest one, not bothering with neatness. I could sort everything when I got to wherever I was going.

I should've known it wouldn't be that easy.

"Reagan!"

His voice startled but didn't surprise me. When the brothers realized I hadn't come back from the bathroom, Finn would've raced home.

Sighing, I sat on the bed with my head in my hands, heels of them digging into my eye sockets. Why hadn't I moved faster? Grabbed only the essentials and bolted?

"Reagan?" he called again, voice closer now.

I *felt* it when he appeared in the doorway. The energy in the room shifted, my body so deeply in tune with his, I'd recognize him deaf and blind in a crowd.

"Belle?" he asked softer. "What's going on?"

I snorted humorlessly. "Isn't it obvious? I'm leaving."

"Like hell you are."

Still refusing to look at him, I got up and headed back to the dresser, kneeling to open the bottom drawer and scoop the clothes out of it.

"C'mon, Finn. We both know I can't stay."

"I don't see why not."

Angrily, I threw the clothes down, pajama shorts and tanks flying all over, landing haphazardly on the floor and bed.

Then I faced him.

"Because I'm the reason your sister is in the hospital right now!" I shouted. "How the fuck can you even stand to look at me?"

All the fight seemed to leave Finn. I hadn't noticed until they relaxed that his muscles had been tense, bracing.

His expression morphed into one of sympathy.

"Is that what you think? That this is your fault?"

I rolled my eyes at his gentle tone. Like I was some scared, wild animal, ready to bolt at the first sign of aggression.

"It *is* my fault. The piece of shit who attacked her was here for *me*." I emphasized the word with a finger to my chest. "You know it, I know it, your whole fucking family knows it."

"*Baby*." Finn crossed the room in three long strides and pulled me in, crushing me against his chest. My arms hung limply at my sides. "*None* of this is your fault. The only person responsible is the one who attacked Aria."

I shoved out of his embrace, stalking across the room, though the few feet of space between us was not nearly enough. There wasn't anywhere in the world I could go that was far enough for me to not feel pulled to him, like a magnet drawn to a metal surface.

Crossing my arms over my chest, I stared him down.

"You can say that until you're blue in the face, Finn, but we both know it's bullshit. That man was here for *me*. And Aria got caught in the crossfire. I will *never* forgive myself for that."

"So you're just going to run?"

"I'm not running. I'm removing myself from the situation in order to protect you and your family."

"Bullshit," he spat. "You're *running*, just like you did seven years ago."

I gasped, rearing back like he'd slapped me.

"How *dare* you? I left because I had to. *You* didn't even stay! We agreed to one night."

"Maybe so, but you stayed away because you were afraid. You were scared then, and you're scared now."

"Scared of what, exactly? The worst has already happened, Finn. My sister is *missing* and will probably die without us ever knowing what happened to her. Your sister was *attacked.*"

"You're scared of what you feel for me. Of what's happening between us. Of how fucking *right* it feels when we're together."

"I don't know what you're talking about."

A weak, hurtful lie.

Finn only laughed.

"I *know* you feel it, Reagan. So stop lying to yourself, and stop lying to me."

My gaze narrowed on him. "Did you ever stop to think that I'm doing this *because* I care about you? And your family? And refuse to be the reason another one of you winds up hurt?"

"Afraid you don't have a choice, belle," he said. "I knew what I was getting into when you came here, and you are not responsible for the safety of my family." In a flash, he was in front of me and hauling me into another crushing hug. "Aria is going to be okay, and so is your sister. None of what's happened is your fault."

"All of it is my fault," I mumbled into his chest, but my argument was quickly losing steam.

I didn't *want* to run. I'd never felt more at home than I did in Finn's arms.

But once again, I faced the cost of our being together, and if people continued to get hurt, it wasn't a price I was willing to pay.

"Stop punishing yourself, Reagan. You're only hurting us both."

Though I hadn't stopped to consider it, I had to admit, since I'd made the decision to leave, my heart felt like it had shattered in my chest. Finn's proximity was a balm, drawing the broken parts back in and piecing them together.

"Do you want me to beg?" he asked when I didn't immediately respond. "I'll get on my fucking knees and beg. *Please*, belle. Don't go."

"I don't want to," I admitted.

"You belong right here with me," he said softly, pressing a kiss against my hair. "I know staying when every fiber of your being is begging you to run isn't easy, but I need you to. For me. For *us*."

I retreated enough to look up at him. "You know what that's like?"

He chuckled. "Baby, I was in the Army. In active warzones. Of course I know what that's like."

Rolling my eyes, I said, "That's totally different."

"You're right," he agreed. "Then, my and the lives of West and our team were on the line. Here…well, I have to admit, I don't think I could survive without you."

I shook my head. "No, Finn. You'd be fine without me. But me? Right here, in your arms? It's where I'm safest. And if I didn't have it anymore, who knows what would happen to me."

"Yet you tried to run," he said, slightly teasing.

"I'm scared," I admitted. "Of how…*big* I feel for you. And how my staying could only get more people hurt."

"Me too," he agreed. "But I'm right here with you." His hands shifted from where they were banded low on my waist to grab my hands, bringing them between us and pressing a lingering kiss to my knuckles. "What can I do to make it easier?"

"Everyone I've ever loved, ever felt like I couldn't live without, I've been forced to learn how to. First my parents, and now Lainey—"

"Lainey is coming home," he cut in, but I ignored him.

"I can't lose you too," I whispered. "So please be patient with me."

"I can do that," he promised.

For a moment, we clung to each other in the silence, swaying back and forth to music only we could hear.

Then Finn said, "Feel free to tell me to fuck off but how would you feel about moving into my room?"

Resting my chin on his chest, I stared up at him. "You sure?"

"Positive," he replied easily. "I don't want to go another day without waking up beside you or falling asleep next to you."

I grinned, and he ducked a bit to kiss me.

When he released me, I hooked my thumb over my shoulder at my suitcase.

"Guess it's a good thing I already started packing."

thirty-one

. . .

FINN

A **PHONE RING** cut through the dark stillness of the bedroom.

Instantly, my hackles rose.

Nothing good came from phone calls after midnight.

Rolling away from Reagan, who stirred when I shifted, I swiped my phone off my nightstand, ready to answer.

Mine wasn't ringing.

"Baby," I whispered to Reagan as I flipped the lamp on. "It's yours."

Reagan sat up in a flash, the sheet pooling around her waist, revealing the oversized Lawless Rescue & Dude Ranch tee of mine she'd thrown on before we passed out only a few hours ago.

"Hello?" Her voice shook on the single word.

"It should've been you."

I could hear the speaker clear as day, though they were distorted by some sort of voice altering software.

"Who is this?" Reagan hissed, tone stronger, eyes steely.

"Only one way to find out."

"Which is?"

"Come to me. Lainey is waiting for you."

"Tell me where you are."

"Not until you agree."

Reagan let out a harsh laugh. "That will never happen."

"Then we'll have to do this the hard way."

My hand whipped out, taking the phone from Reagan before she could protest.

"Listen here, fucker. Do you know who I am?"

"Finn Lawless," the mechanical voice spat. "The bastard my girl is shacking up with."

"She's not your girl. She. Is. *Mine*. And since you know who I am, you can trust me when I tell you this: when I find out who *you* are, the things I will do to you for causing Reagan this pain and stress will make the interrogation techniques I used as a Ranger look like child's play. Do you understand me?"

The laughter that followed my statement was nothing short of menacing, sending cold tendrils of fear down my spine.

There was no warmth to it. I could describe it as nothing but pure evil.

"Happy hunting."

Then the line went dead.

Rage overtook me as I whipped the phone across the room, where it slammed into the wall, leaving a dent in the drywall, before falling to the floor.

Too late, I realized it was Reagan's.

"Fuck," I breathed, my chest heaving from exertion like I'd run a marathon and not had a simple phone conversation with, arguably, a crazed psychopath. "I'm sorry."

Reagan rose and shuffled to the phone, picking it up and inspecting it for damage.

"It's okay," she murmured when she returned to the bed. "No harm done."

I huffed out a laugh and gestured at my ruined wall. "A *lot* of harm was done."

Reagan flopped backward, turning on her side and curling into a ball. Her eyes focused on some middle distance, here with me physically but not mentally.

"I fucking hate this, Finn. I want Lainey home. And I want to feel safe."

"Do you…not feel safe with me?"

She shook her head. "No, that's not what I mean. There's this invisible threat to *all* of us. And Lainey has to deal with this fucker *every day*. Who knows what he's doing to her."

Tears sprang forth from her eyes immediately, like a faucet turned on full blast. The flood gates had opened, sobs racking her body hard enough that the entire bed shook with the force of them. I curled myself around her, shielding her, holding her together while she fell apart.

I could not imagine her pain. Could not comprehend what it would be like to have my twin missing, like half of my being had been ripped away.

I wished there was something I could do to carry this burden for her. I didn't like feeling useless, hated that the best I could offer was giving her a soft place to land when she needed to break.

When she at last quieted, I brushed her hair out of her eyes and pressed a kiss to her forehead.

She smiled, grateful but also a touch rueful. "I'm sorry."

"*Never* apologize for your feelings, belle. I want you to always be honest with me, and that includes not hiding your emotions. Big, small, happy, sad. Everything in between. I want them all."

"Greedy."

"Care about you," I retorted.

"In the interest of full transparency then," she started, and I had a feeling I wasn't going to like what came next. "There's more I need to tell you."

I groaned. "Out with it then."

"This isn't the first time I've gotten a call like this," she admitted quietly. She didn't look at me, and her fingers traced nonsensical patterns across my chest, as though that would distract me.

Once again, rage seized me.

"How many?" I ground out, trying to keep my composure.

"A couple times a week since I got back to town. There have been texts too."

"Do you still have them?" She nodded, waving her phone at me. My hand moved between us, to her chin, clasping it between my thumb and forefinger. Tilting it back until our eyes met. "Nothing and no one is going to hurt you, Reagan. I promise you that. But I can't protect you if you don't tell me what you need protection from."

"I know, and I'm sorry. I was hoping they would go away."

"None of this will go away until Lainey is home and the fucker responsible is dead."

She nodded emphatically in agreement.

"Whatever it takes."

"We need to loop Lane in on this."

"Fine," she said. "But can it wait until the morning?"

Her voice had gone sleepy, and she burrowed deeper into my embrace. I shifted only enough to grip the comforter and drag it over both of us.

Reagan was already out.

I sent a text to Lane before trying—and failing—to do the same.

THE FOLLOWING MORNING, we headed over to the big house for our meeting with Lane. Naturally, all of my brothers, except Crew, who was on shift, were already there and fussing over Aria. My baby sister sat in the den, the white bandage wrapped around her head stark against her tan skin. Dark shadows had taken up residence under her eyes.

I walked right to her, dropping down at her side and gingerly pulling her into an embrace.

"I am so sorry," I murmured into her hair, doing my best to keep my emotions in check.

"Shut up," she said, completely with an eye roll that had her wincing. "It's not your fault."

Reagan came and knelt in front of us, hands on Aria's knees. "You're right. It's mine."

Aria and I groaned in unison.

"Belle…" I warned.

"It's no one's fault," Aria stated firmly. "I should've told you I was coming over."

"And I would've told you not to."

Aria nodded in agreement. I could tell there was more she wanted to say, but not in a room full of her brothers.

Pressing a kiss to her temple, I said, "We'll talk about it later."

She nodded, burrowing deeper into my side. Reagan sat down on my left, and I swung my arm around her.

Lane walked in, steaming Lawless Rescue and Dude Ranch mug in hand, and took stock of the room. West and Trey sat on the other side of the couch, Mama in her easy chair.

Shaking his head, he muttered, "Whole fucking family for a victim statement."

"That *victim* is our baby sister," Trey ground out. "Of course we're here."

"I'm not a victim," Aria said. "Stop calling me that."

Lane raised his hands in surrender, then sank into the armchair across from the couch. He pulled out his work phone and placed it in the center of the coffee table on which Aria's feet were propped, already recording. The rest of us went silent.

As he ran through his usual spiel with file number, date, time, and interviewee, he also withdrew his trusty spiral-bound note-book from his pocket and clicked a pen open.

"Can you tell me what happened the other night?"

Aria took a deep, preparatory breath, and Reagan reached across my lap for her hand.

"Mama and I got in a fight," Aria started, eyes avoiding the part of the room where Mama sat.

"It wasn't a *fight*," Mama said. "Just a disagreement."

Aria waved her off. "The particulars aren't important. I needed out, and you all know Finn's guest house is my favorite place to go. And since Reagan had moved in with him, I knew it was empty."

"You also know the only reason Reagan moved in with me is because someone broke in and left her a threatening message," I ground out.

"Yeah well, I wasn't exactly thinking clearly."

"So you went to Finn's," Lane stated, getting the interview back on track.

"Right," Aria said. "I was working on a new song, and when I came out of that haze, I realized how late it had gotten. So I got up to get something to drink before going to sleep, and—"

Her breaths increased, and her eyes slammed shut. I wrapped her up tighter, and Reagan's fingers blanched white from Aria gripping them so tightly.

"Sorry," she said hoarsely, sniffing back unshed tears.

"It's okay, Ari," Lane said. "Take your time."

"I didn't really see anything," she finally managed to gasp. "I was at the sink in the kitchen, and an arm came around my waist, and something cold and hard pressed against my temple."

"Describe them," Lane prompted.

"It was definitely a man," Aria said slowly, eyes unfocused, as though she was a thousand miles away. "Deep voice, thick, dark hair on his forearms. A few inches taller than me."

Aria was on the tall side for a woman, only a few inches shy of six feet, so that gave us a good estimate of her attacker's height.

"What did he say to you?"

"'Make a sound, Reagan, and I'll kill anyone who tries to save you.'"

"Fuck," Reagan breathed. "I told you this was my fault." Then to Aria she said, "I am so sorry, Ari."

"Stop that!" Aria pulled her hand away from Reagan. "It is *no one's* fault but the asshole who did this."

"What happened next?" Lane asked.

"I told him I wasn't Reagan, and he spun me to face him." Aria held up her hand before Lane could speak again. "He was wearing a ski mask. Best I can tell you is he was white and his eyes were an unremarkable shade of brown."

"Better than nothing," West muttered as Lane jotted down notes.

Trey said, "Height at least matches the figure on the security footage."

"You looked at footage from the house?" Reagan asked.

Trey answered for me. "Yeah, but I meant from the bar the night Lainey was taken."

All attention shot to him. Even Lane appeared surprised.

"How long have you been sitting on *that* information?" the sheriff asked.

"Since the day Benny handed over the tapes."

"And why didn't you tell me?"

"Because it didn't show anything actionable. Her assailant was dressed head to toe in black, and he pounced on her as soon as she left the bar. It was pretty dark, and you know that lot isn't well-lit, but if I had to guess, he drugged her somehow. One minute she was fighting him, and the next she slumped in his arms. He carried her out of frame, and that was it. None of the other cameras in town picked up a vehicle immediately afterward, so I had to guess he took one of the lesser traveled routes. The whole thing was over in less than three minutes."

Next to me, Reagan's face had gone white, but not from distress.

No, she was vibrating with rage.

"I'm going to find him, and I'm going to kill him."

thirty-two

. . .

REAGAN

EVERYONE CHUCKLED AT ME, but judging by the way
Finn's hand tightened around mine, he knew I wasn't joking.

Lane theatrically stuck his fingers in his ears. "I didn't hear
that."

"Stiff," West muttered, too low for anyone but me and Finn
to hear. Finn choked on a laugh, but I remained still.

So much anger coursed through me, making it difficult to
focus on what was happening around me. All I could do was
imagine Lainey in those moments she was being abducted, fear
sending ice through my veins as though I was living through the
ordeal myself.

"Where are we at on the footage from seven years ago?"
Lane asked Trey suddenly.

"I managed to locate a tape from April of that year, but it
didn't have anything from the day in question. I'm close,
though," he added, flexing his fingers. "I can feel it."

"Work faster."

All the Lawlesses' eyes darted to me.

"I'm going as quickly as I can," Trey gritted out.

"You're not doing enough!" I exploded, rising to my feet and moving to tower over him. "She's been gone for *three months*, Trey! I don't know why she isn't dead yet, but the longer it takes us to find her, the lower the chances of her coming home alive. And I will not survive if that's the case. Do you understand me? If she dies, *I die*."

The truth of that statement settled over the room like a thick shroud. I'd surprised even myself by how deeply I meant that. Finn or no Finn, without my sister, I could see no point in living, no reason to carry on without her.

A gentle touch found the small of my back, and I turned into Finn's embrace instantly. He banded his arms around me as I buried my face in his chest and fell apart.

Goddesses, please grant me strength.

I was so fucking tired. Mentally and emotionally. I felt like a pendulum swinging between happy and sad, joy and rage. I wanted normalcy, to go back to a time when Lainey was home and safe.

And I wanted to be able to enjoy this budding romance with Finn without guilt hanging over my head like a guillotine.

Once I managed to collect myself, I pulled back from Finn and gave him a watery smile, brushing my fingers over the dampened front of his shirt.

He rested his forehead against mine and whispered, "I've got you, baby. But you have to fight. For Lainey, and for us."

All I could do was nod.

Then Aspen piped up. "Where are we at on those journal pages, Sheriff?"

Finn helped me wipe my tears from my face before I faced his family again.

Lane appeared surprised. "How do you know about the journal?"

Aspen grinned. "You didn't think you were the only one working this case, did you?" She rolled her eyes. "Get to know me already, big brother."

"I'm not your brother," Lane muttered, pinching the bridge of his nose.

"Not yet!" Aspen sing-songed.

The sheriff released a world-weary sigh and looked at me. "I'm assuming this is your doing?"

I shrugged. "I thought it couldn't hurt to have another set of eyes on this thing."

"And, in the interest of full disclosure," Finn started, turning away from me to look at his brother, "West and I have also been working on it too."

"You fucking people," Lane said under his breath, catching a stern look from Mama.

"You love us," West grinned.

Lane raised a hand and folded his fingers over his palm in an *out with it* gesture.

"We received a…tip," Finn started, cutting his eyes to me. I appreciated the discretion. There was no fucking way Lane would approve of what they'd been doing based on a dream I'd had.

"What kind of tip? Why didn't the department receive this 'tip'?"

"Don't worry about the why of it all," Finn said, waving a dismissive hand. "The point is, West and I have been doing some aerial recon of farmhouses and land in the area where someone may be keeping Lainey."

"And?"

"And," West stepped in, "we've managed to narrow it down to several properties. It's not much, but it's a start."

"Was this tip obtained illegally?" Lane asked.

"No," Finn said quickly. "And it came from a reliable source."

Lane raised his hands in surrender. "Fair enough. I want everything you have on my desk by the end of the day."

"Fine."

"Can we circle back to the journal now?" I asked.

"We're still analyzing them," Lane admitted. "Trying to create a timeline of the harassment by cross-checking texts she received with her journal entries."

Aspen looked at me. "Has anything jumped out at you?"

I swallowed hard. "I, uh…I haven't read them."

"Why not?" Lane asked, a sharp edge to his tone that I didn't appreciate.

Neither did Aspen. She cut him with a look that would've taken down lesser men. To me, she said, "It's gotta be hard."

All I could do was nod.

Facing my sister's inner musings, looking at her handwriting and hearing her voice in my head as I read her words—I hadn't been ready.

But maybe now was the time to bite the bullet.

Maybe I'd be able to tease something out of them the police hadn't been able to.

Facing Lane again, I said, "Aspen is right. It *is* hard. But they could hold some key that only I can decode."

"I doubt there's anything there for you to find that we haven't already, but I can get you a copy."

I held up a hand. "Not necessary. I have my own."

Lane raised a brow but wisely didn't press the issue further. *Smart man.* I found my patience where his bureaucratic bullshit was concerned sorely lacking at the moment.

"Well then," Lane said, rising to his feet, flipping his notebook closed and stuffing it back into his pocket. "We've all got our marching orders." Glancing around the room, he looked each of us in the eye in turn. "*Everything* goes through me. Understood?"

I didn't miss the way he lingered on Finn and West, as if the cowboys of the family had a tendency to go, well, a little cowboy on occasion.

Everyone, including the twins, nodded in assent.

The family dispersed shortly after, Finn leaving me with a

lingering but relatively chaste kiss before he snagged a muffin and walked out the door. I watched him eat up the lawn and head down the hill toward the barn, eyes remaining on him until he was out of sight.

"Did you know?" Aspen asked. "About the twins?"

I nodded. "I went up with them once."

"Did you…ask them to do that?"

"Of course not! I didn't even consider the possibility."

"But they were operating on your 'tip,'" she guessed, and I nodded.

"I had a dream," I admitted. "More of a nightmare, really. About the farmhouse. About Lainey chained up in the basement. I woke up screaming, and Finn came to check on me, so I told him about it."

"Why didn't you tell *me*?"

Snorting, I canted my head to the side and pursed my lips in a *get real* expression. "C'mon, Aspen. Would you have believed me? It was a *dream*. Not a vision or anything kooky like that."

Aspen shrugged, not bothering to refute me. "Obviously the twins think differently."

Even if Finn and West weren't dialed into the same freaky twin frequency as me and Lainey, I somehow knew Finn would've taken me seriously anyway.

Maybe I should've trusted Aspen to do the same.

"Do you have any ideas or leads?" I asked her.

Aspen shook her head. "I've gotten a number of tip calls thanks to your posters, but so far, nothing has panned out." Glancing across the room, she leveled Trey with a look. "We *really* need that security footage from seven years ago."

"I'm working on it."

I rolled my eyes. "You've been *working on it* for months."

"Do you want to try it?" Trey asked, his irritation evident. "Let's see how far you get."

"Knock it off," Birdie said softly. "You're all working so hard on this. Cut each other some slack."

Trey rose from his seat, walked over to Birdie, pressed a kiss to her cheek, then left.

Hopefully to get back to work on that footage.

I had a task of my own to complete and headed home not long after.

As difficult as I knew it would be, being blindsided by any information that may come out about my sister as a result of those journals would be far worse.

I didn't want any surprises, and the time had come to face them.

thirty-three

. . .

REAGAN

FINN'S HANDS were on my waist, his mouth on my neck the second we walked in the house later that evening, smelling like fresh air and hay.

Pushing him away nearly killed me when all I wanted to do was bury my face in the warmth of his skin.

"What's wrong?" he asked when I pulled back, his brow furrowed in concern.

I reached up and smoothed the creased skin.

"I need to read Lainey's journals."

Finn's expression cleared. "Okay, no problem. West and I were going to go up in the plane again anyway."

"This close to sunset?"

He nodded. "We think it's a good idea to check the areas we've flagged to see if there is any nighttime activity. You know, lights on, vehicles in the drive. That sort of thing."

"That sounds like a great idea," I agreed.

"You gonna be okay here alone?"

"Of course."

"Arm the system the second I leave, and call one of my brothers if you need anything."

"Yes, daddy."

Finn stilled, and his pupils expanded, irises going dark and stormy. Reaching for me, he gripped my ass and dragged me against him. I could hardly protest before his mouth descended on mine.

The kiss was crushing and punishing, feral and reckless.

I fucking loved it.

The way his tongue stroked mine, his teeth nipping my lips, his fingers digging into my flesh hard enough to bruise.

When he slowed the kiss and broke free, both of us were breathing hard.

"I'll show you 'daddy' later, belle."

I grinned. "Promise?"

"Promise."

With a final quick kiss to my mouth, he stepped away to call his twin. In ten minutes, the two drove away from Finn's house.

I waited another ten to be sure they didn't come back for anything before I made my move.

What Finn didn't know wouldn't hurt him, and I knew without a doubt he would *not* approve of my own evening excursion.

***

I EXPERIENCED ONLY a moment of trepidation as I parked in the deserted lot at Sunset Ridge. If something were to happen to me, there would be no one to hear my struggles, no one nearby to come if I called for help.

But this was something I had to do, and this ridge seemed like the best place to do it.

Pushing my misgivings to the side, I got out, collected my camera bag and the box of Lainey's journal pages, and moved toward the edge of the cliff.

Delaying the inevitable, I took far too much time setting up my cameras, one for a timelapse of the sunset, and the other to snap shots as I felt like it. Once that was taken care of, I spread out a blanket I'd stolen from Finn's linen closet and dropped onto it.

I dragged the box to my side but didn't open it and withdraw the first stack of pages right away. Instead, I stared out at the horizon, allowing it to soothe me. I highly doubted I'd find anything in the journals that would shock me or turn the tide of the investigation into Lainey's disappearance, but I knew I needed to rip this bandage off.

At last, I lifted the lid and pulled out the bundle representing Lainey's first journal.

The one I got her for that first birthday after Mom and Dad died.

Was I ready to confront those demons?

Never.

But I didn't have a choice.

Inhaling deeply and willing myself to remain calm, I dropped my eyes to the first page.

Dear diary…

It seems so silly to write that. I'm a 23-year-old woman, not a teenager spilling her inconsequential high school dramas onto these pages. Though, at the time, those high school dramas sure felt awfully big and insurmountable, didn't they? Given what I've endured since, I'd give anything to go back…

My eyes blurred with tears almost instantly, some of them dropping free and splashing onto the pages.

Our parents' deaths had hit both of us hard. For me, the survivor's guilt was downright debilitating the first few months afterward. There had been days when I wished I'd died with them, simply so I wouldn't have to endure the unending agony of living without them—of remembering their final words and breaths.

While Lainey and I had talked at length about how we were feeling in those days, and had done our best to talk about the good times with Mom and Dad in an effort to keep their memories alive, I supposed I never stopped to consider what it had been like for her. For the first time, I'd experienced something she couldn't begin to understand. She'd been grieving for them, but also for *me*. Struggling with how to help me, while also recognizing the only way out was through.

Hours passed in a blink, my eyes and mind eating up the words faster than I could turn the pages.

Unsurprisingly, there wasn't anything I didn't already know, but I found myself reliving certain moments through Lainey's eyes. Laughing at her commentary on the morning after a lost night in which we drank too much tequila and danced on the bar at our local dive. Remembering the trips we'd taken in the early days of Twin Flames.

The bad days had been rock bottom, a black pit I wasn't sure we'd ever claw our way out of.

But being reminded of the good days showed me that we *had*. And they were a good reminder that we still had each other.

At least, I hoped that was the case.

Lainey's journals were surprisingly stingy on the details of our time in Dusk Valley, only a few pages in recap of our hikes and the photos she couldn't wait to develop.

Mentions of the guy she'd slept with didn't begin until a few weeks after our return.

He messaged me again. I keep blocking his number, and he just keeps getting new ones. I've considered changing mine, but I refuse to let

him win. I know I need to tell Reagan what's going on, but I don't
think I could stand to see that "I told you so" look in her eyes…

"Oh, Lainey…"

I never would've judged her for that—which she learned when she did finally tell me. After all, I wasn't a saint and had participated in a hook up of my own that night.

But what I'd never understood is why she didn't tell me the guy's name. Why hadn't she given me some sort of identifying information to use in case he ever showed up—or that I could pass on to the police if she ever went missing?

Then again, this kind of escalation had never been on our radar. We thought that, because we lived across the country, we were safe.

I wondered, what would've happened if I hadn't gotten sick? If I'd been the one to come back to Dusk Valley? Would he have taken me? Lainey and I were twins, after all, and this guy had fixated on me since I'd arrived in town.

Once I'd gotten through those first months' worth of entries and past our return from Dusk Valley, I began scanning, knowing I didn't have time to read them all cover to cover. I looked for any mentions of names I didn't recognize or secrets she hadn't shared with me.

So intent on searching for information that stuck out, I nearly missed it.

The entry was dated three days before Lainey left for Dusk Valley, when we both realized I would be too sick to make the trip as originally planned.

I have to go back to Dusk Valley. It's not Reagan's fault. Shitty
timing for her to catch the flu, but it's not like she did it intentionally.
I am equal parts terrified and excited to return to Idaho. Excited,

because I've really honed my craft in the last seven years, and I am excited to shoot the landscape using my new skills. I love meeting new people, so I'm really looking forward to working with the Wallis family.

But I'm terrified because, for the first time since that night, I'll be within spitting distance of <u>him</u>. For all these years, I feel like I've been bracing myself, waiting for some ultimate showdown with my harasser.

And now, I'm willingly entering his ring.

Maybe he left, but I sincerely doubt it.

I hope LT is ready for a fight.

LT?

Who the fuck was LT?

Little turd? Loose trash? Lowly tool?

My imagination supplied childish nicknames, but I had to admit, I felt better for having thought them.

Taking the task more seriously, I ran through my mental Rolodex, searching through the names of all the people I'd met in Dusk Valley, trying to find the one that fit those initials.

Unfortunately, I came up with nothing.

The remaining few journal entries didn't yield anything else. She mentioned the pizza from Mozzy's, giving in to the colder temperatures and moving from her campsite into the motel, and her plan to check out the Swallow again. *I want to see if it's changed,* she'd written. *Maybe I'll run into Rea's soldier too.*

She'd be so fucking giddy to know Finn and I had made our way back to each other, and I couldn't wait to tell her.

When I finally looked up, the lower curve of the sun was kissing the horizon. Knowing I had seconds to capture it, I scrambled to my feet, piled the loose pages into the box, and grabbed my camera.

I allowed my mind to wander while I took photos, but by the

time the sun had fully sunk, the stars blinking to life, I hadn't come up with any ideas for who LT could be.

Having no desire to remain out here alone after dark, I quickly packed my things, stowed them in my SUV, and set off toward the ranch.

Thankfully, my phone remained free of messages from Finn, so I knew he and West hadn't touched back down and gone home yet.

Hopefully, I could beat him there.

thirty-four

. . .

REAGAN

WHAM.

At first, I thought I'd run something over, but I hadn't seen anything in the headlights, and the impact had come from behind. A quick glance in my rear view made my blood run cold.

Illuminated in the glow of my taillights was a truck, its headlights extinguished, grill and brush guard menacing in the red illumination.

"Oh, god," I breathed.

Picking up speed, I groped around my passenger seat in search of my phone. I'd wrapped my fingers around it when another crash came from the back, jolting me forward, the seatbelt digging painfully into my chest.

My phone slipped from my grip and flew out of reach.

Fuck fuck fuck.

I pressed the gas pedal down harder, desperate to create some space between me and the crazy fucker behind me. Glancing around, I searched in vain for some sort of landmark, something to tell me how close I was to the ranch drive.

Surely this person wouldn't follow me all the way home, right?

Likely not—especially not if they knew who I was, who Finn was, and I guessed that was the case. It would make perfect sense for this to be the same person that had been tormenting me for weeks.

The truck rammed into me once again, and it took every ounce of strength I had to keep my SUV steady and on the road.

Fuck, I should've listened to Finn and stayed home. But I'd been determined, certain I was safe as long as the sun was out.

Silly me.

My back bumper must've looked like an accordion by now, but the assailant matched my speed, increasing his, slamming into me once more.

The hit jarred my bones, forcing my hands off the steering wheel. I lost control, going too fast, spinning out on the gravel. I careened off the road—right into a tree.

All the breath vacated my lungs on impact, when the airbag deployed right into my chest.

Time seemed to halt before sensation returned to me all at once.

The hissing of the engine.

The cloud of smoke seeping into the cab and blotting out the night.

The excruciating pain in my left arm.

And beyond all of that…footsteps, growing closer by the second.

I couldn't move, not only because shifting jostled my arm in a way that had me swearing through the pain, but because I was pinned in, both by the seatbelt I couldn't unfasten and the steering column that had moved several feet closer in the crash.

All I could do was sit there and accept my fate.

A masked, shadowy figure appeared in my periphery, and I faced them, willing my brain to latch onto any defining characteristic.

But the darkness was too thick to see anything but an amorphous mass.

They reached for the door handle, wrenching on it, and I breathed a sigh of relief that it didn't budge, that the locks hadn't malfunctioned in the crash. The figure lifted their elbow, clearly about to smash out the window, but stilled when a distant voice cut through the night.

"Reagan? Oh my god, Crew, it's Reagan!"

Aspen. And she obviously had Crew with her.

Thank Hecate.

I'd take any Lawless man I could get right now.

At her voice, the dark figure bolted.

"Help!" I screamed, trying to twist in my seat, hoping they could hear me, pounding on the window with my fist. "I'm stuck! I'm still in the car!"

"Reagan!" Aspen cried when she reached the door, her phone light shining into my eyes, and I lifted my good arm to shield them. "Are you okay?"

I shook my head. "My arm. I think it's broken. And I'm stuck."

Crew appeared behind her. "We'll get you out, Reagan. I promise."

All I could do was nod. I trusted him, and he did this for a living. I was in good hands.

"Aspen?" I asked when Crew disappeared.

"Yeah?"

"Call Finn."

"Of course," she said, bringing her phone down and tapping on the screen, but she paused, tipping her face up. Was she... sniffing? "Do you smell that?"

For a moment, there was nothing but the scent of blood— wait, I was bleeding?

Goddesses, I was reliving the night Mom and Dad died.

At least I was alone this time.

"Gas," I said when I finally located the scent, fear sluicing down my spine.

"Gas," Aspen confirmed in horror. "Hey, hotshot! We've got gas!"

No sooner had the words left her mouth than did a whoosh sound from behind me, illuminating Aspen in a fiery glow a moment later.

"Get back, Aspen!" Crew shouted as he rejoined us.

Oh god, I was going to die in this fucking car. Trapped like a caged animal, burning alive without ever discovering what happened to my sister.

Tears fell rapidly, mixing with the blood I now knew to be coming from a cut above my left eye. I didn't even remember hitting it.

"Cover your face, Reagan!"

Wait, what?

Crew's words pulled me out of my spiral, and I did the best I could, turning slightly and shielding my face with my good arm, squeezing my eyes tightly shut.

A moment later, glass shattered and rained down on me, cool night air sweeping in and caressing my overheated skin.

"What about the fire?"

Yeah, those were the first words out of my mouth when I looked at Crew, his face framed in the now busted out window of my car.

Aspen chuckled, and Crew lifted a fire extinguisher.

"It's out," he said simply.

"He's a fucking Boy Scout," she said with a good-natured eye roll.

"Actually, I'm a firefighter."

"Oh, I know," she replied. "I just live to tease you."

"How are you guys even here? I mean…fuck, thank you. You saved my life."

"I had a meeting with some of my publishing team up in

Boise, and since Crew isn't on shift tonight, he came with. We were heading home when we spotted you."

"You were hit, weren't you?" Crew asked, and I nodded. "I thought I heard another vehicle take off, but I was so focused on checking on you, I didn't give it much thought."

"There was a truck. Big. Headlights off. Brush guard. They —" I cut off as a shiver rolled through me. Goddesses, I'd been so close to a fate much worse than some broken bones and a cut on my face. "I think they wanted to take me," I whispered. "I think this was the same person who took my sister."

"Shit," Crew and Aspen swore in unison.

A siren wailed in the distance, preceding the flashing blue lights from the approaching cavalry. From the opposite direction, a big black truck raced up and braked hard, skidding to a stop on the gravel. Another vehicle pulled up shortly after.

"Reagan!"

Finn.

"Over here!" Aspen called. "I'm warning you, though, take it easy. Looks like she's got a broken arm and a pretty nasty cut on her head."

She and Crew stepped back, and then he was there.

Reaching through the window to gently cup my cheeks, turning my head this way and that, examining me.

"Belle," he croaked out.

"Hey, soldier."

"You're okay?"

"I think so."

"Can you get out?"

I shook my head. "I'm stuck under the steering column."

"The boys will get you out," Crew said from behind Finn, inclining his head. I looked in the side mirror, which was miraculously undamaged, to see the fire truck fast approaching.

"Captain!"

Crew turned to the newcomer. "Tuck?"

Tuck jogged up. "Heard the call go out over the scanner, so I drove out."

Crew clapped him on the shoulder. "Thanks, man. We can assist these guys."

Behind the fire truck, several more vehicles pulled to a stop, Lane at their head, trailed by two more guys I vaguely recognized.

"Reporting for duty, Cap," the smaller of the two said.

"Childers, Burns. What the fuck are you guys doing here?"

They looked between him and Tuck. "Likely the same thing as the rest of you. Heard the call go out, wanted to come help."

"You're not getting overtime for this," Crew said in warning. "And we've still gotta show up bright and early tomorrow."

The guys made no move to leave, so Crew shrugged.

Before he could launch into an explanation of the scene, Lane arrived.

"What've we got?" he asked, all business.

"Why don't you let me be the judge of that, Sheriff?" a female voice said, one that sounded vaguely familiar, but I couldn't quite place.

"Be my guest," Lane grumbled, shifting to the side so Sutton, the paramedic, could examine me.

"Hey, Reagan."

"Hi."

"You doing okay?"

Nodding, I said, "Just want to get the fuck out of here."

"I think we can make that happen," she winked. "I'm going to do a cursory exam, stabilize you, and then the fire department will get you free."

Without waiting for a response from me, she proceeded to shine a penlight in my eyes, checking my pupils for proper dilation.

"I can't do anything about your arm until you're out, so I

need you to keep it close to your body and hold it as still as possible when they pull you out, okay?"

"Okay."

"Great. I'm going to put this cervical collar on you, then hand you over to the boys."

Leaning me forward as far as she could, Sutton slipped the collar around my neck and fastened the Velcro straps. Discomfort with the unnatural position set in, and I was already counting down the minutes until I could take it off.

At last, satisfied with her work, Sutton moved out of the way, and the firefighters took her place. There were a lot of machine sounds, drilling, slamming, and winching. Finally, the door popped open. Someone reached in, cut my seatbelt, and weaved it away from my body.

There was a halt in progress as the team debated the best way to extract me, Crew ultimately coming to my rescue with a suggestion that sounded like it would cause me the least amount of distress.

"They're going to put a hydraulic jack down here," he said, motioning to the space by my feet, "and lift the steering column off your lap enough to pull you out. It's going to hurt, but it'll be quick, okay?

I nodded again. I was grateful he and everyone else around was keeping me in the loop on what was happening. It went a long way to quelling my nerves.

"You're gonna be okay, belle," Finn said, giving me what I'm sure he thought was a reassuring smile that was more of a grimace.

The men continued to work, the sounds of the jack filling the space as it lifted the steering column. I hadn't realized how heavy it was, how much feeling I'd lost in my legs, until the weight disappeared and that prickling, pins and needles sensation took over.

With that out of the way, a backboard appeared and was situated at my side. On the count of three, three men gripped me, turning me and pulling me out.

A cry left me as my arm jostled, and I breathed harshly through my teeth, waiting for the worst of the pain to abate.

Finn was at my side a moment later, helping load me onto a stretcher, then grabbing my hand as Sutton and her partner wheeled it across the grass toward the ambulance.

thirty-five

• • •

FINN

TO SAY I was furious with Reagan would've been an understatement, but my rage was tempered by my worry.

When we arrived at the hospital—Dusk Valley Memorial, thankfully; her injuries weren't serious enough to warrant a trip to Boise—they wheeled her back for examination and tests. I was forced into the waiting room.

My mind ran rampant with worst case scenarios. Obviously, she'd broken her arm. The bones had been visible, for fuck's sake. But what about her legs? Back? *Head?*

Dropping heavily onto one of the world's most uncomfortable chairs, I propped my elbows on my knees and my head on my hands. Digging my palms into my eyes. So lost in my own thoughts I hadn't noticed my family come in.

Mama and Aria. Trey. Lane. Crew, West, and Aspen.

My twin sat beside me, hand falling to my shoulder.

He didn't speak, but I knew what he'd say if he did.

She's going to be fine. It's not your fault.

I shot him a glare, and his hand lifted.

The fuck it wasn't my fault. I never should've left her alone.

Then again, what had *she* been thinking, leaving the house by herself and not telling anyone where she was going?

And where the fuck had she been?

I had so many questions, and Reagan would be lucky if I ever let her out of my sight again—at least until we found the fucker who was after her.

A gentler touch found my opposite shoulder, and I shifted my head to find Aria.

"What are you even doing here?" I asked, my gentle tone at odds with my distress.

"Reagan is family," she said with a shrug.

Looking around the room at my siblings and mom gathered, I realized she meant that, and they all thought it. None of them would be here otherwise.

"Finn?"

I rose and turned in the direction of the voice, finding Sonya, a nurse who had worked here for most of my life, standing in the doorway.

"Is she okay?"

Sonya nodded. "She's asking for you."

Without another word, she left, and I rushed to follow her.

"She's really okay?" I asked when I caught up.

"Yes, but she did sustain a few injuries. I'll let her explain it all."

As long as she was breathing and would make a full recovery, I didn't give a fuck.

Even better news was that she wasn't in a private room, which meant they wouldn't need to keep her for observation. Instead, she was in a bay of the ER. When Sonya pulled the curtain back, I found Reagan laying on the bed in a hospital gown, looking so small and ghostly pale against the bright white sheets. An equally stark bandage wrapped around her head.

"Belle," I murmured, rushing to her side and taking her hand in mine.

"Soldier," she replied softly, eyes instantly welling.

"Shh," I breathed, cupping her face and brushing the fallen moisture off her cheeks. "You're okay."

"I was s-so scared," she whispered, her teeth chattering.

"I'm here, baby. I've got you."

"Miss Lindsey?"

"Yes?" she said to the doctor, eyes not shifting from my face.

"Your tests came back clear, so the good news is you don't have a concussion or any other brain injury."

"What's the bad news?" I asked.

"Unfortunately, based on the x-rays, surgery will be required to properly set her broken arm."

"*Surgery?*" Reagan croaked in disbelief. "It's that bad?"

"Afraid so. You snapped both your radius and ulna. The radius is the one that came through the skin, but the x-rays showed some bone fragments floating around in your arm. A surgeon will need to go in, clean those up, and set the breaks with pins."

"Fuck," Reagan breathed.

The doctor, at least, appeared sympathetic.

"Is that something you can do here?"

Doc shook his head. "She'll have to go up to Boise."

Reagan's eyes widened, face draining impossibly further of blood.

"I don't want surgery."

"I'm sorry, Miss Lindsey," Doc said, though she'd been speaking to me. "I'm afraid we don't have any other options."

"It's okay," I told her, trying to reassure us both. "You'll go under, they'll clean you up, and you'll come out good as new."

"You'll come with me?"

"I won't leave your side unless I absolutely have to," I promised.

The same vow I'd made myself earlier, but the tone was different now. My anger had dissipated entirely at seeing her in this bed, brow scrunched in obvious pain despite the IV on her skin pumping meds through her system. None of that mattered anymore. Not where she'd gone or why she'd been out alone.

All that mattered to me now was helping her heal in any way I could.

———

THREE DAYS LATER, we returned home—to my entire family waiting with balloons and food and far too much enthusiasm for Reagan to face in her post-surgery exhaustion.

I cleared them all out quickly while Reagan disappeared into our bedroom.

She was asleep before the last of my family members drove off.

We passed the next week in much the same way. Reagan had little energy and a lot of pain, so I spent a lot of the time quietly moving around the house, completing what little work I could remotely while Abel covered things at the ranch.

Despite the fact that we were home together all day, every day, I could sense her pulling away. I hoped this was merely her way of dealing with the pain, drawing into herself while she healed, but I had a bad feeling there was more to it than that.

Nine days after her operation, I woke up to find the bed at my side empty.

"Reagan?"

No answer.

Louder, I called for her again.

Still no response.

Rushing from bed, I first peeked into the bathroom and found it empty.

Checks of the kitchen, living room, and even the basement yielded the same result.

At last, I found her in the guest room, curled into a ball in the middle of the bed, her casted arm jutting out from her body and tucked awkwardly under her head.

"What're you doing in here?" I asked softly as I approached.

"Thinking."

Her voice was so small, so quiet, she might as well have been in a different dimension.

I sank down onto the bed at her side, but didn't touch her, somehow knowing that pulling her close would only drive her further away.

"Thinking about what?"

"About how this wouldn't have happened if you'd let me leave in the first place. Actually, I should've never come back here in the first place. My presence has done nothing but cause pain and problems for all of us."

I thought, after Aria's ordeal, we'd turned a corner. That she'd given up on this desire to protect us all by taking herself out of the equation.

Inexplicably, my anger rose.

When some people got mad, they exploded.

Me? I stilled, my entire body settling into a deathly calm.

Coddling her, whispering sweet nothings, making all the grand promises in the world clearly hadn't been enough for her to knock it off with these thoughts.

Maybe tough love would work.

"I can't keep doing this with you, Reagan," I said, tone even. "You pull me in then push me away. You let me fuck you like you belong to me, say all the right things, convince me you're mine, then try to run the next second. There are a lot of things I will endure for you, but I'm not some puppet whose strings you control. I'm a person with feelings, and right now, you're hurting them."

"You survived a *war*, Finn. I refused to be the thing that costs you your life now."

A derisive laugh escaped me. "Don't you see? You *are* my life now."

Reagan sat up abruptly, as though she'd been forced into position. Her mouth gaped, opening and closing as she searched for a response.

"I've lost everything," she finally said. "My parents. My sister." Her eyes swam with tears. "I draw the line at losing myself."

"Is that what you think is happening here? That being with me means losing yourself? That loving me means you don't love yourself?"

"I told you before that I couldn't do this with you. That Lainey had to be my top priority. And since I've gotten here, I feel like all I've done is get further away from that promise to myself. I'm losing myself in you, and I think by extension, I'm losing Lainey too."

"You think I haven't lost people too?" I exploded, losing the grip on my fury at last. "As you so helpfully mentioned, I've been to fucking *war*, Reagan. And lost my dad long before that. I know *exactly* what this feels like, so don't try to use your losses as some bullshit excuse to push me away."

"It's not bullshit," she said stubbornly.

But she'd softened slightly, as though her indecision between whether to stay or go balanced on a razor's edge, and my anger deflated like a pin stuck in a balloon.

We weren't getting anywhere screaming at each other.

There was a simple way to settle this, a single question I needed to ask. The answer would determine our future.

"Reagan?" I murmured in question.

"What?"

"Do you love me?"

I was certain I knew the answer, but acknowledging how deep her feelings for me ran would alter reality as we knew it— would force her to confront she was in too deep to run now. We were living one of those moments that we'd look back on, point at, and say, "*That's it. That's when it all changed.*"

"What does that matter?"

"Answer the fucking question, belle."

She was silent for long enough that I thought she'd ignore me altogether, wash her hands of us, and leave without another word.

Instead, she crossed the room and threw herself into my arms.

"You know I do," she said, the words muffled by the fabric of my tee.

"Then that's *all* that matters."

thirty-six

IN THE DRAMA and aftermath of my accident, I'd completely forgotten about the discovery I made in Lainey's journal.

Finn was blessedly at work, leaving me to my own devices for once. With, of course, strict instructions not to go outside.

"I'll be watching you," he'd promised as he left.

I'd rolled my eyes.

I was still in enough pain that my leaving wouldn't be a problem. I couldn't even shower without Finn's help, not that I'd tried. Plus, I had no desire for another showdown with my attacker.

Instead of going out, I'd make people come to me.

Lifting my phone from the couch at my side, I made my first call.

"Reagan?" Lane asked when he picked up. "You okay?"

His concern surprised me, but maybe all of the brothers were on high alert after I'd been run off the road and nearly killed.

"I'm fine," I assured him. "I'm calling because, before the accident, I finally read Lainey's journals, and I think I found something. Would you be able to come out to the house?"

"Sure…" he said, slowly. Skeptically.

"When should I expect you?"

"I'll leave the department now."

"Great, see you soon."

Next, I called Aspen, relayed the same information, and made the same request.

She beat Lane to the house, but only by a few minutes.

"Alright, what's this critical piece of info you found?" Lane asked dubiously.

Ignoring his tone, I flipped through the pages of Lainey's most recent journal until I located the section in question.

Then I passed it to Lane.

"Where did this come from?" he asked. "I've never seen this one before."

I waved him off, not having the energy to argue. "Not important."

He eyed me warily but flipped to the page I'd bookmarked and began to read.

Aspen scooted closer, reading alongside him.

"Know anyone with those initials?" I asked, tapping near the line that mentioned "LT".

"Not off the top of my head," Lane admitted, and Aspen nodded in agreement. "But I can run some census records and see what pops."

"What about the couple Lainey was supposed to shoot? Any luck there?"

Lane shook his head. "To be honest, I don't even think they exist."

"What?" I asked dumbly.

"The number has been disconnected. Emails bounce back. Addie hasn't been able to track down any Idaho residents—or even residents of adjacent states, for that matter—with those names."

"You don't think..." I trailed off, a horrifying realization occurring to me.

Lane nodded solemnly. "I think it's a safe bet whoever booked this photo session did so as an attempt to lure your sister out here."

"That makes no sense, though."

"What do you mean?" Aspen asked.

"We traded off trips. It was the one 'rule' we had. Alternating who got to travel. This one was supposed to be mine. But I came down with the flu a few days before I had to leave, so Lainey took my place last minute."

"I don't think that matters," Lane said. "I'm not a profiler, but...I think he wants both of you."

Before Aspen or I could respond, he pulled out his phone and made a call.

A woman answered.

"Caldwell."

"Hey, Addie. It's Lane."

"Hey," she replied, tone softening. "What's up?"

Lane shot both me and Aspen glares as if to say, *not a word*.

She and I exchanged a knowing glance but kept our mouths shut.

"We're working on the Lindsey case, and I've got a question I'm hoping you can answer from a profiler's perspective."

"Hit me."

"We've got an unsub here who has kidnapped a woman. Blonde, thirty..."

I tuned out while Lane gave Addie the background. Already familiar with the particulars, I allowed my mind to wander. Mainly, I hoped like hell Addie would be able to help us. Aspen was the best in the business, as far as I was concerned—she had, after all, been instrumental in taking down a serial killer who had been operating for over four decades—but even she struggled to find any leads. While Aspen wasn't cuffed by the same bureaucratic red tape as law enforcement, Addie, as an FBI agent, had resources even Lane, as the county sheriff, couldn't access.

Plus, her background in profiling could tell us *why* my sister had been taken, which could bring us one step closer to discovering *who* had taken her.

"Lainey has been missing for three months," Lane was saying when I mentally tuned back into the conversation. "But since Reagan's arrival, she's also been the target of harassment and two abduction attempts."

"He wants them both," Addie said quickly when he finished.

"That's what I was thinking too."

"They're likely surrogates for someone from his past. Either someone he loved and lost, or someone who dealt him some sort of soul-deep emotional trauma."

"If it was trauma-related, wouldn't she already be dead?" I asked before I could stop myself. Lane hadn't bidden us to speak, nor had he alerted Addie to my and Aspen's presence.

Oops.

Addie sighed. "You know I hate being put on speaker in front of other people without my knowledge, Sheriff."

"Sorry," he replied, though he didn't sound it at all. "Hey, Addie?"

"Yes?" the FBI agent clipped.

"You're on speaker, and I'm here with Lainey's sister, Reagan, and Aspen, who I'm sure you remember from the Prom Night Arsonist case."

"Hoping to upstage law enforcement again, Miss McKay?" Addie asked lightly.

Aspen chuckled. "Just doing a friend a favor."

"Fair enough. Now back to the matter at hand…in my expert opinion, yes. If this abduction and holding Lainey captive was related to past trauma, she would likely already be dead." She paused, and I knew what she'd ask next. "I don't mean to be insensitive here, Reagan, but are you *certain* she's still alive? From what Lane has told me, there's nothing to suggest otherwise, but it could be that her remains haven't yet been discovered."

"I don't have any tangible proof," I admitted, giving into a shiver at the image she painted. Remembering the poor woman in the county morgue whose identity was still a mystery. "But… we're twins. I'd know."

"I believe you," Addie said, surprising me, and I relaxed fractionally. Aspen squeezed my arm reassuringly.

"You keep saying 'he,'" Aspen pointed out to Addie.

"Given that Lainey is likely still alive, and someone is coming after you, Reagan, I am confident we're dealing with a male unsub."

"The same one Lainey slept with all those years ago."

"Yes, I think that's a safe bet."

"So what do we do now?" I asked.

"I'm still working through the journals—"

"Oh!" I exclaimed, cutting her off. "I found something."

I explained the initials and my thinking that they likely belonged to our "unsub", as Addie had called him. Lane took a photo of the page and texted it to Addie, a faint *beep* across the line a moment later alerting us it arrived.

We waited while Addie read, and she said, "Okay, yes, I see. How long before her disappearance was this?"

"About three days before she left Tennessee." Then I reminded her that Lainey had gone missing on her fourth day in town.

Keys clacked on Addie's end.

Lane asked her, "Could you run down those initials?"

"How broad?" More keystrokes.

"Start with Owyhee, Canyon, Ada, and Elmore. If nothing pops, we keep expanding."

"Anything specific I'm looking for in terms of ruling people out?"

"Isn't profiling your specialty?"

"You're right." She spoke as she typed. "Male, early to mid-thirties. Do we have any physical characteristics?"

"Brunette," I supplied. "Somewhere around six feet. Otherwise, I've got nothing."

"Any property?"

Closing my eyes, I remembered the big truck with the brush guard that ran me off the road a few weeks before and relayed that info to Addie.

"Potentially owns or rents a farmhouse too," Lane added. "Could've purchased outright or, more likely, took possession as next of kin when parents or grandparents died. May also own a truck or large SUV."

"Alright," Addie said. "I'll get some techs on this and see what pops up."

"Thank you so much for your help," I said.

"Anytime. But Sheriff?"

"Yeah?"

"You owe me."

The line died, and Lane grinned at me and Aspen.

"So…that's Addie."

Aspen and I crossed our arms over our chests—well, as best as I could with one of them encased from knuckles to mid-biceps in plaster—and leaned back against the couch, pinning Lane with identical stares.

Lane growled a warning, wordlessly urging us not to press it.

Aspen merely said, "We're all looking forward to meeting her at the wedding."

"Yep," I agreed, looking at Aspen. "Though I wonder how Sutton will react."

Lane ignored that comment. "Can we get back to work?"

He tapped his middle finger to his notebook in obvious *fuck off* gesture, and Aspen and I laughed.

"I suppose," I said airily.

Lane looked at me like he wanted to call out my tone but wisely didn't. Instead, he said, "I want to try a cognitive."

Aspen blinked in surprise. "You haven't yet?"

"It's been so long, I didn't think it would help."

"Well, it definitely can't hurt."

"What the fuck is a cognitive?" I asked.

"Cognitive interview," Lane explained. "It's a technique law enforcement uses that will hopefully allow us to get more information about that night seven years ago."

At this point, I was willing to try anything.

"What do you need me to do?"

"Lie down," Aspen said.

"I didn't make you lie down for yours."

"No," she agreed. "But I was also reliving a traumatic event. This is going to be easy for Reagan, so she might as well be comfortable."

Easy? To recall the events of a single night seven years ago? Or, at the very least, remember anything about that night except for Finn?

I didn't have high hopes.

But if they both thought it would help, I'd give it a go.

Fluffing a pillow, I reclined my head onto it, feet straight out, hands resting against my stomach, my cast a heavy weight at my left side.

"Relax," Lane directed. "Clear your mind as best as you can and, when you're ready, bring up that night."

All too aware of my limbs, the lingering pain in my arm, and the gentle *whoosh* of my breath in and out, accompanied by the rise and fall of my chest, it took me several minutes to do as Lane asked.

But then, the present went hazy around me, my mind's eye instead focused on the battered wooden door of a bar and the neon sign above that glowed like a beacon in the night, twisting to spell THE SWALLOW.

As if sensing the shift in me, Lane softly said, "First, I want you to immerse yourself in the scene. What do you hear, smell, see?"

My voice seemed to reach my own ears from a great distance as I replied.

"We haven't gone in yet, but I can hear the bass of the music thumping and the overlapping voices of a lot of people. Lainey moves ahead of me and opens the door, and I'm hit with a wave of sound. Everything was muffled before, but now it's loud. As soon as I cross the threshold, I can smell stale beer and lingering cigarette smoke. I thought smoking indoors was illegal?" I asked absently.

Distantly, I registered Lane's chuckle. "It is, but the Swallow has been open for a long damn time. Now, what do you see?"

"People. *Lots* of people. How are we ever going to get to the bar through this?"

My mind seemed to flash at me, reminding me I'd had that same thought all those years ago.

"Can you tell me what you're wearing?"

"You were there. You already know."

"Humor me."

"A red dress," I said. "And black cowboy boots I'd bought that day."

"What about Lainey?"

I described her denim skirt, white blouse, and matching boots —though hers were brown. We purposely purchased different colors so we could share them.

"Somehow, Lainey found us a table. In that sea of bodies, impossibly, no one had claimed it, so she did. I went to the bar and got our first round."

"What were you drinking?"

"Vodka sodas, same as always."

"Was this when you met Finn?"

"No. I got drinks after waiting for what seemed like hours,

then went back to the table. Lainey and I stood there, sipping and taking in the scene."

We were from the south, you know? Country bars weren't uncharted territory for us, especially not when one of the biggest country stars of our generation happened to be from our same hometown. But the vibe at the Swallow was…different. No one made any effort to impress anyone else. Back home, eyes would've followed us everywhere, accompanied by whispers of the shitty hand we'd been dealt with the loss of our parents. But in Dusk Valley…no one knew us. No one gave a fuck who we were.

"When did you meet Finn?"

"The next time I went to the bar. I begged Lainey to go since I got the first round, but she insisted she was better suited to 'protect the table.'" I chucked as I recalled her words. "I was on my way there when some guy touched my ass."

"Tony Walters."

I'd never learned the creep's name, but it made sense Lane had.

"Finn and I chatted for a bit, then I headed back to my sister. When I got there, she told me she was leaving with the guy she'd just met."

"Was that out of character for her?"

I snorted. "No. Lainey was the queen of one-night stands."

Meanwhile, the only time I'd ever participated in one, the man had haunted me for seven years, re-entered my life unexpectedly, and I'd fallen in love with him.

Lainey, on the other hand, was the fuck-'em-and-leave-'em type.

"Let's talk about this guy. He was tall, right?"

"By normal standards, maybe? Like to Aspen, yeah, he'd be considered tall."

Aspen made a noise of protest but didn't refute me.

"But not to you?" Lane asked.

"Lainey and I are five ten. This guy was *maybe* two inches taller than us."

"What about the rest of him?"

"Brown hair, muscular build."

"How muscular?"

"Like he used his hands for a living. Not as trim as Trey, but not as stacked as you."

"Anything else? Eye color?"

"I never saw his face."

I explained how he'd had his back turned to me when I arrived at the table. How he was chatting with some other guys, but I couldn't remember anything about them.

"Any idea how old he was?"

"Not a clue," I admitted. "But Lainey never mentioned he was older or anything, so I'd guess somewhere around our age."

"Was he local?" Lane asked me.

"I don't know that either."

"How about the morning after? Did you have to pick her up?"

Jolting upright, I stared wide-eyed at Lane.

"He dropped her off."

Sitting back against the couch, I pulled my knees to my chest and allowed my eyes to flutter closed again, squeezing them tightly shut, as though that would make my memory clearer.

"He drove a truck."

"The same one that ran you off the road?"

I wanted to say no, but I couldn't be certain. "Maybe?" It sounded more like a question than an answer. My eyes popped open again. "I remember a dark color. Black, maybe brown, maybe navy?"

"I don't suppose you got a plate." I glared. "*Try*," he prodded.

Eyes fluttering closed again, I focused my mind's eye on that truck. On the glow of its taillights, bright in the fresh dawn of a new day. The roads were deserted, and he'd pulled away so fast, kicking up dust from the motel lot.

"E," I gasped. "But that's it."

"That's amazing, Reagan. Truly."

"Thanks." I beamed, pleased by a job well done.

Lane didn't look at me; his attention was focused wholly on scratching furtive notes in his spiral-bound pad. When he finished, he got to his feet, closing his notebook and stuffing it into the pocket of his uniform shirt. "Well, I think that's everything. I'll pass this new info onto Addie and start running down some leads myself."

"Keep us posted," Aspen said.

Lane tipped an imaginary hat and left.

"I suppose I should head out too," she said when he'd gone.

"You should stay. Crew is on shift, right?"

"Yeah, and I do hate being in that house alone. Especially now, with this stalker on the loose."

"Stay for dinner." I checked my watch. "Finn will be home any minute."

"You sure?"

"Of course," I insisted.

"Okay, fine. On one condition."

"What's that?"

"You let me cook," she said, glancing pointedly at my casted arm.

I laughed. "Deal."

While she moved around our kitchen with the ease of someone who had likely done so before, we chatted about my sister's case and the upcoming wedding. When Finn arrived home, we had a full spread of spaghetti, garlic bread, and a salad on the table.

Over the food and a few glasses of wine, Aspen and I shared all of the new info with Finn. After that, conversation flowed easily until we realized how late it had gotten. Not wanting to take any chances with her safety, we convinced Aspen to stay in the guest room.

Once she was settled, Finn and I went through our own nighttime routines and got into bed ourselves, him drawing me tight against his chest and falling asleep almost instantly.

Sleep didn't come as easily for me, but when it did, for the first time in months, I wasn't plagued by nightmares of a creepy, abandoned farmhouse.

thirty-seven

. . .

FINN

AS BADLY AS we all wanted to keep chasing these new leads in hopes of bringing Lainey home sooner, everything was put on hold a few days later.

Wedding week had arrived—along with Owen, his wife, Delia, and my nephew, Jace.

They were staying in my guest house, which had been professionally cleaned after Aria's attack. The likelihood of Reagan's stalker coming back to the house was minimal, but one could never be too safe, so I had Trey upgrade the security system. Plus, I trusted Owen—and Delia, for that matter—to take care of themselves and their son. They'd both go down swinging if it meant keeping their family safe.

Reagan did what she could to help me prepare for their arrival, which mostly consisted of standing by barking orders while West and I rearranged furniture.

When they pulled up, we greeted them on the front porch.

"Quite the welcoming committee," Delia joked when she got out of their rental SUV.

"Whiskey…" my eldest brother warned his wife as he collected my nephew from the backseat.

"What?" Delia asked, feigning innocence, complete with exaggerated fluttering of her lashes. "Normally the whole fucking cavalry is here."

My brother had caught a live wire with this one, but they loved each other fiercely, and we loved her right back.

Still, I ignored them both and beelined for Jace, slapping Owen's arm away when he attempted to give me a side hug in favor of sweeping my nephew from his hold.

Jace Leon Lawless—named for both of his grandfathers—was the perfect blend of his parents. With Delia's dark brown hair and olive skin, and Owen's bright blue eyes, he was the most beautiful baby any of us had ever seen.

This also happened to be the first time I'd met him, and I purposely didn't give the rest of the family an ETA for Owen and Delia so I could have some time with Jace and not have to share him with my thousand siblings.

Delia approached with a diaper bag slung over her shoulder and reached for her son. I turned my body away from her, shielding him, which had both her and Jace giggling.

"I'll give him back," she promised. "Unless *you* want to change his shitty diaper?"

I held Jace out to his mom. "I thought the smell was coming from O."

My brother smacked me upside the head as Delia disappeared into the house. Then Owen and I moved to the back of their vehicle and began unloading and carrying their luggage inside.

Once that was done, we found ourselves gathered in the living room, me sitting on the floor with Jace, rolling a ball back and forth, while Owen, Delia, and Reagan gathered on the sofa and chairs around us.

At one point, I glanced up at Reagan, our gazes locking longer than was normal. Likely having similar thoughts.

I'd always wanted kids. Being in the Army, though, I'd never considered the possibility of a family when I'd been in my twenties. War had a habit of making widows, and I never wanted to leave any wife and potential children heartbroken from my loss.

All too well, I knew how devastating it could be.

Now that my time in the service was long over, however, I was more than ready to settle down and build the kind of life my parents had given me and my siblings.

And I wanted to do it all with Reagan.

Her chin dipped slightly, excitement glinting in her eyes, telling me she wanted all of that too.

When the time was right, we'd make those dreams a reality.

"You must be Reagan," Delia said without preamble, cutting into my visions of the future, and I realized I hadn't formally introduced them.

"Yes," my girl squeaked in response, which was entirely out of character for her. Delia, however, was a big personality, and she took some getting used to.

"I'm sorry about your sister. I have four myself, and I have no idea what I'd do if one of them went missing. Likely tear the world apart then burn it down searching for them."

"Thank you. We recently came across some new information that generated more leads," Reagan replied, her voice gaining confidence. "But everything is on hold because of the wedding."

"Fuck the wedding," Delia said emphatically.

Frankly, I agreed with her. Crew and Aspen vowing themselves to each other forever was important, especially given all the shit they'd endured both together and apart. But I failed to understand why we couldn't continue working on Lainey's case. Why did all of us have to drop everything for an entire week leading up to the ceremony? Wasn't there an event planner better suited to put out any fires that arose?

"You wouldn't be singing the same tune if one of your sisters was getting married," Owen retorted.

"All of my sisters are already married, QB," she reminded

him. "But you better believe, if the choice came down to celebrating a wedding or finding a missing sister—it'd be no contest."

I glanced at Reagan, finding the truth of that statement reflected in her eyes.

Knowing without a doubt she was only putting on a brave facade in the face of all this wedding stuff because she loved me. It had absolutely nothing to do with anyone else.

WE SPENT the first few days after Owen and Delia's arrival running around the ranch like chickens with their heads cut off. Mainly, we were getting the barn ready for the reception. West had even closed the dude ranch for public bookings, instead offering his cabins at a discounted rate to anyone traveling long distance to Dusk Valley for the wedding.

On Thursday, two days before the ceremony, we finally handed over control of things to the wedding planner—which we should've done from the start, if you asked me, not that anyone did.

Family dinner that week had been moved up a day in deference to the big rehearsal dinner planned the next night, so afterward, we decided to go out to celebrate. A joint bachelor-bachelorette party of sorts. And where else would we go but the Swallow?

"You okay with this?" I asked Reagan. We'd come home after dinner to change before heading into town, and Crew would be there to pick us up shortly. The question was prompted by her still casted arm and the haunted expression she'd been wearing since that first conversation with Delia five days before.

"Of course," she replied easily, and I didn't detect any hint that she was lying.

"If it gets to be too much, emotionally or for your arm, say the word and we'll—"

She cut me off with a finger to my lips, which she shortly replaced with her own.

"I know, Finn. You got me."

When she tried to pull away, I held fast, capturing her mouth with mine again, taking the kiss deeper than the one she'd given me.

"Have I told you how incredible you look?" I asked against her lips, snaking a hand up her thigh.

I nearly swallowed my tongue when she walked out of the closet earlier. Her dress was a blue and white gingham pattern, tight across her chest and torso, flaring out at her hips. Paired with brown boots and her hair in long, soft curls down her back, she was the sexiest thing I'd ever seen.

Outside, a car horn beeped, derailing my hand's path to her cunt.

Reagan pushed me away with a giggle, both of us gasping for air.

"C'mon," she said, tugging me toward the door. "If we don't leave now, we never will."

"I'm okay with that."

"Your family won't be."

To punctuate her point, Crew laid on the horn again, far longer than was necessary, alerting us to his impatience.

"Saved by the bell," I muttered.

Reagan stopped dead in the doorway and turned to me, curling her fists in my shirt, expression surprisingly stern.

"You're saving me, Finn. I don't need saving *from* you."

I covered her hands with mine and leaned in for a light kiss.

"Love you."

"Love you more."

"Not possible."

THE BAR WAS PACKED, and I knew Aria's upcoming performance tonight had a lot to do with it.

Thankfully, someone had called ahead to reserve our usual table.

Déjà vu hit me *hard* when we walked in, being back here with Reagan for the first time since the night we met. With her hand in mine, towing her through the mass of bodies—the lines between past and present blurred, transporting me backward seven years while I remained in the moment.

Reagan and I had lost so much time together, and I vowed not to waste anymore.

I was going to ask her to stay. To build a life with me here in Dusk Valley. To make my house our home.

We'd barely settled around the large table before the bartender appeared, a younger girl I'd never seen before, carrying a tray of beers. Even Aspen, who normally didn't drink out of solidarity with her fiancé, reached for one and slammed half before coming up for air.

"What?" she asked when she found us all staring at her. "I'm ready for this fucking wedding to be over."

"Rude," Crew muttered, though he leaned over and pressed a kiss to her temple.

"It's not you, hotshot," she reminded him in a way that suggested they'd had this conversation before. "I can't wait to be your wife. I just hate the production of it all. We should've eloped."

Crew snorted. "And risk the wrath of Mama?"

Aspen softened. She loved our mother fiercely, and Mama loved her right back.

"Birdie is the *only* reason we're doing the big reception," she said to the rest of us. "That was the only concession I'd been willing to make."

Though the guest list was over two hundred people, the bulk of them were only invited to the reception. They'd wanted to keep the ceremony small, so only close family and friends would be present.

"Smart," Delia said, raising her beer in toast, which Aspen clinked with her own. "When we told Birdie we were doing a destination wedding in the Bahamas, QB thought she was going to disown him."

"She must've forgotten how much of my money keeps this place afloat," Owen chuckled.

"Hey!" West and I protested in unison. I added, "The rescue is doing well."

"And the dude ranch is booked solid year-round," West said, proudly puffing out his chest.

Our oldest brother laughed heartily now. "Easy killers. I'm just fucking with you."

He wasn't entirely off base, though. After Dad died, Owen left college a year early, forgoing his senior season to declare for the NFL draft. A sizable portion of his signing bonus went toward keeping us fed, clothed, and the ranch running smoothly. The cash infusions continued until West and I returned from the service and ultimately took over operations. But we hadn't needed money from Owen in a long ass time.

"The point is," Delia said. "We all know how Birdie gets when she's disappointed."

I'd been on the receiving end of it myself more than once and knew Delia spoke the truth.

"Like when we told her we were enlisting?" West said to me with a grimace, plucking the thought right from my head.

"She didn't speak to us for a week."

"I remember that!" Aria said. "She made me be the go-between when Crew refused."

We all burst into laughter, reminded of our eight-year-old sister acting as liaison between her mother and eighteen-year-old brothers.

"See!" Aspen exclaimed. "I do *not* need that kind of karma."

Loud, obnoxious feedback from the nearby speaker cut off further conversation, and Aria grinned.

"That's my cue."

We all turned so we faced the stage, and pride surged in my chest as I watched Aria confidently stride to the mic.

"Good evening, Dusk Valley!"

A cheer rose from the crowd, and I grinned. Reagan tucked herself closer into my side, tilting her head to speak directly into my ear.

"I've never seen her play or heard her sing! Is she good?"

I smirked, knowing my girl was in for a treat. "Just watch."

"How we doing tonight?" Aria asked the crowd, eliciting another happy yell. "Good, good," she continued when they quieted. "Well, as I'm sure most of you know, my brother, Crew, is marrying the love of his life this weekend." Another cheer. "And my whole family is in town!" Chants of LAW-LESS rang out, and I dropped my head with a shake. We were fucking notorious in this place, and I wasn't sure if that was a good or bad thing.

"I'm going to kick us off with a fast one," Aria said, then turned to nod at the drummer, who launched into a steady beat.

When the guitars joined in, I recognized the song as "Selfish" by Jordan Davis. Aria had changed the arrangement, raising the key to better suit her range, but no one seemed to mind. The dance floor filled with people immediately.

I turned to Reagan, who stared at the stage in awe.

At last, she looked at me. "She's *incredible*."

"I know," I said, grinning proudly.

Each time I watched my baby sister perform, I was reminded that her talent was too fucking big for this tiny town. If she wanted to leave to pursue her dreams like she'd been talking about for years, I'd be the man behind the wheel of the getaway car.

Aria plied the masses with several pop and country songs,

including a high-energy rendition of "Shivers" by Ed Sheeran that had the residents of Dusk Valley easily dropping into formation for an impressive display of line dancing.

While baby sis was doing her thing, the rest of us Lawlesses stayed gathered around the table, shooting the shit and cheering her on. I knew being surrounded by my family had to be difficult for Reagan, who was entirely without what remained of her own, but she was either truly enjoying herself or putting on an impressively brave face. I didn't try to figure out which, merely kept her close and let being in the company of my favorite people in the world soften the sharp edges of my worry and fear and anger from the last few months.

"For this next one, we're going to slow it down," Aria said into the mic.

Within a few notes, I recognized the next song.

"The Bones" by Maren Morris.

Getting to my feet, I extended my hand to my girl.

"May I have this dance?"

Reagan slid her palm against mine and let me lead her to the center of the floor.

Once again, déjà vu washed over me.

As if reading my mind, Reagan tilted her head to look up at me and said, "This feels so much like that night, doesn't it?"

"Exactly like it," I agreed, then shifted my mouth to her ear. "But so much different too. I *know* you now, and I love you so much. That only makes me want you more, which I didn't think was possible."

I felt more than heard her breath hitch.

"Fuck, I wish we could get out of here," she murmured.

An idea took shape in my mind, and I pulled back a bit to grin down at her.

"We don't necessarily have to leave to...*come*." I wiggled my eyebrows suggestively, and she burst out laughing. "Do you trust me?"

"With my life."

In the middle of the song, I pulled her from the dance floor, through the crowd, and down the hallway that led to the restrooms. Beelining for the back door, I led us outside into the night, the cool, fresh air a welcome change from the heat and stale beer scent of inside.

"Finn, what are we doing?"

I didn't speak until I'd pulled us deep enough into the shadows that the dim glow cast by the lone exterior light couldn't reach us.

"I need you."

Any reply she would've made was cut off when my mouth crashed to hers. Thankfully, she met me fervently, our tongues gliding messily together, teeth clacking as we nipped at each other's lips.

"Hard and fast," she begged when I pulled away for a moment, knowing where we were headed.

My hand slid down her side until it connected with bare thigh, then slipped under the hem of her dress, higher until I collided with her pussy—her *bare* pussy.

"No panties? I thought you were supposed to be a southern belle?"

"For everyone else maybe," she said, the last word rising in pitch as my fingers parted her slit. "But not for you."

"That's right, baby," I murmured. "You're my little slut, right?"

"Yes," she gasped. "Now fuck me."

She was already wet, her desire slicking the insides of her thighs and coating my hand.

"Fucking soaked," I mused, then licked my fingers clean. Reagan reached for me, yanking down my zipper and unbuttoning my jeans, shoving them and my boxer briefs down enough to free my cock.

Gripping my length, I speared the tip through her cunt then

spread her arousal down the shaft. I notched my head at her entrance. Before I could even ask the question, Reagan was nodding vehemently, hands finding my hips and urging me forward.

I surged into her, a strangled moaning leaving me as I buried myself in her wet heat. Reagan's head fell back against the brick exterior of the building, sighing. Her casted arm hung awkwardly between us, so I lifted it to my shoulder, and despite their limited movement, her fingers found their way into my hair—anchoring herself.

Grateful she was as tall as she was, I hooked her leg higher on my hip, providing the perfect angle to drive even deeper.

My strokes were slow, savoring. I'd never tired of being connected to her like this.

"You're fucking perfect, belle," I muttered, tipping my forehead against hers. "Like your pussy was molded specifically to fit my cock. Fuck, I love you."

"I love you," she gasped. "But Finn...*hard and fast.*"

Remembering her earlier request, when I pulled out next, I shot my hips forward, slamming back into her.

"*Yes*," she hissed. "Just like that, baby. *Please.*"

"Goddamn, I love it when you beg."

I set a relentless pace. Where Reagan was concerned, it took little more than a single look to get me going, and this was no different. After a few minutes, that telltale pressure coiled at the base of my spine. Reagan's inner walls squeezed around me tightly, telling me she was close too.

Though we were pressed tightly enough together that not even a millimeter of space could be found, I wedged my hand between us and found her clit.

That little bit of pressure was all it took.

Right as the floodgates on our respective orgasms opened, so did the sky, the storm that had been darkening the clouds all day finally breaking free.

We were doused in seconds, but we barely noticed.

Reagan came with a cry, drowned by the boom of thunder, pulsing around me, triggering my own release.

"That's it, baby," I gasped as I unloaded into her. "Milk my cock."

When we stilled and came down from the high, I pulled myself free, tucked my dick back into my pants, and stepped away to readjust my clothes, difficult given the wet denim of my jeans had no give.

Reagan's hair hung in heavy, damp strands across her shoulders and down her back. The pale blue and white of her dress was now damn near transparent and clinging to every dip and hollow of her body. In this state, her curves were positively sinful, and her nipples, tightened to peaks and pressing distractingly against the fabric, begged for my mouth. If I didn't know my family would likely be wondering what happened to us, I'd take her again.

Reagan merely smoothed her palms down the skirt of her dress and watched me with a smirk.

"You look like you've got a secret."

"I do," she agreed, stepping forward to press a single hard kiss to my mouth. Then she whispered against my lips, "I've got your cum dripping down my thighs."

thirty-eight

. . .

REAGAN

WHEN WE'D GONE BACK INSIDE after our tryst, Finn's family gave us endless shit. It had only been too obvious what we'd been up to, and being soaking wet certainly didn't help matters. Though the night was still young, Crew agreed to bring us home under the guise of changing and heading back in our own vehicle.

We all knew that was a lie.

Especially since, the moment we were through the door of the house, Finn swept me into his arms, and I had no doubt how we'd be spending the rest of the night.

Burying his face in my neck, he took an exaggerated inhale of my skin then nipped my flesh with his teeth.

"I'm fucking *hungry*, belle."

"Oh really?"

"Yes. *Starving.*"

"Kitchen's that way," I said, pointing behind him when he bypassed it to head down the hall.

"Not interested in that kind of meal," he assured me as he entered our room and gently placed me on the bed.

"What kind of meal then?" I asked, propping myself up on my elbows and grinning at him.

He glanced pointedly at the apex of my thighs, still sticky from our earlier fuck. "You're a smart woman, Reagan. I think you'll figure it out."

His words struck true, right in my core, lighting me up from the inside out.

Outside the bar had been the first time we'd had sex since my accident—Finn's insistence, not mine. I'd been ready to go a week ago, but he'd refused until I could go a day without my pain meds.

I supposed it was a blessing. With the ugly black cast and dull throbbing as my constant companions, I wasn't feeling particularly sexy these days.

But the way he looked at me…

I must have said the words out loud, because Finn canted his head to the side and said, "How do I look at you?"

"Like I'm the only woman in the world. Like you never want to *stop* looking at me."

"I *don't*," he assured me. "I *love* you, Reagan Lindsey. I love you more than anyone and anything in this world. And…I want you to stay."

Emotion clogged my throat, but I managed to get out, "I love you too, and I'm not going anywhere."

He shook his head. "No, I mean…after we find Lainey. Whatever happens, I want you to stay with me. Build a life here. I don't ever want to spend another second away from you."

His admission was surprising—but also not. We'd been heading in this direction for a while, likely since a few months ago, when we'd seen each other for the first time again in the sheriff's department.

Did I *want* to stay in Dusk Valley? Make this town and Finn permanent?

I didn't even have to think about it.

"Yes."

Like an excited kid on Christmas, Finn hopped on the bed and hovered over me, grinning happily.

"We'll decorate the house however you want," he said quickly. "And we can do up the guest room for Lainey. Hell, I'll bulldoze the whole fucking thing and build a new one if that's what you wa—"

I pressed my finger to his lips. "We can worry about that later. Right now, I need you."

"Ah, yes. How could I have forgotten about my meal?"

With a wicked gleam in his eyes, he retreated and lowered to his stomach until his face was eye level with my pussy. His hands snaked under the hem of my dress, calloused palms rasped higher and higher, closer to the place I needed him most.

"Finn?" I whispered.

"Yeah, baby?" he asked, not looking away from my core, merely flipping my skirt out of the way, eyes on his prize.

"Be gentle."

I hated asking, especially after the hard and fast fuck—which I'd asked for then—outside the bar. I *loved* the frantic, reckless fucking our sex life consisted of before my accident. I loved the way Finn threw me around like a rag doll. He never treated me like something fragile and breakable, because he knew I wasn't. Knew I could handle everything he threw at me—and give it right back. I loved the bruises he'd sometimes leave on my thighs and breasts and proudly bore the reminders of the pleasure he gave me.

But tonight, I needed something different.

"Always," he promised.

And then he left the room.

What the fuck?

Before I could get too worked up, he returned…with a bottle of tequila.

Propping myself up on my elbows, I asked, "What's that for?"

"We're celebrating."

"With…tequila." I was unsure if I was asking a question or making a statement.

"Kind of our thing, isn't it?"

He was right. When I thought of our first night together, those memories were inextricably linked to the burn of tequila as Finn and I pounded shots with his brothers.

"Plus, I had an idea earlier," he continued, setting the bottle on one of the nightstands.

"Oh yeah?" I asked as he climbed onto the mattress. Taking my good hand, he helped me sit up until I was on my knees. Then he grabbed the hem of my dress and peeled it off—leaving me completely naked. Goosebumps erupted as air hit my still slightly damp, newly exposed skin.

"Fuck, you're beautiful."

Grabbing the front of his tee, I hauled him in, capturing his mouth in a hungry kiss.

"You are the most gorgeous man I've ever laid eyes on."

"You're just saying that," he retorted.

I pursed my lips. "When have I *ever* done that?"

He chuckled. "True."

"The first time I ever saw you, I thought you were the hottest man I'd ever seen," I said. "Still do. Still can't figure out how we ended up here."

Finn cupped my sex. "Your pussy is just that good."

With a laugh, I shoved him playfully, then reached for the hem of his shirt and drew it up over his head. Needed to have his warm, solid vitality beneath my fingers.

"So what's this idea?" I asked, nodding at the liquor.

"Lie back."

I reclined, my head resting on the pillows, legs straight out, arms thrown up over my head.

Finn uncapped the bottle.

"Want some?"

Nodding enthusiastically, I parted my lips.

"Good girl," he grinned.

But instead of tipping the bottle over my mouth, he brought it to his own and took a healthy pull.

Then he grabbed my face, fingers digging into my jaw to hold it open as he spit the tequila into my mouth.

Finn let go, and I swallowed. The liquor—slightly warm from his own mouth, which I found incomprehensibly sexy—burned all the way down, settling in my stomach, stoking the fire already crackling in my core.

Before I could move or react, he tipped the bottle over my chest. The chilled liquid was a frigid contrast to my flaming skin. He dipped his head, running his tongue in a long line across my collarbones. Moving lower to my breasts, his mouth closed over each nipple in turn, swirling his tongue around them until they tightened into peaks.

"Finn," I gasped when he pulled away, blowing air across the places his mouth had been.

Goosebumps broke out on my skin, and I shivered in antici- pation of what might come next.

Tequila found its way into the hollow of my belly button and, eyes on mine, Finn lowered his mouth, sucking it up, tongue swirling the divot like it had against my nipples.

By the time he made it to my pussy, the cold neck of the bottle parting my slit and nudging my clit, I was ready to combust.

My back arched, the difference in temperature between the bottle and my hot flesh sending a delicious tremor coursing through my body. A breathy moan escaped me.

"Feel good?" Finn asked.

"*More.*"

With a chuckle, he obliged, tilting the bottle so tequila

cascaded over my slit. Finn wasted no time diving in, once again repeating the flicks and swirls of his tongue he'd used on my nipples and belly button.

I was so keyed up from the slow, exquisite way he'd tortured each of my erogenous zones that I soon clawed at Finn's shoulders and tugged his hair, neither of us caring when my cast clunked him in the forehead. I shifted my hips, angling my pussy closer to his mouth, riding his tongue until I detonated.

Finn slowed but worked me through it, gently tracing and kissing my clit.

"You okay?" he asked when he had his fill and I came down from the high.

"Amazing."

Finn grinned and climbed off the bed. "Hold that thought."

As he stripped off his jeans and boxer briefs, I marveled at his physique. His body was *perfect*, the kind of muscles you only saw in magazines or online—never in real life. There wasn't an ounce of fat to be found, each of his muscles hard-earned and perfectly defined. He was sculpted like an ancient Greek god, made sexier by the ink that covered his arms from wrists to shoulders and continued across his chest to the dip between his pecs. Light blond hair dusted his chest, disappeared across his upper abdomen, and reappeared darker below his belly button before trailing to his cock.

And his *cock*.

My mouth watered at the sight of it—it's thick, steely length, skin impossibly smooth despite its hardness. Knowing how *full* and complete I felt when he was inside me.

"You're drooling."

Nodding at his dick, the tip of which glistened with precum, I said, "So are you."

His grin was feral as he rejoined me on the bed, hovering over me and fitting his hips between my thighs.

One of his hands found my cheek, brushing back a lock of still damp hair.

Staring deeply into my eyes, so deep he cut straight to my soul, he said, "I love you, Reagan."

"I love you, Finn."

With those three words, he drove into me.

"*Fuck*," I groaned. Despite having taken him earlier and the orgasm he'd just given me, the fit was deliciously tight, my pussy stinging slightly as I tried to adjust to his size.

Finn withdrew slowly until only the head of his cock remained inside me.

"Say it again." *Thrust.*

"I love you." *Thrust.*

"Promise me you'll stay." *Thrust.*

"As if I could ever leave you." *Thrust.*

Words left us as we were lost to the slow rocking of our hips. I intertwined my good hand with his, and he pressed them into the mattress by my head as the other gripped my hip. Finn drove us higher and higher until the pressure in my core burst forth, a wave of pleasure cresting and crashing down, pulling us both under.

thirty-nine

. . .

FINN

FRIDAY PASSED in a flurry of activity. Mainly, I did what I could to avoid helping with last minute wedding stuff by putting in some much-needed time at work. Reagan had taken a lot of my focus in recent months, and while I knew my foreman, Abel, and the rest of my ranch hands were happy to pick up the slack —and extra hours—I had always been a hands-on business owner. I didn't enjoy not being in the loop. Before the sun had fully risen, I kissed a still-asleep Reagan goodbye and headed to the barn.

First, I fed all the animals and spent some time grooming them. I let the goats and two Highland cows out to roam in the paddock while I did the same for the horses. Next, I collected eggs from all the chickens and brought them up to the house for Mama, refusing her offer of breakfast for the first time in my life. I knew if I stayed, I'd be roped into hanging ribbons or arranging flowers, or some other stupid shit I wanted no part of.

When that was all done, I took a couple hours to work with the one rescue horse we currently had stabled. Though still a bit skittish, she was far more sociable than she'd been when we'd taken her in the month before. Abel and the team had done great work on her so far. However, we all agreed the Arabian mare, whose name was Capricorn, would be better suited away from the hustle and bustle of the wedding festivities, so I took her with me when I headed home shortly after eight.

Then I made love to my girl—on the bed *and* in the shower.

Around midday, I left to help my brothers haul the archway West and I had built ages ago out to Crew and Aspen's ceremony spot.

We dicked around out there far longer than was necessary, none of us keen to return to the mayhem back at the big house and big barn.

That evening, rehearsal dinner passed in a blink of good food —catered, though, so not as amazing as Mama's cooking— drinks, and time spent with the best family a guy could ask for.

Since Crew and Aspen would be spending the night apart in observation of the old and, in my opinion, antiquated tradition, the girls and Jace were staying at the big house while the rest of us retreated to West's.

I pulled Reagan aside before we left.

"You gonna be okay?" I asked her.

She rolled her eyes in a way that had me wanting to fuck the attitude right out of her. "I'm fine, Finn."

I sighed, knowing she was right; she was safe here. "I just hate being away from you. If something happened…"

"Nothing is going to happen," she assured me. "This place has more cameras on it than a casino floor, and I don't doubt Trey will be keeping an eye on us no matter what you guys get up to tonight. The only place safer is our house."

Our. Damn, I loved the sound of that.

"What exactly do you think we're going to do?"

She smirked. "Get drunk and talk about your feelings?"

"Nah, baby. We'll save that shit for you guys."

"Finn!" Owen hollered. "Let your girl go and get your ass in the truck!"

Groaning, I bent and pressed a quick kiss to her mouth. "Duty calls."

"I love you," she murmured against my lips.

"I love you."

BEFORE WE KNEW IT, Saturday had arrived.

Crew and Aspen's wedding day.

Thankfully, the weather was perfect. Though it rained for a bit in the morning, by the time we finished getting ready, the sun was shining brightly, the temperature hovering in the low seventies. I was grateful we were wearing linen pants and shirts, though I was no stranger to working in higher temps in heavier clothing.

Because Aspen's only sibling had passed away long before she'd ever met Crew, who had more brothers than he knew what to do with, they opted not to have anyone standing up for them. Once the ceremony was complete, Owen and Aria, as the oldest and youngest of our siblings, would serve as witnesses on the marriage certificate.

The ceremony was taking place at three, so my brothers and I spent most of the day bumming around. It'd been a minute since Owen had been back to Dusk Valley—in fact, one of Delia's sisters had been here more recently than our oldest brother—so West showed him around the dude ranch. My twin was proud of how he'd taken this section of ranch land that sat unused for ages and turned it into a thriving, authentic western experience. And, of course, we were proud of him.

"I have to admit," Owen started when we returned to West's house. "I didn't think you had it in you." He clapped West on the shoulder. "But you've done an amazing job."

"I'm not sure if I should be flattered or offended," West said.

"Definitely offended," Trey piped up.

Owen shook his head at our antics in that way he always had, but his expression quickly turned serious.

"All jokes aside, I'm proud of you." He studied each of us in turn. "I'm proud of *all* of you."

Awkward shuffling and throat clearing followed Owen's statement, but I knew without words that each of us appreciated it more than we could ever say anyway.

After Dad died, Owen kept our family afloat. Mama…she's the strongest woman I've ever known. And she did her best. But dealing with the unbearable pain of losing her soulmate while also trying to keep four boys and a little girl fed, clothed, and with a roof over our heads hadn't been easy. By then, both Owen and Trey had graduated and gone to college—but Owen was the one who stepped up. As the oldest, he became "the man of the house" overnight. Even while finishing up his final semester of college in Eugene before moving halfway across the country to Michigan to start his NFL career, he made time for us. Face-Timed us regularly to check in. Came home when he could. And, of course, provided for us financially.

As far as brothers went, there wasn't one better in the world than Owen Lawless, and we were fucking lucky he was ours.

Trey broke the silence—by completely changing the subject.

"As much as I love this little emotional moment we're having, I've got some news."

"You're dying," West said, jokingly lifting his hand for a high five, which I obliged.

Owen smacked us both upside the head.

"You wish," Trey told my twin with a grin. Then he looked at me. "Actually, I finally located the footage from that day at the Swallow seven years ago."

"Holy shit!" This time, I raised my hand for a five from Trey.

"Way to bury the lead, brother!" Lane shouted, clapping

Trey on the shoulder and shaking him, like a teammate celebrating a touchdown in a big game.

"Well, I debated saying anything at all, because I don't have anything to report yet. The place opens at an ungodly hour, so I've still got several hours to comb through. But…we're close."

"Why the hell aren't you working on it then?" Lane asked.

"Uhh…hello?" Crew said, joining the conversation for the first time. "Your baby brother is getting married?"

Lane rolled his eyes. "Please. There are five of you. We'll catch the next one."

Crew pouted.

"How much longer will it take?" I asked Trey, steering us away from an argument.

"Less than a day once I have the chance to sit down and work on it."

Glancing at my watch, I clocked the time, realizing we had to leave shortly to make it out to the ceremony location on time. Which was perfect, in my opinion, because I couldn't wait to tell Reagan we were one step closer to finding her sister.

UNSURPRISINGLY, Crew and Aspen's wedding ceremony was beautiful and heartfelt. The love between the two of them radiated out over the family and friends gathered. I had to admit, I wasn't immune.

With Reagan at my side in the front row, watching as my little brother vowed himself to the woman he'd been through hell and back with, who made him a better man, it was easy to imagine myself doing the same one day with our twins at our sides. Because now that Trey was so close to uncovering the identity of who had taken her, I was confident Lainey would be home in no time.

On my right side was Lane, his arm draped across the back of the chair next to him, where the infamous Addie Caldwell sat. She was about what I expected: tall, tan, and brunette, with bright, almost honey-colored eyes that cut right to the core when she looked at you. I supposed that was part of what made her a good agent. Despite her beauty, she gave off a no-nonsense air that assured you she was not someone to fuck with. Sutton sat somewhere behind us, and the one time I turned around to check out the crowd, she'd been staring at the back of Lane's head. No, *glaring*. But the expression was edged with pain too.

Lane's life was his to do with as he pleased, but he was certainly making a mess of things.

At Reagan's side opposite me was West, his arm similarly placed around Tyler Atwood. Tyler was a decorated barrel racer, so she wasn't home much, but when she did come back, she blew through town like a tornado, twisting West up in knots it would take me weeks to untangle. Personally, I thought he should tell her he was in love with her and let the chips fall where they may.

Past them sat Trey and Wyatt Saunders, who wasn't exactly his date but here as his best friend—though I knew my big brother would change that in a heartbeat if she gave him the green light. Given the fact that her mother was responsible for the deaths of eleven women, a man, and had nearly killed both Aspen *and* Crew, things between them were complicated. It had only been a year since the explosion that took Kelly's life and landed Crew in the hospital, and I could imagine Wyatt was still dealing with the fallout.

All that to say, each of my single brothers had some shit to figure out. I squeezed Reagan's hand tighter, grateful I'd found her.

After the ceremony, we spent far too long posing for pictures. Reagan, still in a cast for at least another three weeks, felt horrible she'd been unable to photograph the wedding as promised. Thankfully, she found a suitable replacement in Sloane Wilder, a friend of a friend who Reagan had followed on Instagram for ages whose work greatly impressed her. After perusing her profile and a lengthy phone call, Aspen agreed.

Once we were released from picture duty, we headed over to the reception. The barn looked better than it ever had. The wedding forced us to finally deep clean it, something that hadn't happened in years.

"You know," Mama mused as we gathered around the long table reserved for Crew and Aspen's immediate family, which included the seven thousand members of the Lawless family... and Aspen's parents. Mama continued, "Now that it's all spiffed up, we could rent this out to the public for events."

West and I shared a look over her head.

Guarantee she's been sitting on this idea for ages and waiting for tonight to spring it on us.

No doubt, I silently agreed. *But you have to admit...it's a damn good one.*

Though West and I were co-managing partners of the ranch, each of our family members held a stake beyond the parcels of land we each owned. Next to me and West, Mama's share was the largest, and West and I would do whatever it took to make her happy. That's how we ended up with fields of flowers and soybeans, goats, and *bees* so she could start making self-care products.

Out loud, West said, "We'll talk this week."

Mama beamed, knowing it was already a done deal.

"And on that note, can I talk to you guys about something?" Aria asked.

We all stilled. Aria's tone was far different from Mama's— nervousness creeping into her voice.

"What's up?" Owen asked.

With a deep breath, eyes squeezed shut, Aria blurted, "I'm moving to Nashville."

Immediately, expletives and refusals spilled from Trey, Lane, and West's lips.

"It's already done," Aria said, loud enough to be heard over them. "I already paid the deposit, and first and last months' rent on an apartment."

"I can get it back," Lane said, pulling out his phone as if to make the call right then. "Give me a name and number."

Aria shook her head. "I don't want you to get it back. I'm moving, and that's the end of it."

"That's *hardly* the end of it," Trey gritted out, then looked at Mama. "Did you know about this?"

"Of course," she said. "I helped her find a place."

"And you're just…letting her go?" Lane asked, incredulous.

"Like I just *let* you boys go off to college?" she said with a raised brow to Trey and Lane, then cut to me and West. "And *let* you two go to *war*?" Pursing her lips, she glared at each of us in turn. "And I surely *let* Owen send us hundreds of thousands of dollars over the years to keep this family and ranch afloat!"

Mama rarely got worked up about anything; she was as even keeled and steadfast as they came. But right now, she was *pissed*.

"I don't *let* any of you do anything," she continued. "The second you turned eighteen, you became adults. And while I'll always be your mother and always want to parent you in the way I think is best, you're a stubborn lot who does whatever they feel like. So while I am nervous and will worry constantly about Aria," she said, taking her only daughter's hand and giving it a squeeze, "I would be the worst kind of parent if I didn't do everything I could to support her while she chases her dreams—just like I did for all of you."

Honestly, I couldn't have said it better myself, and what I'd been trying to implore my brothers to understand the first time Aria brought up the idea of moving.

Lane looked at Aria. "You really want this?"

Aria didn't waver in stance or tone when she said, "Yes."

He shared a look with Trey and West, the three of them coming to some silent agreement. Then Trey said, "I guess we're taking a trip to Nashville."

Aria groaned, knowing we were about to make a whole fucking production out of her cross-country move.

Reagan let go of my hand to pull Aria toward the bar, presumably talking to her about Tennessee and how much she was going to love living there.

I never wanted Reagan to feel like she was giving up everything—her entire life in the only place she'd ever known—for me, so I'd always planned to encourage frequent trips back, going along as often as I could. But now that my sister was moving that way, it gave us even more of a reason to make those trips happen.

Soon, guests started pouring through the open doors, and I was drawn further away from Reagan, into conversation with a few of Lane's deputies—the ones Crew could stand—and Crew's work buddies.

"How's Reagan doing?" Tuck asked. Momentarily confused, I frowned at him. Then it dawned on me that though they hadn't been on shift when the call had gone out about Reagan's accident, Crew's entire team had shown up to help.

"Better," I said. "She's still got her cast on, but she's on the mend."

"Any idea who ran her off the road?" Childers asked.

I shook my head. "Lane is still looking into it, but there wasn't a whole lot to go on. Big, dark-colored trucks with huge grills and brush guards are a dime a dozen around here."

"True enough," Burns piped in. "Well, I hope they catch the son of a bitch who's been tormenting her. You think it's the same guy who took her sister?"

"We're not sure," I replied evasively. Anyone could be listening. The unsub could be standing ten feet away from me and I'd never know it.

Tuck grinned knowingly. "We get it. Information is on a need-to-know basis."

"Exactly."

Before conversation could turn elsewhere, Aria's voice rang out across the barn.

"If you'll all find a seat, the bride and groom are about to make their grand entrance!"

Everyone scrambled toward tables, though we all remained standing. I found Reagan deep in conversation with Mama, but they stopped talking when I appeared and wrapped my arm around my girl's waist.

"What mischief are you two getting into?" I asked softly, eyes darting between her and Mama.

"We were talking about her barn venue ideas," Reagan replied. For the first time in a long time, there was a glint of excitement in her eyes. "I offered my services."

"Services?"

"Photography, duh."

I pinched her backside as punishment for the sass but said, "How's that going to work?"

"Well, if I'm making Dusk Valley home, I'm going to need to find work—"

"You don't have to," I cut in quickly.

She glared, as if she'd ever let me support her. I held up my free hand in surrender. *Fair enough.* The truth was, Reagan's self-sufficiency and at times reckless independence was one of the things I loved most about her.

"I figured, if we're going to open the barn up to events, it might be a good idea to offer up a photographer as well. A sort of package deal."

"That is genius," I agreed, kissing her soundly.

Reagan beamed.

Crew and Aspen finally entered to raucous cheers and whistles, the sound system we'd installed around the barn for tonight booming out some high-bass song I'd never heard before.

Dinner and speeches passed without incident.

At last, the real party began, kicked off by Aria, serenading Crew and Aspen through their first dance with "Something I Need" by OneRepublic.

Once the rest of the guests were welcomed to the floor, I extended my hand to my girl and spun her around. Despite her cast and missing sister, Reagan seemed genuinely happy, and it made *me* happy to see her letting loose and enjoying this night.

Tomorrow, we'd go back to work on locating Lainey.

Tonight, we were simply two people in love, celebrating the union of my baby brother and his bride.

Other men—particularly the single ones—routinely cut in on my dancing time with Reagan, twirling away with her. Normally, it would've pissed me off, but I knew Reagan would be ending the night with me and was mine forever.

While Burns, Childers, Tuck, several of Lane's deputies, and even a ballsier few of my ranch hands took their turns with my girl, I danced with Aria when she wasn't singing, Mama, Delia, Aspen, and even Sutton.

When the band started strumming another slow song and Aria returned to her place at the mic, I stole Reagan back from Tuck.

Her cheeks were flushed. Tendrils of hair had escaped the simple twist she'd pulled it into at the base of her skull, sticky with sweat and clinging to her forehead and temples.

I brushed them away as Aria started to sing a Shania classic. "Hey, belle."

She grinned in response, her expression alight with pure joy. "Hey, soldier."

For a moment, we swayed to the beat. With her in my arms, her chin on my shoulder—even her casted arm tucked awkwardly between us—I couldn't remember a time when I'd ever been happier.

"What do you think?" I murmured in her ear before I could stop myself. "Think you want to get married some day?"

She pulled back, eyes dancing with mischief as she replied, "If the right man asks."

I chuckled. "Honey, I'm the *only* man."

forty

. . .

REAGAN

HONEY, *I'm the* only *man.*

Well, he was right about that. Now that I'd found my way back to him—now that we'd found our way back to each other—I knew without a doubt there would never be anyone else for me. He was *it*. The elusive *one* I'd searched for my whole life.

Goddesses, I couldn't wait for Lainey to meet him.

The thought pulled me up short, timed perfectly to the end of the song.

Finn didn't seem to notice my mind was a million miles away as he led me off the dance floor.

But when he bellied up to the bar to order us fresh drinks, and he turned to see what I wanted, his brow creased in concern before he ever got the question out.

"Are you okay?" he asked instead.

I wanted to lie, to not ruin the perfect moment we'd shared with my mental struggles. But I'd never get away with it; he knew me too well.

"Yes and no," I answered honestly. "Today has been wonderful, but…"

"Lainey."

"Yeah."

He wrapped his palms, warm and steady, around my upper arms. "We *will* find her. *Alive*. I won't rest until it's done."

My eyes flooded with tears, a few slipping down my cheeks, and I nodded.

"I love you."

"I love you too, baby."

Finn pressed a kiss to my forehead, and when he pulled back, I said, "I need a minute. I'm going to go up to the house for a bit, if that's okay?"

I knew he wasn't keen on letting me out of his sight, especially not after dark. But there were enough people around that he ultimately relented—then stood in the open barn door, his tall, broad frame silhouetted by the lights from inside, watching until I made it inside.

I was suddenly so fucking *tired*: emotionally and physically. My arm ached, my feet were killing me in the damn heels I'd decided to wear, and a headache was beginning to form behind my right eye.

A few weeks ago, Finn had shown me his childhood bedroom, and I headed there now, knowing being surrounded by something that was his, even if I needed a moment alone, would help improve my mood.

Slipping my shoes off, I perched on the edge of Finn's bed and rubbed at my feet, groaning at the delicious release of pressure against my toes.

The room was a time capsule, seemingly unchanged from a time sixteen years ago when the twins called it home. I could imagine Birdie keeping everything as it had been when the boys enlisted. A shrine to the sons who may never come home. The walls were decorated with sports posters, including one of their own big brother in an advertisement for Nike. A small shelf in the corner displayed awards earned by the twins over the course of their own athletic careers. I'd been surprised to learn they'd played baseball, not football like Owen, Trey, and Lane. Framed family photos decorated the other flat surfaces, the two simple dressers and closet still filled with Finn and West's teenage clothing.

I couldn't get over how different our upbringings had been—but the similarities of growing up with a twin were impossible to miss. My bedroom back home was the one I'd grown up in, but it had changed over the years, shedding its skin like a chameleon, morphing as I did from girlhood to teenager to collegiate life to the woman I was now.

Lainey and I had never shared a room. Our family farmhouse had more rooms than people to fill them, and after conceiving twins on the first try, Mom and Dad didn't have any more children.

Even though we hadn't *needed* to share, we'd fall asleep together more often than not.

As little girls, Mom and Dad would put us in separate beds, only to find us together in the morning, one of us drawn from our room to our twin's. We'd slip under the covers with a flashlight to play with dolls or tell silly stories. As teens, gossip and overly dissecting the day's happenings carried us until sleep pulled us under.

Then it was Mom and Dad's deaths and my inability to sleep alone. Nightmares would dig their claws in and hold me hostage, forcing me to relive the final moments of their lives, over and over, until Lainey's screams finally dragged me awake.

It had always been us against the world.

Without her, I was unmoored. Adrift. Like a ship lost at sea, unable to return to shore until she returned home.

"Reagan?" someone called from downstairs.

With a sigh, I headed down, my brief reprieve over—and found Aspen waiting at the base of the stairs.

"Shouldn't you be celebrating?" I asked.

"Needed a breather," she admitted. "Likely for the same reason you did."

I nodded in understanding. "I'm sorry."

"Me too," she said, smiling sadly. "Unfortunately, I can't bring Lola back. She is gone forever. But Lainey won't suffer the same fate. We *will* bring her back."

"But what if we don't?"

For the last several months, I'd refused to entertain the thought. Hadn't wanted to consider the possibility that watching her climb into that car in front of our house back in April was the final time I'd ever see her. I knew deep in my heart she was still breathing, but the longer she remained missing, the harder I found it to remain hopeful. Even now that Trey had managed to locate the footage from our first visit to Dusk Valley, I held myself back from truly believing this was the break we needed.

So much time had passed. *Too* much.

Aspen reached for my hand, steadying me.

I hadn't realized I was crying until a tear caught on my top lip. I snatched it with my tongue and sniffed loudly.

"I'm so sorry," I said to her. "That your sister isn't here to celebrate this with you. To see how beautiful you look, how perfect today was. How much Crew loves you."

"It's okay," she assured me. "I've long since come to terms with Lola's absence from my life. It doesn't get easier, of course. But it's one of those things I've come to accept because I know I can't change it." She smiled and squeezed my hand. "Besides, I gained some new sisters today."

I pulled her into a hug, both of us laughing as our height difference smashed her face into my chest. Still, she wrapped her arms around my waist and clung to me. We stayed there like that for a while, both of us allowing the tension of our grief to bleed into one another—allowing someone else to carry some of the load.

At last, we broke apart, and I swiped at my face.

Aspen, of course, still looked pristine.

"I'm going to head back," she said. "You coming?"

"In a minute." I gestured to my face. "I need to clean myself up. Tell Finn I'll be right behind you."

Aspen nodded. "See you down there."

When she left, I made my way to the powder room on the backside of the main floor, where I'd stashed my makeup after getting ready here earlier. I touched up my mascara, dabbed some extra concealer under my eyes, and reapplied my lipstick. Then, shoes in hand because I was *not* putting the infernal things back on, I was ready to head back to the barn.

The day had cooled considerably with the disappearance of the sun, and I wrapped my arms around myself to ward off the worst of the chill until I returned to the warmth of the reception —and Finn's body.

I'd cleared the edge of the gravel drive, my feet sinking into the soft, damp grass, when I sensed movement behind me.

Before I could turn, I went flying, landing face down on the ground. My cast was wedged beneath me, doing little to break my fall. I tried to scramble away, but a hand caught my ankle, tugging me backward. The entire front of my dress was soaked with dew, and the gravel of the drive scraped against my skin, opening tiny, stinging cuts all over my legs and good arm.

My scream was cut off by a hand over my face, muffling my pleas for help. I did my best to scratch and claw and kick out, but with only one hand, it was useless. There was a sharp prick to my deltoid, followed by a sensation like ice flooding my veins. The edges of my vision blurred, and strength seeped slowly from my body.

And then there was nothing but blackness.

forty-one

FINN

THE MOMENT ASPEN walked back into the barn, I rushed to her side before Crew could whisk her away.

"Where's Reagan? Is she okay?"

"Easy, killer," Aspen chuckled. "She's fine. Said she'd be right behind me."

"Okay," I said, relaxing a bit.

With her out of my sight, I was a bit on edge, unable to fully release the tension in my muscles until she was back at my side.

I followed Crew and Aspen to the bar, eyes routinely darting toward the door even as we took a celebratory shot with my brothers.

When ten minutes passed without Reagan reappearing, I began to worry. Excusing myself from my family, I did a lap around the reception, wondering if maybe she snuck in without me noticing. But then, why wouldn't she come right to me? Unsurprisingly, I didn't find her inside, so I stepped out into the night, squinting toward the house, not seeing anyone. After a lap around the barn during which I only succeeded in startling West and Tyler out of a compromising position, my panic had risen to nearly unbearable levels.

My intuition told me something was very goddamn wrong.

I returned inside, West and Tyler hot on my heels. Not wanting to raise the alarm yet, he encouraged her to join the rest of our brothers' dates on the dance floor to do the Cupid Shuffle, the newlyweds leading the charge, while West and I headed for the bar, where Lane, Trey, and Owen stood, shooting the shit.

"Has anyone seen Reagan?"

Their jovial expressions from a beat before fell instantly at my tone.

"Not since she went up to the house," Trey said, craning his neck to search the crowd for her. I barely leashed my irritation. As if I hadn't already done the same thing.

"What's going on?" Lane asked. "Why do you look like someone just died?"

"Reagan is missing," I managed to choke out.

"Are you sure she's not still up at the house?" West asked.

Shit. I'd merely taken Aspen at her word that Reagan was right behind her.

I took off, sprinting from the barn and up the hill, calling for her as I went.

When I received no response, I tried to assure myself she was still in the house.

Everything was fine.

Only…it wasn't.

I reached the spot where the hill plateaued onto the driveway, tripped over something laying in the grass, and nearly fell on my face.

Once I steadied myself, I pulled my phone out of my pocket, clicked on the flashlight, and probed the ground until they landed on the offending object.

My blood ran cold.

Reagan's shoes, carelessly tossed down.

My girl didn't care much for material possessions, but I knew she'd never leave her shoes lying around—especially not in the middle of the yard, and especially not the expensive pair of red bottoms she'd been wearing tonight.

Not unless she'd been forced to.

My flashlight caught a reflective surface as I swept it over the grass, and my blood ran cold as I approached the object.

Half on the lawn, half on the gravel drive lay a phone. Reagan's, I recognized from the beige and black polka-dotted Loopy case.

I flipped it over. The screen was cracked, bits of rock smashed into the fissures.

Even though I knew deep in my bones Reagan was no longer on this ranch, I rushed into the house, calling her name as I raced through every room, nook, and cranny.

She was nowhere to be found.

My brothers followed me inside, and we silently gathered in the foyer.

"I don't know what the fuck to do," I admitted to them, my tone edged with hysteria, gripping my hair in fists, needing something to do with my hands that wasn't throwing my fist into Mama's drywall.

Lane, of course, took charge.

"First things first, we're in agreement Crew and Aspen don't hear of this. The last thing we need to do is ruin their night."

We all nodded, though I knew both of them would be pissed as hell when they eventually found out.

"Secondly," Lane continued, checking his watch, "the reception is about to wrap up. As soon as we send Crew and Aspen on their way, we convene at Trey's. Deal?"

"Deal," the other three said. I was mute, numb, afraid if I allowed what was truly happening to sink in, I'd spiral.

"Now we're going to go back to the barn and put on the fucking show of our lives."

"Someone here *took* her," I ground out. "And you want to act like nothing is happening? What the fuck!"

Those final three words echoed back to us, and West put a steadying hand on my shoulder. Lane's expression turned stern, though edged with sympathy.

"I have a plan," he said, placing his palm on my other shoulder. "Trust me to do my job, Finn. Okay?"

All I could do was nod. The longer we waited, the further away Reagan got. While I was chomping at the bit to tear this fucking ranch, town, the world beyond apart until I found her, the last thing I wanted to do was pop the bubble of Crew and Aspen's perfect day.

Even in the face of my worst nightmare come true, I refused to destroy their dreamlike reality.

Doing my best to put on a brave, happy face, I trailed behind my brothers to the barn. Thankfully, as we crossed the threshold, Aria was up on the mic telling everyone to gather outside for Crew and Aspen's sparkler send-off.

I merely went through the motions, allowed Lane to shove one of the stupid, sparkling sticks into my hand, pasting on a bright, fake smile as Crew and Aspen danced down the aisle formed by the guests still remaining. He helped her into his truck, both of them blowing kisses and waving like the fucking King and Queen of England, basking in the attention of their adoring public.

When their taillights faded into the distance—they were heading to Boise for an overnight before flying out to Hawaii in the morning for their honeymoon—I turned to Lane.

"*Find. Her.*"

Though his eyes narrowed, and I was sure he would scold me, he merely sighed deeply through his nose and faced the crowd.

"Excuse me!" he shouted, and the guests who had started to peel off, moving toward their vehicles, stopped. Under normal circumstances, Lane wasn't a man you wanted to ignore, but *espe-*

cially not when he adopted his sheriff tone. Everyone watched him expectantly.

"First, on behalf of Crew, Aspen, and our entire family, we want to say thank you all for being here tonight. It's been the perfect day, and I speak for all of us when I say we couldn't be happier for our baby bro and his new wife. Unfortunately, though, something…unimaginable happened here tonight."

A collective gasp rose from the crowd, murmurs kicking up and filling the silence in the wake of Lane's words.

"One of our own, Reagan, seems to have gone missing. So before I can let any of you leave, I'm going to need everyone to come back inside so we can conduct some interviews and searches."

"You can't hold us!" someone shouted from the back.

"You're all under suspicion," my brother replied. "As far as the law is concerned, holding you is *exactly* what I'm entitled to do."

Several people grumbled in annoyance but didn't put up a fight as my brothers herded them back into the barn. In their absence, Mama, Aria, Delia, and Owen approached me. Owen held a sleeping Jace against his chest, and all of their faces were lined with concern.

"She's really gone?" Mama asked.

I nodded, not trusting myself to speak.

Owen inclined his head to where Lane had flipped on his sheriff mode, organizing people into little groups and directing Trey and West to question them.

"They'll find her."

They.

I should be—*needed* to be—involved, but at the moment, I was completely useless. All of my training had vacated me the moment I needed it most, needed it to save the woman who meant *everything.* Whose loss I would not survive.

"What do you need from us?" Aria asked.

"Stay—" I started, but my words were cut off as the roar of an engine filled the quiet night.

A beat later, headlights flipped on, illuminating a section of the drive and yard beyond the house, where we'd instructed guests to park. Tires spun and gravel flew as the vehicle peeled out.

I burst into action, racing down the road after it. But of course, the driver was speeding like a bat out of hell and put too much distance between us too quickly.

I didn't think as I turned to Owen, the only one who had followed me, despite carrying his dozing son.

"Keys."

"You've been drinking…"

"Keys, Owen!" I shouted.

The longer he stared at me, delaying giving me what I asked for, the further away the escapee got.

And so did Reagan.

Because I knew without a doubt she was in that truck against her will and being taken away from me.

Finally, Owen dug in his pocket and passed the keys to his rental over.

I clicked the lock button to locate it, then rushed toward it and threw myself behind the wheel, peeling out exactly as the fucker who had taken my girl had.

While he had a headstart, there wasn't anyone on the planet who knew this land better than I did—except, of course, my family—and that gave me an advantage. I drove on autopilot, navigating the curves and hills of the access road that connected our ranch to the county road ahead, pressing the speedometer to sixty, seventy, eighty.

Was it reckless? Absolutely.

Did I give a fuck?

Hell no.

Reagan's life was on the line. At the moment, mine didn't matter.

When I reached the T formed by the ranch drive and the county road, fields expanded in all directions.

Nothing but silence and stillness greeted me. Not even a flash of taillights.

"*Fuck!*" I screamed, slamming my fist over and over against the steering wheel.

Taking a stab in the dark, I headed right, where the road would take me further away from town, deeper into Lawless ranch land. My head was on a swivel as I sped down the dirt lane, whipping toward trails and two tracks that cut into the woods and fields in either direction. I gave myself five miles before I had to accept the driver—and Reagan—had slipped through my fingers.

I reluctantly turned around and headed back to the ranch.

"What the fuck was that?" Lane asked when I parked near the barn and climbed out of the SUV. "You can't just go all cowboy and take off whenever you feel like it!"

"Let all these people go," I said. "None of them are responsible."

"How do you know?"

"Because one of them snuck free of your little round up and took off down the road. I was trying to catch them. I think it's safe to assume they have Reagan."

My words were flat. I couldn't even consider where my girl was now, what state she was in, what she was enduring at the hands of some unknown creep.

"Fuck," Lane muttered, scrubbing a hand down his face.

"Yeah. Great work, Sheriff."

Lane lifted his finger into my face and stepped closer, but Owen stepped in and shoved us apart before fists could fly.

"What we're *not* going to do is turn on each other," our eldest brother said.

"He's being a prick," Lane retorted.

"Some asshole just took the love of my life away from me!" I screamed in his face. "How do you think you'd feel?"

Lane stilled, as though he hadn't stopped to consider that—hadn't reminded himself that Reagan was now the center of my universe.

"Fair enough," he said, backing off, then raising his voice to speak to the guests. "Sorry about that, folks. Everyone can go home."

A mass exodus ensued, and when the final car disappeared down the drive, we gathered in a loose circle.

"So now what?" West asked.

"Now, we head to my house," Trey said.

AN HOUR LATER, I sat in Trey's living room while he and Lane were holed up in Trey's office, combing through the Swallow footage from that day and night seven years ago and tonight's from the big house. I barely noticed what was happening around me, my eyes focused on some middle distance while I tried not to think about what was happening to Reagan.

"How's it going in there?" Owen asked when West rejoined us.

"They started with the cameras from the big house. Whoever attacked Reagan did a hell of a job hiding their identity."

"What about the truck? Did they get a plate?"

West shook his head. "Tag lights were disconnected. All we can be sure of is the truck was big, dark in color, and had a huge ass brush guard."

"Which describes over half the vehicles in this fucking state."

I didn't bother joining the conversation. The truth was…I was barely holding it together.

Images of the present, of being here, in Trey's living room

with my brothers, seemed to cut in and out of focus, replaced in blips with memories from the past.

A briefing room on the other side of the world.

Coordinates to a safe house where several members of our team were being held as prisoners of war.

More lives I couldn't fucking save.

My chest tightened, like a fifty-pound weight sat on my sternum. I gasped for air, but it barely made it into my lungs.

The harder I tried, the more constricted my airway became.

One of my brothers scooted next to me, put a hand on my shoulder, and said, "Breathe."

Owen, using the same tone of voice he'd used to command offenses for years.

The word seemed to reach me from a thousand miles away.

I *couldn't*. I sank further below the surface. The edges of my vision went hazy, darkness slowly creeping in.

Finally, I let it win, let it drag me into the deep and block out everything else.

forty-two

. . .

FINN

"*FINN.*"

Why was that name so familiar?

The earth beneath me quaked, but I couldn't see anything to figure out why.

"*Finn.*"

My name, I realized, and spoken more insistently now.

I blinked my eyes open to find West and Owen hovering over me, Owen gently shaking me.

"What the fuck?" I said softly. "What happened?"

"You had a panic attack," Owen said. "And kind of passed out."

"There's no 'kind of' about it," West said, grimacing. "Your eyes rolled back in your head, and you went limp. Fucking scary. I'm going to have nightmares about it for the rest of my life."

Pushing them both away to get some brother-free air, I sat up, rubbing my temples.

"Sitting around like this isn't good for me," I admitted.

"PTSD is a bitch," West agreed.

"I have panic attacks too, you know," Owen murmured.

"Great," I muttered. "So we're all fucked in the head."

"Mental health struggles are perfectly normal and nothing to be ashamed of," Owen said diplomatically.

"You sound like a shrink."

"He definitely sounds like my old therapist," I agreed with West.

During our time in the service, I'd heard too many horror stories of guys who let their internal issues—the shit they'd seen in war—eat them alive when they left active duty and returned home. Neither West nor I wanted to be another statistic. I worked incredibly hard that first year to confront and banish my demons. Since then, I'd been doing well.

But Reagan going missing? It brought all of that old shit, that same helplessness I'd experienced when some guys had been taken as prisoners of war.

No. I shook that thought off. I hadn't been helpless then, and I sure as fuck wasn't now.

But sitting here on my fucking hands was *not* helping matters.

I leapt to my feet and stalked to the other side of the house, where Trey's command center was, and burst through the door.

"Anything yet?"

"We're working on it," Lane replied. Trey's focus remained on the screens in front of him.

"Well work faster!" I shouted. "My girl is out there somewhere!"

I wanted to shake them both, to demand Trey's stupid little fingers worked quicker, but an arm hooked around my shoulders and dragged me backward, out of the room.

When I faced him, Owen was chuckling and shaking his head.

"Nothing about this is funny."

He held his hands up in surrender. "It's not that." He nodded toward Trey and Lane. "Dad always said when one of us went down, the rest of us would fall like dominoes."

I frowned. "The fuck are you talking about?"

"You're down so bad, brother." He clapped me on the shoulder. "Trust me, I know the feeling. And it's the scariest goddamn thing in the world. If I was in your shoes, and Delia was out there somewhere, I'd be tearing the fucking world apart."

All I could do was stare at him blankly. "What's scary?" I asked dumbly.

"Being in love. You *do* love Reagan, right?"

"More than anything," I agreed, throat clogging with emotion.

Fuck, I didn't know what I'd do if we didn't find her in time, if this sick fuck harmed her and Lainey in ways they couldn't come back from.

"They'll find her," Owen said, gesturing to the war room. "It's what they do. What *you* do."

Owen was nothing if not a master of the pep talk, and his reminder that *all* of my brothers except him had trained for situations exactly like this put me a bit more at ease.

I knew Trey was working as quickly as he could, but standing around like a dumbass waiting for that big break was slowly sapping the remaining vestiges of my sanity.

I had to do *something*.

"West."

"Yeah?"

"Let's take a ride."

My twin's brow curved upward. "Wheels or wings?"

I grinned. "Wings."

"I'm coming."

None of us had heard the door off the garage open, nor had we clocked the footsteps as they approached.

I was *shocked* to find Crew and Aspen standing there.

"What the *fuck* are you two doing here?" Lane asked, emerging from Trey's bat cave, tone echoing my own surprise.

"Aria called," Aspen said. "The real question is, why the *fuck* didn't one of you tell us what was going on?"

"Because it's your wedding night," I said. "And finding Reagan is not your problem."

Crew snorted, and Aspen rolled her eyes.

"Please, Finny," she said, breaking out the nickname she knew I hated. The only ones who got away with using it were Mama and Aria. "She's your girlfriend. And as your sister-in-law, that basically makes her *my* sister. Of course she's our problem."

There was no sense arguing with her. Aspen McKay—no, *Lawless*—put our own stubbornness to shame.

Sensing I wasn't going to fight her further, she stepped up and rose onto her tip toes to give me a hug, though she was so short I had to bend to greet her. When she let go, she said, "We'll find her."

"How can you be sure?"

She hooked a thumb over her shoulder at her new husband. "We got him back, didn't we?"

Fair point.

She strutted into the war room like she owned it. Trey didn't look away from the screens, but Lane handed her a sheaf of papers, which Aspen greedily accepted, settling at the small, square table at the side of the room and instantly going to work.

"What are those?" I asked.

"Property records," Lane supplied.

"We'll find this fucker, Finny," Aspen said, attention on the top sheet. "Promise." Then she raised her hand to shoo us. "Now leave us alone."

"You caught yourself a live one with her," Owen said to Crew with a chuckle.

"Takes one to know one," Crew grinned, looking like the happiest motherfucker on the planet.

Annoyed, I growled, "Are we going to do this or what?"

"Do you want to change first or something?" Crew asked, brow curved as he took in my and West's clothes—the creamy linen pants and button up shirts we'd been wearing all day. I'd shed the bowtie and unbuttoned the top few hours ago, but changing would waste time we didn't have.

"No."

And that was that.

Crew and West followed me out of the house, and we took off for the airfield.

On the way, we called the air traffic controller from Boise, and to say he was pissed would've been an understatement. But when I explained the situation in the barest details possible, he agreed to get out of bed and head to the airport.

"Any idea how long you'll be up?"

"As long as it takes."

"Noted."

"You're being an asshole," Crew said when I disconnected.

Before I could chew him out, West told him, "If someone took Aspen, you'd be doing the same fucking thing, baby brother. Cut him some slack."

Wisely, Crew shut up, and we passed the rest of the drive in silence.

I'd parked when my phone rang with a call from Lane.

"What?" I answered.

"We've got something. Get your asses back."

Though West and Crew were halfway out, I shifted into drive and peeled out of the lot, and they barely threw themselves back inside in time.

"Warn a guy next time," our little brother grumbled. "I almost pissed myself."

"You run into fires for a living," I said with an eye roll. "Grow a pair."

I drove too fast back to Trey's house, barely remembering to put the truck in park before flying out from behind the wheel and racing inside.

"What's this news?" I asked without preamble when I stalked into the war room.

For a moment, Trey, Lane, and Owen shared an unreadable look, as though having the same sort of wordless conversation West and I often had.

I looked to Aspen for answers. If anyone in this fucking room would shoot me straight, it would be her. But my tough-as-nails new sister-in-law was curled in on herself in the chair we'd left her in, face white as a sheet.

"Little phoenix?" Crew asked softly as he approached, kneeling in front of her and putting his hands on her thighs.

"Hotshot," she rasped out, immediately shaking her head, as if whatever they'd found after we left was unbelievable. "Fuck."

"Someone tell us what the fuck is going on," West demanded.

"I finally managed to isolate the footage from that night," Trey explained. "Aspen confirmed it with the property records, and a call to the station told us he has a vehicle matching the description of the one that ran Reagan off the road registered to him.

"We found who took them."

"Who the fuck is it?"

Lane scrubbed his hand over his face. "Come see for yourself."

Annoyed as fuck that they wouldn't simply *tell* me, I stalked over until I stood behind Trey and studied the screens, all paused on the same face.

At first, I couldn't believe what I was seeing. *Him?* There was no fucking way.

But there was no denying it.

The face in the image was none other than Lyle Tucker.

Known to his friends simply as *Tuck.*

forty-three

. . .

REAGAN

I CAME TO CONSCIOUSNESS SLOWLY—AND regrettably.

My head pounded, my tongue stuck to the roof of my mouth, which seemed to be stuffed with cotton.

Even without opening my eyes, I knew I was somewhere unfamiliar.

But I couldn't remember how I'd gotten here.

Gathering myself through the jackhammer in my skull, I attempted to take stock of my surroundings with my eyes still closed.

The surface I lay on wasn't soft, exactly, but not as hard as the floor would be. The fingers of my good hand twitched against it, and some sort of rough fabric scratched against them.

I strained my ears and was greeted by the sound of distantly running water.

And breathing.

Fuck. I wasn't alone.

"C'mon, Rea Rea," a voice whispered. "I know you're awake."

My eyes flew open, and I shot upright, the pain in my head

forgotten as my attention locked on my reflection across the room.

No, not a reflection.

My twin.

"Lainey!" I cried.

I scrambled off the mattress, trying to get to her, but my progress was stalled halfway there.

Looking behind me, my blood lit with fury.

There was a fucking manacle hooked around my ankle and bolted to the wall.

"What the fuck?"

"Shut up," my sister hissed. "Keep your voice down."

Quieter this time, I said, "What the fuck?"

"The real question is, what the fuck are you doing here?"

"Oh, right," I snorted. "Because I asked to be here."

My memories came back to me all at once.

Leaving Crew and Aspen's reception to go up to the house for some much-needed silence.

The conversation with Aspen.

Walking across the driveway, the struggle, the prick of pain in my arm, which I now realized had been the sting of a needle.

Goddesses, how long ago had that been? How long had I been here?

My heart rate ticked up, breath growing shallow.

I swept the room, searching for any indication of the time. Nothing hung on the walls, but the world beyond the small, ceiling-level windows was dark.

We were in a basement, then, and I could've been here for mere hours…or days.

The basement, I realized with a start, looked identical to the one from my recurring nightmare. Right down to the floral wallpaper and shag carpet.

"Glad you're not dead, by the way," I said to Lainey absently.

Lainey crawled toward me until she reached the end of her

own restraint, then dropped onto her stomach and stretched out to her full length, a hand extended toward me. I mirrored her, and when we reached for each other, our fingertips barely brushed.

The simple touch was a balm to my soul.

Despite our circumstances, Lainey grinned.

"I fucking knew you'd find me."

I gestured to my restraint. "Not the rescue I imagined."

Lainey asked, "How long have you been in town?"

I returned with a question of my own. "How long have I been *here*?"

"Maybe six hours? Hard to be exact when I don't have a watch, so that's my best guess."

Okay, not as long as I expected.

Squeezing my eyes shut, the ache in my brain penetrating the adrenaline coursing through me at seeing my sister alive, I tried to focus.

"So it's early on Sunday, the…"

"Twenty-seventh," Lainey confirmed. "Now, when did you get to town?"

"June seventh."

"I fucking *knew it*," she crowed happily, then shifted closer to the wall behind her, where I could make out a series of hash marks scoured into the wood paneling.

One of the marks was circled.

"How did you make those?"

Holding up her hands, I took in the state of her nails. Several of them were broken and cracked, but a surprising number of her acrylics had managed to hang on through four months of growth. "If I ever make it back to Tennessee, I'll have to tip my nail girl more next time. These fuckers will *not* come off. But that's not the point.

"I swear to Aphrodite," she continued, invoking her favorite goddess and tapping the gouged oval, "I *felt* when you got here."

Exactly how I'd always known she wasn't dead.

She tapped another, maybe five days later, and stated, "And this night, I—"

"I had a dream," I cut her off. "Of this place."

Clapping excitedly, she said, "Oh my goddesses, it fucking worked?!"

I nodded. "It felt so real, I immediately told Finn about it."

Lainey smirked. "So you did reconnect with your sexy soldier after all."

"I did," I whispered, my heart aching at the thought of him. He had to be going out of his mind, wondering what happened to me.

"You love him."

My sister knew me better than anyone. Even after four months apart, I wasn't surprised she'd immediately figured it out.

"I do. And he loves me," I said, my grin growing to match my sister's. "Which means he'll come for us. Goddesses, it's good to see you. We've been looking for *you* for months."

"Glad to see that worked out well for you."

"I didn't ask to be assaulted and *drugged*," I hissed.

"And I didn't ask to be held prisoner in this *That '70s Show*-looking basement for months, but here we are."

"Are you okay? Did he…" I trailed off, the thought too horrible to voice out loud.

Lainey shook her head. "We've got ourselves a jailer with a conscience and a relatively straight moral compass, all things considered. Says he won't touch me until I ask."

"Which you never will."

"Bingo."

"We'll be out of here soon," I promised.

"I hope you're right," Lainey said. "Because now that *he*"— she pointed toward the ceiling, where I could hear our captor moving around upstairs—"has both of us, I'm afraid we don't have much time."

"Who the fuck is this guy?"

"His name is Lyle Tucker."

The name tickled my brain, but I couldn't figure out why. Did I know anyone with that name? I didn't think so, but something about it seemed familiar at the same time.

"Tell me everything," I breathed.

Before she could, though, the door at the top of the stairs creaked open, and heavy footfalls landed on the steps, descending toward us.

I hadn't known what to expect—after all, I'd never been abducted before—but it hadn't been *him.*

I'd never known his full name, but I knew exactly who he was.

"You son of a bitch!" I screamed, shooting up and rushing toward him, only to be yanked back by the shackle around my ankle. I landed hard on my stomach, the air leaving my lungs in an *oof.*

"Hello, Reagan," he grinned. "Welcome to the Tucker farmhouse."

Tucker.

Tuck.

Tuck, Crew's co-worker at the firehouse.

Tuck, who had come to my rescue after my accident—the one *he* caused, I now realized.

Tuck, who I'd danced with last night—before he attacked me in the dark the second I was alone, drugged me, and chained me up here.

Everything started clicking into place.

The notes, the message on my mirror.

"You attacked Aria," I gasped in horror.

"In my defense, I thought she was you," Tuck explained. "Seems strange Finn fell for a woman who could so easily pass for his sister, but I guess I have no room to judge." He glanced pointedly between me and Lainey. "I am also not immune to your allure."

"I will fucking *kill* you," I seethed. "Of course, if Finn doesn't get to you first."

He grinned, a boyish expression that made it even more difficult to look at him as someone capable of harming me and my sister. He was a *first responder*, for crying out loud. Had dedicated his life to *saving* people.

"Your little boy toy won't be a problem," he said, waving his hand dismissively. "We'll be long gone before they figure out I'm the one who took you."

"Fuck you," I spat.

He turned to go, pausing with his foot on the first ascending tread, and winked at me. "Only if you ask nicely."

Then he disappeared upstairs.

"What the *fuck*."

"My thoughts exactly," Lainey replied.

As succinctly as I could, I explained who Tuck was to me—to the Lawless family.

"I was *dancing* with him at Crew's wedding last night," I hissed, still in disbelief.

Lainey pouted. "I missed all the fun."

Though there was absolutely nothing comical about this situation, I couldn't help but laugh.

"I wish you could've been there."

"I can't wait to meet this whole ridiculous family when we get out of here." She sighed. "And now I suppose it's my turn to spill."

And she did. About the abduction, how she's been locked in this basement for the last four months. She hadn't exactly been living in squalor, she explained, gesturing to the small vestibule off the side of the main room. I got up and walked toward it, finding I could also reach it. Inside was a stand-up shower, toilet, and the rough foundation of a vanity with an aged porcelain sink and copper pipe as a spigot.

That was good, though. Though he'd made it so we couldn't reach each other in the main room, he apparently hadn't considered the possibility that we could within the bathroom.

Lainey reached my side and threw her arms around me, squeezing me to her. I hugged her with equal fervor, tears slipping down my cheeks as I did. We weren't safe yet, but we were together, and that was a major blessing.

The main area and the mattresses we'd both been provided appeared clean. Lainey herself didn't look too worse for wear, though there were deep, dark crescents under her eyes, her cheeks more hollowed out, the bones of her arms more prominent—like she hadn't been eating enough.

Not to mention, she was *pale*, her skin a shade it likely hadn't been since we were children. Like she hadn't been let outside once during the entirety of her captivity.

"Every three days, he'd leave me alone for an entire day," she continued, tapping her crude calendar, where certain hashes were marked with an X. "Now that I know what he does for a living, obviously, those coincided with his shift at the firehouse. But when he was here, he was *here*." She pointed at the nearby armchair, its ugly orange fabric faded and pilled, the cushion sagging in the middle. "He'd sit there and talk to me. Sharing stories about people I didn't know, reminiscing on memories I'd never been a part of. It didn't take long to realize he was pretending I was someone else."

I shook my head. "That actually makes perfect sense." I explained about how Addie had profiled him. "We're likely surrogates for someone he lost."

"You look exactly like her."

So lost in catching up, neither of us had heard Tuck come downstairs until he spoke.

"That doesn't give you the right to hold us here. We aren't yours to keep."

"*She*"—he pointed at Lainey—"already gave herself to me. And, god, it was like having Nadine back in my arms."

"But we're *not* Nadine," I protested, then switched to a different tack. "What exactly is your plan here, Tuck? To keep us locked in this basement forever, hoping we'll eventually break?"

Instead of answering, he took a seat in that heinous orange chair, reclining back and resting his elbows on the wooden arms.

"Nadine and I were only twenty-three when she left. I thought we were going to spend the rest of our lives together. I even bought a ring. Instead, I came home from shift one morning to find everything she owned gone. She'd disappeared. I tried to find her, spoke to her family, and asked the public for information on her whereabouts. But I didn't have much to go on, and she didn't leave a single clue behind. For a long time, I'd convinced myself someone had taken her."

"Like you took us," Lainey muttered.

I snorted. "And all of her stuff? Fucking delusional."

"About a year later, her mother delivered a letter to me at work. *Stop looking*, it had said. *I left of my own free will. I just didn't love you anymore*. Heartbroken, I'd been forced to accept the fact that she was gone for good."

"What'd you do to drive her away?" I asked before I could stop myself. Lainey drove an elbow into my side.

What? I silently asked her. *Women don't just pick up and leave without a word unless they have a damn good reason.*

Maybe she realized he's fucking crazy.

Rolling my lips between my teeth, I choked down a laugh. *Not the time, Reagan.*

"I did *nothing!*" he shouted, his eyes flashing with anger, the tendons in his neck flexing, jaw muscles jumping as he clenched his teeth together. "I *worshipped* her. Gave her everything she could've ever wanted. A beautiful home, an intense, all-consuming emotional and physical connection. I was going to ask her to marry me. We were going to build a family.

"When you walked into the Swallow that night, right after I got that letter, looking so much like her, it seemed like the universe was giving me a second chance. And for my trouble, there were two of you!" He laughed, a bit maniacally, and I had to wonder how no one saw the obvious psychosis he suffered from. Apparently, he was a hell of an actor. "So I set my trap, and Lainey walked right into it."

My sister rolled her eyes and huffed out an annoyed sigh. "I just wanted to get laid."

"I gave you the most passionate night of your life," Tuck argued.

"You gave me nothing but an itch that still needed to be scratched. Which I saw to the second we got home."

Lainey held out her fist for a bump, which I obliged.

Meanwhile, that night *had* been the most passionate of mine —until Finn and I reconnected. If he hadn't flown off to a literal *war zone* after our night together, I had to admit—the chances were high I would've been back for more.

And now, he was all mine for life.

Funny how things worked out.

I thought Lainey's immodest comments would piss Tuck off, but he appeared calmer than when discussing Nadine and her betrayal.

He continued his story unperturbed.

"I'll admit, I was a bit disheartened when she completely spurned my advances after that," he said, talking about Lainey like she wasn't sitting ten feet away from him, his eyes focused on some middle distance. "But I am nothing if not a persistent man, so I bided my time, hoping she would change her mind. When she didn't, I'd been forced to take more drastic measures."

"You're the 'couple' that booked a session with us."

"Yes, Reagan. And I thought it was going to be *you* coming to

Dusk Valley. That I'd have to take you and lure Lainey. Imagine my surprise when Lainey showed up instead."

Though he'd now confirmed my longtime suspicion, I was somehow still surprised by the lengths this man had gone.

"How can you even tell us apart?" Lainey asked.

"I've spent years studying you. I could pick you both out in a crowded room with my eyes closed."

Something oily and...*icky* sluiced down my spine with his words. I was aware he'd been harassing Lainey with the incessant messages over the years, but I hadn't been aware he'd been *watching* us both—studying us like fucking bugs under a microscope. A quick glance at Lainey revealed her to be equally as appalled.

"So now what?" I asked. "You keep us chained in this basement forever like you've been keeping Lainey these last few months?"

Tuck chuckled, shaking his head. "Of course not, dear girl. Now that I've got you both, we're leaving Dusk Valley."

Lainey snorted, and we shared a look, my own thoughts reflected in her eyes.

We're obviously getting the fuck out of here, right?

I dipped my chin in a barely perceptible nod. *As soon as he comes within reach. Do whatever you gotta do to overpower him. Subdue him long enough for Finn to find us.*

For now, we had to keep him talking.

"We're not going anywhere with you," Lainey said.

"I'm afraid you don't have a choice."

With that, he got to his feet and disappeared back upstairs.

"What the *fuck*?" Lainey hissed. "He's even more delusional than I thought."

"We need a plan." My eyes darted around the room, searching for anything within reach we could use to aid our escape. Of course, Tuck had been thorough in removing any potential weapon from the area.

Understanding what I was doing, Lainey said, "You don't think I've already done that?"

I glared. "No need to get snippy. I'm a fresh set of eyes. There could be something you missed."

"I've been down here for *four months*, Rea. Trust me, I know this place better than our house in Tennessee."

Having been so caught up in the current predicament, that I'd now found myself prisoner here as well, I'd failed to consider the exact toll all the solitude and monotony had taken on my sister.

"Goddesses, Lainey, I'm *so* sorry." Unbidden, my eyes welled, tears slipping free and cascading down my cheeks. "I'm so sorry I didn't come for you sooner."

"You came as soon as you could."

"I didn't want it to be like *this*. We were supposed to find you and send the whole fucking cavalry in to get you. I wasn't supposed to end up here too."

"Look at me."

I did, though reluctantly.

Now that we were back together, I was forced to finally confront the thing that had scared me the most about her return: that she would hate me. That she would begrudge me my freedom all these months while she'd been held here, little better than an animal bound to the whims of its master. That she'd be angry I spent these months falling in love while she'd been falling apart.

I saw none of that in her eyes now, felt none of it radiating from her.

There was only…gratitude.

Though a prisoner myself, she was happy I was here, that I'd been looking for her.

"You're here now, and we can't change that. But we've always been better together, and we've *never* needed a man for anything, right? Fuck those Lawless boys. We're the heroes of this story."

I choked on a laugh, vision blurring as I blinked, trying to expel and quell the tears.

"You know what?" I said, angrily swiping at my face, dashing away my weakness. "You're right. Let's fuck this guy up and get out of here."

Lainey's answering grin was downright feral, the kind she'd wear when we were kids and she was about to get us in a fuckton of trouble.

"Let's do it."

forty-four

· · ·

REAGAN

"FIRST THINGS FIRST—"

"*I'm the realest…*" Lainey rapped, like we always did whenever one of us brought up the first line of "Fancy" by Iggy Azalea.

I narrowed my eyes and pursed my lips. "Not the time."

Lainey giggled. "Sorry. Continue."

Though I rolled my eyes, a little chuckle escaped me as well.

Lifting my leg as best as I could, I indicated the shackle around my ankle. "First, we need to get the fuck out of these."

Lainey sighed. "You think I haven't tried? There isn't anything down here to pry them open or pick the lock."

"Do you even know *how* to pick a lock?"

"Obviously not," she said, "but I'm sure I could figure it out if properly motivated."

Fair enough.

"Okay, let's sweep the area."

"Rea Rea," Lainey whined. "I've already done that!"

"Well, I haven't, so let me try, okay?"

She nodded but didn't move, leaving me to my own devices.

In deference to the lingering headache and insistent pain in my broken arm from the struggle between me and Tuck, I gingerly rose to my feet and took shallow steps forward, in the direction of the bathroom. While I was there, I relieved myself—on a toilet without a seat, my weak legs shaking from the awkward hovering—before returning to my task.

Like the main space, the room had been stripped bare. Anything Tuck seemed to have deemed an object that could be weaponized had been removed. In addition to the missing toilet seat, the tank cover was also gone. Doors, drawers, and hardware had been taken off the crudely constructed vanity, leaving an empty, gaping maw of dust-covered OSB. The stand-up shower had no door or curtain and nothing inside beyond a thin sliver of soap. There were no windows, and the door and hinges had also been taken down.

I walked back into the main area, eyes sweeping the large space. Stretching to the full limit of my chain, I walked the perimeter, eyes probing. Lainey watched me silently, pity on her face. She'd been here for months and hadn't found a way to escape; I didn't know who I thought I was kidding, believing my presence would magically change everything.

Despair swept over me like a towering, inescapable wave. My hands went to my face, wiping the tears that had fallen from my cheeks before sliding into my hair. I yanked on the roots, the sharp sting returning some sense.

Falling apart now wouldn't do either of us any good. I had to stay level-headed.

"Okay," I started, more to fortify myself than anything, my good hand tangling in my hair and pushing it backward, out of my face.

A knot formed around the fingers. I withdrew then tilted my head and came at it from a different angle to work it free.

Elation and excitement buzzed in my veins when I teased it out—and a bobby pin fell into my hand.

Holding it up in triumph, I grinned at Lainey.

"Oh, we are *so* getting out of here," she replied, smile equally as wide and proud as mine as she got up and met me in the bathroom.

"Can't believe that stupid fuck didn't think to check my hair," I chuckled.

We sat mirroring each other on the cold linoleum floor, knees bent so our ankles rested between us.

I reached for Lainey's shackle. "You first."

Picking a lock wasn't as easy as hostages made it appear in movies and television. Hours seemed to pass in a blink—though, in reality, based on what I could glean from the slowly lightening sky beyond the windows, it couldn't have been longer than thirty minutes. By the time Lainey's restraint finally popped open, the bobby pin was scuffed and a bit mangled, and sweat beaded on my forehead.

Her shriek of joy was so loud, she clapped her hand over her mouth, both of us stilling as we waited for any sign that Tuck was approaching.

When all upstairs remained quiet, I went to work on my own. Since I'd already done it once, it took a fraction of the time. Soon, both Lainey and I were free.

In celebration, we jumped up and clung to each other, cheering as quietly as we could.

"Now what?" she asked, twisting her ankle, seemingly absent-mindedly, obviously luxuriating in the sensation. Meanwhile, rage rose within me at the sight of the bruising and scarring marring her flesh.

"Now," I said through clenched teeth, "we take that fucker down and get the hell out of here."

"Any idea how that's supposed to happen?"

"Nope," I said. "But now that we're not restrained, I'm sure it'll be a lot easier."

The door at the top of the basement stairs creaked open, and Lainey and I shared a look of horror. Racing back into the main room, we flopped down on our separate mattresses.

"Put it back around your ankle!" I hissed, gesturing at her shackle while I grudgingly coiled mine back in and dropped it over my ankle. "But don't lock it."

"No shit." Lainey rolled her eyes but followed suit.

Not a moment too soon, either, as Tuck began descending, his footsteps followed by the *thunk thunk thunk* of something heavy being lugged down after him. When he reached the bottom landing, he rounded the corner into the room with his back to us. I rose onto my feet to see what he dragged.

At first, I was certain my eyes were deceiving me.

He couldn't be serious.

"*A shipping container?*" I asked. "You can't make me get in there."

Tuck held a clear vial and needle aloft. "Afraid you won't have a choice. And we don't have much time, so don't make this difficult, 'kay?"

"How did you even—" Lainey started.

"I'm a firefighter, honey. The paramedics in our house keep this stuff on hand for sedation in the field."

"And where exactly are you taking us?"

Tuck grinned. "You'll see when we get there, but I know you'll love it."

"What we'd *love* is to be set free."

"Not gonna happen."

"So you're going to hold us against our will forever? You know that'll never work, right?"

Tuck patted the top of the container, which, upon further inspection, appeared large enough to house us both. "I'm confident some time in this box will convince you cooperation is in your best interests."

"You are a sick fuck," Lainey spat at him.

His lips twisted into a frown, but he didn't respond. Instead, I watched in horror as he inserted the needle into the rubber top of the vial and withdrew some of the clear liquid.

The silence was broken by the gentle hum of an engine.

A plane?

Finn?

Hope flared in my chest.

Out of the corner of my eye, I looked at my twin. Lainey's thoughts echoed my own.

Hear that?

Your lover boy made it after all. But if he gets that shit into us, it's over.

When he gets close enough, we attack, I silently responded. *Punch, kick, do whatever the fuck you gotta do, then race for the stairs.*

Lainey's chin dipped slightly.

All my plans changed when Tuck momentarily turned his back on us, and I saw the gun stuffed in the back waistband of his jeans.

"Now," I murmured to Lainey, barely moving my lips.

"But…"

I shifted my eyes pointedly between her and Tuck's back.

"*Now!*"

"What—" Tuck started, facing us. Before he could utter another word, Lainey and I kicked free of the shackles and rushed him.

He may have been stronger than one of us, but he didn't stand a chance against both. Lainey landed a hard punch to his jaw, full of pent-up rage, and Tuck's head snapped back. A second later, I lifted my knee into his groin, then drove it into his nose when he folded forward.

Dropping my elbow into his back, I knocked him over. Lainey was already halfway up the stairs, and I raced after her.

"You're going to wish you hadn't done that!" Tuck managed to gasp out.

Daring a glance back, I found Tuck already getting to his feet. I thought I'd nailed him square in his balls, but maybe I missed if he recovered so quickly. I had bigger problems when he reached for the gun, lifted it in front of him, and fired.

The bullet passed close enough that its heat singed my cheek.

"Run!" I screamed at Lainey.

Lainey disappeared from sight as Tuck reached the top of the stairs behind me. Another shot rang out, the bullet punching a hole in the wood paneling to my left. Covering myself as best as I could, I reached the end of the hall and made a right turn, running like my life depended on it for the front door. Tuck was moving faster now, and he fired again as I burst outside.

"Reagan!"

Finn.

He *had* come—and brought the cavalry with him.

Thank the goddesses.

"I'm okay!" I shouted, sparing him only a glance but not stopping until I followed Lainey beyond the barricade of deputies straight ahead. "He's got a gun!"

"Get clear! We've got this!"

He wouldn't receive any argument from me. Lainey and I kept running past the wall of deputies, who, guns raised, shuffled backward down the dirt two-track serving as the driveway for the farmhouse.

"Get to the ambulance," one of them said to us over his shoulder. Johns, I thought his name was. I'd seen him around.

Lainey and I nodded. Adrenaline pumped through my veins, making me a bit light-headed. I threaded my arm through Lainey's and started up the drive, willing myself not to turn around, unwilling to see what happened next.

I'd have enough nightmares of that fucking basement to deal with.

A brunette woman raced toward us, and it took me a second to recognize her as Sutton.

"Are y'all okay?" she asked, her nitrile-gloved hands going to Lainey first, gently cupping her chin and tilting her head this way and that.

"Fine," I assured her.

Physically, anyway. Lainey would likely need years of therapy to unpack everything she'd endured down there, and I was sure I could benefit from several sessions myself.

Sutton, however, didn't respond. Her hand dropped from Lainey's face, attention fixing on something behind us, eyes wide, face blanching.

I turned and followed her gaze.

Tuck stood at the top of the porch steps, waving his pistol around like a toy. Blood dripped down his face. The line of deputies remained between us and him, and off to the left stood five of the Lawless brothers, Addie staggered behind Lane.

All nine men had guns trained on Tuck. He had no way out.

Lane broke free from his brothers, taking tentative steps toward the porch, keeping his gun trained on Tuck. From this distance, I could see his lips moving but couldn't hear what he was saying. Likely trying to talk Tuck down, convince him to come peaceably.

What happened next transpired so quickly that, looking back, my memory could only conjure a blur of motion and explosion of gunshots.

But one thing stood out, one thing I'd never forget as long as I lived.

The soul-shattering scream of a woman calling out for a man.

"Lane!"

forty-five

. . .

FINN

WE MOBILIZED QUICKLY after the Tuck bomb dropped. Lane made calls, summoning his deputies to the station for a briefing before heading out on our rescue mission.

Owen and Aspen headed back to the ranch, much to Aspen's dismay. She hated to miss out on the action, but as she didn't have any formal training beyond the classes she'd taken to get her concealed carry permit, she was more of a liability than anything.

Lane had imparted that bit of wisdom, which pissed Aspen off so much Crew had to carry her out to the car before she started swinging.

I made all the appropriate noises and said all the right things, assuring Lane we'd meet them there, that West and I had to run home to get geared up.

He didn't need to know I wouldn't be going anywhere near the station—unless he arrested me after the fact for what I was about to do.

I'd been planning on filling West in on the drive, but I was unsurprised when he sidled up beside me and murmured, "You're about to go rogue, aren't you?"

"This is my girl we're talking about here. You didn't really think I was going to let Deputy Dipshit lead the charge, did you?"

West's answering grin was feral, and he lifted his fist for a bump, which I obliged.

Unfortunately, while Lane seemed none the wiser to my plans, I hadn't managed to dupe Trey and Crew.

"We'll ride with you," Trey—who was already outfitted in his tactical gear and weapons—said as West and I went to leave.

"Yeah," Crew agreed. "Mind swinging by my house?"

"We don't have time for that."

Crew snorted.

"We know you're going rogue, brother," Trey said, ruffling my hair. I socked him in the arm. "And we're coming with you."

"No." West uttered the rejection before I could.

"Then we'll tell Lane," Crew said.

"Oh, you're going to tell big brother on us? Get the fuck out of here. I don't have time for this bullshit."

"We get it, Finn. This is your girl, and all of your military training is telling you there isn't time to waste. Lane has to abide by the letter of the law, but none of us are bound by the same oath. Let us help."

I glanced between them, finally landing on Crew. "You don't even have formal training."

He shrugged, then flexed his biceps like a douchebag. "I think I'll be okay."

West caught my eye. *Up to you.*

I suppose the four of us are better than two.

"Fine," I conceded. "But I'm in charge here, got it?"

They both mock saluted, and I rolled my eyes as we got in the truck.

"See you at the station!" Lane called as he pulled away.

After three quick detours for Crew, West, and I to gear up, we were on our way back to the airport.

The sun was cresting the horizon when we parked in front of the hangar. When we walked inside, I began going through my preflight checks while the other three tossed around ideas for our best course of action to get my girl back from Tuck.

Fucking Tuck.

I was still having difficulty wrapping my mind around the fact that *Tuck*, certified goofball and seemingly good guy, was responsible for Lainey's four-month absence and abducting my girl. I never would've imagined him capable of such things.

Although, it did make a certain amount of sense when I stopped to consider it—not that I'd had a lot of time to do so since his identity had been revealed. But Tuck…he'd always floated on the fringes. There, but easily forgettable. He didn't immediately command attention the moment he walked into a room.

Now that I knew he'd been behind everything, the pieces of the whole puzzle started clicking together in my mind. Thinking back, I did vaguely remember him being at the Swallow the night I met Reagan. As a firefighter, he had intimate knowledge of the cameras in town—and their blind spots—which had made it easy to slip that note under her windshield wiper without anyone noticing. Not to mention access to incapacitating drugs.

For each of the major incidents—Aria's attack and Reagan's accident—he'd been off shift. Hell, he'd *responded* to Reagan's accident scene, acting like he was there to help when he'd been the one who caused it.

The second Reagan and Lainey were safe, I was putting a bullet in his head.

Checks complete, we loaded into the rescue chopper instead of my Cessna in case the girls needed to be airlifted out, a possibility I considered with as much detachment as I could muster.

Once we took off a few minutes later, West pulled up the area of the Tucker farmhouse on the nav system. Thanks to the paperwork Aspen had gone through back at the house, we knew the Tuck was the titleholder on an apartment in town as well as family land that had been passed down for generations.

Yeah, the farmhouse Reagan had seen in her dream was real. Though they'd pieced off what had originally been hundreds of acres of land over the years, the old Tucker farmhouse and a few outbuildings sat on the sizable parcel that remained.

I knew without a doubt that's where Reagan and Lainey were being held, and I knew Lane would split his men into two teams. Half of them would head to the farmhouse, half to the apartment.

Maybe I'd get lucky and he'd go to town himself, not finding out I'd taken matters into my own hands until after the fact.

Despite the terror that had been coursing through my veins nonstop since I realized Reagan was missing, my hands were steady as ever on the cyclic stick and controls.

My headset crackled to life as West spoke, gesturing to the navigation screen.

"If we're going for stealth, I'd touch down here." He pointed at a clearing about half a mile from the house itself. "If not, park this bird in the backyard."

"Stealth," I said immediately. "I'm not taking chances with Reagan and Lainey's lives."

As we closed in on the landing point, my nerves ratcheted up again. I took a deep breath, hoping to steady myself, but it accomplished nothing. I tried to remind myself that West and I had pulled off missions more dangerous than this more times than I could count. That Trey had spent nearly a decade guarding the President's back, that Crew walked into literal burning hell every day to save lives. One man was nothing.

But it *felt* different. I felt...*listless* without Reagan. Knowing she was in danger made it difficult to get a full breath of air into my lungs, like a weight sat on my chest that wouldn't lift until she was back in my arms.

I set the chopper down in the field West had indicated, and

we got out, taking a minute to ensure we had all the weaponry we needed, and that our tactical vests were properly secured and covering what they needed.

Before we set off toward the house, West dropped a hand on my shoulder.

"Chill," he murmured. "You're fucking vibrating."

"We've already wasted too much time," I muttered in response, double and triple checking that all of my holsters were filled.

With a single target to contend with, I didn't anticipate a shootout, so I may have gone overboard, but I wasn't fucking around where my girl was concerned.

"While I don't disagree, you're not going to do those women any good if you don't have your head on straight."

Fuck, I knew he was right. His fingers dug into my skin, and I let the pressure ground me, closing my eyes and attempting to marshal my heartbeat. When they popped open again, I was surprised to feel calmer.

Cell signal out here was spotty, but we'd all wore radios tuned to the police frequency. At the moment, we were out of range, but I didn't doubt Lane would chew our asses out the moment he could reach us.

We hiked toward the house, sticking to wooded areas as best as we could. The forest around us was still, the sky a pale golden blanket overhead. Daylight would make this both easier and harder.

At last, the house appeared about a hundred yards ahead. We stopped, and Trey got out a set of binoculars.

"Nothing going on that I can see," he said, lowering them. "I'm gonna do a sweep."

"I'll go with you," Crew volunteered. "We'll go in on opposite sides, then loop back."

"No," I said, stopping them. "We'll get close together and recon from there."

We followed the edge of the forest, which provided excellent cover as we neared.

From a distance, there didn't appear to be anything wrong with the house. Up close, though, the disrepair was obvious. Tuck clearly didn't care about routine maintenance. The yard was beyond overgrown, likely tall enough to reach my knees or higher, and a gnarled apple tree shaded the corner. White trim was chipped and weathered grey, the evergreen-painted siding now faded and buried under several layers of dirt. The porch sagged dangerously in the middle, one of the railings on its steps completely gone, the other hanging on through what appeared to be sheer will and an interesting trick of gravity.

A nearby outbuilding, which had likely once been a garage, was missing its door and had a large crater in the roof.

In the gravel lot out front, about thirty yards from where we stood, sat an ancient camper truck with its tailgate down. I couldn't tell if there was anything in the bed. Otherwise, there appeared to be no signs of life anywhere on the property.

Fury—a rage unlike anything I'd ever experienced before— boiled in my veins. What kind of sick fuck abducted women and held them hostage? And in a place like this, which seemed barely inhabitable for small critters, let alone humans?

"I'm going to kill him," I seethed through clenched teeth, taking half a step forward.

West's arm shot out, barring my progress. "You can't."

"Like hell."

"*Finn,*" West pleaded, and I finally looked at him. "Not without recon. You know better."

I turned to my brothers, ready to direct them out on said recon mission when our radios sprang to life, startling me.

I'd forgotten we wore them.

"Earth to Dumb and Dumber, and the other two brothers," Lane said, his irritation evident. "Where the fuck are you?"

"Took a little walk," Trey replied levelly, relaying what we saw.

When he finished, Lane demanded our exact location, told us to stay put, and went silent.

"He's going to get them killed if he doesn't start moving with some fucking urgency," I said as we waited for the sheriff's arrival, my nerves completely frazzled, energy coursing like electricity through my body.

We must have been closer to the road than I realized because a few minutes later, Lane crashed through the undergrowth, Addie in tow.

"I've got half the team going around back," Lane said when he reached us, not bothering to reprimand us for ignoring his instructions. "The other half is moving up the access road as we speak. Sutton is on standby."

"We came out in the chopper, should we need it."

He nodded. "Has there been any movement?"

I shook my head.

"Okay, here's what we're going to do. We're going to let my team breach—"

I cut him off. "Fuck no. I'm first in the door."

"You're a civilian, Finn. I can't allow that."

I fucking *hated* the bureaucratic bullshit Lane pulled when it came to stuff like this. If he let us go, Trey, West, and I would have Lainey and Reagan home already. But *noooooo*. We had to operate within the constraints of the law.

Well, fuck the law. I may have retired, but I was still a goddamn soldier.

"I'm going in of my own free will," I protested. "No liability on you."

My brother ran his hand down his face. I could tell he wanted to fight with me, but there was no good reason for it— and we were only wasting more time. He glanced at the rest of our brothers and Addie. "You'll vouch for me if this blows up in my face?"

West grinned. "You got it, Sheriff." My twin nudged me with an elbow. "I've got your six."

"Y'all scare me," Addie admitted.

Trey winked. "You get used to it."

To our left, a group of four deputies led by Johns appeared, slowly approaching the structure.

"Alright," Lane said. "Let's go."

We'd barely cleared the tree line before shouts rang out from inside the house—followed by a gunshot.

Moving before my brain had given my body permission, I raced toward the house like my life depended on it. I was halfway across the yard when two figures appeared running for their lives. Lainey first, followed not too long after by Reagan.

I sagged in relief at laying eyes on my girl again.

"Reagan!"

Reagan's eyes landed on me for a beat, but she didn't slow or veer toward me.

"I'm okay!" she shouted back. Then, "He's got a gun!"

I lifted my own in response. "Get clear! We've got this!"

She nodded and kept moving, running straight toward the group of deputies, who parted to let them through, then reformed a wall between them and the open doorway of the house. Knowing she was safe, I returned my attention to the house. Tuck appeared in the doorway, looming like some monster from a nightmare. His right arm swung a pistol, waving it around like something as harmless as a water gun, while he screamed obscenities at the girls.

Blood dripped down his face from his nose, splashing into his mouth, garishly staining his gums and teeth as he grinned maniacally.

Lane took a step toward him.

"Don't," Trey insisted. "He's fucking crazy."

Lane looked at him over his shoulder, then spared each of us a glance in turn.

"I've got this," he assured us.

Breaking further from our line, his gun never wavered as it remained trained on Tuck. When he spoke, Lane's soft tone was entirely at odds with the tension gathered in the air around us like a thick storm cloud.

"Put the gun down, Tuck."

Tuck laughed a bit hysterically, though he lowered his arm. "Fuck no."

"Tuck," Lane insisted. "It's over. Put the gun down and come with us."

"I'm not going to prison!" Tuck shouted. "I didn't do anything wrong! They belong with me!"

My brother inched closer. "It's over," Lane repeated as he reached the bottom of the stairs, putting him within five feet of Tuck—point blank range for the Glock that, for the moment, hung at his side.

Meanwhile, Lane kept his sights on the center of Tuck's chest, finger on the trigger, poised for any sudden movements.

Tuck continued muttering about how Lainey and Reagan were his, how he wasn't giving them up.

Lane didn't move closer or away, simply said, "It's going to be okay, Tuck. I'm going to have one of these deputies cuff you and put you in a car. Then we'll go to the station and talk, okay?"

Johns stepped forward, cuffs out, and climbed the steps.

Too fast. Too fucking fast.

"Stand down!" I shouted at Johns.

The warning came too late.

Before Lane could react, Tuck lifted his gun, pointed it at my brother, and fired.

As Lane was knocked backward from the force, my own weapon discharged, putting a hole in the center of Tuck's forehead, as several more shots punctured holes in his chest.

forty-six

. . .

FINN

NOTHING COULD PREPARE a person for seeing someone they love getting hurt. The trauma, even though you hadn't endured it yourself, felt like a hole being ripped in your chest, shattering your heart to pieces.

I'd felt it the day West, Crew, and I were fucking around on the ranch as teenagers, and Crew fell off his horse, fracturing his leg.

Again the day Owen took the hit that fucked up his shoulder and ultimately ended his NFL career.

When I found Aria on the kitchen floor of the guest house a few months ago, surrounded by all that blood.

When Reagan was trapped behind the wheel of her car, the bones of her arm poking through the skin.

And now, as long as I lived, I'd never get the image of that bullet passing through Lane's chest, his vest doing nothing to stop the large caliber at such a close range. Good luck or poor aim had kept it from going through his head.

Blood sprayed, and Lane fell backward, landing in a heap on the ground while all of the law enforcement present rushed forward, service weapons unloading on the already dead man who lay on the top step, his arms and legs sprawled awkwardly around and beneath him.

I'd fired the kill shot. He'd been dead before he hit the ground.

"*Lane!*" a woman screamed, and before any of us could reach our brother, Sutton raced forward, dropped her bag and followed it to her knees, and pressed her hands over the wound in his chest.

Everything happened quickly after that. Crew, who had gone through paramedic training a few years ago, rushed to Sutton's side. Together, they hooked Lane up to an IV, intubated him, and did what they could to staunch the bleeding from his chest. As a team, my brothers and I carried him the half mile to the chopper and loaded him in. It all seemed to happen in a blur, all of us moving on autopilot.

"Stay with Reagan!" I shouted at West as I fired up the engines, Crew and Sutton getting in back beside Lane to keep working on him. My twin saluted as I lifted off.

"Boise!" Sutton shouted, but I was already on it.

Crew yelled, "We're losing him!" as a horrible, steady *beeeeeeeeeeep* found its way to my ears over the roar of the engines, rotor, and blades.

"No!" Sutton screamed, her breath labored. "C'mon, Lane. Stay with me."

Her words were punctuated by sobs, and I had to admit, I was barely holding it together myself.

I'd evacuated wounded soldiers and civilians before, but I'd never flown as fast as I did that day, knowing my big brother was dying. Knowing I was responsible for getting him to the hospital as quickly as possible because his life depended on it.

Thanks to me radioing ahead, when I touched down on the helipad atop the hospital's singular tower, the trauma team raced out to meet us. There was a lot of shouting of medical terms I didn't understand as Crew and Sutton helped transfer him to a gurney. Crew remained with me while Sutton raced inside with the team.

My baby brother was covered in Lane's blood, his hands stained, his shirt and pants ruined.

"Come on," I said, wrapping my arm around his shoulders. "Let's get you cleaned up."

Ten minutes and a fresh set of clothes for Crew later, we walked into the waiting room, dropping heavily onto chairs side by side.

"One of us should call Mama," he said quietly, his steady tone belying the fear and worry radiating off him in waves.

My hand shook as I took my phone out of my pocket.

I swallowed hard, emotion clogging my throat, then pressed Mama's name on the screen, putting it on speaker, its ringing far too loud in the silence around us.

"Finn?" Mama said when she answered. "Everything okay?"

"Hi, Mama."

The relief in Mama's voice was evident when she said, "Oh, Finn. It's so good to hear your voice. You're okay? What about Reagan and Lainey? Did you get them back?"

"I'm fine, and so are they. We got them," I assured her. "But Lane was shot."

"Where?" Mama asked.

I had no idea if she meant where he'd been shot or where he'd been taken, so I answered both. "In the chest. We're in Boise now."

"We'll meet you there."

An ambulance raced up in front, screeched to a stop, and Trey climbed out from behind the wheel.

What the fuck?

I rose to my feet, moving faster out into the lobby when my twin, a brunette woman, two blondes appeared at his side.

"Finn!" Reagan called, throwing herself into my arms a moment later.

"Oh god, baby," I sighed, unshed tears pricking my eyes and stinging my nose. The last sixteen hours had been too fucking much. I wrapped her up tightly, certain it would be a long time before I could ever let go. "Are you okay?"

"I'm fine," she assured me. "Lainey too."

Her twin approached us, and even though I was a twin myself, the resemblance was…uncanny. Still, I could easily tell them apart. My body came alive in Reagan's proximity, that tether in my chest drawing me right into her embrace.

"I'm going to get her checked out," Reagan said, offering her face up for a kiss, which I gave her, letting it linger longer than I should have in polite company. She gave my fingers a final squeeze before leading Lainey to the admission desk. I was reluctant to let her go, but all danger to her had passed with Tuck's death.

Soon, cops started to arrive, filling the room with Lane's deputies, though I noticed Johns and the three other deputies at the farmhouse were absent.

Likely cleaning up the mess.

"Any update?" Trey asked when we settled in the waiting room.

"He flatlined on the way," I said, "but Sutton and Crew got his heart going again. They wheeled him back the second we landed."

West looked around. "Sutton go with?"

I nodded. "I don't think they could pry her away from his side at this point."

Trey straightened, scrubbing a hand down his face in a move so like the one Lane made when he was stressed, I damn near burst into tears.

"It doesn't look good, does it, Finny?" he whispered.

I reached for his hand, not speaking. Words were useless, and we weren't the praying kind. Instead, I sank back in a chair and closed my eyes. All at once, a bone-deep exhaustion settled over me—the crash after adrenaline receded from my veins, coming down from the constant fight-or-flight I'd put my body through the past sixteen hours.

And I was fucking sick of hospitals. Too many people I loved had found their way through these doors the last few years, and it had to stop.

Commotion had my eyes popping open in time to see Mama, Aria, Aspen, Owen, Delia, and Jace rushing through the door.

Mama sat on Trey's other side. "What happened?"

Seeing her opened the floodgates, and when I opened my mouth to tell her, a sob broke free instead. Shaking my head, I buried my face in my hands and let it all go.

The rage of Reagan being taken from right under my nose. The panic of not knowing where she'd been, of not knowing what was happening to her. The utter relief of seeing both her and Lainey run out of that house. Having her back in my arms, returning the missing piece of my soul. The worry over Lane, the sheer terror of potentially losing him that strangled me.

All of it was simply too much to bear a second longer.

A warm hand settled between my shoulder blades as I fell apart, though I knew without looking that it belonged to West.

Through my tears, I saw a figure approach and kneel in front of me, but my vision was too blurred to tell who.

"Baby."

I got up and stalked away, outside and around the side of the building. The last thing I wanted was for *anyone* to see me like that, let alone Reagan.

Naturally, she followed me.

"Don't run away from me, Finn Lawless," she said, tone far too stern for my fragile emotional state.

"Go back inside, belle. I'll be fine."

Instead of listening, she stepped up to me and wrapped her arms around my waist, resting her head between my shoulder blades, and held me. I covered her hands, which rested right above my waistband, with one of mine.

I didn't know how long we stood like that, but enough time passed for me to regain some composure and spin to face her.

Resting her chin on my chest, she looked up at me. "Better?"

I choked on a laugh. "Not even close, but thank you for staying."

"You don't hide from me, Finn. *Ever*. You've seen all of my ugly. The least you can do is show me some of yours."

"It's not that easy."

"I know," she said with a sad smile. "But try, okay?"

She likely understood there were parts of me she'd never see. Not necessarily because I was afraid to show them but because I was *terrified* to unpack them, to bring them back into the light of day. There were parts of my and West's time in the service that neither of us would ever talk about again—not even with each other. Parts I refused to *think* about.

But for her, I could try to be more open about the things that wouldn't rip me to shreds to remember.

"I don't know what I'll do if he doesn't make it," I admitted.

Reagan reached up and smoothed her fingers over my face, clearing away the tears that lingered on my cheeks. "We're not going to talk like that. We don't know anything yet. In fact, for all we know, things might not be as bad as they seem. Let's go back inside and sit with your family, okay?"

I nodded and allowed her to lead me back into the waiting room. Before we walked in, though, I pulled her to a stop as something occurred to me.

"How's Lainey? Why aren't you with her?"

Instead of answering, Reagan pulled me forward. The crowd of deputies parted, and I gaped at the scene before me.

Lainey sat in one of the uncomfortable chairs, a hospital blanket tucked in tightly around her, a pole with an IV drip connected to her arm sitting a few feet away.

"She refused to sit in the back," Reagan said with an eye roll. "Wanted to 'be part of the action.'"

"I just can't believe it was *Tuck*," Mama was saying incredulously. "Like…Lyle Tucker. He was such a goofy boy, but he turned into what I thought was a fine man."

"If it makes you feel better, I spent a lot of time with him, and he did seem pretty normal."

My family, which had gathered around Lainey, gaped at her.

The silence was broken by slightly hysterical laughter.

It took me too long to realize it came from me.

Everyone joined in, and once we composed ourselves, Mama turned to Lainey and said, "You know, that *doesn't* make me feel better, but thank you for the laugh."

Lainey smiled proudly. "Anytime."

A murmur spread through the men and women gathered behind me, and I turned toward the door to see Sutton standing there. She picked her way through, Lane's deputies patting her on the shoulder and offering words of thanks.

"Hey guys," she said when she reached us.

I wondered if she knew her dark blue tee was covered in blood.

Honestly, I doubted it. She looked as wrecked as I felt.

Mama got to her feet and pulled Sutton into a hug. "Thank you," I heard her murmuring over and over.

"I didn't do anything," Sutton said when she pulled back, obviously fighting like hell to keep her shit together. "I almost lost him."

"But you didn't," I said, squeezing her shoulder. "You got him here. You gave him a chance."

Sutton nodded but refused to look at me.

I had no idea what she was going through, and I had to admit, I almost thought being in my shoes was better. With my brother, I knew where I stood. While we gave each other constant shit, we loved each other fiercely. For Sutton…we as a family had always secretly agreed there was more to their relationship, some big piece of the picture we weren't privy to. They'd been friendly when they graduated high school, and both had gone to school at Boise State, right up the road from where we currently sat.

Next thing we knew, there was this…animosity racing like an undertow beneath each of their interactions.

But this reaction—the anguished scream, the despondence in her expression now…this wasn't a woman who hated a man, who didn't care what happened to him. In fact, I thought the opposite was true. She cared *deeply* about what happened to Lane, and she had no idea what to do about it.

That made two of us.

forty-seven

. . .

REAGAN

I FOUND myself caught between a rock and a hard place.

Emotions warred for purchase inside me.

Pure elation that Lainey was back. That she was whole, seemingly no worse for the wear, though I knew she'd have some shit to unpack in therapy.

She'd been examined by an ER doc, who ran a battery of tests and immediately hooked her up to an IV, the fluid loaded with electrolytes and medicine. Despite some obvious malnourishment, the doctor didn't see anything outwardly concerning about Lainey's appearance.

Then there was the heartbreak for the Lawless family, especially Finn.

Was this to be my life from now on? Every instance of triumph and joy balanced by one of utter devastation?

I did my best to stay out of Finn's way, giving him room to feel what he needed to feel, to lean on his siblings and Birdie, while also reminding him I was there if he needed me.

Wanting to feel somewhat useful, I approached Owen and asked for his keys. "I'm going to go get coffee and food," I told him when he handed them over.

To West, I added, "Keep an eye on them, okay?"

"You know I will."

No one noticed as I made my escape.

At least, I thought no one noticed, but I'd barely settled behind the wheel of Finn's big ass truck before my phone pinged with a text.

SOLDIER

Come back.

ME

What? Why? Is everything okay?

SOLDIER

No. I miss you.

ME

I've been gone for two minutes!

SOLDIER

And that's two minutes too long. If I could, I'd handcuff us together so you could never get away from me.

I sucked in a gasp that released as a laugh as another message quickly followed his last.

SOLDIER

...too soon?

ME

I love you. I'll be back soon.

MY EXCURSION for coffee and food took longer than I planned, but I had to admit, moving about freely without constantly looking over my shoulder, feeling like there were eyes on my back, watching me from the shadows, was a welcome change. My stalker was dead, and Lainey was home. I could breathe easy for the first time in months.

Well, if you didn't count the fact that the love of my life's brother was fighting for *his* life.

When I pulled back into the lot, I sat unmoving in the truck for a moment, listening to the tick of the cooling engine.

Truthfully, I was fucking sick of this place. Between Aria, me, and now Lane, I'd spent more time in hospitals the last few months than I had in the years since the accident that took my parents combined.

When this was all over, I was going to convince Finn and my sister to take a long tropical vacation.

As long as Lane pulled through and made a full recovery, the days when we were free of this trauma and pain were coming soon.

Finally, after a final deep breath to steel myself, I collected the bags of food and trays of coffee from the passenger seat and went inside.

Upon walking into the waiting room, I was surprised to find most of the deputies and Addie had cleared out, leaving only the Lawless family and Sutton. Birdie and Aria clung to each other, crying quietly, and the brothers all wore varying expressions of… shock? I hated that I couldn't tell if the emotional uproar meant good or bad news.

"What happened?" I asked Finn, setting the food on a nearby table and approaching him.

He pulled me into his arms, squeezing me so tightly I could barely breathe.

"Lane made it through surgery," he said quietly. "They managed to remove the bullet. It missed his heart thankfully but had lodged itself in his lung. They're going to keep him in an induced coma and on a ventilator to give his body a break while the tissue heals."

"But the prognosis is good?"

"The prognosis is *great*," he breathed, tone full of awe and…hope.

I pulled back to look up at him. His eyes shone with tears, but this time, they were accompanied by a smile wide enough to light this entire city. The shadows in his stormy depths had receded, leaving that crystalline blue I loved so much.

Grinning in response, I said, "Happy looks good on you, soldier."

"*You* look good on me, belle. I wouldn't be able to get through this without you."

Digging the fingers of my good hand into his shirt, I fisted it and pulled him impossibly closer, tilting my head back for a kiss, which he obliged.

"*I* wouldn't have survived these last few months without *you*."

He shifted from my mouth to my forehead, lips lingering. "We can unpack all of this later, all of what happened to you in that basement, but…god, belle. I'm so fucking happy to be holding you."

"In your arms is right where I belong."

AFTER ASSURANCES from the hospital staff that Lane was in good hands, the Lawless family began filing out to head back to Dusk Valley. Birdie planned on packing a bag and spending some time in a nearby hotel, wanting to be close in case something happened. Owen, Delia, and Jace were heading back to Michigan, though Owen would be back in a few days.

Eventually, only Finn, Lainey, and I remained. Lainey's test results had come back clear, but the doctor wanted her to stay overnight so he could keep her on a steady IV drip in an effort to return some of her strength.

The second visiting hours ended, we were promptly kicked

out. Finn tried to convince me to go back to Dusk Valley and sleep in our bed, but I refused.

Now that I had my sister back, I wasn't about to be separated from her again. Even walking out of the hospital and not having her directly in my sight took a Herculean effort.

In contrast to the one roach motel in Dusk Valley, Boise had a number of more upscale options to choose from, and Finn booked us a room at the one closest to the hospital.

When we entered, I flopped onto the bed, eyes drooping closed. Beyond the unconsciousness of being drugged, I hadn't slept in over thirty-six hours. Now that the danger had passed, now that Lainey and Lane were going to be fine, all of my energy ebbed out of me until I was a puddle on the mattress.

"Are you sure you're okay?" Finn asked.

I cracked my eyes open. "I'm fine. Great, actually, aside from being fucking exhausted."

He reached for my feet, peeling off the slippers the hospital had given me and tossing them directly in the trash.

"Hey!" I protested, eyes flying open. "Those are the only shoes I have."

Hell, I was still wearing my dress from the wedding, though Delia gave me the extra hoodie she had in their SUV, which had her family's winery logo on the front. I'd cleaned up my face a bit at the hospital, swiping away the makeup that had streaked down my cheeks and crusted under my eyes, but the rest of me was rumpled and filthy.

"I'll buy you new clothes," he said, all of my protestations forgotten as he dug his thumbs into the arch of my foot. I groaned, eyes fluttering closed again.

"Don't stop."

"My two favorite words," he murmured, and I could hear the smile in his voice.

I cracked an eye. "*That* is not happening tonight."

Never did I think I'd see the day when I didn't want to fuck

Finn until neither of us could walk, but after everything that had happened, I felt dirty. Fatigue had settled so deep in my bones, I didn't want to move from this bed for the foreseeable future.

"Didn't say it was," he agreed.

Dropping my one foot, I thought he'd move to the other and give it the same treatment. Instead, he came to my side and easily scooped me off the bed.

"Finn! What are you doing?"

"Thought you might want to take a bath."

Now that the option had presented itself, I could think of nothing I wanted more.

The hotel was fancy enough to have a freestanding tub in the bathroom, pristinely white and large enough to fit me *and* Finn with room to spare. Finn propped me up on the counter, and the cold marble set goosebumps skittering across my skin. He crossed to the tub, twisting the handles and testing the flow until the temperature was how he knew I liked it—nearly hot enough to boil me alive—before he plugged it. On the vanity at my side was a collection of soaps and lotions, and he lifted one, inspecting it.

"How do you feel about eucalyptus?" he asked.

"Sounds fucking heavenly."

He dumped the entire bottle in the water.

Once the basin was appropriately filled, he turned off the faucet and returned to me.

Reaching behind me, he lowered the zipper on my dress. "Arms up."

I obliged, and he gripped the hem of the dress, lifted it over my head, and discarded it on the floor at his feet.

Though I remained clad only in a pair of panties, there was nothing sexual about the moment. We were merely two people who loved each other deeply, gazing into each other's eyes, happy to be alive and sharing this moment.

I watched as he shed his own clothes, marveling at the strength of this man of mine—both physical and emotional.

Being with him made me realize I'd only ever been with boys before. Even Troy, who was older than Finn, bought into bullshit gender stereotypes about remaining stoic in the face of adversity. To him, real men didn't cry, and he would've been appalled by Finn's earlier breakdown.

In my opinion, "men" who believed that weren't men at all.

Once he was naked, Finn helped me down, then slipped his fingers into the waistband of my underwear and pulled them down my legs. I stepped out of them, but before I could get far, he lifted me into his arms and carried me to the tub, sinking in with me.

The steam and temperature were *divine*, and I moaned as I settled back against Finn's chest, resting my cast on the edge so I didn't get it wet.

For a long while, we sat there, luxuriating in the bath and each other's company.

Then Finn asked, "Can I wash your hair?"

I nodded, shifting away from him so I could dunk my head underwater. He reached for the bottle of shampoo resting on a nearby ledge and poured a healthy amount into his palm, rubbing it around and lathering it up. I tilted my head back, and his fingers threaded into my wet hair, lightly massaging with the pads and scratching with his nails.

"Damn, that feels good," I murmured.

"I'm just grateful I can touch you," he replied. "That you're here and safe."

I looked at him over my shoulder. "I promised you I'm staying, and I meant it."

He nodded but said, "There was a while there, for several hours last night, where I didn't think it was a promise you'd be able to keep. That you'd be taken from me forever."

He removed his touch from my head and stilled, though I noted his fingers shook. I twisted to face him, careful to hold my cast aloft.

"You came for me," I reminded him. "You found me, saved me like you've been doing since the day we met."

"I'll *always* come for you," he reminded me. "I would tear this world apart to find you, shred myself in the process if necessary. There is nowhere you could go where I wouldn't come for you, Reagan." He ran a palm over his face, water catching on his eyelashes, bubbles sticking to his stubble. "It's terrifying, you know? To love someone this much."

I'd had the same thought more than once recently, but especially last night. The thought of never seeing him again—of disappearing without him ever knowing what happened to me was an alternate reality I'd refused to accept.

Lainey—she was my wombmate, my twin flame. My equal, my exact match in every way.

But Finn was my *soul*mate. The other half of my very essence, an intrinsic component of my genetic makeup. I could live without him no more than I could live without air.

"I get it," I promised him. "I feel it too. But there isn't a version of this life that exists where you *don't* love me, where we didn't find ourselves right here. Together."

"You think?"

Grinning, the soapy mess of my hair and cast be damned, I curled against his chest and wrapped my arms around his neck. The steady *thump* of his heart beat a rhythm against my cheek, marching along in time with my own.

"I *know*."

epilogue

. . .

FINN

TWO MONTHS LATER

"YOU FINALLY GOING to tell me where you're taking me?" Reagan asked from the passenger seat.

I made an exaggerated show of looking out the window, at the Smoky Mountains rising up around us, their peaks wreathed in wispy clouds. The sky above was a clear, Carolina blue.

"I'd have thought that was obvious," I said, raising a brow at her.

"You're not taking me home, are you? Like…you're not sick of me and decided to drop me off and wash your hands of me?"

My eyes rolled far enough back into my head that it hurt. "If that was my plan, I would've sent you on that plane to France with Lainey." I reached over the center console of our rented truck and squeezed her thigh. "You're stuck with me for life, baby."

"Then put a fucking ring on it already," she pouted, lifting and wriggling her bare ring finger.

I chuckled. "Patience, belle."

The truth was, there was nothing more in this world I wanted than to be Reagan's husband, to make her my wife. To give her my last name. *Reagan Lawless* had a nice ring to it, didn't it? Thinking about it made my dick hard.

But after the ordeal we'd suffered this summer, I figured we could both use some normalcy and mundanity.

Thankfully, through therapy, the talking kind for Lainey and the physical kind for Lane, both were coming back stronger than ever.

Did I think Lainey taking off to the other side of the world to be *alone* was a bit insane? Of course. But I was in no position to judge the way people coped and healed.

Lane, on the other hand, was staying put in Dusk Valley— and found himself with a houseguest to boot, one who was uninvited but doing a hell of a job at making sure he doesn't push himself too hard.

The GPS directed me down a dirt road, entirely shaded by a leafy green canopy, the sun dappling the windshield as we passed through.

"Your destination is on your left."

The lane was nondescript and cut through more trees, but I knew from photos online that we'd soon break free from the cover into unobstructed and soaring mountain views.

As we did, Reagan gasped.

"It's like a little fairy cottage!" she squealed, smacking my arm excitedly. I grinned at her as I pulled to a stop in the little gravel lot out front.

Perched near the edge of a cliff, the cabin did give fairycore vibes.

I wanted to punch myself for even knowing what "fairycore" meant.

The walls were dark-stained logs, the red tin roof domed, making it look more like the cap of a mushroom than a traditional log cabin. The trim and door were painted a burnt umber that blended in with the fall foliage and made me feel as though we'd stumbled onto the Smurf's village.

We'd visited Aria in Nashville—where, unsurprisingly, she was thriving—and it took some time to convince Reagan to extend our trip. After all the uncertainty we'd recently faced, and how unsettled she'd felt all summer, I thought it mostly had to do with wanting to get home and establish a routine. To start building her business up in Idaho, to settle into our day-to-day lives.

But looking at her now, the sense of awe and wonder shining in her eyes as she stood in the front yard of the cottage and spun in a slow circle, taking it all in, I knew she was glad she'd agreed to stay.

"This is…magical."

"Only the best for my girl," I said with a wink.

I gave Reagan the key, an old-fashioned brass thing with a decorative bow, and she ran ahead of me while I collected the first load of our things.

Despite the logs and rich, walnut stain on the exterior, the inside was dry-walled and painted a creamy white, the floors a gorgeous birch hardwood, brightening the entire space. The entire backside of the living and kitchen was windows with a sliding door that went out to a deck overlooking the valley below and mountains beyond.

Bypassing Reagan's inspection of the welcome basket on the butcher block counter, I carried our luggage to the bedroom, which was situated on the opposite side of the kitchen, offering the same views and private access to the deck.

The bed was decorated in rose petals at my request, a bouquet of them sitting in a vase on the chest at the foot of it.

Walking back into the kitchen, I stepped up behind Reagan and pressed a kiss to her bare shoulder, the skin exposed where the sleeve of her sweater slipped down.

"What've we got here?" I asked, indicating the basket.

Reagan tilted her head so our eyes met, a small smirk playing on her lips. "As if you don't know."

"I may have made a few requests," I conceded, eyeing the bar of her favorite chocolate, the beer—*not* an IPA—from a local brewery, and some homemade self-care products, including bubble bath.

She moved out of the circle of my arms, heading for the refrigerator. When she opened the freezer, I found not one, not two, but *three* bottles of tequila chilling—one for every night we'd be staying here.

Reagan raised a brow. "You wanna play, soldier?"

"Maybe later," I said, instead reaching for the bottle of red wine waiting on the counter. I searched through the cabinets until I located two stemless glasses, then the drawers until I found an opener. I gave us each a healthy pour and pulled my girl out to the deck.

We'd arrived in time to watch the sunset, stepping outside right as golden hour hit, burnishing everything around us in a vibrant glow.

"Gorgeous," she breathed.

"The most beautiful thing I've ever seen," I agreed.

I wasn't talking about the scenery, and when Reagan caught me staring at her, a blush bled into her cheeks. I simply slung my arm around her shoulders and pulled her into my side.

Looking out across the vista, the stillness at the summit broken only by our soft breaths and nearby wildlife, I couldn't remember a time when I'd been happier.

"I don't think I could live anywhere but in the mountains," I told Reagan.

She tilted her head to look up at me. "Me either." Her gaze shifted out over the hills and valleys below us, the peaks in the distance. "But not these ones."

I grinned, easily understanding her meaning. The Smokies were gorgeous, but they weren't home.

"No," I agreed. "Not these ones."

THANK you so much for reading *Distress Signal*! If you loved Finn and Reagan, please consider leaving a review on Goodreads and retailer sites.

If you're not quite ready to let them go yet, follow this link for a special bonus chapter!

acknowledgements

This book was the hardest of my career so far. Not because I struggled with Finn and Reagan's story. In fact, once I cracked their code, their story came to me so easily. But transitioning from working full time to writing full time was *not* easy, and to say I suffered creative burnout would be the understatement of the century.

But I powered through, despite setbacks and health struggles, and I am so *proud* that this is book number 10! I hope you enjoyed your return to Dusk Valley and loved Finn and Reagan as much as I do.

That said, the list of people to thank for getting me here, for getting this book into your hands, is endless.

First and foremost, to my family, whose unwavering support means more than I could ever tell them.

To my sister, to whom I dedicated this book. I couldn't do any of this without her. From letting me run ideas and babble endlessly about the thousands of stories that live in my brain, to speed reading when I'm days from needing to send out ARCs or upload final files. Sissy, I know this isn't what you signed up for. I know I'm a pain in the ass. But I would choose you as my sister in every lifetime.

To Mer, who is truly the best best friend a girl could ever ask for. For talking me off ledges, for letting me complain, for always providing the best insight when I need it. For that early morning phone call on October 11. Even though you're *awful* at replying to texts, I know you're always there for me, and that's all I can ask for. I love you.

To Sarah, who is arguably the reason this book actually got finished. For spending over four hours on the phone with me on a rare day off work so I could run ideas with someone and plot from start to finish. For always cheering me on. For always being so excited to read these characters and their story. For being the kind of friend who doesn't balk at my endless voice notes. For just being *you*.

To my author friends, especially Ava Hunter, Karley Brenna, and Maren Moore, who cheered for me, sprinted with me, and pushed me to keep going when throwing in the towel would've been so much easier. I am eternally grateful for your guidance and friendship.

To Jessi, for reading this story when it was at its messiest (and literally not even done yet) and seeing the bones of what I was trying to accomplish. For loving Finn and Reagan despite the chaos.

To Erika, for the incredible feedback that made this book that much better, these characters and their story that much stronger. Distress Signal is what it is because of you.

To my agent, Jillian, who puts up with all my chaos and is one of my biggest cheerleaders.

To Sarah at Okay Creations, for the *stunning* covers. Forever blown away by your talent, and I can't wait to see what you come up with for the rest of the series.

To Lindee Robinson for the gorgeous couple cover image.

And last, but certainly not least, to my readers. *None* of this would be possible without y'all. Whether you've been with me since the FTB days or are just now joining me, I appreciate you and your support so much. It's because of you that I keep going.

also by amanda chaperon

Dusk Valley Series

Fire Fight

Distress Signal

Love on the Vine Series

Wine or Lose

Pour Decisions

Perfect Pairing

A Vine Mess

Pregame Series

Every Rule Worth Breaking

A Heart Worth Finding

about the author

Amanda Chaperon realized her passion for books and writing at a young age. Growing up, she was rarely found without a book in her hands, a hobby she carried into adulthood and which ultimately gave her the confidence to begin writing her own stories. She writes what she loves to read: heartfelt, passionate characters, lots of steam, and always a happily ever after.

Amanda lives in Michigan with her Golden Retriever, Gryffin. When she's not writing or reading, she can be found hanging out with her niece and nephew.

www.ingramcontent.com/pod-product-compliance
Lightning Source LLC
Chambersburg PA
CBHW020329010826
48973CB00005B/1191